lucky me

saba kapur

Amberjack Publishing
New York, New York

Amberjack Publishing
228 Park Avenue S, #89611
New York, NY 10003-1502
http://amberjackpublishing.com

Publisher's Cataloging-in-Publication data
Kapur, Saba.
Lucky me / Saba Kapur.
pages cm
ISBN 9780692536391 (pbk.)
ISBN 9780692536407 (ebook)

Summary : Gia Winters is accustomed to a life of fame and fortune, but her world is flipped upside down when mysterious phone calls start buzzing daily.

1. Children of the rich --Juvenile fiction. 2. Stalkers -- Juvenile fiction. 3. Teenagers -- Juvenile fiction. 4. Celebrities -- Juvenile fiction. I. Title.

PZ7. K1177 L83 2015

[Fic] –dc23   2015952447

Cover Design and Book Design: Ashley Ruggirello of CardboardMonet.com

Printed in the United States of America

For Mom, Dad & Rahat

c h a p t e r
o n e

THERE COMES a point in everyone's life where you've got to take a step back and consider the hand you've been dealt. I'm not going to lie to you; some people have it way easier. I'm not going to sit back and tell you the world is fair, because truthfully, you'd laugh your head off and throw a drink in my face. I guess it probably won't help to mention that I'm someone who has it fairly good in the luck department. At least, I suppose that's what you would call someone who's been born and raised in a world of glitz and glamour. Lucky. So before you go complaining about how I've got it all, I'm going to let you in on a little secret.

Disaster, as it turns out, doesn't discriminate. It doesn't care if you're rich or poor. It doesn't care how hot your girlfriend is or what car you drive. It sure as hell doesn't care if you're a nice person. It just marches into your life, slaps you across the face and even takes a sip of that cocktail you're drinking, just to really prove its point. This story is about my share of disaster, which struck in my final year of high school and in the craziest time of my life. But you're going to need some background information before we get into that.

Once upon a time there was a beautiful girl named Gia Winters, who lived in the magical land of Hollywood. Gia wasn't your average eighteen-year-old. Not only did she have an impeccable sense of style and long eyelashes she was particularly proud of, her dad was the king of this faraway land. Kind of. Actually, he was a huge movie star, and was basically a big deal, okay? Anyway, King Harry Winters once starred in a super lame movie in the eighties called *A Piece of My Heart,* which sent women around his kingdom into a frenzy over his cheesy romantic dialogues and mushroom haircut. But King Harry already had a queen, a beautiful young woman with perfect hair and a seriously banging body. She left behind her palace, The Playboy Mansion, and they were married in a grand ceremony that wowed the world.

A few years later, Queen Evelyn gave birth to a beautiful baby girl, and very impressively did a swimsuit photoshoot just four months later. The baby girl, a.k.a. me, brought lots of happiness to the kingdom, and two years later a young prince was born. Prince Mike was kind of cute when Gia was small and could squish his little baby cheeks with her tiny fingers. But then they grew up and the prince became a huge pain in the ass and Princess Gia was kind of over it. Either way, King Harry had everything he ever wanted and much more.

Fast-forward to present day and a lot has changed in that perfect little fairytale. The King and Queen, or Mom and Dad as I call them, are no longer ruling the kingdom together. Mom's acting career took off, as did the affair rumors, and they called it quits when I was twelve. When she moved out, it was a time of tears and heartbreak. I hated knowing that I would be part of a broken family, especially when all the details were going to be splashed across magazine covers throughout the country. Our family therapist at the time told my parents that it wasn't healthy for Mike and me to be exposed to all the talk and slander, as if it was something we could have helped. But it didn't matter; I didn't believe the affair rumors back then. Some days I have my doubts.

Mom lives in New York, so I'm used to seeing her every couple of months. At the time of the divorce, we kids were given the option of which city we preferred. Because we've grown up here, Mike and I both chose L.A., even though I really wanted to live with my mother. Now I'm kind of grateful for the space. Dad does a decent job and watching Mom go through men so hungrily is just not something I can deal with on a daily basis. My father hasn't done a movie in a few years, just little roles here and there, but nothing huge. Instead, he's been more focused on "reconnecting with his children," which is a nice sentiment, but pretty optimistic given our lifestyle.

Despite all the bumps in our little story, you could say that for a teenage girl I'd scored seriously big in the game of karma. You just don't get my wardrobe without doing something Mother Teresa-like in a previous life. But this story isn't just about hefty price tags and sipping mimosas on the beach. It begins on the fateful day when everything changed. And trust me, when change hit, it hit *hard*. The bank was still full and the heels were still high. But you can't put a price on drama, and believe me, there was plenty of it.

I walked into the house with my "congratulations on not failing your math test" present in hand, unaware that trouble was right around the corner. My dad, clearly taking advantage of my vulnerable state, took that as the perfect opportunity to announce a *family meeting* in the living room.

Family meetings were Dad's way of keeping us all close and up-to-date with the latest events of his now increasingly repetitive life. As if we needed him to tell us he was slipping into a giant hole of monotony. By now, I've lost count of all the events he's attended about cars, jeans, and cologne. I never even get to go to the events. Usually I'm at home keeping an eye on my brother and pretending to be impressed every time he tells me about "that time he got high and it was dope as hell, son."

Dad isn't too strict but he does have a few sacred rules. The most unbreakable of these is no entering the industry until after I've completed high school. No modeling contracts, no cover shoots for Harper's Bazaar, no acting gigs. Not that I even want to be an actor. I've thought about it, sure, but I don't exactly have a burning passion for it. I don't really have a burning passion for anything, except maybe Daniel Craig. A lot of things burn for that man. But according to Dad, I need to have graduated school before pursuing whatever it is I choose to do. The only things he holds as holy as this are his beloved family meetings.

"Gia! NOW," Dad called from the main living room.

Everyone knows the fun of buying new shoes is immediately locking yourself in your room, prancing around in them, and pouting into the mirror. A solid pair of stilettos can help you take over the world. Unfortunately, I lived in a house with two males, neither of them caring the slightest bit about footwear.

"FAMILY. MEETING. YO," Mike yelled from somewhere down the hall, to which I responded with an eye roll.

The moment my brother hit sixteen, he entered a phase where he thought he was the coolest person in the world and could therefore get away with saying "yo."

"Alright, alright! I'm coming!"

The musical prancing would have to wait until later. Handing my Chanel bags to Stella, one of the many housekeepers, I took my time walking toward the living room. Family meetings usually consisted of one thing: overwhelming boredom. Sometimes we would just run out of things to talk about, and then I'd sit there staring at Dad, wondering why he tried so hard. Don't get me wrong; I love my father. But I would rather not watch him struggle to find common ground with his kids and resort to telling us something completely irrelevant, like geographical fun facts. Friendly tip, there's nothing fun about those facts.

"And here I thought I'd need to book an appointment for five minutes with you," Dad said, as I sauntered into the room.

"Oh come on, Dad," I replied, smiling innocently. "I can always squeeze you in between meetings."

I reached straight for the latest Vogue lying on the coffee table in front of me and flopped down on the sofa, next to a very bored looking Mike, who was concentrating on his phone.

"It's a Monday," Dad said to me, unimpressed with my fantastic sarcasm. "Why do you need to go shopping after school on a Monday?"

I flipped open the first page, caressing the glossy paper without looking up. "I'm running out of things to wear. What do you want me to do, repeat outfits? I'm not an animal!"

"Can we get this over and done with quickly? I sort of have a life, you know," Mike said, checking his watch and sighing with frustration.

Mike's life consisted of nothing but posturing around his friends, getting drunk, annoying me, and failing school. He wasn't really missing out on a whole lot.

"Gia?" Dad said, and I looked up from the Vera Wang bridal spread.

"Yeah?"

"This is a family meeting. Your magazine can wait."

I was about to mention that Vogue wasn't merely a *magazine,* and that he ought to be ashamed of himself for saying that. Especially because he had met Anna Wintour, and she would not have been impressed with that ignorant comment. But he was looking all antsy so I did some exaggerated eye rolling to tell him I wasn't pleased, and placed the Vogue next to me.

"Happy?"

"Look guys," Dad replied. "This won't take long, but this meeting is particularly important so I need your complete attention, okay?" He looked at our blank faces blinking back at him, and continued. "Now, there are going to be some changes around here. It might seem a little strange at first, but I'd like you to keep an open mind."

I'm not a fan of changes. Not unless you count increasing my monthly allowance. But the way Dad kept fiddling with his fingers nervously, I had figured out it wasn't going to be good.

"This isn't one of those *Wife Swap* things is it?" I asked, giving him an unimpressed look. "Because I saw you watching that the other day and I swear some of my brain cells actually died."

"No, Gia," Dad replied, matching my tone. "I promise you, it's not that."

"Oh God . . ." Mike said, sitting up with a panicked look on his face. "You didn't fire Anya did you? Her pancakes are the best, man! We'll never get a housekeeper better than her! Who's going to teach me how to bake?"

The pancakes part I agreed with, but teaching Mike how to bake was questionable. He could barely make toast, and the only definition of "bake" he knew didn't have anything to with cooking.

"No, I didn't fire anyone!" Dad exclaimed impatiently, and Mike sighed with relief. "Just listen! What I'm about to tell you may come as a bit of a surprise, but I promise you, it's a good thing."

"We're not broke are we?" Mike said. "Or trying out one of those things where we pretend we're homeless so we can, like, appreciate what we have?"

"Michael, we are not broke," Dad replied, looking more agitated with every passing second. "Your theories are all off."

"Dude, it's *Mike!*"

"Dude," I repeated. "Nobody cares! Dad, seriously just tell us."

Dad nodded, looking almost nervous. "Right," he said. "Of course. It's not even a big deal. Just think of it as a present."

"OH! Are we finally getting a pony?" I cried, clasping my hands together in excitement.

Mike groaned. "No! I don't want a freakin' horse. Like, what are we going to do with a horse, man? Ride it down Hollywood Boulevard?"

"It's *my* horse, not yours!"

"It's nobody's horse, because I didn't buy one," Dad cut in, crushing my dreams. "It's more of a—"

"Oh, I know what it is!" Mike exclaimed. He turned to Dad with a sly look on his face. "You've got a girlfriend. And she's hot!"

"Uh, no. No, no, no." I shook my head like my brain was rejecting the idea. "Ew! No!"

"I bet she's young," Mike added, nodding approvingly.

"Yuck!"

"Could you just listen to me for one second, please?"

"Like, *real* young."

"Absolutely not!" I exclaimed. "Like, I want you to be happy and all. But how can I show my face in school now?"

"Fortunately for you, Gia, I do *not* have a girlfriend. But thanks for restoring my faith in how supportive you'd be if that ever did happen."

"Yeah, well, we'll cross that bridge when we get to it."

Which would hopefully be *never.* I didn't need to see my father prancing around with some twenty-something bimbo; my mother had already taken that position. All the therapy in the world wouldn't erase those images from my mind.

"You're killin' me man," Mike said, shaking his head. "What the hell is it?"

"I got us each a bodyguard."

Dad was smiling proudly as if he were telling us he'd won the Nobel Peace Prize.

"You got us a what?" I asked, even though I was fairly certain I heard correctly.

"Bodyguards, Gia. I got us bodyguards. *All* of us."

As famous as my father is, we've never once felt the need to have a full time bodyguard. To be honest, Dad's a bit of a hermit. When he's not out cutting a ribbon with a giant pair of scissors in some type of unveiling ceremony, he's usually golfing with buddies or sitting at home watching John Wayne movies. He had a bodyguard once but the whole thing was pointless; Dad never even used him. He was more of a "hire when needed" kind of guy. Also, I think he secretly thought he wasn't important enough to have crazy people throw themselves at him on the street. In fact, the only part of the fame and glory that seems to have really affected my father is the time it takes him to do his hair.

"Each?" I said.

"Yes, each."

"Like, each of us?"

"Yes, Gia. I just said that."

"This has got to be some kind of a joke," Mike said, reading my mind. "We don't need bodyguards! You might, but not us. It's not like *we're* in any danger."

"That's not necessarily true," Dad said, suddenly looking anxious. "I don't want you to panic, but something came to my attention recently that I . . . I didn't like. So I figured a little extra protection wouldn't hurt."

"Is everything okay?" I asked with a frown. "Like, no one's trying to kill you right?"

"Yeah, cause that would suck," Mike added.

He was right. If Dad were dead, I'd have to live with Mom and her boyfriend of the month. Which would definitely have some perks, namely I could steal things from her closet. But my self-esteem would die on a daily basis looking at her perfect hair, and my potential stepfather could be young enough to date me. Oh, and my actual father would be dead of course, which you know, would suck big time.

"As of now," Dad said. "Everything's fine, and that's all you need to know. But that doesn't mean it can't get worse."

"Well what happened?" Mike asked. "Should we be worried?"

"No, I've got the situation controlled. But that being said, the bodyguards do need to be with you at all times, just in case. And that's non-negotiable."

"All times?" I repeated, and Dad nodded. "Like *all* the time?"

"Even at school?" Mike asked.

"Yes."

"No way!" I said bluntly, shaking my head some more. "That's so embarrassing! I can't have some random guy following me everywhere I go! People will stare!"

"Gia, there may be a serious threat here!" Dad looked at me with disbelief. "I think that should matter more than what your classmates think."

Obviously my father had never had to be a teenage girl growing up in Hollywood, so he was in no position to make a statement like that.

"Well which is it?" I snapped. "On one hand you tell us we shouldn't be worried, but then you hire full time bodyguards to stalk us all day long just *in case* something goes down?"

"I—"

"Listen Dad," Mike interrupted calmly, rising from the plush sofa. "I get that you're famous and all. But I think you're taking the idea of a desperate housewife to the extreme. The most they'll do is throw a heel at you. Maybe even underwear if you're lucky. But that's hardly *life threatening*."

"Ew. Never repeat that."

"Thanks Mike," Dad replied, his tone completely dry of any humor. "But this is a little more than some housewife. It's not even me I'm worried about! Look, you're just going to have to trust me on this one. I can't explain everything to you right now, but it's already been decided."

"But, but," I persisted, refusing to back down. "Why would anyone care about harming us? Aren't there a billion more important celebrities to go after?"

Who would waste their time trying to get to Harry Winters's kids when Ryan Gosling was alive? Surely no one was *that* bored.

"Gia," Dad said, his stern parenting voice in full swing. "We're getting bodyguards and that's final!"

He may as well have stamped his foot on the ground and crossed his arms over his chest, like a four-year-old throwing a tantrum in the candy aisle of a supermarket. We all stared at each other in silence for a few seconds, contemplating our next move. Arguing further was probably a waste of time, and I wasn't in the mood to lose a fight. But the whole idea was so ridiculous, I was half expecting Dad to burst into laughter and tell us it was a joke.

"So how do you even get a bodyguard anyway?" Mike asked, clearly beginning to succumb. "Do you just look it up in the yellow pages, or something?"

"Your Uncle Don has two bodyguards. I spoke to him yesterday and he recommended a great agency from New York."

"Uncle Don? As in, the guy who hasn't been in a movie since like, the eighteenth century?" Mike said with a laugh. "Why does he need a bodyguard? No one even knows who he is!"

"Irrelevant!" I help up a hand so Mike would stop talking. "But don't you think it's going to be a little suspicious to everyone if we suddenly show up to school carting around these mean-looking, buff guys? Won't that draw more attention to us and our so-called 'threat?'"

"That's already been dealt with," Dad told me. He had clearly rehearsed some of this talk in the shower. "The agency is sending over their youngest bodyguards for you two, so fitting in won't be a problem. I've already spoken to your school's principal, and they were enrolled yesterd—"

"You enrolled them?" I interrupted, my voice becoming shrill with disbelief. "Like, at our school?"

"As far as the public knows," Dad continued, ignoring me completely. "They're family friends who have recently moved to L.A. I've got all the details worked out."

Couldn't argue with that. He had clearly planned the entire bodyguard scheme out, and very carefully. Whatever this mysterious threat was, it really had him going. The only problem was, I still wasn't fully convinced. The family friend excuse was a seriously pathetic one, and no one was going to buy it. You don't have family friends in Hollywood. You have family, and you have friends. The two don't mix.

"Dad," Mike said with a frown. "This plan just ain't right."

"Stop saying *ain't*," I told him, giving him a judgemental look. "You're not a gangster and you're not a farmer."

"If I want to say ain't then I'm gonna say ain't," Mike replied with a glare. "That's in the Constitution. Look it up."

I'll admit I was a little impressed he knew what the Constitution was. Got to give a guy credit where it's due.

"Look," Dad said wearily, his patience clearly growing thinner by the second. "I know you're confused, but I need you to trust me on this one. I'm only doing this for your own good. I don't ask for a lot from both of you, but I hope you can do this much for me. Just give it a try."

Dad looked like he was just about ready to drop to his knees and start begging. I glanced at Mike begrudgingly, who returned the look with slight guilt. Dad had pulled out the *doing this for your own good* card, which was a hard one to refute. Besides, if my life were actually in danger I would probably need some major protection. I can't even kill a fly without backup.

"Fine." I sighed in defeat.

"Yeah, fine." Mike agreed.

Dad smiled at us gratefully, releasing a relieved sigh. "I appreciate it, kids. I really do."

Alright, fine, so bodyguards weren't the most horrible things in the world. It could have been worse. Dad's so-called present could very well have been that girlfriend. Or worse, another family botany class. He had tried that on me once, saying I should get more involved in the environment and bond with him. It was so boring; I had almost keeled over and died within the first ten minutes. All we did was inspect leaves and talk about greenhouse gases, which I still don't understand to be honest. Needless to say we never went back.

"Are we done here?" I mumbled, reaching for the Vogue.

The doorbell suddenly rang, and my hand froze, mid-air. I looked at Mike, then at Dad, as the chimes echoed off every wall of the house.

"They're here," Dad said, rubbing his hands together like an evil genius.

"The bodyguards?" Mike said, and Dad nodded.

"Wait, you invited them right now?" I asked.

"Yes!"

"What! Why?"

Dad didn't reply. Instead we all stood in silence, shooting each other panicked looks, neither of us going to answer the door. Anya, our head housekeeper and maker of the world's best pancakes, shuffled into the room and announced in her heavy Russian accent that a "Mizter Walterz" had arrived. Almost immediately after she left the room, we heard light footsteps from the hallway approaching us. I felt a buzzing in the pocket of my jeans, and pulled my phone out. It was my boyfriend, Brendan.

"Sorry," I said, giving Dad an apologetic look. "I have to take this."

"Gia!" Dad hissed, but I answered the phone anyway.

"I'll be a minute, jeez!"

I spun around so my back was facing my dad and Mike, putting the phone to my ear. Dad was no doubt going to enjoy lecturing me later on, but the more time I had to delay the bodyguard process, the better. Brendan was supposed to come over for dinner, but it was a majorly inconvenient time.

It's not like I had anticipated my dad was going to hit me with the news of bodyguards like, an hour before our dinner plans. That, and Dad hated Brendan. But that wasn't really important; he hated most people.

Behind me I could hear my father introducing himself to someone named Colin, which didn't sound very bodyguard-ish. His last bodyguard had insisted we call him Bob, which he claimed wasn't short for Robert. He was "just Bob."

"Hello?"

"Hey, it's me, Brendan."

I did an internal eye roll. He said that every time he called, as though caller ID hadn't been invented yet. "Yeah, hey. What's up?"

"I got into it with my dad again," Brendan said, letting out a frustrated sigh. "He's being a real pain in the ass and took my keys. I could take one of the other cars, but I'm kind of not in the mood. I'm going to have to cancel, I'm sorry."

Behind me I could hear my dad introducing Mike to the room. I put a hand over my free ear, so I could block out the noise, and said, "Oh, that sucks!"

Actually it didn't suck, but a tiny white lie wasn't going to kill anyone. Brendan cancelling was perfect timing, what with Dad offering a group of bodyguards refreshments right behind me. Brendan did some more apologizing and promised he'd pick me up for school the next day. I did some more pretend, disappointed sighing and hung up the phone. At least now Brendan had saved himself from a night of death glares coming from my father.

I don't know why Dad didn't like Brendan. He was insanely attractive, sweet, and smart. Well, smart is pushing it a little. But he was genuinely a nice guy. I thought *I* fought with my dad a lot, but my situation was nothing compared to Brendan's. He'd always wanted to make it big in Hollywood, but his dad seemed to think it was a terrible idea, so they spent all their time hating each other. I had once asked my father if he could help Brendan out with a role, even if it was tiny. I even showed him an audition Brendan did for a cheese commercial. Dad laughed so hard I was scared he might have ruptured a kidney or something. Brendan never even landed that cheese commercial. I still don't know why he decided to do it in an Indian accent.

"Gia!" Dad practically barked at me.

Eyes still on my phone, I spun around with a sigh. I'd just say my hellos, do some polite smiling and retreat back to my room. Dad's happy. I'm happy. It's a win-win. I had barely walked three steps before I slammed into a perfectly toned torso I didn't recognize, almost tripping over my own feet.

"Ooof!"

"Woah!"

I felt two hands hold up my arms, steadying me so that I didn't fall over. My gaze followed the grip all the way up to its owner; a young, blonde-haired guy who was standing only an inch away. His eyes were blue, but not piercing, and I was standing close enough to see tiny bits of grey in them. He was the kind of attractive that you don't come across too often, the kind that makes you all excited. He was the type of guy who you'd tell your friends asked for your number at a bar, when really all he did was walk past you. He had a smile on his face as he watched me, his fingers still curled around my arms.

"You alright?" he said, laughing a little.

I nodded silently, and his hands pulled away from me as he took a step back.

"This is my daughter, Gia." Dad stepped in. I stood rooted to the spot, scared to blink just in case the view disappeared.

"Hi," the stranger said.

"Wow!" I breathed.

I mentally slapped myself so hard; I think my cheek actually bruised. With any luck he hadn't heard me.

"Excuse me?"

Yep, he had heard me. My brain kicked into survival gear and I stupidly placed the iPhone to my ear, pretending someone was still on the line.

"Wow! That sounds great. Uh-huh. Okay, bye now!" I hung up on my pretend caller and roughly shoved my phone back into my pocket. "Sorry, phone call. What were you saying?"

"I'm Jack. Anderson," he said, extending his hand to me.

"Me too," I replied, shaking his hand lightly. It was like I was scared to touch his skin, just in case I melted.

"What?" His smile widened.

"What?" I repeated casually. Somewhere to my left I heard Mike guffaw, and I realized the entire room could hear me make a fool of myself.

Jack Anderson was undoubtedly one of the most attractive people I had ever met. Which is a big deal, given the fact that I have shared the same air as Jake Gyllenhaal. He shook his head slightly and pulled his hand away, much to my disappointment. I waited for him to turn around and ask if I were mentally challenged. Thankfully, he just stood there.

"Gia, this is Mr. Colin Walters," Dad said, motioning to the man on his right. "He's head of the agency in New York. They've been nice enough to fly all the way down to L.A. especially for us."

I smiled awkwardly at the kind looking man with white hair and a white moustache. He reminded me of Santa Claus a little bit, and judging by the blonde present standing right next to me, I had been a good girl this year. I walked over to Mr. Walters and shook his hand, brushing past Jack on my way.

"Nice to meet you, Gia," Mr. Walters said, and turned to the two other men standing next to him. "This is Kenny, and that's Chris."

I looked at the other bodyguards, evaluating their appearances as I gave them an awkward wave. Unlike Jack, Kenny looked like a bodyguard. He was dressed in black from head to toe, he was *really* buff, he was bald, and he was African-American. I know, what a stereotype. Chris, on the other hand, looked absolutely nothing like a bodyguard. With his skinny frame and floppy brown hair, he didn't look capable of kicking his own butt, let alone someone else's. Plus, he looked like he hadn't even hit puberty yet. And then there was Jack, who was nothing like I'd ever seen.

"We're all very honored that you chose our company, despite all the fantastic services here in L.A.," Mr. Walters said, practically beaming behind his moustache. "Personally, I'm a very big fan of your movies."

Dad smiled humbly and said, "You were very highly recommended. It's no problem at all."

Mr. Nice Santa Guy started to ramble on about how important it was that we didn't tell even our closest friends about the bodyguards, at least for the time being, but I wasn't really paying attention. Instead, I was concentrating on trying to figure out what was wrong with Jack. Someone who looked that perfect had to have been harboring some kind of crazy secret. If it looks too good to be true, then it probably is. Maybe he was a ribbon gymnastics enthusiast, or had a sock collection stored in his basement.

Kenny was reassuring Dad about how they were the very best bodyguards, as if I even cared about their capabilities. From the corner of my eye I could see Jack evaluating me, which was freaking me out. What the heck was he staring at? It was taking me all the strength I had not to burst into uncontrollable nervous laughter. When I tuned back into the conversation, Santa Man seemed ready to leave.

"I should probably be heading off," Mr. Walters said, shaking my dad's hand.

We all politely thanked Mr. Walters, then Dad walked him to the front door, leaving Mike and me in the living room with the three bodyguards. On the way out of the room, I could hear him asking Dad if he did his own stunts.

"So," Mike began, trying to break the ice after a few seconds of silence. "Which one of you is going to be my bodyguard?"

I silently prayed that Jack wasn't Mike's bodyguard. Someone as beautiful as him could not be wasted on my brother. Baby J wouldn't do me like that.

"I am," Chris said quietly, holding up his hand and giving a little wave. I blew out a sigh of relief.

"I'm your dad's," Kenny told us, in a deep voice.

I looked at Jack. "So that means—"

"I'm yours."

If only he had said that with a bouquet of roses in his hand.

"Yeah. Great. Awesome," I replied.

"Kids," Dad said, reappearing suddenly from the hallway. His eyes settled on me. "Can you show these guys to the guest rooms? Make sure they're comfortable."

"They're staying with us?" I asked.

"Yes, Gia. They're staying with us." Dad said.

"Like in the house? In the house with us? Here in the house . . . with us?"

Dad shot me a look that said, *is there a problem?* and I replied with clear panic in my eyes. Of course there was a problem! I was going into cardiac arrest.

"Follow me, man," Mike said, motioning toward Chris.

On his way past me, he gave me a knowing look. No doubt he was going to enjoy making fun of my nervous flailing later. I narrowed my eyes at him just before he left the room, sending him a warning.

"I'll give you boys some time to get settled in before dinner," Dad told Kenny.

"Thank you, sir," Kenny replied, with a shake of his head. "But we're pretty adaptable. In fact I'd like to spend this time discussing the details of this arrangement, if that's alright."

"Yes, of course. We can talk in the other room."

"We're having apple pie for dessert," I blurted out to the room, and Dad raised an eyebrow. In fact, I had practically yelled it, and very aggressively.

"Great," Jack said, as I forced myself to lock eyes with his. "I love apple pie."

"Yeah, me too," I said with an overly enthusiastic nod. "It's . . . good stuff. Apples, you know. Love 'em."

I absolutely hate apple pie. Fruit should not be warm. It's a sign of witchcraft.

"Gia, can I have a quick word with you?" Dad said, and I gave him a questioning look.

Dad gave Kenny and Jack a tight smile, wrapped his hand around my elbow and gently led me out of the room.

"What?" I said, the moment we were out of earshot.

"Don't," Dad said sternly, dropping his grip from my

arm.

"Don't what?"

"Don't! I'm not an idiot, Gia. I can see that Jack is an attractive young man, and I can see this isn't going to end well."

My jaw dropped so low, I was surprised it actually didn't hit the floor like in the cartoons. "Dad!" I cried, hoping my outrage would mask my embarrassment. The damn apple pie comment had totally given me away.

"I don't want you crossing any lines. I'm serious."

I crossed my arms defensively across my chest. "Oh, so now *I'm* the only one capable of crossing a line? You invite strangers into our house to trail your kids around all day, and I'm the problem?"

"I'm doing this for your own good!" Dad shot back, and I rolled my eyes. "And you can drop the attitude, it's not going to work with me."

I uncrossed my arms and gave him the most innocent look I could muster. "Fine," I said, with a noncommittal shrug. "I was willing to give this a shot for you. But if you don't want me to be nice to the bodyguards, then I won't be."

"That's not what I—"

"I'm just following orders."

"Gia th—"

I spun on my heel before he could stop me and practically ran back into the living room. Well jeez; I wasn't some crazed promiscuous lunatic who couldn't control her hormones. Sure, I spent a lot of time lusting after guys who weren't my boyfriend, but you don't introduce a girl to Chris Pine and then expect that she *won't* start planning an imaginary wedding.

Besides, the bodyguards were a complete joke; it's not like we even needed them. They could leave as quickly as they came in. Kenny and Jack, who were talking quietly, stopped and looked at me expectantly when I suddenly marched back in the room.

"Let's go," I said sharply to Jack. "Look alive."

He gave me a surprised look and glanced at Kenny, who had his eyebrow raised so far up his head, I doubted it was coming down anytime soon.

"Um . . ."

"Did you not hear me? Let's go!"

"Gia," Dad said, coming up behind me. His tone implied a threat, but his weary smile told me he was far too exhausted to make a scene. I was winning by default.

"I'm showing Jack to his room, just like you asked. Because apparently we don't have housekeepers to do that." I batted my long eyelashes innocently. "Right, Jack?"

"Uh, yeah?" Jack said uncertainly. He walked toward me hesitantly, as if he was scared I might rip his head off any second.

"Be nice," Dad whispered, loud enough so that only I could hear it.

I just smiled. "Let's go."

I led my new bodyguard down the hallway in silence, past the two recreational rooms, the cinema room and two more lounge rooms. We hadn't even covered a quarter of downstairs yet, but I didn't bother giving him the full tour. He wasn't going to stay for long, so there was no point wasting my time.

Only now that the rage was wearing off a little, the nerves were starting to kick back in. Jack was standing so close to me, the sleeve of his shirt would occasionally graze my arm and tiny electric currents would shoot through my whole body. There was no way that was healthy. As we walked past a mirror, I eyed my outfit as subtly as I could. Tight skinny jeans and a Zara crop top. Nothing too fancy, but at least Dad had sprung the news on me when I had returned from shopping and not when I was just lounging around the house in my PJs.

"Oh, you have a dog," Jack said finally, more to himself than to me. He was obviously making a sad attempt at small talk.

My Yorkshire Terrier, who was sitting by the stairs, stopped playing a tug-of-war game with his chew toy and gave Jack a half-assed yelp. He trotted over to us to inspect the attractive stranger standing beside me. Jack bent down and scooped him up, holding him close to his chest.

"She's adorable," Jack said. "What's her name?"

"*His,*" I said haughtily, as if by confusing my pet's gender he had somehow insulted my entire ancestral line. "His name is Famous."

"Oh," Jack said. "Interesting."

Oh no. What if he didn't think that was interesting and he was just saying that? Like when someone goes "oh your child is an absolute angel" when everyone in the world can tell that little kid is the spawn of Satan. Not that I could do anything to fix the whole situation. It's not like I had consulted him before naming my dog. Plus, if Famous was a good enough name for Audrey Hepburn's pet, then it was good enough for Jack Anderson.

Jack was going on about how he had always wanted a puppy but someone in his family, I couldn't remember whom, was allergic to dogs. I was barely paying attention. I was focusing so hard on breathing normally; I was scared the veins on my forehead were bulging out. He looked like Mr. January in a *Hot Guys with Puppies* calendar, and my respiratory system was suffering as a result. I allowed myself one minute more of shameless lusting before roughly yanking Famous from Jack's grip.

"He doesn't like strangers."

I placed Famous down on the floor, and he looked up at me. If dogs could give judgemental looks, he had definitely given me one before turning back to his chew toy.

"Your house is incredible," Jack said, eyeing the chandelier hanging above the staircase. He seemed unfazed by my abruptness. "What is it, like, five stories?"

"Six," I said curtly, leading him toward the elevator. The less

I talked, the less chance I had of making a fool of myself.

"You have an elevator in your house?" Jack said, his eyes bright with excitement. It was weird to see him so surprised about something so mundane.

I pushed the "up" button on the elevator, which was positioned next to stairs, and the doors opened immediately. Great. Dad didn't want me "crossing lines" but he had sent me to show Jack a bedroom. Nice thinking.

"Wait," I said, my gaze dropping to Jack's empty hands. "You don't have any bags with you."

"Oh, yeah, that's okay. I don't wear a lot when I'm sleeping," he replied matter-of-factly.

I opened my mouth to say something but no words formed. I just stood there gaping at him. He didn't look like he was kidding. I surely hoped he wasn't.

"Right," I said, nodding. "Of course. I read once that sleeping naked is actually good for your health and like, your brain network formations. I read that. In a magazine."

The elevator doors closed again, as did my window for making Jack fall in love with my quick wit and flirtation skills. What the hell were network formations? It was like my mind had temporarily shut down, due to the image of Jack naked burnt into my temporal lobe. If brain network formations existed, I was missing a lot of them.

"I was kidding. The bags are in the car," Jack said, clearly trying to suppress a smile. "Just . . . breaking the ice."

"Right. Yeah, me too. Obviously."

Somewhere in the heavens above, someone was slow clapping at my stupidity. The proverbial ice wasn't being broken; it was being repeatedly smashed against my head. I clasped my eyes shut for a few seconds, hoping my brain could delete the humiliation from my mind. No luck. We stood there staring at each other for a few seconds in silence, as I struggled to find my way out of the hole I kept digging for myself. Luckily it was Jack who broke the silence first.

"I know this is tough," Jack said, suddenly becoming more serious. "It's natural to want to turn to friends in such a confusing time. But it really is important to keep this all quiet. At least until we figure out how serious this threat is."

I watched him without saying a word, arms crossed against my chest protectively. Maybe that would be my way of putting up a battle. Complete silence. I figured I'd be so silent everyone would be scared that I had forgotten how to speak.

Jack looked at me awkwardly, fidgeting with his fingers. "So, final year of high school? That's exciting, right?"

"Listen, Jack," I began, forcing the attitude back into my tone. "It's nothing personal, but if we're going to do this, then we're going to do this my way."

The silence plan was a long shot anyway.

"Your way?" Jack repeated, giving me an amused look. He looked completely relaxed now, albeit slightly confused.

I nodded and said, "I don't know what my dad's told you, but there's no threat."

"We were just told to keep you all safe, 'round the clock."

"Right, well that's not necessary," I told him. "As you can see, I'm fine. I'm not dead. There's no one trying to kill me. I'm all good, so you can go back to New York now."

I smiled at him warmly, hoping that I had done enough to send him packing.

"I'm sorry," Jack said, looking at me as though he couldn't actually believe he was having this conversation. "But I'm not sure it works like that."

My smile dropped. "Look, if this is going to work you have to stay out of my way, okay?"

"I'm not here to get in anyone's wa—"

"Well, good."

I was putting so much effort into being haughty; I was coming across as borderline constipated. In reality I was scared I was already in love, and I had known the guy for all but ten minutes. My ego was only *just* winning against my hormones, and I didn't know how much longer that would last. I just had to concentrate on what I was saying so I wouldn't accidently ask him to father my children, and everything would be fine.

Jack opened his mouth, ready to say something, but then closed it. We watched each other in silence, waiting for one of us to make the first move.

"Your room," I said, when I had finally had enough of the awkwardness. "Is two levels up. Choose any bedroom, whatever. I don't care. I'm on the floor just above us now. If you need anything, don't come to me. We have the help for that."

I pushed the button on the elevator for what I hoped would be the last time for that encounter, taking a few steps away from it.

"Got it," Jack said. He was smiling again, which was weird because I was coming across as a real psycho.

"It was nice to meet you, Jack." I tried to make it sound like a goodbye; a heads up that he would be leaving as fast as he came in.

"Likewise," he replied. Only he really looked like he meant it too.

Jack's eyes were practically burning holes through my eye sockets, but I couldn't yank my gaze away. My bodyguard wasn't meant to be a love interest in the romantic comedy I had invented in my mind! Not that I needed a new love interest in my life; I had a boyfriend. And we got along just fine. Sure, it wasn't a fireworks relationship, but, you know, I got by in life.

"I think this'll be fun," Jack said, just as I was turning to leave. I stopped dead in my tracks, only turning my head back to face his grin.

Um. Could he not look at me like that please? I was already having trouble coping. I tried not to return the smile, but I think I failed in that department because my lips kind of twitched up anyway, purely out of nerves. The elevator doors began to move toward each other, but Jack caught one with his hand, and they parted once more. We stared at each other for a few seconds, neither of us blinking. I took a deep breath and turned on my heel, only exhaling when my back was turned.

"Yeah, well," I said. "We'll have to see about that."

c h a p t e r
t w o

DAY TWO of hating Jack began as a complete disaster. I woke up the next morning feeling like death, and looking even worse. In movies, *everyone* is a morning person. In real life, we're lucky if we look remotely human getting out of bed. Trust me, I have tried multiple times to wake up looking like Beyoncé. I failed, big time.

I almost broke my alarm clock with the force I used to turn it off, roughly brushed my teeth and jumped straight into the shower. Brendan was no doubt going to be outside the house soon, honking his horn with impatience. He hated it when I was late. For my sixteenth birthday, dad had gifted me a glossy black, convertible Beetle, a car I had wanted since I was five. I use it all the time for shopping and partying purposes, but my house is on

Brendan's way to school. For the past seven months or so, since we had started dating, he'd been taking me to school everyday.

Tripping over my towel, I ran out of the ensuite and straight into my walk-in closet, commonly known as heaven. It's about the size of half my bedroom, smells like happiness and is completely stocked with an endless list of designer clothes and a fluffy pink beanbag that I never use. There are many people in Hollywood that complain about having to dress up. I am not one of those people. Sure, it can be a pain at times, but trust me, life tends to run a whole lot smoother when you're wearing a pair of Louboutins. Take it from someone who's grown up around human Barbie dolls. If you want to survive at my school, you've got to bring something to the table. Even your off days have to be red-carpet worthy.

"Gia! Are you ready?" I heard Dad call from the foot of the stairs.

"Almost!" I yelled back as his footsteps grew distant.

Confidence levels were running low, and time to contemplate outfits was even lower. I grabbed my American Apparel strapless jumpsuit off the hanger and threw it on without a second thought, slipping my feet into my heeled Jeffery Campbell boots. I hadn't even gotten a chance to reinspect yesterday's purchases; I had been too busy hoping the whole bodyguard thing would end quickly and painlessly. I had sort of hoped that I'd get to look like a complete knockout, blowing Jack away with my fabulous looks and sense of style. Unfortunately, that didn't look like it was going to happen. If only I had Mom's personal makeup artist here to help me.

I grimaced at the reflection of my long, brown hair in the huge mirror, pouting at how much of a mess it was. Straightening it would take too long but curling it would take even longer. I also secretly believed that my hair was often a good indication of my stress levels. If that theory had any strength, I was going to be

Disney's new *Lion King* character before noon. I gave a frustrated sigh as I ran my fingers through it, hoping desperately that it would magically transform into a GHD advertisement. When it didn't, I gave up and tied it into a ponytail.

Thanks to Jack and his beautiful face, I would now have to look top notch all the freaking time. This was a major inconvenience, because it meant I wasn't allowed any of those off days I mentioned before. Heidi Klum could wear a garbage bag and still work it like a nine-to-five job. I, on the other hand, needed to put in a little extra effort. Clearly, crippling insecurity wasn't something people tended to advertise with the perfect Hollywood life. What a shocker.

"GIA! YOUR BOYFRIEND'S HERE," Dad called out, sounding annoyed.

I did some mental pep talking and reassured myself that I looked fabulous, given my small time frame. Grabbing my science book and studded Balmain bag off my bed, I ran down the stairs, taking them two at a time. I jogged down the hallway, into the kitchen and straight into Jack, hitting against his arm. I gave a small groan as my hip dug into the tip of the kitchen island.

"Ow!"

"Morning!" Jack greeted me cheerfully, still rooted in the same spot. He eyed me up and down, a smile appearing on his face.

I had chosen my outfit in a minute flat, my eyeliner wings were uneven, I had a little too much blush on, and I had a seventy percent chance of looking like a drag queen. If that smile was to say he liked what he saw, he was hopefully going to see a whole lot better.

"You're still here?" I asked, a little out of breath from running.

"Gia!" Dad said sharply, coming up from behind me. I gave a small jump, startled at his sudden appearance. "Jack is here to help you, remember? Be nice."

"Oh, that's okay Mr. Winters," Jack said, with a humble look. "I can understand that this must be hard on Gia. It's all a process."

I glared at him so hard, I thought my eyes were going pop out of my head. What a kiss-ass.

"I'm going to go show Kenny how our security system works," Dad said, his tone suggesting a warning to me. "Breakfast is on the counter, and your boyfriend is still waiting outside. Tell him not to wake the whole of L.A. up with his car horn."

I silently watched Dad walk out of the kitchen before turning back to Jack the moment we were alone. He was watching me, leaning against the fridge and sipping coffee out of *my* favorite mug. It's pink and has a little Yorkshire terrier on it, just like Famous. Who, evidently, Jack thought was *interesting*, whatever that means.

"I just figured you'd have gotten the hint by now," I said, shrugging casually. "It's not too late to book a flight back to New York."

"I don't scare easy," Jack replied, placing the mug down on the counter gently.

"Oh, really?"

Jack leaned in a little closer, as if he was about to reveal some huge government secret to me. My body stiffened, and I reflexively took a step back.

"No offense," Jack said softly, and I raised an expectant eyebrow. "But I've dealt with a lot worse than a hostile teenager."

I narrowed my eyes at him, crossing my arms over my chest. Hostile? Where did he get off calling me hostile? Okay, so maybe I was being hostile. And maybe that was kind of the point. But still! He didn't get to stand in my kitchen, drink out of *my* mug and call *me* hostile!

"Well . . ." I began, struggling to think of a decent comeback. "Good for you."

Brendan had definitely caused some damage to his car horn from the amount of times he had pressed it. I checked the time on my phone. It was 8.07 am. That was *really* late for Brendan. That was beyond early for me.

"Where is everyone, anyway?" I asked Jack, referring to the lack of housekeepers, who were usually bustling around the kitchen.

"Somewhere around, I guess."

"Where's my brother?" I pulled a plate of pancakes toward me. I took a mouthful, barely chewed and swallowed it whole.

"He left about five minutes ago. Chris drove him to school."

"And you didn't go with them?"

"And give up an opportunity to spend quality time with you?" Jack asked in mock surprise, as if I had just suggested we start eating our feet. "Never!"

I watched Jack silently, fiercely chewing on my pancakes as Brendan continued to honk his horn outside. He was dressed in jeans again, and he was wearing a plain black t-shirt that was a little tight so you could tell he had perfectly toned abs. His hair looked like it hadn't been brushed, but not in a dirty and scruffy way. More in an *I always look this sexy* kind of way. Oh yeah, L.A. City Elite was going to love Jack.

"I have to go," I said, leaving the food half eaten and swiping my bag and book off the counter.

I yelled my goodbyes out to Dad and Anya—even though I had no clue where she was—and kissed Famous on my way to the front door. Noticing Jack was right behind me, I turned to face him abruptly, slamming the front door shut.

"Don't you have your own car?" I asked hopefully, clutching the science book to my chest.

"Of course I do," he replied. "But I have to ride with you and your piece of meat, or whatever your dad called him."

My cheeks flushed. "Brendan is NOT a piece of beef!" I

cried.

"That's the one."

Clearly my dad had shared his personal views on my boyfriend with Jack that morning. I could only dare to imagine what else he had discussed with him while I was battling my bad hair day upstairs. Brendan, who was still furiously honking his horn, seemed to be having a fight with his stereo, and losing. He kept pressing all the buttons and yelling out "Damn you, track fifteen!"

"If we're going to do this then I'm going to set out some ground rules," I said firmly, and Jack raised his eyebrows, clearly amused. It was like I was a skydiving instructor and we were standing on the edge of a plane. "Rule number one, no touching me. Like, ever. Not even by accident. Rule number two, no flirting."

"Well that's not fair!" Jack protested. "If I'm not allowed to touch you then I should be allowed to flirt. It's all I've got!"

I narrowed my eyes at him. "Was that supposed to be a joke?"

"Yeah," Jack replied, looking at me expressionless. "Why, do you not have a sense of humor?"

"Not when it comes to you," I replied. "Rule number three, minimal talking. People at school can get kind of crazy about a new student, and you're . . ." I trailed off, eyeing him up and down. "Just try not to talk to anyone."

"What if they talk to me first? I can't *not* reply. They'll think I'm weird."

"You *are* weird."

"You read articles about people who sleep naked, and I'm the weird one?"

Oh lord. I felt my cheeks begin to blaze up, immediately grateful that my sunglasses were covering the embarrassment in my eyes.

"Just don't talk! Okay?"

"Do you give all your friends these rules, or—"

"Uh," I said, cutting in. "We're not friends. Your time here has an expiration date, and it's coming up."

Jack smiled. It wasn't a full grin or anything, but he was clearly enjoying himself.

"GIA! FOR THE LOVE OF GOD, GET IN THE CAR ALREADY!" Brendan screamed, roughly pulling a CD out of the player.

"He seems nice," Jack said. I couldn't tell if he was being sarcastic or not.

"Rule number four, no insulting my boyfriend."

"I wasn't."

"Good, don't."

"Should I be writing these down?"

"You got a pen?"

The first half of the day had gone painfully slow, and by the time lunch came around I couldn't bear to introduce Jack one more time. I had told the cover story so many times, I was actually starting to forget why Jack was really around. I managed to find my short-lived escape when the lunch bell rang, bolting out of class and away from Jack before he could stop me.

Usually my friends and I would drive off campus at lunch, just to get away for an hour, maybe for a milkshake to brighten our moods. Not that we really need to, there's a Starbucks at school. With Jack around, I needed that milkshake more than ever, but no one was interested in leaving. People were fawning over Jack like he was actually a Calvin Klein model. Even my best friends, Aria and Veronica, were sitting opposite me at our usual table, wide-eyed with curiosity.

"I'm just going to say it," Veronica began, and I looked up from my lunch. "That Jack guy is the most attractive person I've ever seen."

"What about your boyfriend?" I asked, pulling my sunglasses off the top of my head and putting them on the table.

"What about him?"

"I don't think it's even legal to look that good," Aria added, inspecting her heavily rhinestoned acrylic nails. "I couldn't stop staring at him in History. That boy is sex on a stick!"

"In more exciting news," I said, desperately trying to steer the conversation in a different direction. "I've been dying to tell you guys something! It's going to blow your minds, but you have to keep it on the D-L."

"Oooo!" Aria said, leaning in. "This sounds scandalous."

"So Mom called last night . . ."

"She's dating Orlando Bloom?" Veronica said, looking hopeful.

"Even better," I said with a grin. I paused momentarily, just for dramatic effect. "The Hollywood Foreign Press are considering me for Miss Golden Globe this year!"

Aria's jaw dropped and Veronica clasped a hand over her mouth in excitement. My smile widened. It was just the reaction I had hoped for.

"No!" Aria exclaimed. "Shut up! No way! That's amazing!"

I nodded and said, "I practically died! She said the person they chose had to back out last minute so now they have to find a replacement."

"Which could be you!" Veronica finished.

I squealed in excitement, my friends joining in. Mom's phone call last night had started off as the perfect opportunity for me to complain about my dad's stupid bodyguard plan. But before I had even gotten around to mentioning Jack and the gross injustice I was facing, Mom had dropped the news on me about

Miss Golden Globe, the coveted opportunity of a lifetime. Only the children of the very best stars are chosen for the chance to help hand out awards to the winners at the prestigious Golden Globe ceremony, and I actually had a shot! I had been so excited; I had completely forgotten to mention the bodyguards to my mother. I was too busy imagining what it would be like to get to hold the statues in my hands, looking like Grace Kelly, as I helped hand them out to the elite class of Hollywood. Maybe they would consider giving me an award just for doing such a fabulous job.

"So when do you find out?" Aria asked.

"I'm not sure, she didn't say. But it's already been delayed by a few months, so I'm guessing it'll be soon. There's no time to waste!"

"Hey guys," Jack said suddenly, placing a bowl of salad down next to my chicken parmesan. "If I'm going to be your bodyguard," Jack whispered, leaning in close to my ear. "I'm going to need a body to guard. Don't disappear again."

My whole body tensed as he eased into the chair next to me and gave a cheerful smile to Aria and Veronica. All the happiness that had been running through my veins had been replaced by dread within seconds. Even Aria and Veronica had forgotten all about my amazing news and were now beaming at Jack, completely oblivious to my discomfort.

"So Jack," Aria began, looking at him from under her eyelash extensions. "How come we've never heard about you before? I mean, we've been friends with Gia since fifth grade, and she's never mentioned you."

I glanced at Jack uncertainly. He opened his mouth to reply, but I cut in between.

"That's because he used to live in . . . Guam. We barely ever saw his family."

"Oh!" Veronica said, clearly a little confused.

"Guam." Aria repeated. "Isn't that a fruit?"

"Of course not!" I snapped back, my voice becoming shrill. "It's just off the coast of . . . Africa."

Alright, I had no idea what I was talking about. I'm pretty sure I had only ever heard about Guam on TV, and there was a big chance that it actually didn't exist. But it seemed random enough to fit my story. Besides, did Africa even have a coast? What *is* a coast?

"So, Guam. That must have been different than L.A.," Veronica said, turning to Jack.

"Uh, yeah. Africa's, um, definitely different."

I bit my lip, reasoning with myself not to have a nervous breakdown. I could practically feel my organs shutting down from copious amounts of stress.

"So how do you like LAC Elite?"

"It's a huge change from . . . Guam," Jack replied, glancing at me with a smile. I stabbed my chicken with my fork, whimpering a little. "But I like it. I have to admit though, everyone seems a little overdressed for school. All the elite schools in Guam had uniforms."

"Years ago, LAC Elite used to have a uniform policy," Aria explained, tossing her insanely long, brown hair behind her shoulder. "But then all these mothers went all *Real Housewives* on the school and started to complain about how the uniforms weren't good enough."

"Our school is a little different from others," Veronica added. She didn't need to elaborate; we all got the picture.

Jack raised his eyebrows in surprise, and I wanted to kick my friends under the table. Now he probably thought we were all stuck-up, pretentious snobs who wouldn't accept anything less than Chanel. Which was kind of true, but it wasn't a great first impression to make.

"Hello ladies!"

I looked up from my stabbed chicken and saw Brendan

walking toward me with Veronica's boyfriend, Aaron. Veronica and Aaron have been dating for just over two years, and I secretly think they'll get married. To be honest, I'm crazy jealous of Veronica. She's a natural brunette, but in ninth grade she dyed her hair a blood red color and instantly turned into a sexy, supermodel look-alike. I had begged dad to let me dye my hair red as well, but he told me I'd look like Elmo, and he refused to father Elmo. To spite him I dyed the ends of my hair blue with one of those washout DIY packs. I looked liked an idiot. Thankfully it washed out in a couple of weeks.

Veronica has the perfect relationship with Aaron. He's the kind of guy who unexpectedly buys her flowers and quotes poetry to her. But I didn't get any of that. My relationship had been seven months of boredom, decent make-out sessions, and zero common ground. Brendan was great, but he was the anti-romantic. Once, he gave me half of his Hershey's bar and quoted a scene from *White Chicks*. Hardly something to write home about.

"Hi!" I said a little too enthusiastically, as Brendan and Aaron approached the table.

Aaron pulled up a chair and sat next to Veronica, kissing her on the cheek. Aria was concentrating on Jack, and was completely unfazed by the lack of romance in her life. If it was possible, Aria was even more attractive than Veronica. But it was impossible for one guy to hold her down. It wasn't like she went around making out with any male who passed her on the street, but the word "commitment" just wasn't in her vocabulary. Plus, she could do the splits, which I think added to her appeal.

Brendan lowered himself into a chair next to me and kissed me on the lips. I went completely rigid, as if my body had temporarily paralyzed itself from sheer awkwardness. I didn't know if Jack even cared, but I had suddenly become shy and self-conscious.

"Hey man. How're you liking school so far?" he asked Jack.

Jack leaned back in his chair and said, "Algebra was torture, but so far, so good."

"Algebra is definitely not the highlight of LAC Elite. But it gets better, don't worry."

Oh lord, why were they even conversing? Couldn't they both just shut up and let me hyperventilate in peace? The two were clearly continuing their polite conversation from the car ride to school. It had been excruciatingly awkward until I finally got Brendan talking about the fight with his dad, who was apparently making him miss out on a bar hopping adventure with his best bud Danny that night. Instead, he was forcing Brendan to go to some college mixer where he was giving a speech about building a successful empire. Brendan had described it as "giving lectures and drinking expensive whiskey. My father's two favorite things." I'm not a fan of Danny, but I disliked Brendan's dad far more, so I could sympathize.

Dad and I had been to a few of those lame mixers last year, so that I could suck up to the professors and deans well enough to slip into an Ivy League. But people were either extremely excited by my last name or extremely bitter. "It's not a reputation you need, Gia. I've already built one for you," Dad had said, when he finally gave up on his networking plan. "It's really your grades you should be worried about." Apparently my grades weren't the only thing crashing and burning, now that my father had decided to hire full time protection without so much as an explanation.

Fortunately for me, getting lost in thought had allowed me to stop freaking out momentarily. Brendan and Aaron had lost interest in Jack and were talking about basketball, while Aria and Veronica were engaged in a deep discussion about Ellie Saab's latest collection. I couldn't join either quick enough to cut Jack out of the group. He leaned forward in his chair and eyed my untouched food with the fork protruding out of it.

"Not hungry?" Jack asked.

I pushed the plate away from me, frowning. "I've lost my appetite." Jack laughed and pulled the fork out of my chicken, placing it on the tray. I noticed his food hadn't been touched either.

He looked around silently, as if taking a few moments to soak in his surroundings. "It's been a while since I was at school. It feels weird."

Jack couldn't have been much older than I was; he looked to be in his early twenties. He was definitely young enough to not raise eyebrows at a high school. He probably saw me as kid though. The whole schoolyard setting wasn't particularly helping my cause. A thought suddenly crossed my mind, that Jack could potentially be a vampire. I mean, it was unlikely. But he was definitely hot enough to fit the quota, plus his skin was flawless. No sparkles though.

"You guys have a sushi stand at school?" Jack asked, turning to me with an incredulous look.

"Yeah, next to the waffle stand."

"That's crazy!"

"Why? It's just sushi."

"Yeah, but do you really need *four* sushi stands?"

I blinked at him. "We actually have five. There's one the other side of the school."

"Oh of course," Jack replied wryly. "My mistake."

"It's not a big deal!" I shot back, suddenly feeling defensive. "We just have a lot of options."

"You get options at a Burger King, Gia. This is something else."

"Jack," I dropped my voice to almost a whisper, making sure my friends couldn't hear. They were too immersed in their own conversation to notice anyway. "You're a bodyguard. Don't you deal with rich people all the time?"

"Well, yeah," he said. "But not like *this*. I've never seen wealth like this around people so young."

"Jeez, its just sushi," I mumbled, ignoring my phone as it let out a little buzz on the table in front of me.

Actually it wasn't just basic Japanese food. Jack was completely missing the point. He thought he was just sitting amongst spoiled kids with overpriced shoes, eating overpriced lunch. But in my world, it's not just about money; it's about where you're from. And if he was going to be around *and* survive, even if it was for a short while, he was going to learn that a pair of Alexander McQueen stilettos and five sushi stands represented a postcode and not just a dollar bill.

But I just shrugged and played along, not bothering to explain this to Jack. He wouldn't have understood, and I'd have come across looking like a stuck-up brat, which was a reputation I was desperately trying to steer clear of. It hadn't even been a proper twenty-four hours of knowing the guy and my self-consciousness was through the roof. I was so aware of every move I was making, I felt like someone had attached strings to me and was moving my arms and legs like a puppet.

Jack leaned forward and rested his arm on the table next to our untouched food. "So let me get this straight," he said, pointing at Brendan, who was still immersed in conversation with Aaron. "He's the quarterback and you're head cheerleader?"

I looked at Brendan and then back at Jack. "I'm sorry," I scoffed. "Does this look like a *Bring it On* movie to you? We don't do that stuff here."

"Yeah, you're probably right. You don't look like the overly perky type anyway."

I pursed my lips, not sure if that was a compliment or an insult. My phone buzzed again before I could reply, clearly annoyed that I hadn't bothered to check my texts the first time it alerted me. The screen read "Unknown." Without giving it a second thought, I clicked open. It read:

I'm always watching you

- DR. D

Alrighty then. Whoever thought that text was a good way to scare me clearly needed to up their game. Why would someone have secretly sent me a message and then signed it off? Didn't that just defeat the purpose of the anonymity? Granted, I had no clue who this Dr. D was, but still. And how did they manage to mask their number? I had heard of private phone calls, but never a private text message. It wasn't adding up.

"What's the matter?" Jack's voice broke into my thoughts.

"What do you mean?"

"I mean you're glaring at your phone. Is everything okay?"

"Everything's fine, jeez."

And it was. It was just a text, not a bomb threat. Okay sure, it wasn't exactly normal. And Dad had hired Jack for a reason, right? What had he said about that threat to my life, again? I really should pay more attention when he speaks. I put the phone down on the table, but forgot to lock it. Jack leaned closer and read the text before I had the chance to snatch it away from him.

"Gia," was all Jack said, his mouth forming a grim line.

"What's up?" Aria asked me, as I glared at Jack. He clearly had issues with respecting privacy.

"Nothing," I replied, waving a hand as if I was swatting a mosquito. "I just got this weird text. Whatever, don't worry."

"Who's it from?" Brendan said.

"Don't know," Jack replied for me. "It just shows up with *unknown*."

"Unknown?" Veronica repeated. "Can you even do that?"

At least I wasn't the only one lacking knowledge in that department. "Clearly you can," I said. "But it's signed off with 'Dr. D,' which is pretty bizarre."

"Do you know who that is?" Aaron asked, and I shook my head no.

"Try replying," Brendan suggested. "Ask who it is."

Jack leaned forward in his chair, shaking his head. "It won't work. There's no number listed, remember?"

Brendan cut his eyes to Jack. "Right," he said, a few seconds after he probably should have.

"I heard once," Aria said, looking dead serious. "That music producers watch their possible new clients for months in advance to gain more information on the type of person they are. It's all part of a marketing strategy."

We all looked at her blankly for a few seconds before Aaron finally said what we were all thinking. "What? That's ridiculous!" he exclaimed. "Where'd you hear that?"

"Some guy at a party told me!" Aria told him defensively. "He said his dad was a music producer so he knows all about this stuff."

"You really think a record producer is reaching out to me?" I asked, doing a half-assed job of stifling my laughter.

"It's a possibility. I mean, maybe this Dr. D is some guy who's been watching you because he wants to do an album with you."

"Maybe it's Dr. Dre!" Veronica said eagerly.

I gave her a, *you can't be serious* look, but she just grinned back at me so I knew she was only kidding. Aria, however, took it seriously. She slapped her palms down on the bench as her eyes widened.

"Oh my gosh, MAYBE! How cool is that!"

Jack, who was silent through this whole ordeal, cleared his throat and we all turned to look at him. "I think it's a definite possibility," he began, looking at Aria's keen expression. "But I highly doubt it."

"Oh come on, Jack!" Brendan piped up, throwing a muscly

arm across my shoulders and trapping my ponytail underneath it. "Don't be so negative. Maybe Dr. Dre really does want Gia."

I glanced at Jack and craned my neck uncomfortably underneath Brendan's arm. He looked at me without a word and I turned back to Brendan almost instantly. How nice of Brendan to crush me under his arm like I was going to run off into the sunset with Jack at any moment. He may as well have just peed on me. That would have been a more subtle way of marking his territory.

"I wouldn't worry too much about it," Aaron said, stretching his arms out above his head lazily. "This is Hollywood. Someone's always watching."

My phone buzzed in my hand. Another text message popped up, again from an unknown number.

"I got another one," I said, and all my friends leaned in to view the message.

And I'm closer than you think.

"Okay," Aria said uncertainly. She looked at me with a frown. "I'll admit that's kind of creepy."

A small rush of fear climbed up my spine. Couldn't disagree with her on that one. As if we had all rehearsed it, my friends and I looked around the campus in unison, hoping to catch someone suspiciously peering at me with a phone in their hand.

"Well who do you think it is?" Jack asked.

It felt like every student on campus had suddenly had a violent urge to pull out their phones and start texting. Almost everyone I could see was tapping away on their keypads and screens. It could have been anyone.

"Gia!" A voice called out from my right.

I froze, immediately recognizing who it was. "Mystery solved," I said under my breath.

The voice belonged to Meghan Adams, daughter of billionaire magnate Kevin Adams. She's also my arch nemesis.

Don't be fooled by her perfectly styled strawberry blonde hair or her insanely large blue eyes. She looks innocent enough, but in reality she's the most arrogant and self-obsessed human being, like, ever. Her dad owns a B-grade airline called "Air Adams," but still manages to earn what seems like a zillion dollars each day. Over the years I've come up with many theories about how her family must get the money to sustain her shopping addiction. I've decided she uses some kind of black magic. Wouldn't put it past her; she's pure evil.

Not only does Meghan's ego suck the air out of a room, she always acts like a complete angel around Brendan because she knows he's attractive and lacking in the common sense department. But for the amount of people who hate Meghan, which is a lot, there's an equal amount who adore her. Her two best friends, Lori and Mischa, never leave her side, acting more like bodyguards than Jack ever has.

"Meghan!" I said with fake enthusiasm, as she and her friends approached our table. "Come to feed on more innocent people's souls?"

"Yeah!" Aria added, matching my mocking tone. "I didn't know you could come out in daylight hours!"

"That's hilarious," Lori sneered, and I smiled at her sweetly.

"I just came to introduce myself to your friend Jack. Maybe show him around the school if he needed a tour guide or something," Meghan explained with an innocent smile on her face.

Brendan removed his arm from my shoulders and rose from his chair. "That's a great idea!" he said, beaming at her. "Do you guys want to sit down? Should I get some more chairs or something?"

"What are you doing?" Veronica asked him, with an incredulous look on her face. "She can't sit here."

"V, come on," Brendan said quietly.

"Oh that's okay Brendan," Meghan said, giving him a bruised look. "I just came to say hi."

Aria rolled her eyes as I glared at Meghan, slightly impressed that she could play the victim so well. Aaron glanced at Jack, who was watching the scene unfold silently. Brendan sat back down on his chair uncomfortably, avoiding my eye contact.

"I got your messages by the way," I told her, holding up my iPhone. "I must say, I didn't think cyber stalking was your style, but I guess it's not completely unbelievable."

To be honest, I didn't think Meghan would randomly send me a stalker-esque message; it *wasn't* her style. But I wouldn't put it past her to go a little crazy when it came to making my life hell.

"What are you talking about?" she asked, looking genuinely confused.

"You didn't send Gia a message saying you're always 'watching her'?" Aaron asked her.

Meghan put a perfectly manicured hand over her heart and gave me a hurt look. "I am deeply offended that you think I would be behind such a childish act," she said, batting her fake eyelashes at me dramatically.

Now it was my turn to roll my eyes. "Oh give it up Meghan! Everyone knows you're a—"

"Did you know," Brendan cut me off abruptly, fully aware that the situation would escalate if he didn't. "That Dr. Dre wants to do a record with Gia? Isn't that awesome?"

"Seriously?" Mischa said with a scoff. Meghan held up a hand, silencing her like the evil dictator she was.

"Oh," Meghan began, unsure as to how to respond to that. "Yeah. That's cool. I didn't even know you could sing, or rap. Or whatever. Good for you."

I smirked at her. It was clear she was biting back a snide remark to maintain her angelic reputation in front of Brendan, and give Jack a squeaky clean impression of herself. Brendan thought he was helping keep the peace on both sides, but really he was just making things worse for her and better for me. Lori and Mischa glanced at each other, struggling to keep in their own opinions.

"Well it's nice to meet you, Meghan." Jack's voice came from behind me, and I shot him a death glare. He gave me a shrug and his lips curved into a half smile.

"So I'm having a party this Saturday to celebrate Gia's almost record deal. You guys wanna come?" Brendan asked.

It was like he was *asking* me to slap him. "Brendan!" I cried, my voice reaching a new octave.

"What?"

"I'd love to!" Meghan exclaimed, looking painfully smug. "You'll be there, won't you, Jack?"

Jack opened his mouth to say something and turned to look at my warning glower. He closed his mouth and gave Meghan a sweet smile.

"Absolutely."

I reasoned with myself and took a deep breath. Stabbing Jack with a fork wasn't going to help the situation, so I decided against it.

"Nice outfit, Aria," Lori said, looking distastefully at her silver glittery skirt. "Of course, my mother always told me that a lady never wears silver in the afternoon. It makes her look cheap."

"Really?" Aria exclaimed with fake fascination. "Well if I ever meet a lady, I'll let her know."

Veronica gave a bark of laughter and I glanced at my lap, suppressing a smile. At least I was polite enough not to laugh at Lori right in front her. Meghan kept her eyes fixated on Jack with a tight smile on her face, before spinning on her pencil-thin Louis Vuitton heels and walking off silently, taking long strides with her two loyal friends behind her.

"What the hell was that?" I cried, smacking Brendan on the

arm the moment Meghan was out of earshot.

"Ow! What are you talking about? I just invited her to—"

"—a party that you're not even having!"

"Who said?" Brendan rubbed his arm where I had hit him. "My parents are going to Boston for the weekend so I'll have the house to myself. I was just about to tell you before Meghan came over."

I took my bag and whacked him again on the arm. "So then why'd you invite her?"

"Gia," Brendan said reasonably. "Don't you think it's time to give up these childish games? I mean, Meghan's always making an effort and you come across as kind of bitchy."

I gaped at him incredulously. He couldn't be serious; there was absolutely no way. I mean, Meghan was a self-righteous concubine, and Brendan was falling right into her trap.

"Oh come on, Brendan," Aria said, making a face. "Everyone knows Meghan's evil and she only acts all innocent around you because she wants you to get in her last season's Tibi pants."

Brendan shook his head disappointedly and said, "You girls, she's not even that bad! In fact, she's actually pretty funny. The other day—"

"Oh yeah?" I snapped, clutching my bag as I pulled my chair back. "Well if she's so freakin' fantastic, then why don't you make *her* your girlfriend?"

I hiked my bag strap onto my shoulder and pushed past Brendan roughly, leaving my sunglasses on the table. He tried to grab my hand to stop me, but I yanked it away and stalked off toward the lockers. I could hear Jack calling my name behind me, but I ignored him. Stupid Brendan could have stupid Meghan. If he was crazy enough to think someone like that was great, then he deserved her.

On top of that, Jack was proving to be more of a distraction than I had imagined he would be. His blonde hair made me want to read Shakespeare and use words like "glisten" or "scintillate." The last thing I needed was a ridiculously attractive guy up in my face all the time, especially when my boyfriend was being such an ass.

"Gia!"

"WHAT!"

I whirled around and smacked right into Jack's chest, which after all of this bumping into, I had realized was toned *as hell.* Jeez, he was always sneaking up behind me. I reminded myself not to run my hands down his abs, as it would be far too awkward to explain later. I took a step back and brushed a loose strand of hair away from my face.

"Go away, Jack. You can be my bodyguard later."

"What, did she steal your cheerleading routine or something?"

I glared at him. "Was that another joke? Because it wasn't funny."

"Not big on humor, I can see."

"I don't suppose you can have her . . . removed?"

Jack gave me a knowing look and said, "Gia, I'm a bodyguard. I'm not an assassin."

I pouted. "Once again, you're proving to be completely useless."

"Oh relax, she's just a girl. You can take her."

"Meghan isn't just *some girl,* Jack!" I practically exploded. "I hate her with every morsel of my body! This isn't some clichéd high school movie, where we were best friends in second grade but now she hates me, even though everyone knows we'll let it go and become friends again at the end. We've always hated each other, and we always will. Brendan knows that! Or at least he should."

"Well," Jack said, putting his hands in his pockets casually. "Then don't go to the party on Saturday."

I gave a deep sigh. "Well I have to go, now! Meghan will be there for sure, and if I'm not there something's bound to happen between the two of them. I don't trust her at all."

Jack raised an eyebrow. "But you trust Brendan?"

"Of course," I replied quickly. "It's just, Meghan will do something and he won't have time to say no."

Jack gave me pitying look and said, "I don't know what's worse. The fact that you may actually believe that, or that you're trying to get me to believe it."

"I don't pay you to pass judgement."

"Actually, you don't pay me at all. Your dad does. And he doesn't like the guy too much either."

"Well *I* trust him!" I exclaimed, taking another step back. I figured I could subtly inch away from him, far enough to not be able to hear him. The conversation would have to end then. "I mean, I'd practically let him perform heart surgery on me! That's how much I trust him!"

Okay, maybe I had gone slightly overboard with my "I trust Brendan" speech. Jack grinned and my heart started dance battling inside my chest.

"Gia," Jack began, trying not to laugh. "I wouldn't trust him with the game *Operation*. I doubt he even knows where the heart is located."

"It's a difficult organ to locate!"

Jack shook his head, but stayed silent. He didn't need to say anything; his judgement was pretty obvious. I hiked my bag's strap higher up my shoulder just as the bell signaling the end of lunch went off.

"Look," I said, giving a frustrated sigh. "It doesn't matter what you think. I know why I'm going to that party, and that's what counts."

"Whatever you say."

I crossed my arms over my chest, flipping the tip of my

ponytail behind my shoulder. "I bet you're having a great time relishing in my pain."

"I'm just here to do my job," Jack replied, but his smile gave away his amusement.

"A job that isn't actually necessary."

"I think those text messages prove otherwise."

"Seriously?" I asked, my irritation growing by the second. "*That* set you off? That was nothing! If I call Pizza Hut tonight, you're not going to shoot someone are you?"

"Hilarious," Jack said, deadpan. "But you don't think it's a tiny bit suspicious that the day after your dad hires bodyguards for your protection, some random person starts telling you that they're constantly watching you?"

On the word "bodyguards" Jack lowered his voice, aware that we were in full eavesdropping range.

I let my arms fall to my sides, forcing all emotion off my face. "Well, I mean, if you put it like that . . ."

Brendan suddenly walked past Jack before he could respond, pushing him roughly into me. I turned around to look at him, just in time to catch the glare he had shot in Jack's direction. It was Jack's first day at school and he had already left a trail of destruction in his wake. The worst part was he didn't seem to care that he was slowly but surely ruining my life. For him, I was a source of entertainment.

"Perfect," I said, throwing my hands in the air with frustration. "Just freaking perfect!"

"And you thought your life was nothing like a clichéd high school movie," Jack said, tilting his head to one side with a smile.

A jealous boyfriend, a manipulative arch nemesis, a creepy stalker and a frustratingly good-looking bodyguard. Throw in some pom poms and a stolen cheer routine, and I was the definition of a cliché.

c h a p t e r
t h r e e

THE NEXT sign that something disastrous was coming was kind enough to wait a few days before showing itself. It was Friday afternoon and I was sitting on an exercise ball in the indoor gym, letting the ball swivel to and fro underneath me. Ordinarily, there's no way I set foot in that gym unless I *really* force myself to. My love affair with sugar is too strong. Which isn't fantastic, because in Hollywood, your appearance defines you. Luckily, I'm one of those annoying people who can eat their weight in junk food and never gain a pound. That probably won't last forever, but I'm going to enjoy it while I can.

Unfortunately, it seemed that ever since the bodyguards had shown up, the gym was the only place I could really sit and think without being disturbed, despite all the rooms in the house. In particular, there was no escaping Jack and his painfully beautiful face. He was causing a lot of problems in my life, and I couldn't figure out a way to get him out. To make matters worse, Brendan hadn't spoken to me since the fight. Instead, we resorted to avoiding each other in hallways and shooting awkward glances whenever we were near one another. He hadn't even *tried* to talk to me. The day after our fight, he came to my locker before first period as if he wanted make up, but then he took one look at Jack and walked away silently. Which, let's face it, was a major overreaction. Clearly he disliked Jack, or was threatened by him or whatever, but too bad, buddy. He had started the fight with his "I love Meghan" fan club-style speech on how great she was. He could deal with it.

Worst of all, hating Jack was proving to be a major challenge for me. Sure, he was a jerk and all. But as it turns out, he was also really funny and smart, and it was a tough job pretending that I hated him twenty-four-seven. Also, he looked like an Abercrombie and Fitch model, so that didn't hurt either. He was always just *there*, making it hard for me to actually decide what I felt about him. He was like a constant distraction and when I was around him I couldn't breathe properly. If that continues, I might actually just stop breathing one day because I forget how to.

As if that all that wasn't bad enough, Jack had quickly become the most popular guy in school. Everywhere we went, people would flock as though Drake were having a concert in the hallway. It wasn't just the girls who were batting their eyelashes and reapplying lip-gloss when he was around. Even the male population of LAC Elite thought he was the best thing to have ever happened to the world. No wonder Brendan hated the guy so much; Jack had managed to achieve what he couldn't in just a few days. If anything, people were only going to show up to Brendan's party in hopes that Jack might get drunk enough to make out with them, the males probably included.

So there I was, sitting on an exercise ball, plotting my next move. Driving Jack out of the house was turning out to be a huge failure, and I wasn't sure how long I could continue being a psycho freak. It didn't seem to be getting on my dad's nerves at all. In fact, the only person who was constantly annoyed was me. I was considering drawing out my plan of action, stick figures and all, when I heard footsteps coming from the stairs.

"Gia?" Jack's voice called out.

I shot up from the exercise ball, stumbling a little as I regained my balance. Shoot! Jack couldn't walk in on me in a gym not doing anything! He probably dated supermodels in his spare time, supermodels that go on the elliptical machine for fun!

I did some quick thinking and ran my fingers through my hair, trying to add volume to the top. The footsteps were coming closer and I was running out of time. I practically ripped my jacket off me, revealing the spandex crop top and body-hugging tights I had on underneath. I had bought the work-out clothes almost a year ago when the girls and I decided we were going to get into shape, eat our veggies and do more squats. Only Aria really stuck to that promise, but even she gave up after a few weeks. If I was going to pretend that I was a health-goddess with Jack in the house, then I needed to look like one. The spandex had really made the most sense at the time, even if it didn't exactly fit right anymore.

"Hey," Jack said, padding into the gym.

I kicked the jacket to one side, leaning against the treadmill as seductively as I could.

"'Sup?" I said casually, giving him a nod of acknowledgment.

He looked around the gym, nodding in what I hoped was appreciation. I mean, I don't even like working out and I'll be the first to admit that having a gym as awesome as ours in your own home is pretty damn fantastic. The surround sound alone is reason enough to hang out in there.

"Nice," he said, looking at the many flat screen TVs across the walls. I could only hope I was included in that assessment.

I smoothed my hair down a little from the ends, suddenly very conscious of my crop top and super tight pants. The aim was to look sexy, but I was pretty sure I just looked like an idiot stuffed in clothes too small for her.

"Did you need something?" I asked, reaching for my water bottle. I heaved a deep sigh, like I had been working my butt off and had only stopped because of his interruption.

"Your dad wants to know when you're going to stop pretending to work out," Jack said, and I practically spat the water out of my mouth in embarrassment.

I forced it down and said, "Excuse me?"

"His words, not mine."

I put the water bottle down on the floor next to me, hoping the tight pants would hug all the right places as I was bending.

"I'm not *pretending*," I snapped. "I just burnt off like, all of my calories for today on the treadmill."

Jack's gaze diverted to the treadmill, and I shifted uncomfortably from one foot to another. "It's not even on," he said.

"I just turned it off."

Jack looked at me, and I raised my eyebrows. "It's not even plugged in."

Whoops. Why did I have to go with the treadmill? There was enough gym equipment in there to stock a nation, and I chose the one thing that wasn't freaking plugged in.

"What are you, the treadmill police?" I asked. "What do you want?"

"I don't want anything. Your dad wa—"

"Yeah," I interrupted. "But why'd he send you to ask? What are you, his new messenger boy?"

Jack gave a small smile and said, "Actually, he sent Mike. But I don't think your brother was paying attention. And I was bored, so I figured I may as well check out the gym."

If he wanted to check me out while he was it, I had no issues with that.

"Well," I said, putting my hands on my hips. "All checked out. You can go now."

I was suddenly becoming desperate for an opportunity to put the jacket back on and fix my hair. Jack hadn't hit on me once, so I clearly wasn't pulling off the fitness guru look I had been aiming for.

"Woah," Jack said, walking toward a piece of large equipment that had all these weights and handles and scary looking things all over it. "This is pretty heavy duty stuff. Who uses it?"

"My dad, mostly. Although not so much anymore," I replied, watching a clearly impressed Jack inspect the equipment. "And when he wants to impress his friends, Mike will use it sometimes."

Jack looked up at me. "And you of course," he said, his lips curving into a smile.

"Right," I said, crossing my arms over my chest. "I use that all the time."

"Yo, sis!" I heard Mike say from behind me. I looked over at him, just as he walked into the room. "Dad wants to know when you're gonna stop pr—"

"I got it!"

Jeez. Dad was majorly salting my game here. Mike looked at me, my tight as hell outfit, Jack's face, and then back at me.

"Am I interrupting?" he said, and I narrowed my eyes at him as aggressively as I could.

"No!"

"Just asking," he replied, clearly pleased with himself.

Jack came up from behind and stood next to me. I could feel him glance at me but I didn't do the same. There was no way I was looking at him directly in the eye while standing that close to him. The crop top was definitely a bad idea. Hindsight is always twenty-twenty.

"What are you even doing in here, anyway?" Mike asked. "You never work out."

"That's not true!" I snapped defensively. "I exercise all the time."

"You only come in here to sit on the exercise ball," Mike replied, giving me a knowing look.

"Excuse me?" I exclaimed, deeply offended. "I use a bunch of stuff in the gym."

"Oh, yeah? Like what?"

Reflexively, I looked at Jack, as if he could offer some help. He just looked back at me blankly, waiting for me to answer.

"The . . . bench press thing," I finally said, turning back to my brother.

Mike gave a bark of laughter. "Do you even know what that looks like?"

"I know that if I pick up one of these dumbbells and throw it at you, it would probably do some serious damage," I said, smiling sweetly. "How's *that* for gym knowledge?"

"Oh please," Mike replied. "You can't even pick one of these up, let alone throw one at me."

"You really wanna test that theory?"

Jack gave a quiet laugh next to me, and I realized how childish I was coming across. Not at all the poised supermodel I had planned to be. But spend a minute with my brother, and you'll understand. He just brings out the violent side in everyone.

"Whatever," Mike said, turning to leave.

"Oh, and Mike?" I said, just as he made it to the door. "If you prank call me one more time, so help me, I will shove my foot *so* far down your throat tha—"

"Oh my God!" Mike groaned, spinning around to face me. "For the last time, Gia. It's not me!"

I scoffed. "Yeah right!"

Mike gave a frustrated sigh and said, "I don't need a phone to piss you off, Gia. I live with you! If I really want to get on your nerves, I'd just break into your closet and throw your shoes all over the floor."

My jaw dropped in sudden realization. "I *knew* that wasn't a raccoon!" I cried, practically launching myself at Mike.

"Woah, woah!" Jack said, stepping in. "Calm down!"

He extended his arm out, using it as a kind of barricade between Mike and I, just as I lurched forward. I slammed right into his arm, immediately becoming rigid when my bare skin came into contact with his. Stupid, stupid crop top! What the hell was I thinking? Mike, in the meantime, had taken the opportunity to walk out of the gym and leave me to make a fool of myself in front of Jack. I took an almost hilariously giant step back, regaining my composure and trying to stop my cheeks from burning up.

"I'm going to kill him," I mumbled. Jack gave a small headshake.

"What's this about prank calls?" he asked.

"Ugh! It's just my brother has decided that his new favorite hobby is creeping me out over the phone!"

"Creeping you out?" Jack repeated. "How?"

"Super cliché," I replied. "Heavy breathing, occasionally whispering my name. Sometimes it sounds like he's talking to someone else on the phone. Maybe it's his friend Josh. That kid is such a perv, I swear."

"Okay, woah, slow down," Jack said. "Describe these conversations to me."

I sighed, as if talking was such an effort. "The phone will ring, I'll pick it up and I'll say hello. It'll be silent for a few seconds and then randomly people will start talking about stuff that doesn't even make sense. Then I usually just hang up."

"What do they say?"

"Weird stuff. Once, it was two guys yelling at each other. One kept going on and on about how the other one was meant to have his back, or something. Another time, it was like a whole freaking monologue on life! Like, what the hell? It was so messed up."

Jack gave me a confused look. "What? That doesn't make any sense."

I nodded and said, "Told you. Although sometimes I think they sound kind of familiar."

"The voices?"

"Yeah. That's why I think it's Mike, he's pretty good at accents. But mostly it just sounds like someone's watching a movie and they forgot to turn it down when they called."

"When was the last time you got one of these calls?" Jack asked me.

"Maybe an hour ago?" I replied, shrugging.

"Does it come up with a number?"

"Um, it's a prank call. They're not going to put their number on there so I can call back!"

He was hot, but he wasn't very smart, clearly.

"How long have you been getting these calls?" Jack asked, and I tapped my foot impatiently.

"I don't know, a week? Are we done with the interrogation, Sherlock?"

"Gia," Jack said, giving me a serious look. "Did you ever consider that maybe the phone calls have something to do with those texts you got a couple of days ago?"

I stared at him. What? I had been so caught up with everything else; I had forgotten about the messages.

I shook my head and said, "Jack, this is all just some lame joke. There's no conspiracy here. Sorry to disappoint you."

"But it makes sense, doesn't it? What I'm saying?" Jack

replied.

It did, kind of. But there was no way I was telling him that.

"No."

"Gia."

"Whatever, Jack!" I exclaimed. I was getting really tired of talking about the whole thing. "Obviously Mike has nothing better to do right now, but he'll get bored eventually and it'll stop."

"Alright," Jack said. He was clearly not pleased, but he knew there was no way to prove it was something bigger. The scoreboard was finally giving me something to celebrate.

But then it hit me. I wasn't wrong about the random conversations. In fact, I was exactly right. They weren't random at all; they *were* dialogues from movies. My dad's movies, to be exact. No wonder they sounded so familiar!

"What?" Jack said, and I realized my face had probably given away my epiphany.

"Nothing," I replied, looking at the floor inconspicuously.

Telling Jack about the movie dialogues was a terrible idea. It made it seem a lot worse than it probably was, and I didn't need Jack giving me another lecture or questionnaire.

"Gia, you're not fooling anyone," Jack said, and I looked up at him with a glare. "Just tell me."

"Fine! The conversations are dialogues from my dad's movies! Whoever it is, they play random parts of the movies to me. There! Are you happy?"

Boy, I didn't last one second under that pressure. I would be the *worst* in hostage situations where they needed me to divulge secrets. I'd give them everything they wanted before they even finished asking.

Jack looked at me, expressionless. It was so hard to tell what he was thinking. He was always a question mark. "Still think this is just some stupid game your brother's playing?" he asked, challenging me to say yes.

I knew he had a point, but there was no way I was going to give him the satisfaction. Besides, if it wasn't my brother, then there really was some random out there harassing me. Not exactly something that helps you sleep peacefully at night. So I did the mature thing, and completely denied everything.

"Look, forget it," I declared. "I'm over all of this. Let's just forget the whole thing and move on, okay?"

I turned my back to him, giving another sigh. The conversation was never ending, and I was struggling to keep it together in that much spandex. How the hell does Spiderman swing from buildings and save lives in that material? I can barely waddle in it.

"I have a proposal," Jack said from behind me, after only a few seconds of uncomfortable silence.

I stiffened. A proposal? Like a legit proposal! Sure it was a bit soon, and I didn't particularly like Jack, but he was hot as hell. And if he had a nice ring I wasn't going to say no. Hell if he had a crappy ring, I'd still probably say yes. I'd just have to break the news to Brendan later. He'd understand. Maybe.

"Um . . ." I spun on my heel hesitantly, turning to face Jack's extremely serious face.

"Look, it's pretty obvious that, for whatever reason, you don't like me very much," Jack said. "But I know this isn't really about me. I'm not really the problem here."

Okay, so no ring. His proposal was clearly not going down how I thought it would.

"What are you trying to say?" I asked him, putting my hands on my hips.

"I'm willing to help you investigate this whole prank call thing and figure out who's behind it," Jack said, his tone sounding very business-like. "But, you need to accept the fact that I'm not going anywhere. You can hate me all you want, but I'm still going to be around."

"What if I don't want to know who's behind it? What then?"

"I think we both know that's a lie. And you don't have the ability to find out who it is by yourself."

"But you do?"

Jack shrugged. "I could definitely help. Plus, you've got that Golden Globes thing you're so excited about. You don't want to ruin that, do you?"

I raised an eyebrow. "How do you know about that?"

"Gia, I live with you remember? It's all you've been talking about for the past few days."

I narrowed my eyes at him suspiciously. "Let's say I, hypothetically, take you up on this offer. What do I have to do?"

"Drop the act," Jack said simply.

"Come again?"

"Oh come on, Gia," Jack replied. "You can't honestly hate me this much for no reason. You don't even know me! This is probably just to get back at your dad for something."

I stared at him silently for a few seconds. Alright, so he had caught me. I mean, it wasn't like it was a huge secret or anything. But I wasn't exactly expecting him to just blatantly state it like that.

"Well what's in it for you?" I asked, deciding it was a good idea to ignore his very valid points and swiftly move on.

Jack's expression remained completely serious. "The sooner we figure out who's doing this, the sooner you're out of danger. Which also means I'm no longer needed. So I go back to New York, your life goes back to normal, and everyone's happy. It's a win-win from where I'm standing."

I hoped I also looked like a Victoria's Secret model from where he was standing. I took a deep breath, majorly unhappy with where this was headed. He *did* have a point. As much as I would miss his overwhelmingly attractive good looks, having Jack out of my life would bring back a lot of peace to my world. And he was right. Now that I was up for the role of Miss Golden Globe, I couldn't afford for anything to go wrong and ruin my chances. I wasn't about to let some weirdo with far too much free time get in the way of me handing Bradley Cooper a trophy.

"So you'll help me catch this creep, and all I need to do is be nicer to you?"

"Pretty much."

"You know, I could just fire you and all our problems would end."

Jack shook his head and said, "Actually you can't fire me. I technically work for your dad and not directly for you."

I did some mental reasoning, weighing up the pros and cons. Being nice to Jack was going to be tough, but it would lead to a lot of my problems beings solved.

Against my better judgment, I finally sighed and gave a reluctant nod. "Fine."

The corners of Jack's lips twitched as if they were going to curve up, but didn't quite get there. He extended his hand toward me so that I could shake it.

"Deal?" he said.

I looked at his hand uncertainly, and the back at him. The hostility was my only defense mechanism! I was practically signing over my one weapon to my enemy. Unfortunately for me, I needed Jack's help, and his offer worked out pretty well in my favor.

I put my hand in his and shook it firmly. "Deal."

"Great," Jack said, our hands still holding one another.

"Just so you know, this doesn't make us besties."

"Got it."

"And my rules still apply."

"I figured as much."

My gaze dropped to our hands, and suddenly the electric

currents started shooting through my body again. I yanked my hand out of his placed it behind my back, where it wouldn't be tempted to try and rip off Jack's shirt.

"Alright, no need to get emotional," I said.

Jack's grin reappeared as he walked toward the door. "It was a pleasure doing business with you, Miss Winters."

I watched him walk out without saying a word. The moment I heard the soles of his shoes hit the stairs, I exhaled deeply, slapping my palm to my forehead. Jack seemed to have taken all the air out of the room when he walked out. The stupid spandex was killing me, and my pants were so tight I was scared Anya would need to cut them off me.

I had absolutely no clue who was behind all the phone calls and the texts. Maybe they were they same person, maybe not. One thing was for sure, though. I had just made a deal with the devil.

And there was no going back after that.

chapter four

WHEN SATURDAY night finally arrived, I had a game plan set out in my mind and was fully ready to execute it. When I had told Dad I was going to Brendan's party he had looked at me like I was crazy and then flat out refused, even though I hadn't really asked for permission. It might have had something to do with the fact that Jack had opened his big mouth and told my dad about the phone calls and the text. Needless to say, he freaked out and started talking about how he was going to have to lock me away in some tower just to keep me safe. Unfortunately for Dad, he could try and Rapunzel me all the way to San Francisco if he wanted, but I was going to that party come hell or high water. If there was one thing Meghan was brilliant at, it was getting her way. She wasn't an idiot; she knew for sure that Brendan and I had been fighting all week. His party was the perfect setting to flip her hair and throw some playful winks in his direction. And knowing Brendan, he'd fall right into her trap. So I told Dad to take a chill pill and relax, promising I wouldn't be out too late, even though we both knew that was a big fat lie. He did lots of sighing and kept giving me his *I'm a pained parent* look, but couldn't really stop me in the end.

Jack and I rode to Brendan's house that night in almost complete silence, which was good because I still didn't trust myself to not say something stupid around him. I was already on edge because of the party; I didn't need Jack's perfect blonde hair messing with my thoughts. Besides, our little arrangement in the gym meant that I'd have to tone my attitude down around him, which was going to be hard because it was becoming more of a habit now than anything else. Luckily for me, Jack had given up on trying to make small talk about a minute into the ride, and instead turned the radio up as loud as our ears could manage. Apparently pretending the other one didn't exist was working out to be the preferred coping method for the both of us.

When we finally arrived, Jack parked on Brendan's street a little away from the open gates leading to his enormous mansion. He turned the car off, eyes straight ahead.

"Jesus," Jack said. "Did the whole of L.A. turn out for this party?"

There was a sea of luxury cars ahead, as already tipsy teenage girls were making their way past the manicured bushes and into the house, while their boyfriends yelled at each other not to scratch their new Lamborghinis while parking. The music was so loud that we could hear it from Jack's jeep, even with the windows rolled up. I didn't recognize about eighty percent of the people I saw, but that was pretty normal. Big parties always tended to draw attention from the outside.

"I wonder if Meghan's here yet?" I said, scanning the crowd.

"Seriously?" Jack turned to face me. "You're *still* on that?"

"If you're referring to how Meghan Adams is trying to get her slimy fingers on Brendan, then yes. I'm *still* on that."

"You've got a lot of issues."

Yeah, well, who doesn't buddy? Jack shook his head, opened the car door and climbed out. After a few seconds of mental pep-talking I did the same, trying not to fall flat on my face as my five-inch Balenciaga shoes hit the pavement.

"Wait," Jack said, eyeing the area around the car. He stood on his tiptoes, peering over the back of the car.

"What the hell are you doing?"

"All clear," Jack said, slipping the keys into his jeans pocket. "Just checking."

Now it was my turn to shake my head. After our deal, Jack had gone full spy mode. He kept looking out the windows like a hired assassin was going to jump out from behind a bush with a pair of nunchucks. Which was fantastic, because Dad was already hyped enough about it. No really Jack, thanks a bunch. Luckily Kenny, although slightly concerned, kept reminding him that there was nothing we could do until we got another sign from whoever this Dr. D was.

I had even taken it upon myself to do some top secret spy research and Googled the different ways someone could anonymously send a message. I'm pretty sure some of the sites that came up had some illegal content on them, but apparently it was possible to send texts from certain websites. That, and there were single, busty Russian girls in my area who were dying to meet me.

"Can we tone down the whole secret service thing you've got going?" I said. "It's freaking me out."

"My 'secret service' thing is what's going to keep you safe."

"Can't you just, like, give me a can of pepper spray like a normal person and go home to New York?"

Jack smiled. "That wasn't our deal."

I groaned and said, "Ugh, this stupid deal is going to kill me."

And if it didn't, Jack's appearance definitely would. He had his hands tucked into the pockets of his blue jeans, and was wearing a maroon, button-down shirt with the sleeves rolled up to his elbows. He had taken a little extra care with his hair, and his eyes looked bluer than I'd ever seen them before. There was a large part of me that thought I should just give up on the Meghan thing and let her have my boyfriend and focus all my energy on Jack. But there was another part of me, most likely my ego, that wouldn't allow it. At least not yet. I had barely known the guy a week and I had bigger things to worry about at the moment.

Although now that the party was right behind me, I was beginning to have some doubts about my game plan. So many things could go wrong; it was ridiculous. Jack and Brendan in the same place with unlimited alcohol *and* Meghan Adams could only result in something bad happening. The alcohol was inevitable and I doubted I could handle a Brendan-Jack showdown, but Meghan I could deal with. I took a deep breath, giving the air a sharp, determined nod. It was just a party. I had been to a million of these and I'd survived. Of course I had never had to deal with Jack Anderson before, living proof that there is a God and he does love us.

"We should cover a few things before we go in," I told him, leaning against his car.

But Jack didn't look like he was listening. Instead, he was eyeing me up and down, now that my outfit was in full view. I guess he hadn't bothered to notice it when I was in the car.

"You look nice," he said, giving a light shrug.

Wow. Really wasn't expecting that one.

"Are you allowed to say that to me?"

"What? I'm just harmlessly complimenting you."

I scoffed and said, "Yeah, alright buddy. Keep it in your

pants. It's just a dress."

OH. MY. LORD. Jack Anderson had actually complimented me, which clearly meant he thought I looked hot! And good, because I was wearing a two thousand dollar Herve Leger dress. So if a few boys didn't have a heart attack at the party, then I'd be severely disappointed. Sure, it was a tad much for an impromptu high school gathering, but given my circumstances, I needed to pull out *all* stops.

"Fine," Jack said. "You look like crap. Is that better?"

I narrowed my eyes at him, something I was doing a lot lately. "Are you allowed to say that to me?"

Jack rolled his eyes and said, "I can't win with you!"

I clutched my bag to my chest, trying not to shiver as a gust of wind blew past. "I think we need to add a clause to our contract," I told him, hoping my voice was coming across as extremely professional.

Jack looked like he wanted to walk away and never return, but I could see the curiosity was kind of eating at him. I was right.

"Alright, fine. Let's hear it," he said.

"I don't think it's fair that I have to be nice to you but you don't have to be nice to me," I replied.

"I just complimented your dress!"

"So?"

"So that was nice."

"No, that was inappropriate."

"I can't separate the two."

I gave him a knowing look. "Clearly."

Jack gave an impatient sigh and said, "I'm helping you investigate your stalker. Isn't that enough?"

"You haven't even done anything yet!" I cried, half-laughing at how ridiculous the conversation was beginning to sound.

"Gia, I have nothing to go off," Jack said. "We have no phone number, no real name, no way of contacting this person.

I'm doing the best I can!"

"Yeah well, do better," I said, walking toward the loud music.

"Only the best for Harry Winters's little princess."

I stopped walking, turning to face him with a wrinkled nose. It was only okay when I referred to myself as Princess Gia in my flashback story. Coming out of Jack's mouth, it sounded like a huge insult. I considered whacking him with my bag, but then eyed his deceptively toned muscles. They didn't look like Hulk Hogan, but I hit like a sissy. There was no way the bag was going to do enough damage. My stiletto might have, but I wasn't about to let my foot touch the pavement without a layer of protection.

Behind us, the drunken shouts of people singing along to a song I barely recognized grew louder.

"Look, here's the game plan!" I snapped impatiently. "We go in there, I find Meghan, confront her and make sure she keeps her paws off my man."

"Please never repeat that last line."

"I just know she's going to be prancing around Brendan all night in her hooker shoes."

Jack looked like he was slowly losing the will to live. "Wait," he said. "Your grand plan is to find Meghan and start a fight? How's that going to solve anything?"

"It's a working idea, okay?" I said, hands on my hips. "Just go with the flow. Oh, and if someone hands you a bag with white powder in it, it's probably not icing sugar."

"Gia," Jack said, giving me a knowing look. "I know how parties work, and I know what drugs are. I'm not actually from Guam. Which, by the way, happens to be part of America."

"Seriously?" My eyes widened. "No kidding!"

Somehow Dad had forgotten to put that into his geographical fun facts.

"So can we go in now, or do you have any other freaky rules to go over?"

"No, I think that covers it."

As Jack and I walked up Brendan's driveway, I did some major mental pep talking. I totally had the situation under control. I mean, my hair was perfect and my dress was beyond fabulous. Granted I couldn't really breathe all that well in it, but whatever. If you aren't in some kind of pain, your outfit isn't right.

We entered the house and were instantly greeted by a wave of minimally dressed, drunk people. The music was so deafeningly loud; my ears began ringing within seconds. It had been less than a minute and I had already inhaled enough secondhand fumes to last a lifetime. Jack leaned in and said something close to my ear, but I couldn't hear it over the sound of a group of giggling girls holding their heels in their hands.

"WHAT?"

"STAY CLOSE."

He didn't have to ask me twice. I wasn't too keen on getting lost among a raging ocean of strangers, especially ones that couldn't even speak English, based on the two girls standing next to me. They kept yelling in what I could only assume was Swedish, and they didn't seem happy with each other. Jack and I weaved our way through the crowd, which seemed unusually packed given the time. It was just past nine o'clock and I was certain the police would show up within the next hour. I had been to a lot of parties in my time, but the turn out for this one was impressive. You'd have thought Dr. Dre and I really were collaborating on an album.

Unfortunately for me, from the minute we walked in, girls around the room had already spotted Jack as a possible target and were giving him hopeful smiles and waves. There was no way in hell I was letting Jack near the pool and the bikini-clad Barbie dolls surrounding it. Some perky brunette who I always saw around school, but never knew the name of, walked past us with a gentle "hi" to Jack, absolutely ignoring me in the process.

She wasn't fooling anyone with the amount of makeup she was wearing; I still knew she didn't belong.

"Freshman?" I said, smiling at her innocently.

She looked at me nervously and said, "Um, yeah. Bu—"

"Get out!" I said, my smile unwavering.

Her eyes darted between mine and Jack's before nodding sharply, as she slipped back into the crowd without putting up a fight.

"Ouch," Jack said beside me, and I glared at him.

"What?" I snapped.

"Nothing," he replied, suppressing a smile.

Smart move on his part. It's not that Jack wasn't allowed to hit on other girls, or anything. I just didn't need anyone distracting my bodyguard just in case something were to happen to me. It was a matter of personal security and nothing else, okay? Pure and simple logic. Besides, freshmen weren't welcome at senior parties. I don't care what lame excuse she was going to conjure up to try to stay.

We made our way past the staircase and into the first living room on the right. There were plastic cups scattered across the floor and empty pizza boxes shoved into the corners of the room. I had no idea where the furniture had gone, but Brendan had clearly moved it so that he could accommodate the large amount of drunken teens gyrating against one another. A Nicki Minaj song was now blaring through the house, and the people surrounding us all had their hands up in the air, waving them around and fist pumping. The room was dark aside from disco lights that had been put up on all four corners of the room, and the glow-stick necklaces wrapped around a group of boys whose Ralph Lauren polo shirts were well on their way off their bodies. I scanned the room for Brendan and Meghan, coming up short. I had no clue where my friends were either, and calling them up would be useless over this music. Parties suck.

"GIA!"

I spun around and came face-to-face with Lincoln Foster, smiling back at me in the dim lighting. Lincoln was one of the nicest guys in the school and truthfully also one of the best looking. And if that wasn't good enough, Lincoln was an actor, trying to break into the business. He had been in a few movies, usually playing the role of someone's son or another's best friend. He wasn't an extra, but hardly a leading man. I had had a bit of a crush on him back in the day, but after we became good friends I ruled him out as an option. It was actually a surprise that he was at the party. Brendan didn't like him very much, on account of him being way more successful with his acting gigs. Clearly jealousy was a reoccurring pattern with my boyfriend.

"HEY LINCOLN!"

I didn't even bother introducing Jack; I assumed he knew. Jack had been the only thing LAC Elite had talked about all week.

"YOU LOOKING FOR BRENDAN?"

"NO THANKS. I'M NOT THIRSTY."

Lincoln raised his eyebrows in confusion.

"I'LL GO TELL THE DJ TO TURN THE MUSIC DOWN."

I didn't know why he was going to sell CJ a tunic gown, but I smiled and nodded, pretending that I had heard what he was saying. Luckily it seemed to be an acceptable answer, because he nodded in reply, turned on his heel and disappeared in the crowd. I shrugged and turned to Jack, not knowing what to do next. I was far from being in a partying mood, and there still seemed to be no sign of my friends or Brendan among the growing number of partyers. Unfortunately, there was also no sign of Meghan, which was always an issue. That girl is a slippery little thing.

A group of guys I only half recognized pushed past us roughly, knocking me backward into Jack. He moved a little closer to me to let the crowd through, slipping his hand into mine as he pulled to the left a little. My heart rate increased almost immediately to the danger zone, and I was pretty certain there was no way it was ever coming down. Of course Jack wasn't bothered by it all; he had only done it to move me out of the way. I clearly didn't have the same effect on him that he did on me, two thousand dollar dress on or not.

I allowed myself three more seconds of pure bliss before pulling my hand out of his grasp and taking the biggest step back that I could in the tiny space around us.

"What are you doing?" I yelled over the music. Thankfully the volume seemed to have reduced, so my ears weren't in so much pain.

Jack gave me a confused look and said, "What?" I held up the hand he had been holding a few seconds before and waved it at him. He realized what I meant and leaned in so I could hear him. "Gia I'm a bodyguard, remember? I can't keep you safe if I lose you in the crowd."

It *was* a very logical response. Hard to argue with logic, but tell that to my raging hormones.

"You can keep me safe without touching me!"

Jack rolled his eyes as if he couldn't believe how unlucky he was, and I couldn't even blame him. It's not like I wanted to be mean to Jack. It just sort of came out. It was my brain's way of making sure I didn't accidently fall in love with him. But obviously Jack didn't know that. From his eyes, I was just throwing a whole lot of crazy at him and for no reason. No wonder the guy was so desperate to go back to New York.

"Hey, babe!" Some random guy I had never seen suddenly swung his arm around my shoulders, pulling me close to him. "I swear I wasn't making out with her! She was making out with me. I was the victim!"

I widened my eyes in alarm and looked at Jack, who was trying not to laugh. I mouthed *help* at him but he shook his head, an infuriating smile on his face. Really? He was just going to stand there and not do anything? So much for his secret service bullshit.

"Um, do I know you?" I asked, pulling away from the guy in disgust. He smelled like what I could only imagine was cat litter.

He looked at me, his eyes drooping a little. His hair looked completely dishevelled and he had a joint in between his lips, only it didn't look lit. He eyed me up and down, raising an eyebrow. He had a red plastic cup in one hand, with more than one ring resting on each of his fingers.

"My b. I thought you were my girl!" the guy said loudly, so that I could hear him over the music and drunken cheers.

His *B?* I looked at Jack, who was still smiling at me. He nodded at me, giving me a look that said *go for it*. Great. I was being groped by some creep who had his hands all over my extremely expensive outfit, and it was all happening in front of Jack's eyes. By the looks of it, the night was on the right track to crashing and burning.

"We have to go," I declared. "But I'll take that."

I reached over and grabbed the cup from his hand, pushing through the crowd before anyone could stop me. I had no idea if Jack was following me or not, but given his freaky bodyguard conduct, I figured he'd be close behind. When I finally managed to squeeze my way out of the living room and into the main hall, where there was a little more space, I took a deep breath and sipped at whatever was in the red cup.

"Oh God . . ." I sputtered, feeling the liquid burning as it eased down my throat. It tasted *disgusting*, whatever it was.

It seemed to be a mix of something, most likely some type of cleaning liquid and straight up rat poison. Given how sketchy that guy had looked, it wouldn't be surprising if whatever I was drinking had been conjured up in his basement. But I was going to need something strong if I was going to make it through the party. Jack's presence was making little things seem like a bigger deal than they were. How many of these stupid parties had I already been to? How many times had I forced myself to sip a drink and pretend I liked it? How many times had I watched the people around me completely destroy their livers, and at times, pieces of furniture? None of it was new, but with Jack there, it felt like I was suffocating.

"You sure that's a good idea?" Jack said, watching me force another few sips down.

I gagged, forcing more down my throat. "Yes."

Thankfully the music in the main hall was even softer than before, so I could actually hear what he was saying at an almost normal volume. I had no idea where the DJ was, but I could see speakers all around the house. Brendan's mansion was absolutely huge, so the DJ could have been in any one of the several living rooms open to the party animals. Even Lincoln seemed to have disappeared without a trace.

I placed the drink down on a nearby table. Half a cup of liquid death was enough for one night. A group of people who were standing in a kind of circle near the far corner of the room were all cheering loudly. I waited until a bunch of girls, who I recognized from a lower year level, finished stumbling past Jack and me, before looking over at the group.

"What are they doing?" Jack asked, watching them in confusion.

"Suck and blow," I replied, the bitter taste of the drink still lingering on my tongue.

Jack looked at me, widening his eyes. His corner of his lips curved up into a half-smile. "Excuse me?"

I gave him a disgusted look and said, "Get your mind out of the gutter. It's a card game! Haven't you ever seen *Clueless*?"

"Does it look like I've seen *Clueless*?"

Jack turned his attention back to the group of cheering teenagers, who were clearly encouraging two people making out passionately. At least I knew almost everyone playing the game, only now I wish I hadn't. They looked like idiots.

"You suck in air so that the card sticks to your lips," I explained. "And then you pass it on to the person next to you, blowing out air so that it sticks to their lips. Suck. And. Blow."

I pointed at two girls who were demonstrating exactly what I had just said.

"So what happens if you drop the card?" Jack asked.

"You have to kiss."

Jack looked at me, an impressed look on his face. "That's creative."

Creative wasn't exactly how I'd put it, but sure. Creative was a good path to go down.

"Oh, hey Gia!" I heard someone say, and saw Charlie Kingston coming right toward me in a top with the world's lowest neckline. There almost wasn't even a point to wearing anything on top. It wasn't really covering much.

Charlie Kingston's father is a big time music producer, and not the sketchy type that Aria talks to. Like an *actual* music producer. She was always going on about that one time Ariana Grande invited her to her birthday party, or how hot Robin Thicke looks over brunch. Don't get me wrong, I like the girl. Only I don't *really* like her. It's kind of like talking to Kate Upton. I mean, sure she's stunning and sweet and all. But did she have to be *that* good looking and nice, all in one go? Someone like that has to be hiding some huge skeleton in her closet. Maybe she was addicted to smelling shampoo or something. The other shoe has got to drop at some point.

"Hey Charlie," I said, giving her a half-assed smile. "Great dress!"

What little there was of it, of course.

"Thanks Gia! Did you want to play?" Charlie asked, motioning toward the group Jack and I had been watching.

"Uh, no thanks," I said. "I'm good."

Charlie nodded and looked at Jack, smiling at him hopefully. "What about you?"

Jack looked at me and then back at Charlie. I glared at him, making sure his gaze didn't drop any lower than her nose. Boy, was I going to unleash hell if that happened.

"Oh no, I'm okay. Thanks," Jack replied politely.

"Oh come on!" Charlie said, tilting her head to one side so that her blonde curls tumbled all the way down to her hip. "It'll be fun!"

"Wel—"

"He's very busy!" I cut in, and Jack looked at me with an amused smile. "Very, very busy. So busy."

Charlie looked at me uncertainly and said, "Um, okay?"

"Maybe later," Jack said.

"But then again, maybe not," I quickly added. *So busy*, I mouthed, giving her an innocent smile.

"Cool," Charlie said, looking at me like I had lost my mind. "Well, you know where to find me."

She winked at him and walked off without even acknowledging my existence. I watched her through narrowed eyes. *You know where to find me?* Oh please. I did know where to find her, and it was nowhere classy.

"What was that?" Jack asked. I crossed my arms over my chest defensively, bag still in hand.

"What?" I replied, shrugging nonchalantly. "I was doing you a favor."

Jack raised an eyebrow and said, "Oh really?"

"You don't want to go there, trust me," I told him. "For health reasons. Bad idea."

Okay, so that was a total lie. Not a *total* lie, because she really did get around, so the chances of a rash were high. But a little exaggeration never killed anyone.

Jack looked like he wasn't buying a word of it, his smile unwavering. "Oh."

"You're welcome."

A girl I didn't know walked past holding a Jell-O shot in one hand. I pulled it out of her reach as she approached us, gulping it down without thinking twice about it.

"What the hell?" she said, as I placed the empty glass back in her hand.

"Enjoy the party," I told her.

Hey, it was my boyfriend's house. I could do whatever the hell I wanted. And by the looks of it, I was in the mood to make extremely bad life choices. Jack rolled his eyes again and wrapped his hand around my wrist, pulling me away from the girl. This time I didn't bother yelling at him for touching me.

"Where are we going?" I asked Jack.

"Somewhere quiet!" Jack replied. I guess he took the lack of a tantrum as a go sign, because his hand trailed down from my wrist and slipped into my hand as he slowed down to let a few people squish past us.

I looked down at our hands, our fingers intertwined. The birth of my first-born child would probably not match up to how it felt holding onto Jack's hand right after he had met someone like Charlie Kingston. The heavens above really did have an angel watching over me, and boy, that angel was doing one heck of a job.

I mentally slapped myself and pulled my eyes away from our hands. I was at my own boyfriend's party, daydreaming about some other guy's hand! I was a terrible person and there was no denying it.

"I'M DRUNK BITCHES!"

A random guy wearing a Hawaiian printed shirt and a Rasta hat with fake dreadlocks attached to it jumped in front of us with his hands in the air, clutching what seemed to be a Ukulele in one of them. Jack came to a sudden halt and I crashed into his back, steadying myself on my heels. Was it legal for Jack to smell that good? Probably not. Plus, the basement deluxe drink I had downed wasn't settling well with my mind. The Ukulele guy high-fived someone next to him and started chanting the lyrics to the Flo Rida song playing. Jack turned to me and grinned, as if he couldn't believe he was actually at a party like this. I shrugged. I'd seen all this before.

Jack opened the door directly to his right, and having been to Brendan's house many times before, I knew it was one of many lavish bathrooms in the house.

"Oh! Sorry . . ."

Aria and some attractive, slightly exotic guy were sitting on the edge of the empty bath, passionately making out.

"Hey Gia," she said, slightly breathlessly.

"Hey. Who's this?" I asked, glancing at the guy adjusting his shirt.

"Oh," Aria said, looking at him with a sheepish smile. "This is . . . uh . . ."

I widened my eyes expectantly. She didn't even know the guy's name! Typical Aria.

"Marco," he said, with an awkward wave and a slight Italian accent.

"Marco." Aria repeated, with a firm nod. "He's from Spain."

"Italy." He corrected her.

"Oh, Italy."

"Right, well nice to meet you Marco." Jack said, giving me a sideways look.

"Hey, have you seen Brendan?" I asked, still holding onto Jack's hand.

"No, sorry. Try the kitchen? He was there with the caterers before."

"We'll leave you to it then." Jack told her.

I mouthed *nice work* to Aria, motioning to Marco who was looking at his feet, and just managed to catch her wink before Jack closed the door.

"Marco seems nice." Jack said, raising his voice slightly to be heard over the music.

I just smiled. Aria always ended up with some amazing stranger at parties, it was just who she was. What did I always end up with? Putting a drunk Brendan to bed while he sang the *Friends* theme song and completely missed the part where you clap.

"Let's try this room," Jack said, more to himself than me, pushing open the door a little ahead of us.

Again from experience, I already knew that the room was for guests. I'd only ever been in it once, the first time I had come to Brendan's house. I remember falling in love with the golden lampshades and secretly wondering if I could sneak out with one if I hid it under my shirt. I didn't try it though; Brendan was with me the whole time.

"Finally," Jack sighed, closing the door behind us and releasing my hand. "I can actually hear myself think."

"Why are we in the bedroom?" I asked, taking a step away from him. "Brendan was in the kitchen, remember?"

The music was still loud, but at least it was muffled enough that we could have a conversation without shouting. I did some heavy breathing and reminded myself that Jack was just a guy, and not especially crafted by Baby J just for me. The bedroom atmosphere wasn't helping though. Jack moved toward the bed and sat down on the edge of it, eyeing the contents of the room with an impressed look on his face.

"Beef boy's got a nice house," he remarked, caressing the silk bed sheet beneath him.

"Yeah, it's . . . yeah." I put my bag on the table closest to me, tucking my hair behind my ear.

I was starting to regret those drinks I had conveniently downed out of spite and anxiety. I suddenly remembered I hadn't eaten anything since the afternoon, which probably hadn't helped. Jack raised his eyebrow at me, and I shifted from one foot to another nervously. I couldn't help it. His cologne was freaking amazing!

"Where is beef boy anyway?" Jack asked, rising from the bed.

"Kitchen. I don't know. I should go check."

"What's wrong with you?" Jack said, looking at me suspiciously. "I've called Brendan 'beef boy' twice and you haven't said anything."

I fiddled with the ends of my hair and looked at the ground, reminding myself to breathe normally.

"Uh, hello? Are you listening to me?" Jack said.

Oh lord. I was going off the rails, and there was no coming back. Abort plan. Abort plan!

"Uh, mother must be calling us for tea and crumpets! I should check the parlour and find out."

Oh crap. I slapped a hand across my mouth and gave Jack a horrified look. His smile widened and he stifled a laugh.

"Um, do I want to know what that was?"

I continued to stare at him with my hand stopping me from saying anything else that would make me look appalling stupid. That's it. I had reached the peak of embarrassment. There was no coming down from that. Ever.

"Gia?"

"I just—it's nothing."

Okay that was a lie. When I was in fifth grade, there was a British guy in my class called David. He was my first crush, besides Nick Carter of course, and I was convinced I was going to marry him. Things didn't go down too well for that plan though. I only ever spoke to him twice, and the first time all I said was a meek "hello." The second time, we were paired to do an assignment and I was so terrified that I barely said anything to him at all for three lessons. Finally, when he was getting kind of weirded out by me, I rambled on for twenty minutes about things I liked about England in an atrocious British accent. I talked about everything from telephone booths to the Queen, all in a ridiculous accent. It turned out he was Irish, and the only Queen he liked was the band.

He ended up requesting another partner, and eventually moved schools in the next year, hopefully not because of me. But ever since then, I automatically put on a British accent and-slash-or talk about English things every time I get overwhelmingly nervous.

"Earth to Gia?"

I snapped out of my flashback and lowered my hand, still gaping at Jack. The British accent hadn't come out in a while, but it had returned with a bang.

"Yeah, sorry. I just go a little British when I'm nervous. It's a long story."

Jack stared at me blankly for a few seconds, biting his bottom lip. He looked like he was doing some internal reasoning, but wasn't winning the battle. Jack finally began laughing, unable to keep it in any longer. He was laughing so hard; he had to put one hand on the bed to support him.

"British!" He managed to say in between laughs.

"What!" I cried. "Stop laughing at me!"

I had intended for it come off a lot angrier, but watching Jack laugh made me want to laugh too. I only managed a smile and a little giggle, before Jack began composing himself and I forced the happiness off my face.

"Oh my gosh," Jack groaned, wiping a tear from under his eye. "You're unbelievable."

"It's not a big deal!" I argued. "Sometimes when I'm just a little nervous it pops out! Whatever!"

"Wait!" Jack cocked his head to one side, his smile turning to a thoughtful look. "So I make you nervous?"

It was the perfect opportunity to smash a fantastic comeback in his face, and remind him how unimportant he really was. Instead, I gulped and took a step backward toward the door.

"Of course not."

Jack took a tiny step closer. "Really?"

Oh lordy.

"Wow," I said. "It's hot in here! Is it really hot in here? Or is that just me? Because I kind of feel like you're hot. I mean, *it's* hot."

Jack's lips curved into a half-smile. He was enjoying the effect he had on me. No way I could stay in that room for a second longer, I didn't trust myself. Practically launching myself at the door handle, I swung the door open, crashing right into Brendan in the process. I pushed the hair out of my face, painfully twisting my ankle on my stiletto heels. That wasn't about to stop me though. The babbling had already begun.

"Oh my gosh! There you are! I've been looking everywhere for you. Like *everywhere*!" I practically shouted at Brendan, throwing my hands straight up in the air like a maniac.

"Uh," he said, looking a little taken aback by my over enthusiasm. "Hey."

This was not going well. Brendan looked kind of scared of me, Jack's cologne had taken up permanent residency in my nose and I still had my hands in the air like a deranged person. Obviously nothing had happened between Jack and I, but from where Brendan was standing, I was flustered and leaving a bedroom with the guy he currently hated most.

"Hey man," Jack greeted Brendan awkwardly. "Great party."

"What are you guys doing?" Brendan said, ignoring Jack.

I glanced at the empty plate Brendan was holding in his left hand.

"We were . . . looking for food."

"In the bedroom?"

"Yeah. The guy with the ukulele said there was some in here."

I sent my mental apologies to "Ukulele guy" for throwing him under the bus. But desperate times called for desperate measures. I turned to Jack uncertainly, who was looking at the floor. What a load of help he was.

"Well you just missed out. The fried dumplings finished a second ago." Brendan said slowly, looking from me to Jack.

Unfortunately, the music's volume was significantly lower now so I couldn't pretend that I couldn't hear anything to get out of this conversation.

"Listen," Brendan leaned in closer. "Can I talk to you for a second?"

"Sure!" I cried, clasping my hands together as though I had been told we were going to Disneyland.

"I'll let you have a minute," Jack said, nodding at me and pushing past Brendan. "I'll be right outside."

He emphasized the word "right," as a reminder that he was still my bodyguard and I couldn't go crazy and run off when he wasn't looking. I watched him leave in agony. All week I had been dying for a moment without Jack, and suddenly I desperately wanted him back in the room. Brendan shut the room door behind him, and I realized I hadn't had *enough* to drink.

"Nice outfit!" I said, giving Brendan a thumbs up.

I actually gave him a thumbs up. What was I, five? He looked down at his jeans, shirt and unbuttoned vest with a shrug.

"Uh, thanks. Listen, Gia, I get that Jack's amazing and dreamy and stuff, but I don't want to have to compete with anyone. So if something's going on with you two, then just tell me."

I gaped at him for a few seconds before forcing myself to form words. I couldn't believe he was saying this after all the crap he pulled with Meghan.

"Brendan, nothing's going on between us. We're friends."

"You don't act like friends!"

"Yes we do!"

"He's always around you! Like, *always*. Besides, I see the way you look at him."

I crossed my arms over my chest defensively. I could feel my cheeks beginning to heat up, but I continued to keep the glare on my face.

"The way I look at him?" I repeated, angrily.

"Yes!" Brendan replied, as I heard a group of people laugh from behind the door. "And it's really starting to piss me off!"

"Brendan, nothing is happening between me and Jack! I've only known him for like . . ." I trailed off, suddenly remembering the back-story I had told everyone. I was supposed to have known Jack for practically all my life.

"You're lying," Brendan replied, ignoring my almost slip-up.

I was beyond livid at that point. Brendan and Meghan could play footsies all day, but I want to rip off *one* guy's clothes and suddenly I'm the bad guy? What the hell kind of double standard is that!

"This is ridiculous!" I exclaimed, uncrossing my arms.

"Yeah, it is!"

"Well what about Meghan?"

"What about her?" Brendan replied, giving a frustrated sigh.

"You two don't exactly have a sibling relationship!"

"God, Gia!" Brendan cried. "Why are you so insecure?"

My jaw dropped so low, I was scared I had lost it forever. *Insecure?* Had he really just called me insecure? Brendan couldn't deal with Jack for one freaking lunch because he was so paranoid, and he hated Lincoln because he couldn't even land himself a pathetic cheese commercial! And I was the insecure one?

"You know what?" I said, shooting daggers at him with

my eyes. "I hope you and Meghan are very happy together. My insecurities and I will be just fine without you."

"Gia—" Brendan said, reaching for my arm to stop me.

"Seriously Brendan, just—"

I felt his hand slip away from my arm and heard a loud thump behind me. I spun around just as Brendan went crashing to the floor. The empty platter in his hand landed with a heavy thud next to him on the carpet, and he grasped onto the bed sheet as he went down.

"BRENDAN!" I shrieked, dropping to my knees beside him.

His body was shaking; his eyes rolled over inside his head. He looked like he was being possessed by some demonic presence. Sure, I may have learned a medical term or two from watching all those episodes of Grey's Anatomy, but I was no expert. Mostly I just watched it for the scandalous romances. I jumped up and thrust the door open in a panic. Brendan's body had become alarmingly still, and his grip on the bed sheet loosened as his hand dropped lifelessly.

"SOMEBODY HELP!" I shouted, watching a sea of surprised faces turn to look at me.

Jack, who really was standing right outside like he said, raised an eyebrow. "What happened Gia? What's the matter?" he asked.

I scanned the room, my head spinning. Everything seemed to be in slow motion, and those drinks were really messing up my head. I could see Jack's lips forming my name, more urgently this time, but everything seemed to be happening in a different dimension.

"Brendan." I whispered.

"What happened? Did he hurt you?" Jack demanded, eyeing the bedroom.

"No." I said. "I—I think . . ."

"Gia?"

"I think he's dead."

chapter
five

I'M NOT going to lie. I had spent hours if not *days* daydreaming about hospitals and doctors with well-fitted scrubs and perfect hair. But I'll be the first to admit that fictional hospitals are very different to the real thing. Not everyone is Patrick Dempsey, and the nurses aren't nearly as attractive as they are on TV.

It turns out Brendan wasn't dead, which was a serious relief. I had had to sit down for a few minutes and sip water so I'd stop hyperventilating, but at least my heart started beating normally again when the paramedics assured me that Brendan had a pulse. I kept replaying the moment he went down on the ground in my head; he looked so lifeless just lying there, still clutching onto that bed sheet. I was secretly relieved that Jack was there to take control of the situation, or else I probably would have just sat there staring at Brendan and babbling to myself. I'm the last person to call in an emergency situation. I just make everything worse.

Jack and I were sitting outside Brendan's hospital room, waiting for Dad to show up so he could yell at me. I had gotten a chance to sit with Brendan for a while, holding onto his hand like it was a float and I was drowning. His parents had been called and informed of the incident, but it would be hours until their plane landed back in L.A. Aria, Veronica, Aaron and the random Italian hottie had come with us, and they temporarily left Jack and me alone together so they could get some coffee from the cafeteria downstairs.

"Do you need something?" Jack asked.

A hug would have been nice. Maybe some chocolate. Anything that would erase the night from my memory would have been great. I probably didn't need that half a cup of vodka lemonade I had downed while they were loading Brendan into the van. In my defense, I thought it was water. I just didn't stop drinking it when I realized it wasn't.

"I'm okay."

"Gia, he's going to be fine. The doctors said that it would have been really acute poisoning if it wasn't for the alcohol already in his system."

I shrugged. Sure, he was going to be okay. But he was still lying in that bed, poisoned. Like, actually *poisoned*. Where does someone even get poison? It's not like you can just walk into Target and say, "Oh, hi. I'd like a vial of your best poison please."

"I just don't understand how," I said, turning to Jack. "I mean, *how* did Brendan even get poisoned?"

"The doctors said it was from the food, remember?" Jack replied.

"Yeah, but it could've been from anything then. There was pizza and those little pie-looking things and—"

"Gia, I don't need a whole menu. Brendan told the doctors that the only thing he ate were a few dumplings. Weren't you paying *any* attention?"

"Uh, sorry. I was kind of busy freaking out over the fact that I may have killed my boyfriend!"

"Hey," Veronica said softly, returning with the rest of the gang. She handed me a plastic cup full of watery coffee and took a scat next to Jack. "Is your dad here yet?"

"Can you hear anyone yelling at me?" I asked, slumping further down in my chair.

"No?"

"Then he's not here yet."

"Oh come on, G. It's not your fault!" Aaron said, holding a cup similar to mine. "You didn't do anything wrong!"

"Yeah, but didn't you see those reporters?" Aria asked, and I looked up sharply.

"What?" I snapped. "What reporters?"

"They were taking pictures outside while the police were getting your statement. Didn't you see Meghan? She pretty much sprinted out of there, track star style." Aria laughed, taking a seat next to me.

"I don't think daddy would be too pleased if she was photographed at a party, getting questioned by the cops," Veronica sneered.

As hilarious as that was, I was in no mood for laughing. Not only did the coffee taste disgusting, I now had the responsibility of keeping Dad away from any form of media, to stop him from looking at the inevitable pictures that would surface from outside Brendan's house.

"Honestly guys," I said. "Thanks for being here, but it's late. You should head home."

"Aria's sleeping over at mine anyway and Aaron's parents are in the Hamptons for the weekend. He doesn't have a curfew."

Veronica told me.

Everyone's eyes awkwardly fixed on the Italian stallion sipping coffee silently.

"Fabio lives nearby," Aria said with a nod, as if she had solved the problem.

"It's Marco." He said, a sigh escaping amongst his accent.

"Yeah, that's what I said," Aria said, with a nonchalant shrug. "GIA?"

I groaned as I saw Dad burst through the hospital doors, Kenny close behind at his heels. Goodbye cruel world. It was nice knowing you.

"Sir," a passing nurse hissed at him. "I'm going to have to ask you to keep it down. Hey, wait. Aren't you Ha—"

"You're grounded for life! You hear me? LIFE! No leaving the house until you're dead," Dad declared, ignoring the nurse.

I rose from my chair. "But I didn't even do anything!"

"I don't care what you did or did not do. No more going out on weekends, and your curfew for every other night is ten."

My jaw dropped. "Are you joking? That's so unreasonable!"

"When you have an eighteen-year-old daughter who leaves the house in a heart-attack provoking dress and calls you from the hospital, you can tell me what's reasonable!"

"Hi Mr. Winters. Nice to see you again." Aria offered him a bright smile.

Dad eyed her up and down suspiciously; most likely judging her insanely short skirt. He glanced at Marco, who had an amused smile on his face.

"Who's this guy?" Dad asked, jerking a thumb in Marco's direction.

"Mercutio," Aria replied.

"Marco," Veronica, Aaron, Jack and I said in unison.

"Well we were just leaving anyway," Veronica said awkwardly, taking Aaron's hand. "Bye, Jack."

I watched my friends leave with a sinking heart. Dad was going to go Parenting 101 on me in front of Jack and the star-struck nurse who was excitedly whispering into her cell phone.

"You have a *lot* of explaining to do, Gia," Dad said sternly. "Start talking. Now."

I turned to Jack for some help, but he wasn't even looking at me. Jerk.

"Well," I began, still holding my undrinkable coffee. "We went to the party and there was this really pretty bedroom and it was really hot and Brendan was kind of angry and he was holding a tray that had dumplings on it, but I guess he ate all of them, which sucks 'cause I was *really* hungry. But then he was yelling at me and then he kind of just keeled over and died. But not really died, he was just poisoned."

I sucked in some air and exhaled deeply. Wow. What a night. Dad furrowed his eyebrows and turned to Jack for confirmation, as if he couldn't actually believe any of this had happened. Jack nodded at him, supporting my story, and my dad gave Kenny an exasperated look.

"Teenagers," was all Kenny said.

"What's this about a bedroom?" Dad asked, turning back to me.

"Where's Mike?" Jack asked, finally jumping in to save my life.

"He's at home with Chris," Kenny replied. "Should we get out of here, sir?"

"Yes please," I sighed, completely exhausted from the whole drama of the night.

Dad did some more *I'm a very angry father* glaring before he and Kenny began walking toward the exit. Jack rose from his chair but I stood in front of him before he could walk away.

"What?" he asked.

"Do I look okay?"

"What do you mean?"

"Well there are probably people with cameras outside. I want to look good just in case I end up on Perez Hilton tomorrow. Plus, I might be a little drunk. I don't know, I can't really tell."

Jack raised his eyebrows and turned to look at me, clearly amused.

"Let me get this straight. You dragged me to this party so that I could get groped and you could keep an eye on this psychotic chick who's after your boyfriend, who ends up in hospital because of poisoning. And your biggest problem is what you look like in front of the paparazzi?" Jack asked, his smile widening.

I stared at him silently for a few seconds.

"Wait a minute. You got groped? By who?"

When I woke up several hours later it was just past noon, and I was snugly wrapped between my silk sheets. My head kind of hurt and my eyelids still felt heavy, but my brain had reached the stage where it was wide awake and not willing to go back to sleep without major coercion. I sighed and propped myself up on my elbows, taking in my surroundings. Everything seemed normal enough, but there was something off. Something I couldn't quite put my finger on.

Famous was sleeping on the edge of my bed as normal, my math books were still untouched on my desk, my walls were still pink, the walk-in wardrobe doors were closed, Jack was asleep on my couch, and my Audrey Hepburn poster was still hanging neatly above my bed. The heels I had worn the night before were lying next to my bed and I was still dressed in the tight dress, so I guess I hadn't bothered to change. I was way too tired after the whole poisoning misadventure.

Wait a minute. Jack was asleep on my couch? I shot upright

and watched him silently, putting a hand to my lips in surprise. He was facing me, still dressed in the outfit he had worn to the party. One arm was dangling across his chest and off the couch, and I winced at how uncomfortable he looked there. He was still fast asleep by the looks of it, his chest rising and falling gently.

I crawled out of bed as quietly as I could, tip-toeing over to him. I carefully picked up a cushion from my bed and clutched it to my chest, eyeing Jack as he slept peacefully. He was in my room! What was I supposed to do? He was just lying there looking like perfection, while I stood there with smudged mascara all over my face. I slowly crept toward the couch, stopping when I was right above him.

"Jack?" I whispered, but he didn't move. "Hello? Jack?" With the pillow still pressed to my chest, I poked him on his shoulder. "Jack! Wake up!"

His head looked like it twitched a tiny bit, but he was still in slumber land. I sighed and clutched the pillow some more. He definitely wasn't dead because I could see him breathing. But he didn't look like he wanted to get up anytime soon. Which wasn't very convenient for me, or my mission to not fall in love with him. I took a deep breath, raised my hand and slapped him hard across the cheek.

"OW!" He yelled and woke with a start.

I gave a yelp and leapt backward, digging my nails into the pillow. Jack looked a little disoriented as he rubbed his cheek. He looked up at me, sleep still evident in his eyes.

"Hi." I said.

"Gia! What the hell?"

"What the hell is right!" I said, the moment my heart went back to its normal rate. Almost. It was never normal around Jack. "What are you doing in my room?"

"Well," Jack said, groaning a little as he swung his legs off the couch. He ran a hand through his hair, stretching a little. "I *was* sleeping, until you decided to attack me with that pillow."

"Don't blame the pillow."

"Oh, sorry. I'll blame your hand instead."

I dropped the pillow to the floor. It hit the fluffy rug with a barely-audible thud. "You have a bedroom!" I exclaimed. "Go sleep there!"

Jack looked up at me in disbelief. "Are you kidding? You were the one who asked me to stay until you fell asleep because you felt sick, remember?"

Just as he said it, the memory of me asking him to stay came crashing back into my mind. Oh shoot. It was almost like the alcohol had kicked in *after* the party, and my brain broke or something. That is the only explanation that would make sense for asking Jack to stay and watch me until I fell asleep.

"I—I may have asked you to make sure I was safe." I said, putting my hands on my hips. "I didn't ask you to spend the night!"

"It's not my fault *someone* is a lightweight," Jack replied, rising from the couch with another stretch. He was standing right in front of me, closer than I was comfortable with. "You took forever to fall asleep, and I was tired."

I took a giant step back. "If you even *tried* to touch me—"

"Yeah, Gia," Jack said, giving me the world's most sarcastic look. "I completely took advantage of you, and then fell asleep on the couch!"

Okay, fine. Not one of my better theories. The memories of last night were becoming a little clearer now, particularly the part when I asked Jack to make sure no one tried to poison me in my sleep. So I had been a little drunk last night, but thankfully not enough to make my dad notice. Unfortunately, just drunk enough to wait until my dad had gone to bed, after another thirty thousand lectures he had delivered when we got home, and practically beg Jack to keep an eye on me. I was wrong. The embarrassment levels had managed to hit a new high.

"Well the sleepover club is over now," I snapped. "So get out!"

"Hey!" Jack replied, his irritation growing. "This wasn't a slumber party for me either, you know. That couch practically broke my back in two!"

I gave him a pleased smile and said, "That actually folds out into a huge ass bed."

Jack looked at me, expressionless. "I really wish you would have mentioned that before you fell asleep."

"My bad."

"Yeah. Right."

I pointed to my room door and said, "Get out before Dad sees you."

Jack obediently began walking toward the door, as I watched him with a glare that seemed to be perpetually on my face. "Isn't that ideal for you? That way your dad could fire me and we'd all go back to living our lives?"

"Uh, no," I replied, coming up behind him and opening the bedroom door. "We had a deal, remember? I need you to help me, especially now that Brendan's been poisoned. You need to hold up your end."

"Because you're doing such a good job of holding up yours," Jack said as I scowled.

"Oh!" I heard someone say to my right. Nadia, one of the housekeepers glanced at Jack and I standing an inch away from each other, and then looked at the floor. "Sorry to interrupt. I'll come back later!"

Eyes on Nadia, I pushed Jack away from me lightly. "No!" I exclaimed. "This is a perfect time. Nothing's happening here."

"Really, I can come ba—"

"I said it's fine!" I turned to Jack, who looked like he was having a crazy amount of fun. "Get out!"

"Alright, alright. I'm going," he said, smiling at Nadia on his way out. "Thanks for last night, Gia!"

"Shut up, oh my God!"

"I can keep this between us if you'd like," Nadia said, nodding at me understandingly.

"There's nothing to keep between us, Nadia," I replied, trying to look as casual as possible. "Honestly, I have no idea what you're talking about."

She looked like she wanted to say something, but instead gave me a sharp nod and began making my bed without a word. I watched her for a few seconds, wondering just how bad it looked between Jack and I. When the awkwardness was becoming too much, I gave up on damage control, locked myself in the ensuite, and did some heavy breathing for a while.

By the time I had finished battling with the tangles in my hair, showering and putting on clothes that made me look like a human being, it was already past one. Nadia and Jack were both gone, leaving my bed neatly made, and the couch looking flawless. The idea of Jack sleeping in the same room as me was giving me heart palpitations. At least now the couch would smell like his cologne. I made my way down the stairs and through the silent hallway into the kitchen, where Mike and Chris were eating lasagne.

"Where's Anya?" I asked, not bothering to greet the boys with a hello first.

"I don't know," Mike said.

"Where's Dad?"

"Don't know. He went somewhere with Kenny. He said he'll be back soon and that you're not allowed to leave the house," Mike replied, shovelling pasta into his mouth.

Sabrina, one of older housekeepers, walked out of the kitchen shooting a glare in my direction. I always had a feeling she didn't like me. She's always shaking her head around me, although

I can't figure out why.

"How am I supposed to see Brendan?" I asked, turning my attention back to the boys.

Mike shrugged and said, "Take that up with Dad."

I helped myself to some lasagne and took a seat on a barstool next to Chris. That boy *never* spoke. Like, ever. It was actually kind of worrying.

"So what's up?" I asked Chris, attempting to break the ice and show him speaking was actually allowed in the household.

His glanced at me from the corner of his eye and gave a tiny shrug. I raised my eyebrows. Okay then.

"So, you wanna tell me why Jack walked out of your room this morning wearing the same clothes he wore to that party last night? Moving a bit fast, eh sis?" Mike asked, smiling in between bites of pasta.

"You wanna tell me why I shouldn't squish you like the insect you are?"

Mike turned to Chris and gave him an understanding look. "It's probably her time of month. Don't take anything she says personally."

Jack walked in before I had a chance to reply, catching me off guard with blue jeans and red flannel shirt. I had to actually remind myself to chew my lasagne so that I wouldn't start drooling.

"Hey guys," Jack said, without looking up from his phone.

"Oh, hey Jack!" Mike said, a little too enthusiastically. "Anything interesting happen last night after the party?"

"Um," Jack began, giving me a confused look. "Not really, Mike. How was your night?"

I was going to squeeze the life out of Mike the next time I caught him alone. Chris was going to come in handy if he didn't stop hinting at Jack and I doing the nasty.

"It was alright," Mike said. "Probably not nearly as wild as what was happening in my sister's bedroom."

"Mike!"

"Okay, I've pretty much established that crazy comes along with this family, so I'm going to ignore all these weird comments," Jack said, and Chris nodded in agreement.

"Lasagne?" I pushed the dish of pasta toward Jack, hoping it would change the topic.

"Thanks," he replied, serving himself a piece. "So I've got some info about last night's poisoning debacle."

I looked up from my plate. "What did you find?"

Jack broke off a piece of lasagne and scooped it up with his fork. "The dumpling had Chinese poison in it. Nothing too strong, but it did the job."

"Was it in all of the dumplings?"

"Nope just one, and that's why no one else was poisoned."

"Freaky coincidence?" I suggested, hopefully.

Jack swallowed his bite. "Not likely. That poison was put in there."

I nodded, still processing the information. Why would anyone want to poison Brendan? "So now what?"

"I called Brendan an—"

"You *called* Brendan?" I cried, dropping my fork in surprise. It hit the plate with a loud clatter.

"Yeah, why?" Jack said, looking at Mike as if he could answer for me.

"I got nothing," Mike replied with an apologetic look.

"Did you forget that massive fight I had with Brendan about *you* last night? He hates you!"

"Damn!" Mike exclaimed, turning to Chris. "As if we missed that!"

"Relax, he was on a bunch of meds," Jack said, putting his plate down on the marble kitchen island. "I called him, told him I was just checking up on him and made a few lame jokes about mystery meat. He said everything's cool and that he's learned his lesson."

"What lesson?" Mike asked for me.

"Never to get catering from the Dumpling Hospital again."

"The Dumpling Hospital?" I repeated, making a face. "What the hell is that?"

"Oh, I know that place!" Mike piped up. "It's in China Town. My friend Dave said that it's really sketchy! His dad got diarrhea once after eating there."

I looked at Chris, who was *still* silent. "You got nothing to add?"

"No," he replied.

One word, two letters. It was all the proof I needed that Chris actually could talk.

"Anyway," Jack resumed. "If I were you, I would do some more research on this Dumpling Hospital place. If the name isn't suspicious enough, their food definitely is."

"That's great and all," I said, pushing my plate away from me slightly so that I could lean my arms on the counter. "But who was that dumpling for? I mean, why would they just poison one dumpling? It doesn't make any sense."

"Well when I asked how the whole thing happened," Jack explained, "Brendan said the waiter was actually heading in our direction to offer us some food."

"Offer us food inside a bedroom?" I said. "Sounds a bit creepy, doesn't it?"

"Bedroom?" Mike said, his smile returning.

Jack paused for a few seconds, as though he was thinking about smiling, and then deciding against it.

"He said he took the tray off him right before he saw us walk into the room."

"I didn't see any waiters," I said.

"Me neither," Jack replied with a nod. "In fact, Brendan

didn't even hire any waiters. Whoever this guy was, he was planted there in disguise."

"That," Mike said, "is some Mission Impossible shiz!"

"No one says *shiz,* Mike," I said abruptly. "Did Brendan say what the guy looked like?"

"No, and I didn't want to ask. I already seemed super suspicious with all my questions. You can ask him later."

Jack put his plate in the sink, and the room was silent for a moment as everyone considered his story. It was possible that the waiter was out for Jack, but it was unlikely. Especially with the creepy calls and texts in play, I had a pretty good idea that it was me he was after. Jack clearly agreed.

"So what you're saying is," I began slowly, "this random guy was disguised as a waiter to potentially serve me a poisoned dumpling from a sketchy Chinese restaurant that gave Dave's dad diarrhea?"

Jack nodded. "It definitely looks that way."

"Well that's just dandy!" I exclaimed, hopping off the barstool. "No, really! As if I didn't already have enough to deal with! Let's just throw in some psycho freak stalker who's trying to kill me!"

"Chill out, sis," Mike said, pushing his empty plate away from him. "It's not a big deal. So you're getting stalked a little! Big whoop."

I spun on my heel to face Mike, eyes narrowed into a steely glare. "Leave now if you value your life," I told him, and he slid off his chair.

"Clearly Jack didn't relax your psychotic nerves last night," Mike said, shrugging lightly. He turned to Jack. "Dude, try again. She's going to need a few sessions to crack."

With that he strolled out of the kitchen, leaving me to stare at his empty seat in shock and embarrassment.

I glanced at Jack. "Don't say a word. Don't you dare."

"I didn't say anything."

"Good, don't."

Chris, who was watching us quietly from his bar stool, gave a small cough. I looked at him expectantly, hoping I'd get another word out of him. He just gave me a tiny smile like he was scared of showing any sign of happiness and looked down at his plate awkwardly.

"So," Jack said, resting his elbows on the kitchen island as he leaned in. "What do you want to do about this dumpling?"

"What can we do?"

"Well it's not like we really have any proof. So, nothing really."

How insanely helpful of him. No, really.

"So let's go get some proof," I said. "How do you feel about taking a little after-school excursion tomorrow?"

Jack raised an eyebrow. "Excursion?"

"I want to check out the restaurant," I told him. "Go straight to the source."

"I don't think that's a good idea, Gia."

"In case you forgot, last night my boyfriend was poisoned by some creep who was really aiming for me. I want to know why! I *would* go alone, but then I'd be depriving you of an opportunity to be crazy overprotective, which I know is your favorite thing to do."

Jack was silent as he considered his next move. Beside me, Chris ate another forkful of lasagne.

"Alright fine," Jack said finally, and I gave him a pleased smile. "We can go check it out quickly. And I mean *really* quickly."

My smile faltered a little. "Wait, just the two of us?" I said, as the realization hit me. Images of Jack lying on my couch were flashing at the front of my mind like my thoughts were at a nightclub.

"Yeah?" Jack replied with a shrug. "Why?"

"No. Nothing. It's all good."

Jack gave me a knowing look. "Are you going to go all British on me again?"

Boy, don't tempt me.

chapter
six

GOING TO school isn't exactly buckets of fun on a normal day, but after the events on Saturday night, it had become unbearable. Brendan was of course absent, but had been released from the hospital, which was a step in the right direction. Truthfully, I don't think Brendan was at home for his own health and recovery. I think his parents needed all the time in the day to yell at him for the party.

In the meantime, I was stuck dealing with people constantly showing me pictures of Jack, Dad, and I outside the hospital, as if I had forgotten the entire incident. Al, Dad's manager and best friend for as long as I can remember, had done some damage control to make sure TMZ didn't pick up on the news and make it a bigger deal than it was. But most of the partygoers fled the moment they heard sirens, so this was all new to them. Meghan, of course, had denied even being at the party. She claimed she was at some charity banquet, which resulted in me laughing for about three hours straight. Meghan considered just speaking to the people outside her clique an act of charity.

With an impressive amount of self-control and breathing exercises, I had somehow managed to get through the day without punching someone in the face or having a full Britney Spears-like meltdown. The same can't be said for my emotions after school however, as I eyed myself in the mirror with disgust.

"And you're *absolutely* sure that you couldn't find anything that would make us look like food inspectors?"

"I thought we would blend more like this."

Blend? Maybe the beauty hadn't gotten to his brain and broken it or something, because Jack's idea of "blend" was very different than mine. Jack was wearing baggy white basketball shorts paired with a loose, purple and yellow Lakers jersey. Large gold chains hung around his neck, knocking against each other every time he adjusted the angle of his black snapback.

"You look like you were raised by Lil' Wayne!" I exclaimed, motioning toward his baggy pants.

"Hey!" Jack said, sitting on the edge of my bed. "I look like Marky Mark."

"You look ridiculous!"

Jack ignored me, inspecting my outfit with an approving nod. "At least your outfit fits. I had to guess your size."

I wheeled around to face the mirror again with a grimace. Jack had forced me to put on this stupid golden mini-skirt and a similar basketball jersey that hung so loose off, it almost covered my skirt in length. That should be a good indication of how well he guessed my size. As if that wasn't bad enough, Jack had insisted that my ponytail be extremely high up, almost to the point where I looked like I had a unicorn horn. To top it all off, the only thing keeping me from being classified as semi-naked was a heinous black, puffy, plastic-looking jacket with a fur hood.

"I couldn't get shoes for you, you'll have to wear your own," Jack told me, as I glared at my reflection in the mirror.

"What shoes are you wearing?"

"These."

Jack pulled out a pair of white sneakers from a backpack lying next to him. The shoes looked a little old and worn out, and had the word "Pimp" written once on each shoe in glittery gold permanent marker.

I raised my eyebrows. "You're kidding, right?"

"What?" Jack smiled at me, slipping his foot into one of the shoes. "I think I may wear these more often."

"And I think I may go run myself over now."

"Little extreme don't you think?"

"So now I have to wear this heinous outfit with a pair of Louboutins?"

Jack shrugged and said, "I can't help that you only have fancy shoes."

I groaned. "Where do you even get these clothes from? They're a crime against humanity."

"I don't reveal my sources."

Clearly Jack's so-called "sources" were blind, or just really hated the fashion industry, because these clothes were offensive to my entire existence. I shook my head firmly, my ponytail swinging side-to-side.

"I can't be seen in public like this!" I said firmly. "Why can't I just wear something I already have? We can still go as food inspectors. I'll just put on a blazer and—"

"Gia! That'll take too much time. Now suck it up, put some overpriced shoes on and let's go!"

Slipping out of the house had thankfully been a less painful process than getting dressed. I had run into Anya on the way out, who looked at me like she couldn't believe I was actually planning on going out in public like that, and I couldn't blame her. The ponytail height had managed to crawl down a little, but I had still somehow ended up in the ridiculous homie getup at the end of all the arguing. Feeding Anya an impromptu lie about how we needed to attend an emergency dress rehearsal for a school play, we practically sprinted out the front door. Dad was out for lunch with friends, so I didn't have to worry about dealing with him directly. Ironically, he had been spending a lot more time out of the house and away from me ever since the bodyguards had moved in. Suspicious, but definitely convenient for me.

About twenty minutes later, and lots of arguments on the way over, Jack and I were sitting in an almost deserted parking lot gaping at the Dumpling Hospital that was just ahead.

"No, seriously," Jack said, hands still wrapped around the steering wheel. "What the hell is that thing?"

I didn't reply. I couldn't reply. The Dumpling Hospital kind of spoke for itself. The whole building just screamed sketchy. They may as well have painted over the crooked, first aid cross and plastered "Death Chamber" all over the place. The restaurant was definitely old, but run-down was an understatement. Whoever chose to voluntarily eat there clearly had a death wish.

"Well . . . let's go." Jack said, pulling the car keys out of the ignition.

I turned to face him with my eyes widened. "I don't think this is a good idea anymore."

Jack sighed, resting his hands on the top of steering wheel. "This was your brilliant plan!" he exclaimed. "We drove all the way over here, so we're going in now."

I glanced at the Dumpling Hospital with a grimace. "I changed my mind. Take me home."

"No."

"What do you mean 'no'? Look at this place! Look at what

we're wearing! Look at what *you're* wearing! I'm not leaving this car."

"Yo woman! I ain't gon' hear no crazy talk from you!" Jack replied, bobbing his head so aggressively that his hat almost slid of his head.

I gave him an incredulous look and said, "Are you having a seizure or something? What the hell was that?"

"It was my gangster talk! I'm getting into character."

"Oh my God, we're going to die in this place."

"Well," Jack said cheerfully, pushing open the car door. "No time like the present."

There wasn't going to be much more of a present if we went in there. I groaned and pushed my car door open, stepping out in my far too expensive shoes.

"Jack, there's no one here!" I cried, staying as close to the car as possible. "Look around. It's all deserted! They probably killed them all inside!"

"Gia, don't be such a drama queen. There's a family going in right now. See? They have little kids with them and everything!"

I followed his gaze toward a family walking into the restaurant. There were two parents and three little boys. One of the boys had a little action figure in his hand, but I couldn't tell who it was from the distance. He was waving it around in the air and yelling out "DIE. I KILL YOU." I spun back around in panic and slammed right into Jack, my arm roughly brushing against the cold chains hanging around his neck.

"Are you insane?" I cried. "Even the kids are violent! It's a breeding ground for serial killers, I'm telling you!"

Jack rolled his eyes and grabbed onto my hand, firmly walking toward the restaurant as his chains clanked against each other.

"Come on, Princess," he said in a bored voice, practically dragging me through the entrance doors. "I won't let the mean little kids touch you, don't worry."

"Hi, welcome to the Dumpling Hospital." A young Asian girl with a hint of an accent greeted us as we walked in.

She was dressed as a nurse and stood behind a small podium that read *Reception*. She had a name-tag attached to her outfit that read Cindy.

"Yo!" Jack said, releasing my hand and forming his fingers into a peace sign. "We'd like a table yo. For like, two, yo," Jack told her.

"Just you two?" She asked uncertainly, eyeing us up and down. She looked half amused, half scared.

"Uh, yeah. That's what I said, dog. Ya feel?"

"Uh, follow me please," she replied, and I knew she was judging us big time in her mind.

"Ease up on the homie talk!" I hissed to Jack. "And a peace sign? Really?"

"It's what homies do, Gia!" He whispered back fiercely.

"No it's not!"

"Oh, forgive me. I'm not exactly fluent in gangster sign language, you know!"

"Here you are," the waitress said, motioning to the booth to her right.

"Thanks, G," Jack replied, holding out his fist as if encouraging her to bump it against hers. She didn't.

"We'll take a minute to order," I said, yanking Jack's arms down and forcibly sliding him into the booth.

She sized us up once more, her gaze lingering on the pimp shoes planted on Jack's feet, before finally turning on her heel and walking away.

"Would you relax?" I snapped the moment she was far enough. "She thinks we're crazy!"

"She works at a restaurant modeled after a hospital, and we're the crazy ones?" Jack replied, adjusting his chains.

Well, there was no arguing with that. I picked up a menu

and scanned the surroundings. The Dumpling Hospital was a seriously messed up place, but you had to give it points for creativity. The tables were long and had pale blue tablecloths over them, so they looked like gurneys without wheels. Above the kitchen door there was a sign that said *"Operating Room"* and all the waitresses were dressed in white nurse uniforms and the waiters in scrubs. I took a wild guess that the chefs were dressed as doctors, and was actually surprised at how impressed I suddenly was with the décor. All creepiness and shabby furniture aside, it had something cool about it. But the restaurant wasn't particularly full, even though it was getting close to dinnertime, which told me the place wasn't doing too well. It wasn't very large either, and I doubted it would fit more than thirty people at most.

"Hi, I take order please?" A young "nurse" asked me, her ponytail swishing to and fro. Her accent was heavy and her English was clearly broken, but I could make out what she had asked.

"Uh, sure," I said, picking up the menu.

I looked down at it with a frown. The paper looked like it had been printed a million years ago and I hadn't thought to bring any hand sanitizer. Not only was I probably going to get food poisoning, they were going to throw in tetanus for free. The top of the menu read *Dumpling Hospital—Dumplings are the best medicine.* I ran my finger down the list of dishes and looked at the waitress who was tapping her foot impatiently.

"Could I please have a—" Jack, who was kicking me under the table, cut me short. He shot me a look that told me I was out of character and I cleared my throat. "Oh right. I mean, girl, what's your special today?" I exclaimed, startling the waitress with my fake ghetto accent.

"Dear God," I heard Jack whisper, closing his eyes.

She mumbled something and pointed to the top of the menu. I looked down at where her finger was pointing. It read:

Kong Bao Kidney Stones—served with rice

I re-read the special dish two more times just so I was sure that I hadn't made a mistake, and looked up at the waitress uncertainly.

"Great," I said, with zero enthusiasm. "I'll have one of those, please."

Jack ordered the "Guong Zhou Gallbladder," matching my lack of excitement at the dish names. The waitress directed us to the self-serve cutlery area before taking one last long look at our outfits, and finally walking away.

"Okay," Jack said in a hushed voice, as we both leaned in. "I want you to go to the self-serve place and pretend to get us plates and spoons and forks and stuff, but take a look around while you're walking up."

"Got it." I nodded. "Wait a minute. Why do I have to do it? I'm the one being targeted here!"

"You literally have to walk three yards. No one's going to jump up and attack you, I promise."

"Boy you're going to be so sorry if that isn't true."

"We'll deal with that if it happens. Now go pretend to get us stuff! But actually do get cutlery, because we need it to eat our kidney stones."

"I'm not actually eating any of this!" I exclaimed, surprised that he even thought that was a possibility. "What if it's poisoned?"

"Do you want to say that any louder?" Jack asked, and I scowled. "Just go get some cutlery!"

I glared at him and begrudgingly slid out of the booth, catching a glimpse of Jack's shoes in the process.

"Remind me again why we're dressed like this?" I said, frowning as he adjusted his snapback with frustrating amusement.

"I'm going to be really honest here," he said with a smile. "I was totally just messing around with the costumes and I never thought you'd go along with it. But it turns out, keeping up the act was way more fun!"

I rested my palms flat onto the gurney and leaned in toward Jack, eyes narrowed. "So you're saying I'm dressed like the female version of Vanilla Ice for *fun?*"

Jack blinked back at me, expressionless. "Well, yeah."

I did some quick reasoning with myself and decided slapping Jack was probably not a good idea. For one, it would draw more attention to us, and we didn't need any more attention in those outfits. Secondly, it would probably come up later if Jack and I ever decided to fall in love. But the chances of that happening were looking slimmer than shady at the given moment. Grumbling to myself, I stalked off toward the cutlery, smoothing down my marshmallow jacket as best as I could. A waiter dressed in "scrubs" was refilling the small baskets when I approached. He looked up at me and dropped a bundle of forks into the tub in surprise, causing them to make a loud clattering sound. He was most likely just taken aback by my outfit, but his eyes widened as if he recognized me. I tried to act cool, convincing myself that he probably didn't know who I was. I doubted he even knew who I was without the homie gear. There was no way he was recognizing me with it on.

"'Sup?" I asked him casually, bobbing my head back and forth in an attempt to seem tough and street.

He just looked at me blankly, before silently readjusting the forks and walking away. I turned back to look at Jack, who was immersed in the menu. Some bodyguard he was. I could have been kidnapped and transported to Yemen by now and he hadn't even glanced at me yet. I picked up two spoons and forks, made sure no one was watching me, and casually walked behind the cutlery bench, where there was a door that read "Staff Only" directly behind. A couple steps forward revealed a dimly lit hallway to the right, conveniently out of the patrons' sight.

I was guessing diners weren't meant to be back this far, which made it the perfect place for an evil genius to set up shop, and the perfect opportunity to bust out some *Homeland* worthy spy moves. I looked around carefully to make sure no one was watching me and I took a step toward the deserted hallway. To my surprise, my heel had barely made contact with the floor before the sound of *Soulja Boy* escaped from beside me somewhere. I immediately backtracked out into the main dining area, where people were beginning to stare at me with confused and judgemental looks. I threw my palms up as if to say *it's not me, I swear* but the vibrating in my skirt pocket told me otherwise.

Pulling out my phone, I did some big time death glaring at Jack, who was now in uncontrollable fits of laughter. Shoot. It was Dad calling. I blew out a sigh and turned my phone on silent, allowing it to continue buzzing. Slipping it back into my pocket, I stalked toward Jack, spoons and forks in hand.

"Don't," I said, putting the cutlery down with more force than required. "Touch. My. Phone. Ever."

Jack, who was having a hard time composing himself, said, "I'm sorry. It was just such an easy target!"

"I can't believe you bought that stupid song just to change my ringtone!" I exclaimed. "What are you, three years old?"

Jack responded with more laughter, as I crossed my arms over my chest and did some more glaring.

"Okay," Jack finally said, his laughter dying down. "I promise. No more ringtone pranks."

"Anyway, forget that right now!" I leaned down close to him, lowering my voice. "I need your help."

Jack, still smiling, said, "With what?"

"There's a creepy hallway at the back of this restaurant with a room at the end of it. And I want to know what's in there."

Jack looked at me incredulously, all traces of laughter instantly disappearing. "Are you insane?"

"Shhh!"

Jack lowered his voice, but his expression remained the

same. "Gia, I'm not helping you sneak into some random room!"

"You promised me you'd help me investigate! That was the deal."

"Yeah, and I drove you here, didn't I? That's helpful."

I rolled my eyes and said, "Oh come on! You were the one who told me to look around! Well I did, and I found something."

"Yeah bu—"

"Do you want your great driving abilities to go to waste?" I added, pulling out my famous puppy dog eyes. "I'll be quick, I swear."

Jack did some frustrated sighing and fiddled with his hat while he considered his options. I tapped my foot impatiently as I waited for the inevitable to occur.

"Fine!" he said finally, looking less than pleased. "What do I have to do?"

I turned to look over my shoulder, cocking my head toward the waiter that had been at the cutlery station. He was serving a table on the far side of the room, but kept glancing over at us.

"You see that guy over there?" I said, and Jack nodded. "Distract him so I can sneak into the room."

"What if someone else sees you?" Jack asked. "I can't distract all the waiters in here!"

"Yeah, but he's the only one who keeps looking over here. No one else cares."

"Maybe he keeps looking over here because we're dressed like idiots."

I put my hands on my hips and said, "And whose fault is that?"

"Alright fine, whatever!" Jack exclaimed, sliding out of the booth. "But make it quick! I mean it."

I smugly watched him walk toward the waiter, mumbling something as he repositioned his chains. The waiter was now near the kitchen, which unfortunately was located opposite the patron-restricted door, and of course, the secret hallway. Jack was going to have to do some major distracting if I was going to sneak past unnoticed.

As casually as I could, I weaved my way through the restaurant, smiling innocently at all the families who were enjoying their potentially poisonous meals. Practically tip-toeing toward the cutlery station, I watched Jack approach the waiter.

"Uh, hey man," I heard Jack say. He clapped his hand over the waiter's back and turned him in the direction of the kitchen, keeping me out of sight. "I was just wondering if you got a toilet, ya know what I'm sayin? 'Cause them kidney stones ain't settling well, ya feel? A brotha can't handle it."

What was I so worried about? The boy was a freaking natural. Jack turned his head ever so slightly and caught my eye. I clapped a hand over my mouth to stop the laughter from escaping, and he widened his eyes at me in disbelief. He mouthed *go!*

"Uh . . ." The waiter began, attempting to turn his head. But Jack was too quick, and directed his attention back toward the kitchen.

"Is it over there?" he asked, randomly pointing to nowhere in particularly.

Alright Gia, go time. Now even if the waiter turned around, he wouldn't be able to see me. Phew. I stared down at the hallway, biting on my lip. So it was just a creepy ass hallway with minimal lighting in a sketchy restaurant that may or may not have poisoned my boyfriend with a dumpling that was actually meant for me. No biggie.

I took a deep breath and told myself not to be such a wimp. I mean, it was possible to have incredible hair and still be badass. Just ask Charlie's Angels. I had made it about halfway down the hallway when I felt my phone vibrate in my pocket once more.

"Oh for cryin' out loud!" I mumbled, pulling it out. It was my dad, calling again. "Hello?"

"Gia, where are you?"

"Oh, hey Dad! How's it hanging?"

"Where are you? And why are you whispering?"

"I'm, uh, picking up lunch for Brendan. He gets discharged today." I said, cautiously taking another step forward. "I'm talking quietly because . . ." I trailed off, hoping he wouldn't notice.

He didn't. "Anya said you were in a play?"

"Oh, right!" I cried, smacking the heel of my palm against my forward in realization. "Yeah. I'm picking up lunch for Brendan *and* I'm in a play."

I really need to step up my lying game. This was pathetic.

"Oh really?" Dad replied. "Which one?"

"Um . . ." Shit. Why couldn't I think of any plays! "Macbeth?"

"Macbeth." Dad repeated, clearly not buying anything I was throwing his way. "Really? Who do you play?"

I rolled my eyes in frustration. The man was practically a trained interrogator. "Uh, I play Macbeth."

"Macbeth. The male lead, Macbeth."

"Dad," I said, feigning a disappointed tone. "Our school doesn't discriminate based on gender. Frankly I'm offended by th—"

"Gia, come home. You're grounded remember? I was picking you up from the hospital just last night, and you're already off God knows where with God knows who!"

"I'll be home soon, jeez!"

Dad continued to drone on about how inappropriate my behavior was, but I was barely paying attention because I had finally reached the end of the long hallway and was standing in front of a small, dimly lit room.

"Gia, are you even listening to a word I'm saying?" Dad's voice rung in my ears.

"Of course I am." I lied and peeked into the room.

"Good, because I really need you to be prepared. You know

it's always chaotic with her."

"Prepared?" I said quietly into the phone, scanning the room for anyone secretly hiding in the shadows. All clear.

"Yes, prepared! So, tomorrow at—"

"Dad, hang on a second." I cut him off and covered my phone with my hand.

"Hello?" I called out softly into the room. No reply. I found a light switch next to me on the wall and I flicked it.

"Gia, tomorrow at one. Be ready." Dad simply said as I put the phone back to my ear.

"Got it. Bye Dad," I said, cutting the phone before he could say anything else.

The room was empty with barren walls, except for a small coffee table and three plastic chairs. It looked like some sort of room available to employees on their lunch breaks, but it was so empty I couldn't seem to find any plausible use for it.

I hurried over to the table, which had a half-empty glass in it, its contents resembling green tea. Next to the glass was a photograph and a nametag. The nametag read Ao Jie Kai, a name that I knew I would have trouble remembering when I recounted my findings to Jack. I put the nametag down and picked up the photograph, almost immediately dropping it back on the table in surprise.

No. There was no way. It couldn't be. Yet there it was. There was no doubting who was in the picture, but *why* it was in the room was still a question.

Why was there a photo of *me* at The Dumpling Hospital?

c h a p t e r
s e v e n

"ARE YOU sure that's even me?"

"No, Gia. There's just someone else who's pretending to be you in your exact clothes, standing next to your parents at one of your dad's movie premieres. Alert the feds! You have an imposter!"

"Is the sarcasm really necessary at this moment?"

"Oh come on, Gia. Denial isn't going to get us anywhere."

Speak for yourself, denial seemed like a pretty fantastic idea at that point. Jack and I were sitting on my bed, attempting to make sense of the photograph and the nametag I had managed to steal from the Dumpling Hospital. We hadn't stuck around to eat our kidney stones; I had been too freaked out. And it was probably for the best anyway. I didn't need a creepy stalker *and* violent urges to throw up. I hadn't told my dad yet, and I assumed Jack hadn't told Chris or Kenny. This was the perfect opportunity for Dad to lecture me about my "irresponsible behavior" for the millionth time that week, and I just wasn't in the mood.

"So are we going to tell my dad?" I asked Jack, looking up from the photo to him nervously.

"Well, yeah I guess so." He replied with a shrug. "I mean, legally I have to tell him."

I groaned and said, "Do you have to? Like, can't you just wait for a couple of days, or something? Just until we find out some more? He's going to put me on lock-down mode if he finds out!"

Jack frowned. "Technically, I work for your dad, so I answer to him."

"But you're *my* bodyguard," I told him, pushing the photo away from me in frustration. "Which means you should be protecting *my* body. And I need protecting against my father."

"It doesn't work like that, Gia."

"Please?" I begged. "Just for like, a day? You can tell him everything after we go to the police tomorrow."

Jack's eyes widened. "Are you insane? You want to go to the police first and *then* tell your dad? He's going to kill you! Hell, he's going to kill me! Where's my bodyguard, huh?"

"Look, I'll deal with Dad when the time comes. Tomorrow we go to the police, tell them everything and then we can tell my father. That way, I have some more time to search for possible stalkers online, and Dad can't go crazy on me because I was responsible and went to the police for help."

Jack blinked at me, expressionless, and I narrowed my eyes as if to say *what?* He closed his eyes and took a deep breath, as if reasoning with himself not to completely lose it.

"You're a lunatic!" Jack cried. "Like a full-fledged, certified crazy person! You can't just Google possible stalkers! There's not some kind of website or blog called *Stalkers R Us*, where everyone shares stories from their boundary challenged adventures!"

"Jack," I said calmly. "This is the Internet we're talking about. You'd be surprised at what you can find."

"And secondly," Jack continued, ignoring me. "You have school tomorrow. Where exactly does your perfect police plan fit in there, huh?"

I shrugged and said, "So we skip school. It's not like I've never done it before."

Jack put his head in his hands shook it lightly, as if he couldn't believe he was actually having this conversation with me.

"Oh my God, you're going to get me fired," came his muffled voice from within his hands.

"Oh please!" I scoffed, and he looked up at me with another sigh. "You'll be fine! Tomorrow we'll tell Dad that we went to the Dumpling Hospital during school with the cast from the play. Like an excursion! See? Problem solved."

"No." Jack said incredulously. "Problem not solved! What play?"

"The play that Dad thinks we're in at school!" I replied impatiently. "Never mind, you weren't there for that part. So basically we say we went on a little trip with the cast, totally legit, and I just happened upon the picture and nametag so we went to the police. I mean, half of it is true."

Jack rose from the bed, shaking his head in disbelief. "I can't have this conversation anymore. I can actually feel parts of my brain shutting down."

"You're such a drama queen."

Jack had one hand on the bedroom door as he swung around to face me with an exasperated expression on his face. "I don't understand why we have to go to the police first!" he exclaimed. "What's the point?"

"Because," I said impatiently, placing the nametag and photo safely in my bedside table drawer. "Then it makes me seem responsible to my dad."

"As opposed to telling him straight away which is completely careless?" Jack asked, raising an eyebrow.

I put my hands on my hips, refusing to give up. Okay fine, he had a point. And let's face it, I was no Veronica Mars. Finding answers on the Internet was far too hopeful, but admitting that to Jack was more painful than an appointment with the dentist.

"Fine!" I said, giving a defeated sigh. "Have it your way! Let's go tell Dad."

Jack followed me down the stairs and into the living room where Dad was pouring himself a glass of wine, an old edition of GQ magazine lying next to him.

"Hey daddy! Can I talk to you for a second?" I asked, taking a seat on the couch next to him. I smiled brightly as Jack stood next to me, hands in his jeans pockets. "Your hair looks fab by the way. Did you do something new?"

Dad put the wine bottle down on the coffee table and looked at me with a raised eyebrow. "What did you do now?"

"Excuse me?" I asked with a deeply offended look. "What makes you think I did something wrong?"

Dad looked at Jack and said, "What did she do now?"

"In this case, nothing actually," Jack replied, as Dad took a big sip of his wine. "Well. Sort of."

"'Sort of' is not reassuring," Dad replied.

"Gia and I did some . . ." Jack paused and glanced at me. "Research, and found ourselves at the Dumpling Hospital this afternoon."

"The Dumpling Hospital?" Dad repeated. "That creepy little restaurant in China Town? That place is a dump! What were you guys doing there?"

I looked at Jack, who gave me a tiny nod of encouragement. "Well," I began, fiddling with my iPhone nervously. "I had a suspicion that the poisoned dumpling that Brendan ate was meant for me."

"Why would you th—"

"So then," I intervened, cutting him off before he started to grill me on specific facts. "I asked Jack to do some research and we found out that Brendan had ordered catering from the Dumpling Hospital. So after school today, Jack and I went to the restaurant just to check it out, and I was looking for the toilet when I came across this break room type of thing. So I went in there and found a picture of me, lying on the table in the room."

I took a deep breath and leaned back expectantly. About ninety-seven percent of that had been true, which was a lot more than I thought I would blurt out. Dad gently placed his wine glass down and I glanced at Jack uncertainly. He opened his mouth to say something, probably in a yelling voice, but luckily the chime of the doorbell cut him off. Saved by the bell.

"I'll get it!" I cried, jumping up and practically sprinting out of the room.

"Gia!" Dad called from behind me.

Stella was already near the door when I got there, but I told her I would get it and that she could continue going about her business, whatever that was.

"Mom?" I said, swinging the door completely open. "What are you doing here?"

"Hey, kiddo!"

If there's one thing you should know about my mother, it's this: she *always* looks amazing. To the point where you want to curl up under your blankets with a giant tub of Ben and Jerry's ice-cream and *Sex and the City* reruns so that you can soothe your self-esteem back to a healthy level. Needless to say, she was never allowed to come to a parent-teacher meeting. Not that she would have been into that anyway.

"Well, are you just going to stand here gaping at me or are you going to invite me in?" she asked, already pushing past me.

She spun on her velvet Prada pumps to face me, her blonde locks sliding gracefully over her shoulders.

"What are you doing here?" I repeated, closing the door behind me.

"I know, I know. I was supposed to get in tomorrow afternoon, but those morons canceled my meeting so I thought, why not take an early flight?" she said casually, handing me her handbag like I was a bellboy.

I took the bag from her and held it against my chest like it was a baby. "You were supposed to get in tomorrow?"

"Your father didn't tell you I was coming? Typical. That man has the memory of a goldfish." She paused, inspecting my face. "What happened to your hair?"

I put my free hand to the ends of my hair, lifting it up consciously. It looked normal to me. "Nothing. Why?"

Mom gave me a look that was almost sympathetic and said, "It looks a little dead at the tips. I'd put something in it, sweetie."

Dad entered the main hall just as I did some frustrated eye rolling, and looked at my mother in surprise, wine glass in hand.

"Evelyn! I thought you were coming to stay with us tomorrow?" Dad asked, walking over and giving my mom a hug.

So that's why I had to be prepared! Mom explained once more that her meeting with some director got canceled right as Jack walked in, and I immediately began to panic. If Mom hit on Jack, which she most likely would, I was pretty certain I would die. And if it wasn't bad enough that my hot, forty-something mother was going to make a move on my hot, twenty-something bodyguard, she actually had a chance!

"Hi!" Mom greeted Jack with a bright smile. The smile of a lion right after he's spotted his prey.

"Ev, this is Jack, he's Gia's bodyguard." Dad introduced, and I looked at him in alarm.

"Dad!" I said sharply, giving him a quizzical look. "I thought we weren't supposed to tell anyone about our bodyguards!"

"Yes, well I'm not just anyone, kiddo. I'm your mother," Mom replied for him, eyes still on Jack.

"Nice to meet you Ms. Winters," Jack said politely. "I'm a big fan of your movies."

I dropped Mom's bag to the floor. Of her movies? Yeah right. Mom was a former Playboy bunny. He was a fan of something else, for sure.

"Nice to meet you, Jack. I'm Evelyn, but you can call me Eve."

I cringed, mentally praying that she wouldn't crack some type of Adam and Eve sexual innuendo. Luckily, Mom decided to play it cool and took Dad's wine glass from his hand, taking a sip as we all walked back into the living room. She stopped me just as we re-entered the room, pulling me to one side.

"What's the deal with Jack?" she whispered. "Is he your boyfriend? I wouldn't mind a piece of that."

I resisted the urge to throw up and said, "Mom! I'm still dating Brendan, remember?"

"Still?" Mom asked, with a look of disappointment on her face. "Really? I mean he's sweet and all. Great body too, but the boy is dumber than a box of hair."

"Mom!"

"I'm just saying!"

"Well now that you're here," I said, looking hopeful. "Do you think we could have that mother-daughter spa session we never got around to last time?"

"Sweetheart I have so much on my plate this trip," she said, and I pouted. "And I'm only here for a few days! But I promise I'll try and squeeze you in."

Well gee, just what every daughter wants to here. What an honor to be "squeezed" in to see your own mother. Mike suddenly appeared out of nowhere and Mom's attention immediately diverted to him. She thrust the wine glass in my hand and ran right over to Mike, enveloping him in a big hug and ranting about how tall he was getting. All I got was a smile and a job as her personal bag-holder. I handed the glass back to Dad and sunk onto the sofa with a sigh. After a few seconds, Jack took a seat next to me.

"What are you all pouty about?" Jack asked, watching my parents talk.

"Just look at her! She's perfect. She makes everyone look like dog food," I said bitterly. "It's so unfair."

"Oh come on. You're not too bad yourself."

I cocked up an eyebrow. "Oh, really?" I said, turning to Jack. OH MY LORD, BE STILL MY POOR HEART.

"Sure," he replied, giving no indication that he was joking. "I know Chris is always going on about how hot you are."

"Chris?" I exclaimed, giving him an incredulous look. "You mean Mike's bodyguard, Chris? You mean Mr. Silence?"

Jack gave a light shrug. "Yeah. He was talking about it the other day. He asked me what I thought about you."

"And?"

"And what?"

"And what did you say?"

Actually, I wasn't sure I was really ready to hear the answer to that. Jack's grin formed slowly, but he didn't say anything to add to it.

"Gia!" Dad said suddenly, and I snapped my attention back to my parents. "I think it's time to resume our little conversation, don't you think?"

"Ooo!" Mom said, looking almost excited. She lowered herself onto one of the throne chairs. "Your dad has his strict parent voice on. What did you do wrong?"

"Is Gia getting in trouble?" Mike asked, looking up from his phone.

"No," I said, glaring at him.

"Yes," Dad said at the same time, and I sighed.

"I didn't even *do* anything wrong! If anything, I helped us. Now we have more clues about this Dr. D person."

"Wait, somebody fill me in," Mom said, wide eyed as though she were watching her favorite soap opera.

"Your daughter received a text message last week from somebody named Dr. D. It said he was 'always watching,'" Dad told her.

"What?" Mom cried, turning to me with a look of disbelief.

"And don't forget the creepy phone calls," Mike added.

"Right," Dad said, as I shot Mike a death glare. "And she's been getting suspicious phone calls."

"Gia, honey!" Mom said. "Is everything okay?"

"Yes," I said.

"No," Dad said at the same time.

"So what happened?" Mom asked, crossing a perfectly toned leg over the other.

I rolled my eyes and said, "Brendan got poisoned and Jack and I went to the place that supplied the food. At the restaurant, I snuck into a room that had a picture of me lying on the table, so I took it. Along with a nametag of one of the employees."

"That's badass!" Mom said.

"No!" Dad shot back. "It was *wildly* dangerous!"

"But still helpful!" I argued.

"Is that why you were dressed like a weirdo?" Mike asked me. "Anya said you looked ridiculous."

"Okay," Mom cut in before I could reply, clearly trying to calm us all down. "So what are we going to do about it now?"

"Gia wants to go to the police tomorrow," Jack replied for me, finally speaking up during the argument. "We'll give them the nametag and the picture, and hopefully they can do something about it."

"Well alright then," Mom said, shrugging. "So it's settled. Jack and Gia will go to the police tomorrow."

"I'm not going to le—" Dad started, but Mom cut him off.

"This isn't your problem, Harry. You can trust our daughter enough to go to the police station and responsibly deal with this whole thing. She's practically an adult now! Besides, she has Jack."

"Yes, bu—"

"Here!" Mom said, reaching for the wine bottle. "Have some more wine. Take a chill pill."

Dad sighed but didn't argue anymore, even though he was mumbling under his breath. Mom winked at me, and I gave her a relieved sigh. I really missed having one fun parent, as frustratingly attractive, busy and, at times, inappropriate as she was.

Mike, after noticing that Dad was in fact not getting mad at me, got bored and left the room. My parents began talking about the bodyguards, a conversation Jack and I politely stayed and listened to for about two minutes before we too left the room.

"Well that went well," I said sarcastically, climbing onto the first step of the stairs.

"Could have been worse," Jack said. "At least your mom helped."

"Yeah, about that," I said, taking a seat on one of the marble steps. I looked up at Jack, who was still standing in front of me. "She can be a little . . ."

"What?" Jack said, but he was smiling so I knew he knew what I meant.

"Forward," I finished lamely. "I'd watch out for that one."

My phone buzzed in my hand before Jack could reply. The screen told me I had a new text message from an unknown number. It was either Dr. D, or Channing Tatum was messaging me to let me know he had left his wife for me. Unfortunately, the first option seemed to be more likely.

"Who's it from?" Jack asked, watching me expectantly.

"It doesn't say."

"Well," Jack said, eyeing the screen. "Go on. Open it."

I obediently opened the message, biting my lip. It read:

I spy with my little eye, something beginning with T.

Okay, so it wasn't terrible. I still had a chance with my Channing Tatum fantasy. I mean, he could have been talking about anything really. Like tacos, or Tiffany and Co. Jack leaned in close and read the message, while I focused on not inhaling too much of his cologne. He smelled amazing, as usual. Seriously, I needed to sneak into his room when he was asleep and just spray that scent all over me.

"This one isn't signed off," Jack said. "Maybe it isn't him."

As if perfectly timed, the phone buzzed again as a picture message sent through.

It was a photo of me at the Dumpling Hospital, the suspicious photograph in my hand, along with the nametag. The picture was terrible quality and if I hadn't been in it, I would never have been able to tell what was going on. It was as if someone had paused security camera footage of me in the room and taken a photo of it on their phone, which was most likely what had happened. A few seconds later, the word **THIEF** appeared in capitals underneath the picture.

"Oh crap," Jack said.

"I told you the homie outfits weren't good disguises!"

"Hey! Don't hate on the outfits. The outfits were great."

"Yeah, clearly!"

"This guy's good, I'm not going to lie," Jack said to me, handing me the phone.

"So now what, genius?" I snapped. "My dad is going to kill me!"

"Gia, none of this is your fault!" Jack said, shaking his head. "Sure, you're annoying as hell and you clearly have issues with obedience, but it's not *your* fault you're getting stalked."

"Obedience issues?" I echoed. "Excuse me? You were there too!"

"Yeah! Because we made a deal, remember? This is a good thing, Gia. The more we have on this guy, the better."

"Well, that's all well and good. But what do we do now?"

"We do exactly what we told your parents. We'll go to the police tomorrow morning, sort this whole thing out, and make it back in time for the last few periods of class. Everyone wins."

Yeah, except me. I had to be stalked *and* I had to deal with school? No, thank you.

"Fine," I said, blowing out another frustrated sigh. "Whatever. Let's just finish this."

"You're so worked up all the time!" Jack said. "Just relax."

I stared back at him blankly. "I'm going to hit you soon."

Jack smiled and said, "Wouldn't that involve breaking one of your rules? I thought we couldn't touch."

"I'm willing to make some amendments."

It would come in handy in the future, no doubt.

chapter eight

NOW I know I made a big deal about talking to the cops, but I'm not so big on police stations. I mean, aside from the fact that police officers always make you want to admit to murders you didn't even commit, and there are public urinators being booked everywhere, I've had my personal share of bad experiences with the LAPD. And very conveniently, I may or may not have chosen the exact moment we arrived at the station to let Jack in on that little secret.

"I cannot believe you," Jack said, shaking his head. "Yesterday, you made the hugest thing out of going and talking to the police, we finally convinced your dad to let you skip school and now we're standing outside the station and you're telling me I have to do the talking?"

"What?" I said defensively. "Cops make me nervous and guns make me queasy. All I asked you to do was talk. That really shouldn't be a problem since you can't shut up around me!"

We were standing right outside the police station, eyes narrowed at each other in steely glares. Every time one of us would take a step, the glass automatic doors parted to allow us to enter, then closed again when we didn't. Jack looked at me like he wanted to strangle me, to which I replied with a lot of hair flipping.

"They're just cops! What's your problem?"

"Jack, I don't want to talk about it, okay?"

"I highly doubt it was any worse than a speeding ticket. You're the furthest thing from a badass," Jack said, and I scowled. "You may as well just tell me."

I did some haughty sighing before finally giving in. "Oh, alright!" I snapped. "When I was fifteen I had a little run-in with the police and I got into crazy amounts of trouble. Ever since then I've been kind of freaked, okay?"

"Wait," Jack said, furrowing his eyebrows as if he were trying to make sense of da Vinci's code. "Define *run-in.*"

"Well," I began reluctantly, fiddling with the belt loops of my skinny jeans. "There was this stupid bet and my friend stole some alcohol from her dad's bar and we ended up getting super drunk, even though it tasted gross."

"And?"

I rolled my eyes. "And then she went kind of psycho hyper and we found this abandoned shopping cart and she got in it and we were rolling around on the streets. And then we hit a bump and the cart fell over and she went rolling out, and I freaked out and we didn't realize there was an LAPD car *right* there, and then they took us to the station because we were super drunk and they called our parents and my dad *flipped.*"

I sucked in a huge amount of air, allowing my lungs to recompose themselves after the mini story-time session they had just endured. Jack looked at me as if contemplating whether or not the story was ridiculous enough to be true, opening his mouth and then closing it again.

"Um . . ."

"Yeah," I said, nodding. "I was grounded for, like, a year after that."

Jack looked at me curiously and said, "Who was the friend? Aria? I bet it was Aria."

"I really can't say."

Jack smiled excitedly, as if I were giving him the biggest Hollywood scoop of the year. "It was someone famous, wasn't it?"

"I can neither confirm nor deny if—"

"Whose kid was it?"

I shook my head and said, "I *really* can't say."

And I couldn't. There was a contract and everything.

Jack looked at me suspiciously but he was smiling a little. "I'll get it out of you eventually."

Yeah, good luck with that, buddy.

"Alright, fine. I'll do the talking," Jack told me, giving a defeated sigh. "But can we actually go in now? I'd like to still be in my twenties by the time we finish."

"You really should be nicer to me. I can have you thrown out of the house any time I want."

"Actually," Jack replied, "I'm pretty sure your dad likes me better than he likes you. So . . ."

"Excuse me? My dad doesn't like *you* better than he likes me!"

"It's okay, Gia," Jack said, in the most condescending voice imaginable. "There's no need to deny it. I know you have strong feelings for me."

"Yeah, *hatred.*"

"But sadly, you're not my type."

Jack moved to the right a little, causing the automatic doors to open once more. The people inside were probably getting super annoyed, but I stood rooted to the spot.

"What do you mean?" I asked.

"What?"

Shut up, Gia. Shut up!

"I'm not your type? What does that mean?"

Jack's smug smile didn't falter once. "Let's go talk to some cops," was all he said.

Fine. As if I cared what Jack's type was. I didn't need him; I had Brendan. I was his type. Please, I was *everyone's* type. Oh gosh, maybe he didn't mean specifically me. Maybe he meant women in general weren't his type. No, probably not. He wasn't giving off any of those vibes.

Awkwardness still hanging in the air, we walked through the glass doors. Inside the police station was far less chaotic than the cogs turning in my mind. In fact, the police station looked like the entrance to any corporate building, complete with a receptionist and waiting chairs near the front door. There, closed rooms running along the right of the station were pretty daunting, but I was still far more relaxed than my last run in with LAPD, three years ago. The left side of the building had an elevator and a set of stairs, leading to an upstairs level. There were police officers everywhere, and some very tired, run-down looking people sitting on the chairs, half asleep by the looks of it.

I glanced at Jack, who looked completely at ease, and took a deep breath. Alright, so it wasn't as terrifying as I remembered it to be. I didn't need Jack to fight my battles. I was Gia Winters, fabulous and proud. Sticking my chin out, I stalked up to the front desk just as the thirty-something receptionist replaced the phone on the receiver.

"Excuse me," I began, flipping my hair behind my shoulder. "I have a stalker."

Jack came up next to me with a light sigh and mumbled

something I couldn't quite make out. It was probably something to do with needing therapy.

The receptionist looked at Jack skeptically and then turned to me. "Is . . . that him?"

I gave Jack a glance and shrugged. "No, but feel free to arrest him anyway."

"Uh," Jack cut in quickly, shooting me a glower. "We'd like to speak to an officer please."

The lady looked at Jack and then back at me, eyeing me up and down with disapproval. Clearly she wasn't big on jokes. I looked away awkwardly, glancing at the officer behind Jack with his back to me, leaning on the front desk filling out what I guessed was a police report.

"I'm sorry, Miss . . .?" The receptionist asked, obviously unaware of who I was. I snapped my attention back.

"Miss Winters," I finished for her. "Daughter of Harry Winters."

Jack glanced at me and suppressed a smile. No harm in throwing in the family name. What use was it going to come to otherwise?

"Miss Winters," she repeated, clearly unfazed by my father's fame. "You say you're being stalked?"

"Yes."

"We get a lot of people claiming they're being stalked, Miss Winters, and most of the time there's nothing we can do about it because there aren't actually any laws being broken. Are you sure the behavior of this person can actually be classified as stalking? Could you describe what's been happening?"

I gave her my most unimpressed look and sighed impatiently. "You know," I said. "That's a really stupid question. That's like asking someone with a gaping bullet wound if they *actually* got shot. I mean, of course they got shot! They didn't poke a hole through their body for fun!"

The receptionist raised her eyebrows and said, "Milo?"

I gave her a frustrated look, glancing at Jack who was as usual, expressionless. Milo? Like Milo chocolate milk? "Thanks," I replied. "But I'm really not thirsty. Besides, I don't see how chocolate milk is going to solve my problems."

"What if chocolate milk was a police officer?" said a voice to my right.

"Excuse me?" I spun around to face the police officer who had his back to me before.

Okay, I'll be the first to admit it. Maybe I had been a tiny bit in denial about my obviously raging attraction toward Jack. But Mystery Police Officer standing a few feet away was freaking beautiful, and I was ready to shout it from the rooftops. There was no chocolate involved, but he was definitely hot.

"Milo Fells." He introduced himself, his smile revealing a set of perfect dimples.

Jack introduced himself and shook Officer Fells's hand. When he extended it to me, I clasped my hands together and let out a nervous laugh. There was no way I was going to touch him. I would never have let go, and then he would have arrested me.

"So you're being stalked?" he asked, lowering his hand awkwardly.

"Yes, yeah," I said softly, proud that I could form even one word.

The receptionist rolled her eyes and answered the phone that had been ringing for the past minute. Milo moved away from the desk a little to escape the noise, and Jack and I following close behind. As we walked to one side, I took the quick opportunity to evaluate what we were dealing with.

Milo Fells looked to be in his early twenties. He was fairly tall; about the same height as Jack. He was, of course, dressed head to toe in his uniform. There was no gun holstered to his hip, but my heart was still racing. His hair was dark brown and, like Jack's, a little messy. It was somewhere between just-got-out-of-bed and I-should-probably-comb-this-someday. His eyes were dark brown and soft and his teeth were perfect. If Jack had ever decided to transfer his perfection into a brunette form, Milo Fells would be the result.

"So do you want to tell me a little more about this?" he asked, breaking into my thoughts.

"Oh, you know!" I exclaimed, waving my hand as if to tell him that it really wasn't a big deal. "Some random guy has been freaking me out. Harassing me a little. It happens!"

"I'm Gia's bodyguard," Jack intervened, and I gave a sigh of relief. Screw it; he could do all the talking he wanted. "And last week she received a threatening text message from an unknown number, from a person who calls himself Dr. D. Neither of us, nor anyone she knows, has ever heard of anyone by that alias. There have also been a number of phone of calls, but they're always anonymous."

Milo nodded and said, "What did the text messages say?"

"That they were 'watching' Gia, and that they were close by."

"And did they send you any other messages?" Milo asked me, his eyes burning right through mine.

I gave another nervous laugh and patted Jack encouragingly on the back, like he had just scored a goal in a soccer match.

"Oh that's a good story, you tell it Jack."

Jack looked like he wanted to half laugh and half yell at me, but continued to tell Officer Fells about Brendan's food poisoning, the Dumpling Hospital, all the creepy phone calls and last night's text message. I watched Milo closely, examining every nod and shift from one leg to another. How was it possible that in eighteen years I had never come across someone who made my heart want to explode, who wasn't one of the Hemsworth brothers, and in just over a week I had come across two!

"Miss Winters?"

"Yeah!" I snapped out of my lust session and focused my eyes on Milo, who had clearly said something that I had missed. "Gia. It's just Gia."

"Gia," he repeated with a small nod. "I just asked for the photograph and the nametag from the restaurant."

"Oh, right."

I pulled the photo and the tag out from my bag, handing it to Officer Fells. I practically thrust it at him like I hated him, which was really not helping my already faltering reputation with this guy. He examined the picture for a few seconds and then looked at the nametag.

"And can you show me the photo he sent you last night?" he asked.

My eyes widened as they flickered toward Jack, who was watching me questioningly. The picture Dr. D had sent me had been pretty bad quality, but you could still see me in my ridiculous disguise! I had kind of been hoping no one would ever have to see me in that homie get-up, and I was practically handing Milo that opportunity on a gold-plated iPhone. Reluctantly pulling the photo up on the screen, I handed my phone over to Milo. I watched him in anticipation as he looked at the picture, the corners of his lips twitching into a small smile.

"This is you in the picture?" he clarified, looking up at me.

"It was his idea," I replied quickly, pointing at Jack.

"Do you think we have a case?" Jack asked.

"Well I'm actually just a cadet," Milo said. "But if you wait here for a second I can get someone who'll be able to better help you."

He handed my phone back to me and I clutched it to my chest as if he had handed me a love letter. He walked behind us toward an older man in a suit, his police badge holstered on his belt. He motioned toward us and the two began talking.

"Hey, Gia?" Jack said.

"Yeah?"

"Do you think you could maybe not make a fool of yourself for like two minutes?"

I turned to Jack with the most offended look I could muster. "How dare you? I'm not doing anything!"

"What's wrong with you?" Jack asked. "You sound like you're mentally challenged."

"Uh, that is extremely insensitive, and I do not appreciate it."

"Oh you're right, sorry," Jack said, looking completely unapologetic. "You would give mentally challenged people a bad name."

I decided to ignore Jack's little remark and instead gaze longingly at Milo, who was still immersed in his conversation with the older man.

"He's so amazing, Jack," I sighed.

Jack followed my gaze. "Who?"

"The receptionist. Who do you think? Officer Fells of course!"

"He's technically not an officer. He's just a cadet, so it doesn't count."

"Yes it does!" I looked at Jack self-consciously. "I can't believe he saw me in that gangster outfit. I could literally die right now! Am I really making a fool of myself?"

"Well it could be worse," Jack told me with a shrug. "I mean, your British accent hasn't come out yet."

Oh crapola. I had forgotten all about the accent! Great, it was bound to slip out now that it was in my conscious mind, which I'm about ninety-seven percent sure is an actual psychological theory. Something to do with some guy called Freed, or Fraud or something. Freud! That's it. I had seen something about it on a boring as hell documentary that ran over time while I was waiting for *True Blood* to start.

Unfortunately, I didn't have time to push the accent back into the darkest corners of my mind, as Milo and the man in the suit had walked back toward us, looking all official and business-like.

"Gia, Jack, this is Detective George Reynolds," Milo said. "I've just filled him in on your case, and he'll be taking the lead on this."

"Nice to meet you two kids, even if it is under unfortunate circumstances. I'm a big fan of your father's work, Miss Winters," Detective Reynolds said, shaking our hands. I watched his perfectly shaped moustache move as he spoke, giving him a small smile. "Milo here has gotten me up to speed and I definitely think there's a case here."

I turned my head toward the receptionist who was clearly pretending like she wasn't listening. I raised an eyebrow and slipped her a sly smile as if to say *told you so*. Sure, there was a big chance they were only taking me seriously because of my last name and not based on the evidence, but you've got to choose your battles.

"Unfortunately," Detective Reynolds continued with a frown. "The photograph that you swiped from the Dumpling Hospital gives us a good place to start, but we can't rely too heavily on it due to the method it was obtained."

I gave him a sheepish smile and looked at the floor. Good one, Gia. I had finally managed to find enough evidence to start a case and it couldn't even be used because it was done through trespassing and stealing.

"Can you send someone undercover, or get a search warrant?" Jack asked, and I nodded in agreement with the ideas.

"We'll most likely send someone undercover. Do a little research," Detective Reynolds told us.

"We should be able to get a warrant," Milo added. "But this Dr. D person obviously knows you've been in his restaurant, so he's had enough time to hide anything incriminating."

"Exactly," Detective Reynolds said with a nod.

Needless to say, I was extremely impressed. I mean, he was the definition of perfection. Not only was he ridiculously hot, he was smart too. Logic was a necessary part of life. Therefore, Milo was a necessary part of my life. It was just basic reasoning.

Detective Reynolds looked down at this phone with a groan. "Damn it! Carl's been booked for indecent exposure again! I swear, if he weren't my brother-in-law . . ." Milo offered him a sympathetic smile. "I'll give it to Davis. He's been slacking lately." Detective Reynolds nodded at Jack and I. "Let me know if you receive any more texts or calls."

"We will, sir. Thank you," Jack replied.

"We'll get our best guys on this, Miss Winters, I assure you," Detective Reynolds said, making me feel pretty good about dropping my surname into the conversation before. "I'll personally be handling the case, and Cadet Fells will be assisting me. This will be a great training experience for him. I do hope that's not a problem."

I looked at Milo, who was watching me with zero expression on his face.

"Right!" I exclaimed. "No problems here! Don't have any problems in my life. Except, of course, the stalker . . ." I trailed off as Jack coughed awkwardly beside me.

Detective Reynolds blinked at me for a few seconds. "Milo will give you our contact details," he finally said, nodding at Milo before finally walking away, leaving Jack, Milo and I alone once more. Milo asked the receptionist for a pen and wrote down two phone numbers on a post-it note, handing it to me after he was done.

"The second number is mine," he told me, and I smiled. "Just call us if you need anything."

"Thanks," I barely managed to squeak out.

Officer Fells gave me a smile that was kind of making me think he was a tad out of my league, so I focused on breathing like a normal person. At least I was wearing a push up bra under my Dolce corset top. That's got to count for something, right? There was silence for a few seconds and I looked at my boots, trying desperately to avoid eye contact with Milo.

"Oh!" Jack said finally, looking at his phone in surprise. "I'm sorry, I have to take this call," he told me, holding up the blank screen to show me.

I grabbed onto Jack's arm and dug my nails into him as hard as I could. Jack's phone hadn't even let out as little as a buzz; there was no way someone was calling him. I knew exactly what he was doing and I wasn't going to let him leave me there with Milo just so he could watch me act like an idiot.

"Jack," I said through a gritted smile. "Your phone's not even ringing."

"I know." Jack smiled at me innocently and put the phone to his ear. "Hello? Yeah I'm here."

I watched him walk off in despair. I was going to *murder* him when I was done ruining my chances with the amazing guy in front of me.

"So . . ." I said, awkwardly rocking back on my heels. "Top of the morning, eh?"

Oh lordy. It was going to be a long road downhill from that.

"Yeah, the weather's holding up," Milo said, thankfully choosing to ignore the initial signs of my anxiety coping mechanism.

"Busy day so far, Officer? I mean cadet . . . sir?"

What the heck was I meant to call him? Future husband?

"I'm technically not an officer yet, but I'm getting there!" he replied with a friendly laugh. "I'm almost done with my training. I've got the uniform, just not the title."

I pointed at his uniform and said, "Well you look really hot in it." I slapped a hand over my mouth and cringed.

Milo smiled, widening his eyes. "Uh . . ." he began, clearly trying to figure out how to respond.

"No! I didn't mean it like that! I mean, do you ever get hot in that uniform? Okay, that sounds bad too. I just mean, it's pretty warm outside, shouldn't you be wearing a t-shirt? You don't have to wear a t-shirt, there's no law saying you have to. Of course you'd know; you're a police officer. Almost. I'm just saying you can just wear something hotter. I mean warmer!"

From the corner of my eye I saw Jack standing at a slight distance, his phone still pressed to his ear, laughing as silently as he possibly could. In fact, he looked absolutely hysterical, and I can't even blame him. If I hadn't been mentally bashing my head against a wall, I'd probably have been laughing at me too.

"It's not too bad," he replied, watching me with a curious smile. Oh great, he was probably trying to figure out which mental disorder I had. "You should try wearing a bullet-proof vest. That thing suffocates you!"

"Yeah," I said, with unnecessary amounts of enthusiasm. "Getting shot at has got to suck, right?"

"I've been lucky on that front so far," Milo admitted, his dimples coming into full view. "But yeah, I've heard it sucks."

Yeah well, it can't be any worse than having this conversation. Luckily, Jack seemed to have given up on his phone call charade and was walking back toward us.

"I'm sorry to interrupt," he said. "But we should probably be heading off now."

"Of course," Milo said. "Just let us know if you get any other texts or calls. We'll see what we can do about the Dumpling Hospital."

"Thanks Officer . . . um . . ." I said, grabbing onto Jack's arm and heading for the door. I could not *wait* to get out of there and stop embarrassing myself.

"Just Milo," he replied, and I momentarily stopped making

a mad dash for the exit. "Like the chocolate milk, remember?"

"Right," I said, giving a nervous laugh. "Well, see you 'round!"

I had Jack's wrist in a death grip as I led him out of the police station, and didn't let go until we were far enough from the building to start breathing normally again.

"Okay, are you going to explain what happened there or should I just go ahead and guess?"

"Oh my gosh!" I groaned, slapping a hand across my eyes in embarrassment. "I totally blew that!"

"Princess, it was like watching a lamb waiting to get slaughtered." Evidently Jack had decided his new nickname was going to stick around.

"I cannot believe how crazy I sounded!" I exclaimed, replaying the conversation in my head.

"Well it doesn't matter," Jack said. "You've got Brendan, remember? Your one and only true love?"

I lowered my hand and looked at Jack. Yep, just as I suspected. A smug and sarcastic look was planted firmly on his freaking perfect face.

"Of course," I said, composing myself. "Brendan and I are great together! Whatever. I don't care about Milo."

"Your denial becomes more amusing every day."

Okay, obviously he was totally wrong. I wasn't in denial! Sure, Milo was so dreamy it made me want to cry a little, but I already had a gorgeous boyfriend. I mean, Brendan was a fine gentleman. Any lady would be lucky to have him as a potential suitor. Why am I talking like Jane Austen? Oh whatever, I give up in life.

"You think they'll find anything in the restaurant?" I asked Jack.

"I doubt it," he replied, shaking his head. "That place is probably cleaner than a hospital right now." He smiled proudly.

"Did you get it?"

"Dear God."

"See, that was a joke. Because the place is modeled after a hospital!"

With the amount of eye rolling I was doing, I was going to give myself a brain aneurysm.

chapter nine

IT WAS bad enough that I had a crumbling love life and a psycho who was stalking me; the last thing I needed to deal with was school. With only months before graduation, it was clear I wasn't getting into *any* colleges with my grades, let alone the Ivy Leagues my father had his sights set on. I had applied just about everywhere, but I couldn't decide what I really wanted. Hollywood was all I knew, all I was comfortable with. But moving to the East Coast would give my dad and I a lot of freedom from each other. Mom had always encouraged me to try out a career in acting, but I was a terrible liar, and acting was pretty much the same thing. Besides, it's a nerve-wracking job, and with my volatile British accent, my luckiest bet was an acting career in England. And that climate just isn't for me.

If I wasn't already worried enough about my future, my friends were beginning to pick up on something being wrong. I couldn't even blame them. Jack had appeared into my life so suddenly, and hadn't left my side since. Plus he was still set on doing his freaky secret service-style surrounding checks no matter where we were, as if Dr. D was going to come bouncing out of my locker and attack me. There was no way I could be around the girls *and* have to deal with the whole bodyguard situation.

"Where were you yesterday?" was the first question I was asked by Veronica before I had even made it to my locker.

"Oh," I had replied, "Um, Anya forgot to separate the whites in the wash again so poor Jack didn't have any clothes to wear. I had to go buy him some."

Needless to say, my friends had both been skeptical about that excuse.

"Jack didn't have any other colors he could have worn?" Aria had asked, giving me a funny look.

"He's . . . crazy about his whites."

Yet another reason for them not to believe me, considering Jack had worn a white t-shirt all but once since they'd met him.

"Oh," Veronica had said. "I thought you were going to say it was because your mom was in town. I saw it online."

Right. That would have been a pretty understandable excuse, but no. Jack wanted his whites.

Brendan, who had finally returned to school, was trying his best to keep his jealousy in check. Unfortunately for him, I was slowly starting to get used to Jack always being around, which wasn't great for our "we're just friends" campaign. I mean, we *were* just friends, but sometimes I felt like I could see us as more. It was a terrifying thought, considering I barely knew the guy. All I'd managed to pick up from short conversations was that he had a younger sister, Scarlett, his favorite color was grey, he was from New York, and his favorite movie was *Fight Club*. He'd practically had a heart attack when I had told him I'd never seen it, but he'd never seen *Breakfast at Tiffany's* so we called it even. Jack or no Jack, I was pretty convinced that Brendan and I were on the road to breakup. But there was never a good time to pull him aside and say "we need to talk, because this clearly isn't working out, buddy." So I kept up the charade, hoping that when the right time arrived, it would present itself.

It had been a few days since the police station misadventure, and I was lying on my bed, staring at the ceiling blankly. Mom had come in almost a half hour ago to tell me that her, Dad, and of course Kenny, were going out with Al and his wife Melissa, and that they'd be late. Personally, I thought it was nice how my parents could stay in the same house and keep mutual friends, even despite all their bad blood with the divorce. But I wasn't an idiot. I knew a lot of that was to do with making sure Mike and I weren't too mentally affected by their separation. Kids in Hollywood are crazy enough as it is. They didn't need us blaming their broken relationship as an excuse for our behavior.

Not that I really even had time to do something crazy. I was too caught up with thoughts about Dr. D and the Dumpling Hospital. I couldn't figure out why he was interested in me, and only me. It was my parents who were the famous ones, not me. I wasn't part of the Kardashian family, where even the pets were celebrities. It didn't really make any sense. My only claim to fame was my last name, and even that wasn't reason enough to harass me.

The real problem was, Dad was being super sketchy about everything. Every time I asked him what he thought about the whole thing, he would just get mad at me or act like he was busy and he didn't have time to talk. Who did he expect me to turn to in my time of need? Mr. Santa Claus guy from the bodyguard agency thing had made it pretty clear no one could know, which wasn't exactly helping my wild curiosity about what had made

Dad hire the bodyguards in the first place. Plus, it's not like I could sit down with Jack and start telling him all of my concerns over margaritas and manicures.

When my half-assed attempts at getting up and doing something productive failed, I finally gave up and scooped up Famous, who was asleep next to me. Grabbing my phone, I made my way down to the TV room, walking in on Jack, Chris, and Mike sitting on the couch watching a Victoria's Secret Fashion Show from a few years ago.

"Really?" I asked, standing in front of the TV with a disapproving face.

"Yes, really!" Mike replied. "Now move."

I put Famous down and moved away from the TV screen so that the boys could continue ogling the genetically flawless women.

"Move over," I told Jack, putting my phone in the pocket of my shorts.

He pointed to the floor with a smile. "There's a spot over there, next to Famous."

I put my hands on my hips with a scowl. "Excuse me?"

Almost immediately, Chris rose from his seat, moved past Mike, and slowly sank onto a beanbag, leaving a space for me in between Mike and Jack.

"See," I said, taking a seat in between the boys. "Chris is nice! Thanks, Chris!"

I suddenly remembered what Jack had said about Chris thinking I was hot and went a little rigid. I mean, it was totally flattering, but it was Jack I had my eye on, not Chris. No offense. He seemed great and all, but he wasn't my type. Mostly because I wasn't a hundred percent sure his vocabulary consisted of more than ten words. Jack clearly had the same thought as I did, because he grinned, mouthing the word *aww*.

"Don't say anything."

"I'm not."

"Good. Don't."

"Is pizza okay for dinner, or should we ask one of the girls to make something?" I asked the boys.

"Pizza," Jack and Mike said simultaneously.

I looked at Chris, sitting inches away. "Is pizza okay?" I said, almost encouragingly.

He gave me a nervous smile and shrugged. I took it as a yes.

"Mike," I said. "Don't you think it's weird that Dad's been going out a little extra since the bodyguards moved in?"

Mike shrugged, never moving his eyes away from the screen. "No."

Wow. His helpfulness was overwhelming.

"Heard from the cops?" Jack asked.

"Why would I hear from Milo? I didn't give him my number. Do you think he has access to that information?"

"Milo?" Jack pulled his eyes away from the TV and fixated them on me. "First name basis already?"

"He said his name was Milo! You were there for my humiliating milk comment."

"Yeah, that was hilarious."

"Well what should I call him then?"

"How about Cadet Fells?"

"How about," Mike cut in. "You both take this conversation outside, and let me watch Adriana Lima in peace."

There were a billion "how about" scenarios I had in mind for my brother, all ending in some form of violence. But instead of wasting my time and energy, Jack and I rose from the sofa and left the room without putting up a fight, leaving Chris, Mike and Famous to continue watching their favorite underwear models on a TV the size of a movie theater screen.

Jack and I headed to the kitchen, a place I happened to be spending way too much time in ever since the bodyguards had moved in. Being near the pantry seemed to be one of the only places that truly brought me peace. Jack went straight for the drinks fridge before I had even entered the room, opening a can of Sprite and handing me one. I placed my phone on the counter, opened my can and took a sip as Jack called for four large pizzas to be delivered. With a house full of boys, four probably wouldn't have been enough. Anya was standing by the sink, shaking her head disapprovingly.

"Gia," she said. "Why you call for pizza? I make for you!"

"Oh don't worry about that," Jack replied for me, hanging up the phone. "You and the rest of the girls do enough around the house! You deserve a night off."

Anya smiled so widely, I was pretty much certain she was mentally filling out adoption papers to officially make Jack her son. She thanked him, said something in Russian, smiled some more and hurried out of the kitchen. Great. Evidently it wasn't just me who was always on the verge of falling for Jack.

"How come you're never that nice to me?" I said.

"When you learn to make chocolate chip cookies like Anya, I'll be that nice to you."

Fair enough, those chocolate chip cookies were the bomb. I took another sip of my drink, the cold can freezing my fingers. "Do you think the police have found anything on that Ao Jie Kai guy?" I asked Jack.

He shrugged and said, "Probably not. It's only been a few days."

"Well, should we do something to help speed up the process?"

Jack gulped down a large sip of Sprite, eyes bugged in alarm. "No," he said, shaking his head fiercely. "Your last expedition got us into this mess!"

"What happened to 'the more we find, the better it is,' huh?" I placed my can on the countertop with more force than required.

"I take it back. I can't be held responsible for your bad life choices."

"My life choices are great, thank you very much!"

Jack opened his mouth to reply, but the sound of my phone vibrating cut him off. I looked at the caller ID that told me it was Brendan calling.

"Dr. D?" Jack said, snapping into action and leaning in close.

"No, Brendan."

"Even better!" he said with a smile.

Unfortunately for me, Jack has fantastic reflexes. Before I could move, he snatched my phone of the counter and swiped the screen to answer the call.

"No! Jack!"

"Gia's phone," he chimed, taking a huge step away from me.

"Jack!" I hissed. I climbed off the barstool I had been sitting on, launching myself at him.

"She's a little occupied right now doing . . ." he smiled. "Things. Can I take a message?"

My jaw dropped, which was clearly the reaction he had been hoping for because it only widened his grin. I pushed Jack against the fridge and wrestled him for the phone. He was obviously stronger than I was, but he finally let me have it after he was done laughing.

"Hello!" I practically yelled into the phone.

Oh great, I sounded breathless from all my fighting with Jack. This wasn't rubbing salt on the wound; it was taking the wound and pouring a four-pound bag of salt over it, and then jumping on it as if it were a personalized, salty bouncy castle.

"Gia?"

"Yeah, hi. I'm here."

"What's going on?" Brendan sounded reluctant, as if he really just wanted to hang up and never think about speaking again.

"Nothing much, we're ordering pizza. In the kitchen. Fully dressed and standing yards away from each other. In fact, I don't even know where Jack is? Huh, what's that? Is that you Jack? Nope, it isn't!"

I slapped a hand to my forehead and glowered at Jack, who wasn't even attempting to muffle his laughter, his head leaning against the fridge for support. Brendan must have been on some intense drugs at the hospital when he had given Jack all that information about the catering for the party. There was no way these two were ever going to get along if one of them wasn't heavily sedated.

"Right," Brendan replied. I could practically hear his frown through the phone. "Listen, we need to talk."

"Oh yeah?" I said, trying to sound as casual as I possibly could. "What's up?"

I knew what was up. I couldn't have been the only thing feeling like things weren't working out. Brendan wasn't Einstein, but he was smart enough to realize that something was off base. Only, I had always figured I'd be the one to doing the breaking up. Jack had finally calmed down his laughter, but was still smiling widely.

"Not right now." Brendan's voice came through the receiver. "Tomorrow at school."

"Okay."

"Cool. See you then."

I hung up without saying bye, releasing Jack from my death grip and taking a few steps back.

"What was that about?" Jack asked, adjusting his shirt.

"Why can't you be nice to him?" I demanded, ignoring his question.

"I am nice to him!" Jack replied.

"No you're not! You were implying that you and I were . . ." I trailed off uncomfortably.

"Doing what?"

"You know."

"Do I?"

"Oh shut up."

"Hey," Jack said. "I said you were 'doing things.' If he has a dirty mind then I can't help that."

I felt my phone vibrate in my hand, and I looked down, expecting it to be Brendan calling back and dropping in a casual "Oh hey, I forgot to tell you that I think Jack is an ass." But the screen read *No Caller ID*.

"Jack!" I said, showing him the screen. "What if it's Milo?"

"Don't you have his number saved?" he asked.

"Well, yeah. But maybe it's on private."

Jack shrugged and reached for his drink. "Then answer it."

Easy for him to say, but much harder for me to do. If it really was Milo on the other end, then that meant he probably had answers for us, which was kind of scary. But more importantly, I needed to make myself sound sexy over the phone.

"Hello?" I said into my phone, my voice husky and low. I glanced at Jack who had his eyebrows raised questioningly.

"What are you doing?" Jack whispered, and I pressed a finger to my lips motioning for him to be quiet.

"Guess who?"

The voice on the other end of the line was definitely not Milo, unless he had suddenly decided to get a creepy, robotic *The Shining* vibe about him.

"Hello?" I repeated, dropping my sultry voice. "Who is this?"

"An old friend," the voice said.

I looked at Jack, who was giving me a quizzical look. He mouthed *who is it,* and I shrugged. The voice wasn't clear at all. It was up and down, almost melodic in a strange way. Either the connection had decided to go crazy, or the voice on the line was auto tuned. Jack mouthed *speaker* to me, and I put the phone on loud speaker.

"Who is this?" I asked again, Jack coming up beside me.

"Oh I think you know, Gia."

Jack and I looked at each other in realization. My eyes widened and looked back the phone with uncertainty.

"Oh my God! T-Pain? Is that you?"

Jack took a deep breath and turned around to face the fridge, making an action of banging his head against it in frustration. Clearly we weren't on the same page about who the mystery caller was.

"Uh, no," came the reply through the phone. "But good try. Let me introduce myself. My name is Dr. D."

I clapped a hand over my mouth. Oh. My. God. He was calling me. He was actually talking to me in this weird, auto-tuned voice! It was definitely a guy; I could tell that much. Well, maybe. Probably. I looked at Jack nervously, and he nodded in reply, encouraging me to go on.

"W—What do you want?" I asked in a shaky voice.

"Oh, Gia," came the robotic reply. "I don't want much. But your dad took something from me, a long time ago. I think it's time I got something back."

"Like how long ago are we talking, here?" I said, eyes on Jack for validation. He gave me a warning look, but I ignored him. I was about to start babbling, and probably go British. It was too late to salvage the situation. "'Cause, if it was a *really* long time ago can't we, like, just pretend it never happened and move on with our lives?"

Jack closed his eyes and took another deep breath. He had that look on his face again, the one that told me he was struggling not to strangle me. And fair enough, I was an idiot.

"No, I don't think that's going to work for me Gia," Dr. D said. "Pretending won't get us anywhere."

The auto-tune was really starting to get on my nerves, but

whoever this guy was; he was doing a good job of keeping his identity hidden. Even if I did know who he was, I'd never be able to recognize his voice.

"Right-o," I said, watching Jack shake his head in disbelief. "Uh, so what exactly did you want?"

"Oh I'll get to that eventually, Gia. But for now, my concern is April twentieth. Save the date."

April twentieth? That meant nothing to me. Was he telling me his birthday? Even worse, was he inviting me to some twisted, psychotic birthday party?

"W—What's on the twentieth?" I asked, scared that this birthday party may have a theme.

"I would suggest leaving the police out of this matter, Gia." Dr. D continued, ignoring my question. "There's no need for this to get messy."

A part of me wanted to poop my pants but a very large part of me wanted to laugh. I couldn't stop imagining T-Pain on the other end of the line, with his dark sunglasses and huge hat. I'd seen the guy on talk shows before and he was super nice. There was no way he was stalking me, but the image in my mind was hilarious.

Jack and I looked at each other as we waited for him to continue. There was an eerie silence hanging over us, as if we were all quietly waiting for the worst of it to come. A few seconds passed and I checked to see if we were still on the line. We were, but he just wasn't talking.

"Hello?" I said, just to make sure he was still there.

"Here's to getting what we deserve."

And the line went dead.

chapter
ten

I'LL BE the first to admit, I am quite possibly the last person anyone would ever choose to go on a secret mission with. I mean, if by some miracle I managed to get into the CIA, I'd just be that one person who can't be trusted with guns or top-secret weapons. Hell, I'd barely be trusted with a stapler. But due to the evident lack of James Bond-ish men in my life to take my place, I was forced to pursue Dr. D's phone call alone. Well, not entirely alone, I had Jack and Milo after all.

After the phone call we called Detective Reynolds immediately, unable to even touch a slice of pizza when it arrived, due to the butterflics in my stomach. Of course, I had snuck into the kitchen when everyone was asleep and had my share in secret, but that's not the point. I had been so frantic on the phone, I had forgotten to sound sexy. I was too busy checking the cupboards in case Dr. D was about to jump out at any second and throw a spatula at me.

Luckily, Detective Reynolds had adhered to his promise of taking my case seriously. He had calmly explained that he was sending a police car to check outside my house, on the off chance Dr. D was somewhere close by. Now I'm not going to lie to you, I was a little disappointed that Milo and his perfect dimples were nowhere to be seen when the police finally showed up. Wasn't this meant to be a good training exercise for him, or something? I was practically making his career here, and he didn't even have the courtesy to stop by and make sure I was alive! Now that's just plain rude.

But even after the police officer assured me that no one suspicious was outside the house, or inside it, I didn't stop panicking. I had even considered asking Jack to sleep on my couch again, but then thought against it. I didn't entirely trust what I'd do in my vulnerable state, and besides, Jack didn't look like he could scare anyone away. He was more likely to attract them. If Dr. D was somewhere in the house stalking me from behind a shower curtain and *wasn't* gay, one look at Jack would definitely send him swinging in another direction.

Mom and Dad obviously had to cut their dinner date a little short, which really set Dad off. He had pretty much banned me from going anywhere past our mailbox, including school, which admittedly wasn't the worst possible thing that could have happened, even if it only lasted a few days. Hey, if he was giving me a few days off from my busy schedule, then I wasn't going to complain. Dad had been absolutely no help when I had asked him what he had supposedly "taken" from the auto-tuned stranger. He just kept shaking his head as if he was trying to rack his brains for anytime he stole a doughnut or something off a friend.

But as it turns out, Detective Reynolds *had* found some

answers on the Dumpling Hospital. As expected, the place was free of anything that could link the restaurant to my family, and apparently the food there really did suck, which I didn't need reassuring about. They had also managed to find out a little more about the nametag. The mystery waiter, Ao Jie Kai, came to L.A. when he was in seventh grade and was now in his third year of college at UCLA. He was also a member of a fraternity, which was great and all, because at least now I knew my stalker was fairly socially accepted in society. Good for him. He had no previous criminal history besides a couple of minor parking ticket fines, and he'd been working at the Dumpling Hospital for about ten months. It was just he and his mother at home, no father. Detective Reynolds said he doubted that Ao Jie Kai was directly related to my stalking, but he was the only lead that they had. It wasn't much, but it gave Jack and me a starting point.

After carefully devising a plan that was followed by lots of arguments and flat out refusals on Jack's part, I finally convinced him to sneak out of the house with me and head off to UCLA to check out this Ao Jie Kai in person. With Dad in the shower and Mom at the spa, we had a small but perfectly timed window to make our escape. I was pretty certain Dad wasn't expecting Mom to stay with us for as long as she was, which wasn't helping his already high blood pressure, but she said there was no way she was leaving until things settled a little. Luckily for me, poor Anya had come down with some type of flu and was bedridden so she couldn't play spy for Dad, and the rest of the housemaids didn't care what I was doing as long as they were getting paid. Mike was too bothered with his own life to notice. Kenny was a slight problem because he was all buff and scary, but it turns out he was a sucker for Oprah reruns. The perfect distraction.

Of course father dearest wasn't going to be too pleased when he got out of the shower, but by that time we'd already be long gone. Just in case, I'd left a note on the kitchen bench telling him that we'd gone to school to pick up some books for studying, promising to be back soon. We all knew that I was a massive liar, but at least I had been nice enough to leave a note with my fake story on it. Not many kids would do that, you know. I was basically Daughter of the Year.

Practically pushing Jack out the door, as I tried to gain control over my excitement and nerves, we finally set off. It was just past noon when we were sitting in his Jeep in one of the many University of California campus parking lots. I had seven missed calls from Dad, two from Veronica and three from Aria. If my life didn't revolve around my phone, I would have run over it myself. Brendan had sent me just one text, asking why I wasn't at school for his little "talk." Not only did our absences make Jack and I look extremely sketchy to my boyfriend, I was pretty certain Meghan was going to be responsible for spreading ridiculous rumors about what we were doing instead of coming to school.

"This doesn't seem like a great idea," Jack told me uncertainly, watching students walk past, clutching books to their chests.

"You always say that."

"Yeah, because your ideas always suck."

"Well then why did you even agree to come?"

Jack leaned his head back against the headrest with a sigh. "Our freakin' deal. The sooner we find out who Dr. D is, the sooner our lives go back to normal, remember?"

"Oh," I said, crossing my hands over my chest. "And here I thought it was because you enjoyed my company."

"I don't know about that, but I *am* going to enjoy the paycheck your dad hands me when all this is done."

Gee. He really knew how to give a girl the warm and fuzzies with his overwhelming sensitivity and affection. I'll admit, I was a little offended. I mean, sure, Jack and I weren't exactly besties for life. But I wasn't *that* bad was I? It wasn't a comforting thought that Jack's mind was only on the money when I spent about eighty percent of my time trying to figure out ways to get him to love me.

"Well," I said, holding my head up high. "I'm not leaving here until I find some answers."

And with that I practically kicked the car door open, climbing out and slamming the door shut behind me. Jack took a few seconds before doing the same, probably doing some mental reasoning with himself not to have a breakdown. A group of girls walked by, their conversation almost coming to a stop as they eyed Jack slipping the car keys into his jeans pocket. Inevitably, their gaze drifted to me, standing with a smug smile on my face and shiny Tom Ford heels on my feet. They raised judgemental eyebrows as they continued on their way, no doubt wondering how and where they were going to find a guy like that.

Jack wasn't paying attention to my little victory. Instead he ran a hand through his hair, which was sexier than I thought it would be, and turned to face the campus ahead.

"Shall we?" Jack said, squinting in the sunlight.

"Give me a sec." I unzipped the leather jacket I was wearing and shimmied out of it. "Can you unlock the car?"

Jack nodded, eyes still on the campus. He glanced at me as he pulled the keys out of his pocket, doing a double take as he sized me up.

"What?" I said, looking down at my outfit.

Okay, I knew what.

"What the hell are you wearing?" he said, eyes scanning me in alarm.

I had kind of been hoping the outfit was hot enough to give Jack one of those electric shocks I always got around him. He definitely looked like he had been electrocuted, but not in the way I had hoped. I had opted for some casually tiny denim shorts and the hideous Lakers jersey that Jack had given me when we were disguised as gangsters. Only I had cut it that morning to make it a crop top, revealing my belly button. Basically, I was barely dressed, but had been using the jacket to keep some suspense.

"What's wrong with what I'm wearing?" I asked him innocently, sliding my phone into my tiny shorts pocket.

Jack looked at me as if I had told him I was running away to herd sheep for the rest of my life. "I'm not going to take you around campus like that!" he exclaimed. "You're not even wearing clothes!"

"Jack," I began impatiently, folding the jacket across my arm. "We're going to go talk to frat houses. No one's going to talk to us if I'm dressed like a nun."

"So nun and stripper were the only two options that came to your mind?" Jack exclaimed, taking the jacket and draping it across my shoulders, attempting to cover as much as he possibly could. "What about dressing like a normal person?"

Well jeez. Put a bunch of leggy supermodels in angel wings and lacy underwear, and the boy had no problems. But the moment I wanted to wear a crop top and shorts it was like, alert the feds! He was so focused on trying to cover me up; he was missing the brilliance of my plan. If I showed up to a frat house with Jack, who was of course an attractive male, the boys would presume that he was my boyfriend. We'd never get any information out of them that way! But if I was minimally dressed, then they wouldn't care if he was my boyfriend. They'd be too busy ogling at me to notice my relationship status. Pretty damn clever, if I may say so myself.

"Would you stop complaining all the time?" I said, hands on my practically bare hips. "You're worse than I am."

Before he could reply, I began walking toward the buildings ahead with the jacket still draped across my shoulders. Jack hadn't gotten around to unlocking the car doors so I wouldn't be able to put it back. Plus, I had no doubts in my mind that he would send me home kicking and screaming if I didn't come to some compromise with him. So the jacket stayed.

Jack kept looking down awkwardly, talking about how people were staring at me weirdly and how I just sent three people into cardiac arrest. But I was too busy concentrating on how beautiful the campus was to pay attention to him. UCLA was full of old-fashioned buildings with rustic brick walls and square roofs. There were lots of grass lawns and the entrances to the corridors were arched. I wasn't sure it was the right place to go to college for me, but it would definitely have made one heck of a wedding venue. There were students everywhere, lying on the lawn and lazily soaking in the L.A. sun. Others were running, clutching stacks of books as they rushed to get to class on time. Jack was right; I was definitely turning heads with my inappropriate outfit, which should have embarrassed me, but it didn't. It was nice to be getting all the attention for once. Jack was a pain to go out with. I was the daughter of an Academy Award winning actor, and nobody even cared when Jack's blonde head was bobbing around the place.

We stopped a nerdy looking guy walking alone across the lawn and asked him to direct us toward the fraternity houses. His eyes practically fell out of their sockets when he saw what I was wearing, but he finally got it together long enough to give us some directions. After ten minutes of aimless loitering and getting majorly lost, we had finally entered the world of sorority and fraternity houses. I looked around, taking in as much as I possibly could. Veronica, Aria, and I had toured universities a few months ago to get a better idea of possible colleges. I had never gone to UCLA, but my friends had. Surely there was some excellent reason for missing out on the most obvious choice, but I can't remember it now. Oh yeah, that's right. Louis Vuitton was having a sale on handbags.

Standing on the street lined with white houses was like being in a slightly shabby part of Greece. It didn't even look like part of a university, with cars parked along the sidewalk as if it were any random street in L.A. and not on a college campus. I had always been a little creeped out by the infamous stories of sorority loyalty gone too far and the emotionally scarring things they made you do to become a member. Mostly, I was going off things I had seen in horror movies and teen TV shows. I mean, it made one hell of a storyline. But there was a part of me deep down that thought it would be kind of cool to be able to call myself a sorority sister.

A group of four guys were jogging down the road, making lots of noise as they went by. They were dressed exactly alike, in blue jeans and black t-shirts that had Greek symbols on them. To me, it just looked like scribbles, but clearly it made sense to the other students around us because they were all cheering the four boys on.

"Local celebrities?" I said to Jack.

"Looks like it."

I had a sudden image of Jack in a fraternity. If you were going off looks, he'd have been the president of his frat. But based on personality, Jack wouldn't have lasted one day in a house full of boys with egos as big as his. His own pride would take up the entire campus.

The four boys passed us, as we stood rooted to the road, watching them work the small crowd of onlookers as if they were at a rock concert. Less than ten seconds after they passed, one of the boys jogged backwards so that he came up behind me to my left, beaming at me. He had sandy blonde hair and perfect teeth, and I was beginning to think that I should just drop out of school and pretend to be a student at UCLA for a while. He jerked a thumb toward Jack.

"Is he your boyfriend?" he asked, eyeing me up and down.

Jack and I looked at each other. "No," we said simultaneously.

"Great!" The blonde guy said, thrusting a flyer in my hand. "We're from the Kappa Alpha Psi house, and we're having a party this Saturday night. We would *love* for you to come."

I looked down at the flyer. It was black and had a picture of a cartoon vampire on it and another of a cauldron. In block, red letters it read:

HALLOWEEN PARTY

Saturday 9 PM

Kappa Alpha Psi House—INVITE ONLY

You should really know the place by now. It's the cool one with the palm trees and white gate.

B.Y.O but no drugs, we almost got shut down last time. Dress up. Or down. No ugly people.

PARTAY!

Well, I had to give them some points for creativity. And really, they got right to the point, which is useful for those of us who can't read or just don't have the time to get through a whole invitation.

"Halloween?" Jack said. "That's months away."

"So?" The blonde guy replied with slight hostility. "People celebrate Christmas in July all the time. It's just like that." He turned back to me with a broad smile. "Besides, costumes are more freeing. They help people get their freak on!"

On the word "freak," he did a little seductive shimmy in my direction with his pelvis. I took a step back and bit my lip, hoping I wouldn't burst into laughter and offend the poor guy's very talented hips.

"We'll try to make it," I told the blonde guy politely. "But I can't promise anything."

I put a hand on Jack's shoulder, urging him to keep going so that the blonde frat boy couldn't hit on me any further. I gave him a little finger wave as a goodbye and Jack and I continued walking down the road.

"See you there!" I heard the blonde guy say from behind me.

He wouldn't, but I didn't have the heart to tell him that. Jack and I continued on our heroic quest, past groups of sorority girls batting their eyelashes at Jack, and frat boys doing a double take at my outfit. The sorority houses weren't in the same area as the fraternities, but it was clear that the girls knew the right places to hang out. After what felt like another hour of walking, when truthfully it had been about five minutes, Jack pointed out the fraternity house we were looking for.

"Phi Kappa Psi." I read from the sign attached to the top of the large, white house. I couldn't have understood the Greek symbols if you had paid me, but thankfully they had it written out.

"That's what Milo said, right?"

"I think so."

The Phi Kappa Psi house that stood in front us was a bit of a sight for sore eyes. Compared to its surroundings this fraternity was a rundown band geek amongst the jocks and cheerleaders of Greek housing. There was a narrow set of stairs leading to the front door, with two boys standing on them, seemingly having a deep conversation. One of the boys had brown hair and had his back to me, but the other brunette in desperate need of a haircut looked over at Jack and I as we approached them.

"Hi," I said, turning my charm switch on. If my short shorts didn't work on these guys, then nothing would. "Is this the Phi Kappa Psi house?"

The other guy turned around to face us, his eyes practically bulging out of his head as he saw my outfit.

"Uh," he began, trying to peel his eyes away from my legs. "Can we help you?"

Jack rolled his eyes and said, "This is the Phi Kappa Psi house, right?"

Both boys nodded silently, eyes still glued on me. My smile broadened as I turned to face Jack. I mentally sent him a *ha! In your face* message, but he was purposely avoiding my victorious expression.

"Yeah," the boy with over-grown hair said to me. "Can we help you with something?"

"Well," I began, careful to stick to what I had rehearsed in the shower this morning. "Jack here wants to join a fraternity house, and we heard this one had a good reputation."

"Really? A good reputation?" He turned to his friend in surprise. "Dude, I told you handing out money would work!"

Well then. Clearly Ao Jie Kai didn't have good taste in fraternity houses. If the brothers had actually resorted to bribing people to join, something was obviously wrong with them.

"Hey you look a little familiar," the Jesus look-alike said, peering at me. "I feel like I've seen your face in a magazine or something."

I opened my mouth to say something, but nothing came out. Dad could stop me from covering Cosmo if he wanted, but there was no stopping me from occasionally appearing in Us Weekly, especially now that the Miss Golden Globe role was up for grabs. I turned to Jack with a panicked look. No one had recognized me in my shower rehearsal!

"Uh, no. You must be thinking of someone else," Jack said as smoothly as he could. "This is my sister, Miranda."

I forced myself not to whack him on the arm. Miranda? I looked nothing like a Miranda, let alone Jack's sister. He was blonde, I was brunette. He was a sex-god who was a clear ten out of ten at all times. When I wore extra eyeliner, I was an eight.

"Anyways," I continued before they could start questioning us some more. "Jack and I, Miranda, Jack's sister Miranda—"

"I think they got the point, Miranda."

"—talked to a few fraternities and we were considering yours."

Jack nodded and said, "Do you have many members?"

"Well," the guy with long hair began, finally coming to terms with my provocative get-up. "We're one of the smaller frat houses, but we have a really strong brotherhood."

"Yeah," the other guy agreed. "We'd invite you in to meet some of the boys, but three of them are probably still asleep, and the rest are at class or out at the moment."

"I'm Ryan, by the way," the guy with mop-hair said.

"I'm Lou," the other one said.

"Nice to meet you guys."

"So do you go to UCLA, Miranda?"

I gave them a tight smile. "Uh, no."

The two boys standing on the stairs looked at me expectantly, waiting for me to elaborate, but I didn't. Hey, I didn't have to write them an autobiography on my fake Miranda life. There was an awkward silence for a few seconds as I thought of my next step. Clearly my shower rehearsal sucked, because it hadn't helped me at all. I couldn't exactly just blurt out "Hey, do you know someone called Ao Jie Kai, because he may be stalking me?" Actually, I could.

"So—" Jack began, but I intervened.

"Oh!" I cried in fake surprise. "Phi Kappa Psi! That's why you sound familiar! Do you guys know someone called Ao Jie Kai?"

"You mean AJ?" Ryan asked, raising his eyebrows in surprise. "Yeah, he's one of the brother's here."

Jack's eyes widened as if to say *what exactly do you think you're doing?* I ignored him, concentrating on my new plan of action.

"How do you know him?" Lou asked me.

"I have a friend who goes here," I explained, impressed with my impromptu skills. "She introduced me to him at a party. Great guy. Super nice."

I sent a mental message to the heavens above, hoping that Ao Jie Kai actually was a nice stalker.

"Oh yeah?" Ryan said with a smile. "Yeah, he's great! Who's your friend? Anyone I'd know?"

"Oh, I doubt it," Jack cut in, shaking his head. "She does fashion designing."

"Hey, my girlfriend does that!" Ryan replied, and Jack and I looked at each other. What were the odds? "What's your friend's name, she may know her?"

"Um—" Jack began, but I got in first.

"Scarlett," I replied quickly. "Scarlett . . . Johanessburg."

Jack let out a sigh next to me. The boys probably wouldn't have picked up on it, but I knew exactly what it meant. He thought I was an idiot.

"Hunh," Lou replied thoughtfully. "Isn't that an actress?"

"Uh, no, it—it's really not," I said truthfully, shaking my head. Hey, it wasn't technically a lie.

Ryan shrugged and said, "The name doesn't ring a bell, but I'll ask my girlfriend."

"So," Jack continued, his fake smile reappearing. "Is AJ around? I know Miranda and him really hit it off."

I forgot for a few seconds that I was Miranda and Jack nudged me lightly with his elbow as a reminder he was talking about me.

"Oh right!" I said. "Yeah, we really hit it off. Is he home? I'd love to catch up with him."

"He's at class right now and then he's got work right after," Lou told us with an apologetic smile.

"Today's a pretty packed day for him, but you can stop by sometime later tonight if you'd like. He should be home after eight."

The two boys looked at each other hopefully and I raised an eyebrow. It's amazing what minimal clothing will do to the human mind.

"Oh that's okay, we may stop by when we're in the neighborhood next," Jack replied, grabbing onto my wrist. "But thanks anyway."

I gave the two boys one last killer smile and could almost see birds circling their heads. The trip had been kind of a waste of time, my feet were killing me and I actually did feel a little ridiculous in those clothes. It had been nice to have my fifteen minutes of fame amongst the testosterone packed males of UCLA, but I just wanted to go home.

"Are you going to the party?" Ryan asked, and Jack and I turned around to face him.

"What party?"

Lou pointed to the flyer that was still in my hand. I looked down at it in surprise.

"I haven't really thought about it," I told them, folding the flyer in half.

"Well they have great parties and all," Lou said. "But the guys aren't the friendliest. I mean, it's great if you want rich boys in Tommy Hilfiger shirts with fancy cars and alcohol. But you know, our brotherhood is real. Plus, they don't have Pictionary night like we do!"

Truth be told Tommy Hilfiger shirts and fancy cars sounded like just my type, as long as they weren't as immature as Brendan's friends. But the boys were really pulling out the fireworks to try and convince Jack to join. Sure, it was probably because they hoped his all too liberal sister Miranda would visit frequently in her tiny clothing, but all the same.

Jack nodded politely and said, "I'll keep that in mind. Thanks guys."

"You know," Ryan said, right as we turned to leave again. Beside me Jack gave an impatient sigh. "We were planning on going to their party this Saturday, if you're interested. AJ's going to be there. You guys could always catch up there?"

The hopeful look on both of their faces returned, but I wasn't celebrating my newfound attention anymore. Jack and I were already exchanging glances that told me we were thinking along the same lines.

"I'll consider it," I said simply, trying my hardest to be non-committal and suppress my excitement.

We said our goodbyes, I smiled some more and we finally left, making our way back down the fraternity house street.

"So what do you think?" Jack asked.

I weaved my arms through the arms of my leather jacket, deciding my outfit had completed its job for the day. I unfolded the flyer and tried to smooth out the creases.

"About the party?" I said, and Jack nodded. "Well Ao Jie Kai is going to be there. It may be worth it to make an appearance."

Jack nodded in agreement and said, "That's what I was thinking."

"Wait," I said, genuinely shocked at how easy that had been. "You *actually* agreed to go to this party without complaining?"

"Oh don't gloat," Jack replied, but he was smiling a little. For some reason that made my insides do this little hip-hop crunk thing that was extremely unsettling.

"Now we just have to figure out how to get out of the house on Saturday without Dad making a big deal out of it."

"We'll figure it out," Jack said. "Your dad loves me."

The sad thing was, my dad *did* love Jack. I was always getting yelled at and grounded, but Jack could throw a puppy off a bridge and my dad would still think he was incredible. It was super depressing, but also convenient if Jack and I ever did decide to take whatever we had to the next step. Oh lord. Now *that* was a scary thought.

"Miranda?" I asked him, and his smile widened. "Really?"

"What?" he said. "I was thinking about Miranda Kerr and it kind of just came out."

Trust Jack to be thinking about Miranda Kerr while we were on a secret mission. Although, if Miranda Kerr had ever met Jack, I doubt she'd be able to walk the runway without him in mind.

The two of them would have fantastic children, which is a little heartbreaking.

"Why not just say Scarlett! It wouldn't have even been lying because she's actually your sister!"

"Maybe it was because you turned her into a fictional student with a real actress's name!"

"Hey! That's not her actual name! I changed it a little." I felt my phone buzz in shorts pocket and pulled it out with a groan. "It's probably Dad. Yet again."

But it wasn't Dad. And in a snap second, being grounded for all eternity actually seemed pretty ideal after I saw the increasingly familiar title of *No Caller ID* staring back at me.

"Pick it up," Jack said, after leaning in and reading the caller ID.

I thrust the phone at him and shook my head. "I don't want to."

He sighed and took the phone, taking me by the wrist and leading me to a corner of the sidewalk, out of everyone's way. He answered the phone and put it on loudspeaker, holding the phone out of my reach when I tried to hang up in a panic.

"Say something," he hissed.

"You say something!"

"Gia!"

"I can hear you, you know," came the auto-tuned voice through the speaker, and Jack and I froze.

"Hey man," I said, and Jack closed his eyes, shaking his head. "W—What's going on?"

"I suggest you stop this childish investigation, Gia." Dr. D said.

Jack held the phone between us and we listened silently, waiting for him to continue. When he didn't I looked at Jack and he shrugged.

"Hello?" I said, leaning in closer to the phone so Dr. D

could hear me.

"You need to stop searching for answers. You'll get them eventually. Investigating will only get you hurt."

I would have been shitting myself if it hadn't been for the auto-tune. Don't get me wrong, I was still freaked as heck. But the editing of his voice kept making me want to laugh. It's hard to take someone seriously if they're threatening you in singsong.

"Are you here right now?" I asked him, scanning my surroundings.

I couldn't see any creepy lurkers, peeping out from behind trees with binoculars, dressed in black from head-to-toe. There was silence for a few seconds and I looked at Jack expectantly. He was staring intently at the phone in his hands, waiting for Dr. D to reply.

"Let this be a warning call," Dr. D finally said. "Or else I'll be forced to put the *pain* in T-Pain."

The line went dead and Jack and I stared at the phone for a few more seconds in silence before he handed the phone back to me. I replaced it in my pocket shakily, as Jack put a comforting arm around my shoulder. Under other circumstances, I would have been overjoyed, but my heart could only deal with one extreme emotion at a time, and fear was definitely winning over lust.

"He didn't actually just say that, did he?" I asked Jack.

"It was super lame, but I think he did."

"Well what do we do now?"

He thought about it for a beat as I gave a defeated sigh. Jack looked at me, almost smiling but not quite. A part of him was secretly enjoying the thrill, I could tell.

"Well," he said. "Get your party shoes on."

c h a p t e r
e l e v e n

THE WINTERSES' household was packed with cops the next afternoon. They were scattered across all rooms, searching for any electronic bugs that may have been planted anywhere in the house, allowing Dr. D inside access into everything I do. Everything had been arranged the night before, when Detective Reynolds had suggested that we let the LAPD do a scan of the house for any listening devices or cameras that shouldn't be there.

Dad hadn't believed for one second that I was just at school, but he'd been surprising cool about the whole thing, losing interest after a few questions. It was probably because Mom had told him to suck it up and let me live my life. He did, however, tell me that I was still under house arrest and needed his permission to even open the window, which I promised I would adhere to. And

I really meant it for five minutes. Maybe it was because Jack was always around so he knew I'd be safe, or maybe he had just given up on me. Either way, he had given me a pleasant surprise, but I made a mental note not to push my luck.

Jack and I couldn't tell my parents about the latest phone call from Dr. D because that would involve us going into detail about where we were and what we were doing. But Jack had assured me that he had informed Kenny and Detective Reynolds in private. The party on Saturday was still our little secret though. It probably wasn't a brilliant idea to keep secrets about this particular issue, but really, Dad was leaving me no choice with his psycho protective behavior.

But he was the last thing on my mind as I watched in dismay as two complete strangers dismantled my phone on the kitchen island. I know he was just doing his job, but if that cop so much as scratched my specially made gold back cover, there would be hell in all forms coming his way. I was concentrating so hard on the destruction of my phone that I didn't realize Milo had quietly slipped into the room and taken a place next to me, leaning against the entrance of the kitchen.

"Hey," he said with a smile. "How's it going?"

My whole body tensed as I mustered an animated smile. "Good I guess. Not sure how I feel about this guy destroying my phone though."

Milo gave a light laugh and said, "We're just double checking to see if there are any listening devices embedded in it. You'll have it back in no time, don't worry. These guys are experts."

I frowned at the officers who were still working on removing the back of my iPhone. I looked away before I started yelling about his lack of care with what I considered to be my lifeline.

"So how's the investigation going?" I asked Milo.

"Pretty good. We still don't really know how everything ties together, but if we find anything in your house today we can get a better idea of who we're dealing with."

There was a big chance Milo was sounding optimistic just to keep me from freaking out any more than I already was. Because from where I was standing, finding listening devices in my home was by no means a good potential outcome. But what did I know? He was the officer-in-training, not me.

Milo walked further into the kitchen, the other officers ignoring him completely. I didn't follow him, choosing to stay put near the entrance. Getting in close proximity to Milo would involve a lot of restraint on my part, and I wasn't sure I had it in me. The further the distance, the safer my hormones were.

"I like the Hepburn poster," he said, fiddling with the cuff of his uniform.

"The what?"

"In your room," Milo said. "The one above the bed. It's nice."

My face drained of color. Milo Fells had been inside my bedroom, and I hadn't even gotten a chance to enjoy the special moment! What kind of cruel joke was the universe playing on me? Even worse, what if I had accidently left a bra lying on the floor or something? I mean, you got to at least take a girl to dinner before you check out her Guia La Bruna.

"Um, thanks. She's my favorite."

"I just knew you'd be into the girly stuff," Milo said with a teasing smile. "I took one look at you and thought, yep, that's a Tiffany's kind of girl."

Hopefully he would remember that analysis when he was buying me an engagement ring. I took a couple of steps into the kitchen, deciding I was brave enough to test the waters of this conversation.

"Oh really?" I said, as if challenging him. "What about you, smarty-pants? Are you a Tiffany's kind of guy?"

Milo's smile widened. "I'm more of a *Diehard* kind of guy. It goes with my cop image."

I froze, racking my brains but coming up short. It's like my mind had decided to temporarily go on holiday to the Bahamas. There were so many random violent movies with macho names that I had lost count.

"Oh," I said, as if I knew exactly which one he was talking about. Fake it 'til you make it. "Yeah. Yeah! I love that movie! That's the one with the guns. And the fighting. And the guys, you know, and that chick."

Milo was clearly suppressing a laugh when he said, "You've seen *Diehard*?"

I gave him my best deeply offended look. "Of course I've seen *Diehard*! It's only like my fourth favorite movie!"

"Okay. Who's the main actor?"

Oh crap. He got me there!

"Um . . ." I said, wondering if he would notice if I Googled it quickly. "It's um, that guy . . . Harrison Ford."

Milo just stared at me for a few seconds, looking amused. "You mean Bruce Willis?" he said.

"Yeah, that's what I said."

"Well what d'ya know? We found one," one of the officers said.

I sighed with relief. If Random Cop One hadn't stepped in, I would probably have resorted to making up facts about Bruce Willis just to keep my cover, and I wasn't so great at fake trivia.

"You found a bug?" I asked, leaning in closer. My phone was now unrecognizable as it lay completely dismantled on the kitchen island, tiny silver pieces scattered around it.

Random Officer Two held up a small pair of tweezers with a tiny black thing attached at the tip. "There it is."

"He bugged my phone?" I exclaimed. I had been totally convinced they were wasting their time. "How could he have gotten to my phone? I always have it on me!"

"Clearly not," Random Officer One said, and I scowled.

"It might have been the UCLA kid," Officer Two said, placing the bug on the counter next to the rest of my phone's insides. "He's a tech student, so he'd know his way around your phone."

Well that was dandy and all, but I was more worried about how he *reached* my phone. Fear crept up my spine. What if he had snuck into the house while I was asleep? Our security was great, but this guy was clearly crafty. Officer One reached into his LAPD jacket and pulled out a similar black device to the bug, placing it inside the back of my phone, exactly where the other one had been.

"What are you doing?" I asked. "Didn't we just take out a bug?"

"Yeah." Milo said. "Now *we're* bugging your phone."

"I don't get it. Isn't that the bad guy's job?"

Milo's lips curved into a half-smile. "Usually. But sometimes the good guys can use it to their advantage too."

"So . . . what does that mean?"

"It means," Officer Two said, restoring the small silver objects to their original places. He must have worked part-time at Apple in a previous life. "Next time Dr. D calls you, we'll automatically be alerted and be able to listen in on the call. And if you keep him on the line for at least sixty seconds, we'll be able to trace the call."

Alright, that was a little badass. Plus, it seemed simple enough. If bugging my phone meant that we'd be able to end all this drama in sixty seconds, I was down for that. The only problem was, those golden sixty seconds could still be ages away, and just the idea of that was making me restless.

"So what do I do in the meantime?" I asked the officers. "While we wait for him to call, I mean."

"Sit tight," Officer Two said, sliding my now completely intact phone across the counter toward me. "Don't stress. Maybe invest in a guard dog."

"I already have a dog," I told him.

As if perfectly timed for the moment, Famous shuffled past the entrance of the kitchen and disappeared down the foyer. He seemed completely unfazed by the strangers dispersed around the house, and was concentrating heavily on sniffing the polished floor.

"Yeah," Officer One said with a snort. "Trained killer that one is."

I narrowed my eyes at the two officers, fighting back an aggressive eye roll. I sincerely hoped Milo's police training didn't involve cracking lame jokes, or else my love story would have a big problem.

"I'm going to go update Reynolds," Officer One said, after he had finished chuckling. "You guys check out the study; see if there's anything there."

"You coming, Fells?"

"Yes, sir."

The two officers left the kitchen, leaving Milo and I alone in silence, except for the distant noises of the many cops shuffling around the house.

"I better go check out the study," he said, finally breaking the awkward tension.

"Right." I nodded. "I better go check the . . . fridge."

"Right."

Milo headed for entrance, and I slapped a hand over my eyes, my back to him. Fridge? Real smooth, Gia.

"Hey, are you going to that Halloween party this weekend?"

I lowered my hand and turned to face him. "What?"

"I didn't mean to pry," Milo said. "I just saw the invite on your desk, and I was curious. I've got a few friends who go to school at UCLA, so I got an invite too. Are you planning on going?"

I blinked at him for a few seconds, unsure of what the right answer was. Jack and I had thought about going, but hadn't come to a decision yet. But if Milo was going to be there, I definitely needed to re-evaluate my options.

"I don't really know too many people there," I told him. "But I might. How about you?"

"It's not really my scene," he said with a smile. "But if you wanted some company then I'd be happy to tag along."

Um, YES. That would be fabulous, thanks. A night out with Milo Fells would make my life. I just needed to work around the whole bodyguard dilemma. There was no way I could get Milo to fall in love with me with Jack always standing an inch away. Plus, there was still the issue of Brendan, who at the end of the day, was still technically my boyfriend. Technicalities. They'll always get you.

"Well," I said, "I'm always up for a good shindig!"

Oh good God. Why couldn't the ground just split into two and swallow me up? Never in my entire life had used the word "shindig" like some kind of hippie living in a van, and my brain had chosen *that* exact moment to make a life change. Jack appeared suddenly in the doorway, allowing me a second to cringe as the attention shifted to him. He looked at Milo, then at me, and back at Milo.

"The officer with the unibrow is looking for you," Jack told him. "I think he wants to check out the fourth floor."

"Thanks," Milo replied. He glanced at me with a smile. "I'd better go check it out."

My over-enthusiastic smile didn't drop until he had left the kitchen, and his footsteps were no longer audible in the foyer.

"What?" I snapped at Jack, who was clearly itching to pass some judgement.

"I didn't say anything."

"Yeah, but you're going to."

"Gia," Jack said, giving me a knowing look. "He seems a

little more interested in getting in your pants than actually solving this case."

I stared at Jack for a few seconds. "Is that bad?"

Jack rolled his eyes. "You're beyond help."

"What's it to you anyway?" I demanded.

"*I'm* actually doing something to keep you safe," Jack replied, looking annoyed. "He's just playing footsies in the kitchen while everyone else is doing their job."

I crossed my arms over my chest and said, "What, are you jealous?"

"I don't do jealous, Gia," Jack replied with a scoff. "Besides, he's not even a real cop! It's like playing dress-up."

There was an awkward silence as Jack and I glared at each other. What the hell was he so worked up about? Jack was acting way out of line for someone who didn't seem to give a damn about my personal life on any other day.

I opened my mouth to continue fighting, but the sound of a familiar voice calling my name out caught me off guard.

"Brendan?" I said, more to myself.

"Gia?" Brendan repeated, his voice coming from somewhere near the front door.

"Oh my God," I said, eyes widened. "Brendan!"

Speaking of jealousy, Brendan really did have the *worst* timing. My boyfriend was in the same house as Jack, my extremely attractive but equally frustrating bodyguard whom he hated, as well as my perpetually annoyed father *and* the future love of my life, Milo. My L.A. mansion had turned into the House of Horror in the blink of an eye.

I pushed past Jack roughly, passing four LAPD cops as I ran to the front door in a panic. If I got to him before Dad, then maybe I could do some damage control. Unfortunately for me, Dad was already at the front door, alongside an officer I had forgotten the name off. He was watching Brendan disapprovingly,

Aria and Veronica unexpectedly standing by his side.

"Oh!" I exclaimed, a little out of breath. "Hey guys."

"Hey Gia!" Brendan replied. He looked like he wanted to hug me, but kept glancing nervously at Dad who was now eyeing the gun holstered on the officer's belt.

"Can we talk?" Aria said, giving me a little smile.

"Nice to see you kids again," Dad said politely, and frowned at Brendan one last time before making his way down the hallway.

I led the gang into the closest living room, awkwardly watching two cops make their way past me. I had no clue why we needed so many officers to search the house! Sure, six stories is a lot, but Dad had practically ordered the whole of the police department to conduct the process.

"So what are you guys doing here?" I asked once the police officers had left the room. Brendan took a seat uncomfortably on the edge of the sofa, but the rest of us remained standing.

"I needed to talk to you about something but my car broke down at school," Brendan explained. "So Veronica and Aria gave me a lift."

"You're never at school anymore," Aria said, as if I hadn't noticed. "So we figured we'd all stop by and see what's going on."

"Nothing's going on," I lied.

Veronica raised her eyebrows and said, "Gia, you and Jack are always AWOL, you never reply to our texts or calls, there are cops all over your house and a giant police van parked in your driveway. Want to tell me again how nothing's going on?"

"I've been sick. Super sick," I said nervously. "So has Jack. I think he caught it from me."

Brendan, Aria and Veronica evaluated my appearance as I fidgeted uncomfortably. An Alexander Wang romper and a full set of makeup didn't exactly scream illness. The outfit had been planned with Milo in mind, not an impromptu high school reunion!

"You don't look sick," Veronica said.

"Well, I am."

"And then what?" Aria asked, crossing her arms over her chest. "You decided to kill someone? What's with all the cops?"

"Does this have something to do with Dr. D?" Veronica asked, and my eyes widened in alarm.

"Who?" Aria asked, and Veronica gave a little sigh.

"Cops?" I exclaimed, as if it was ridiculous for them to even think that way. "Dr. D? No! That's crazy talk! These guys are . . . the Los Angeles Pest Department. I think we have termites."

It was definitely one of my better on-the-spot explanations. It deserved a gold star at the very least. Aria made a face and inched closer to Veronica, as if bugs were suddenly going to burst out from under the floorboards and attack her.

"Oh, hey guys," Jack padded into the living room with a relaxed smile on his face. Aria and Veronica both greeted him with genuine warmth, but Brendan actually groaned a little.

"Don't you have a house of your own?" he snapped at Jack.

"Is that an invitation to move in with you?" Jack replied. "Because I accept."

Aria and Veronica both gave quiet laughs, but I didn't even crack a smile. It was hard enough dealing with the two boys when they pretended to like each other. Now that they were being open about their hatred, it was going to be ten times worse!

"Isn't there somewhere private we can talk?" Brendan asked, giving me an exasperated look.

"The house is kind full right now with the pest department . . ."

"Pest department?" Jack said, raising his eyebrows.

"Yes, Jack," I shot him a *go with it* look. "The pest department. We can talk outside if you want."

"The pest department's van is blocking your driveway," Veronica told us.

"Yeah, good luck getting past that thing," Aria added, inspecting her nails. "Besides, I'm staying for this conversation. I drove you all the way over here, Brendan. I'm not your chauffer."

I caught Veronica's eye but looked away immediately. Aria may have bought that lie, but Veronica could see right through me. I was waiting for her to call me out, but she stayed silent, and I found myself more grateful for her than I had ever been before her.

"Oh for cryin' out loud!" Brendan exclaimed, throwing his hands in the air. "Fine! Everyone can stay." He turned to me with an intense look and said, "Gia, I'm dropping out of school."

"*What?*" everyone in the room said at once. We all looked at each other, as if our brains had suddenly connected and morphed into one.

"I'm moving to Texas."

"I'm sorry, what was that?" I said, scared that I may have heard correctly.

"I got a job on a cowboy TV show!"

"What in the actual—" Aria began.

"Hell?" Jack finished for her. "*You* got hired to be on TV?"

"Dude," Brendan said, trying to remain calm. "I play a lot of sports. I will not think twice about kicking your ass. You want to take this outside?"

"You can't, the pest department van is blocking the driveway," I reminded him.

"'Cause I will take this outside if you want me to!" Brendan continued.

"You can't," I repeated, rolling my eyes. "The pest department van is—"

"What are you going to do?" Jack sneered, ignoring me. "Throw your ping pong ball at me?"

"Hey!" Brendan cried, rising to his feet. "I am a four-time champion!"

"Enough!" I exclaimed. "Jack, shut up. Brendan, are you insane? You can't drop out of school! We only have a few months left!"

Brendan glared at Jack for a few more seconds before reluctantly turning his attention back to me. "Gia, this could be my big break. I've been trying to get into the industry for forever, and I finally scored this opportunity. It's not a big role, but it's enough for me to take a risk."

"Brendan," I said, trying to be patient with his stupidity. "That's great and all, but I don't think you've thought this through. I mean, it's Texas! *Texas!* You've lived in Hollywood your entire life! How are you going to live in Texas?"

"I'll adjust!"

"So when you say it's not a big role . . ." Jack prompted, and I shot him a warning look.

"If you must know, I play a horse trainer on the show. My character's name is Cowboy Stan," Brendan replied haughtily.

"Stan?" Aria said, making a face. "Boy, that's unfortunate."

"No, *cowboy*, that's unfortunate," Jack told her, and Veronica and Aria giggled at his lame joke, despite half-assed attempts to keep it in.

Okay, that one had been kind of funny. But poor Brendan was clearly not enjoying the conversation, and I didn't need to make it worse. But seriously, who's ever heard of a cowboy named Stan? Doesn't the Big Book of Cowboy Baby Names only contain Bill, Billy, Bob, Bobby and Howard? There's no Stan on that list!

"You can laugh all you want," Brendan said to my friends and Jack. "But when I'm famous, you'll all be sorry."

"What do your parents think about this?" I asked, fully aware that it could not have gone down well in his house.

"They weren't pleased," he admitted. "I don't think my dad will ever speak to me again. But I have some relatives who live in Austin and I'm moving in with them. My parents don't really have a choice. I'm eighteen; I can do what I want."

Somehow I thought that the police and parents around the world would disagree, but hey, he had made up his mind. There was obviously no way I was going to stop him now.

"So, I guess we're breaking up, then?" I asked, taking a wild guess.

Two police officers walked past the living room and disappeared through the front door. Hopefully they were almost done with their inspection so I could kick everyone out and bury my head under a pile of pillows.

"Well, I was thinking," Brendan said, suddenly looking excited. "Why don't you come with me?"

Everyone in the room was silent for a few seconds. Jack coughed quietly.

"Come again?" I said, checking to make sure I had actually heard that correctly.

"You don't have to drop out," Brendan explained. "But you could apply to colleges in Texas and come live with me! I think it could really work!"

I couldn't think of a nice way to say "hell no, you must be absolutely delusional," so I kept quiet for a few seconds. I didn't want to hurt his feelings or anything, but if Brendan thought I was going to become Cowgirl Stan, he had another thing coming.

"Brendan, I'm not moving to Texas with you. I'm sorry but that's just never going to happen."

"Can I just say something?" Jack asked, raising his arm as if he was in elementary school.

"No!" Brendan and I said at the same time.

"Fine," Jack replied, making a motion of pulling a zip across his lips, which were curved into a wide grin.

"Just think about it!" Brendan pleaded.

"Brendan, I can't," I said, shaking my head. "I—I'm sorry, but I just can't!"

Brendan gave me a defeated look. "So this is really it then?"

"Looks like it."

"Does it have to be?"

"I'm sorry, Brendan."

Aria and Veronica awkwardly exchanged looks with Jack, who was finding this whole situation incredibly amusing. I actually felt a sudden wave of sadness sweep over me. Okay, so Brendan and I didn't have an amazing Katherine Heigl-worthy love story. But we had a pretty good "like story." I had spent all this time thinking Brendan and I were going to have a mutual breakup; end things as friends because we both knew it wasn't working out. But clearly we hadn't been on the same page. I had just dumped someone! I had never done that before.

"I think I should go," Brendan said quietly. "I leave next week, so I've got a lot of work to do."

"Next week?" Veronica asked him in surprise. "That's so soon!"

Brendan shrugged and I felt even worse. He looked so sad, and I didn't feel nearly as guilty as I should have for neglecting him ever since Jack had moved in.

"I'll walk you to the door," I told him, even though it was about fifteen seconds away.

"No that's okay," he said. "I know the way out."

I opened my mouth to protest, but Milo walked into the living room and cut me off.

"We found a total of eight bugs so far; two in your bedroom," Milo informed me. He turned to look up at my friends in surprise. "Oh! Sorry, I didn't know you had guests."

"Oh my gosh, EW! Bugs?" Aria cried, running for the front door. "I'm waiting in the car! Just don't come near me!"

It took me a few moments to overcome the fact that Aria had actually believed the pest department cover-up before finally turning my attention back to the real issue at hand. Aria must really hate bugs if she hadn't even noticed how hot Milo was. Brendan gave me one last sad look and followed Aria, leaving Milo, Veronica, Jack and I standing in the living room.

"Was it something I said?" Milo whispered to me.

"No, that's okay," I assured him.

"That's my cue. Good luck with the bugs," Veronica said and gave me a quick hug. "Call me."

I promised I would and watched her walk out the door, my head spinning in confusion. *I* had ended things with Brendan. I was prepared for this. But for some reason, I still felt so empty and sad. Maybe it was because I knew Brendan hadn't taken it well, or maybe it was because he was one of the very few normal things left in my life. I didn't mind all the new entries, particularly the good choice in men that the LAPD had. But my life had gotten pretty crazy in the last few weeks, and it felt like everything was passing me by at an incredible speed.

"Well that was . . ." Jack began, struggling to find the right word to describe what had just happened.

"Abrupt," Milo finished for him.

I wheeled around to face both of them with a defeated look on my face. Both men were looking at me expectantly, waiting for me to cry or laugh or just say something. To be honest, I wasn't really sure what I could say. Some psycho freak had somehow managed to get into my house and plant listening devices all over the place, I had just dumped my boyfriend who wanted to make me his cowgirl bride, and now I was very much single and had two painfully attractive guys standing a few feet away from me. I was a complete and utter mess.

"Who was that?" Milo whispered to Jack.

"Who?

"The sad one."

"Nobody!" I replied for him. Milo didn't need to know about my relationship with Brendan. Or lack thereof now.

"Are you okay?" Jack said finally, actually looking a little scared that I was going to throw a lamp against a wall or something.

"Yeah." I said with a shrug, struggling to keep my emotions in check.

The LAPD seemed to have completed their job because they were slowly making their way out of the house and loading up their van with their intricate devices and black thingy-ma-bobbies.

"Any more?" Milo asked a passing officer.

The officer held up two tiny electronic bugs in his gloved hand, exactly the same as what was in Milo's hand. "One in the master bedroom. I think Andrews has some more with him" he replied, before leaving along with his fellow cop friends.

"That's insane!" I cried, turning to Milo. "How could he have even gotten into the house?"

"Was there anyone who came over recently? Someone that isn't a good friend, or maybe an unexpected visitor?" Milo asked.

"Not really," I said with a frown. "Not that I can remember."

Milo nodded grimly and said, "Who has access to your entire house besides your family?"

"Just Anya and the housekeepers. But they're completely harmless. I mean, Anya has been with us for almost eight years!"

"We'll need to interview all the housekeepers anyway, just to be sure. Anyone else?"

"That's it," I replied with a shrug. "Oh, and the bodyguards I guess."

Milo looked at Jack thoughtfully, before nodding slowly. He had an assessing look on his face as he sized Jack up. Surely he didn't think one of the bodyguards was to blame! I mean, Jack was annoying and frustrating and probably capable of some form of evil, but I highly doubted he'd gone around my whole house planting listening devices for himself or anyone. Kenny, I'd probably believe a little more. He was really scary with his beady eyes and his bulging muscles. But every muscly, beady-eyed guy can't be presumed an evil genius just because of his unhelpful features.

My parents were standing in the hallway near the front door, talking to another police officer that was filling them in and most likely asking the same questions Milo had just asked me. Up 'til now, it seemed that Ao Jie Kai was the prime suspect. But Milo looked like he had just found another one. Jack wasn't an idiot; obviously he had noticed the intense look Milo had been giving him. But thankfully he kept his mouth shut and pretended to be overly interested in a painting hanging in the living room.

"We'll send these to the lab," Milo told me after a few, excruciatingly awkward minutes of silence. "Maybe we can find some fingerprints. But mostly it gives us a good indication of how far this guy is willing to go, and how high-tech."

I nodded, even though I didn't really understand what he was talking about. If planting listening devices didn't already tell us Dr. D was a lunatic, then I don't know what would have. Milo's lips curved into a half smile and my heart did its break dancing thing for a few seconds, before he left the living room and walked toward my parents.

"He thinks I did it, doesn't he?" Jack asked, the moment Milo was out of earshot.

"Jack!" I exclaimed. "That's ridiculous. Of course he doesn't."

"He gave me a look!"

"Don't be so dramatic. He didn't give you anything."

Jack looked at me knowingly. "Gia."

"Okay fine! He gave you a look."

"What would you do if I actually had done it?" Jack asked, and I looked at him.

"What?" I replied. "Planted all these listening devices in my house for some psycho freak to listen in on everything that happens so that he can call me later on and freak the living daylights out of me?"

Jack thought about it for a few seconds. "Yeah, that seems about right."

"I'd kick your ass."

"I'd *love* to see you try that."

Whatever sadness I had experienced five minutes ago had passed and I was actually really glad it was over. I mean, yeah that was a bit quick, but whatever. You can't dwell on the past. Now I could focus on the more important things in life, like my stalker, my schoolwork, and potential colleges. Oh, and my future life with Milo Fells, and naming our two children. I may even name one of them Stan, in honor of Brendan. Okay, that's a joke. I'm not naming my kid Stan.

"He can run all the background checks he wants on me," Jack said, as we both watched closely as Milo and other officer talked to my dad. "But he's not going to find what he wants."

I cocked up an eyebrow. "Is that so?"

"Well," Jack replied, with a nonchalant shrug. "You dig deep enough you can find anything on anyone."

"Even on you?"

Jack smiled, his gaze still on Milo. "Especially on me."

chapter
twelve

IT WAS already past noon on Thursday, and I was still lying in bed, half asleep. Only two days had passed since the Brendan break-up and I was already contemplating making plans to go partying with another guy on Saturday night. Congratulations to me, I am a terrible person. A terrible person that would, however, still go party with another guy, despite accepting that it may be considered insensitive. Especially because it was the same night as said ex-boyfriend's farewell party. Look, he was running off to become a cowboy and leaving me behind with all my troubles. Brendan wasn't allowed to be offended.

In the meantime, I *needed* to get my act together and do something productive with my life, because lying in bed all day, eating junk and watching Netflix, was not a good use of my time.

Mom had pointed out that strawberries did not count as a healthy snack if they were drenched in chocolate, but as long as there was fruit involved, I was making good life choices. If my borderline dangerous levels of fitness weren't bad enough, my extreme lack of motivation to catch-up on schoolwork was really becoming a problem. Staying at home and procrastinating had resulted in a pile of homework the size of the Empire State Building to mount on my desk, only nobody proposed or filmed romantic movie scenes at the top of it. Plus, Famous needed a bath, I was still not allowed past the mailbox and I was still being stalked. Good times all around.

What I really couldn't deal with was why Milo suspected Jack to be involved in the stalking. I even reasoned with myself that he didn't, and I had just taken his look the wrong way. I mean, people give each other looks all the time! That doesn't mean they always convey what they're meant to. His thoughtful nodding could have meant anything really. Like, maybe he liked Jack's outfit, or he was thinking about what to have for dinner. Maybe he was thinking about making Jack a groomsmen at our wedding. Who knows?

Either way, there was no way Jack planted those creepy listening devices, and there was even less chance of him actually being Dr. D himself. Absolutely no way in heck. Okay, maybe a slight way in heck. Maybe it was Chris. He barely spoke! He was always just present, but never really a participant. It made sense. Lurking in the background? Check. Thought I was attractive but never outright showed it? Check. Had full access to my house? Check. Those were all features of a potential undercover stalker. Then again, maybe it was Kenny. But being buff and scary looking wasn't a crime. Plus, anyone who gets teary when Oprah gives away a free car can't be evil. Oprah brings out the best in all of us.

The sound of my phone violently buzzing on my bedside table broke into my sleepy thoughts, and I clumsily reached for it with a groan. Without opening an eyelid, I answered the call, sliding the screen like a pro.

"Hello?" I said groggily, my voice partially muffled by my pillows.

"You missed one."

My eyelids fluttered open as I propped myself up onto my elbows, squinting at my phone screen. It read *No Caller ID.*

"Hello?" I repeated.

"I must say," came the deep robotic voice. "The police did a good job of finding the rest. But they missed the most important one."

Oh crap. I shot up to a sitting position and did some heavy breathing. Evidently, as if he wasn't scary enough, Dr. D had decided to trade his auto-tune for some good, old-fashioned Darth Vader. Where the heck was Jack when I needed him? He was always around when it was inconvenient, but the moment I actually needed his assistance he wasn't there. I bit my lip, evaluating my next step. Maybe I was wrong. Maybe it was Matt Damon. Although, why Matt Damon would be calling in a creepy edited voice, talking about the police, is questionable.

I sucked in some air and put the phone back to my ear. "You're talking about the bugs, right?" I said.

"Of course."

"How'd you get in the house anyway?" I said, hugging my knees to my chest. "There's no way you would have gotten in without being seen."

There was a low rumble on the other end, and I figured he must have been chuckling. "What if it wasn't me?" Dr. D asked.

"Ao Jie Kai then," I said, trying to stop my voice from shaking. "Or someone who works for you. If you tell me how then I promise I won't go to the cops."

Okay, that was such a pathetic lie and we both knew it. But the way I saw it, there was only one of these mystery bugs left in the house. Wherever it was, chances are it wouldn't have picked up on Milo putting a bug into my phone. What Dr. D didn't know wouldn't kill him, but it would get him arrested. According to the police officers and pretty much every crime-related movie or TV show I've ever seen, sixty seconds is enough time to trace the call. After that its bam! Bye-bye mister creepo forever. I felt like my heart was going to collapse from the nerves, but I trusted that someone at the police station, hopefully Milo, had my back.

There was silence on the other end of the line for a few seconds as Dr. D considered my deal. "I like you Gia," he finally said. "You've got an attitude that I admire. You're brave, which is a quality I never saw in your father. You two differ there. And just for that, I'm going to tell you."

"Um, thank you?"

It was a bit of a backhanded compliment, but I took it. No need to get into the semantics of it all. It had only been just over thirty seconds. I needed him to stay on for at least thirty more, but he suddenly seemed eager to answer all my questions.

"A month ago your father called a professional cleaning service to steam clean your carpets and clean the drapes and what not," Dr. D explained. "One of those cleaners was working for me and planted the bugs around your house."

I stared at my feet, processing this information. I could barely understand the man through all of that voice editing, but I had managed to get what was important. Whoever this maniac was, he was good. He had to have been watching my family even before the cleaners were called, or else he'd never have been able to plant his person in the right position to do the job.

"Just one of the workers?" I reconfirmed. I considered taking notes; all of that information would probably come in handy later.

"Do you enjoy it, Gia?" Dr. D said, ignoring my question.

My eyebrows furrowed together. I couldn't keep up with the constantly changing nature of our conversations. "Do I enjoy what?"

"Getting everything you want?"

It had to have been a minute now, but something didn't seem right. Dr. D was obviously much smarter than I had first anticipated. If he was bold enough to put listening devices all over my house, then there was no way it wouldn't have crossed his mind that the police would have done the same to him. But he didn't seem bothered by it at all.

"I don't—" I began, but was cut off immediately.

"You truly are your father's daughter."

"Okay, but—"

"Enjoy it while it lasts," Dr. D said, as I climbed out of bed. The deep, robotic voice was a million times scarier than the auto tune, and I was having a tough time coping. "In the meantime, stop looking for me. You're going to get hurt. I'm trying to help you."

Oh gee, that was great coming from the insane guy who was preying on me like he was a hunter and I was a deer. It was all well and good to keep warning me, but at the end of the day he was still going to stick a spear in my butt and steal my antlers, no matter how fast I ran.

"Wait, bu—"

"Until next time," Dr. D said, cutting me off. "Goodbye Miss Winters. And goodbye to you too, Officer Fells."

Milo had called seconds after my shaky call with Dr. D had ended. The good news was the call was long enough to trace the location, but the bad news was the location was a pay phone in downtown Beverly Hills, so anyone could have been the caller. The police were using security cameras to try and identify a face, while still trying to figure out how he could have edited his voice using a public phone, but that was the last thing I was worried about.

After yelling at Jack for a good twenty minutes about why he was showering when I needed him most, I had a grim realization that Dr. D really did know the police would be listening, but he was still giving away his trade secrets. Either he was the world's stupidest stalker, or he was ten times more dangerous than anyone had first thought. Addressing Milo straight on before hanging up was a pretty clear indication that this lunatic knew exactly what he was doing, and had his twisted little plan all worked out. I had been tempted to add that Milo was in fact not an officer yet, but actually just a cadet. But Dr. D had hung up before I got the chance. Plus I don't think he would have cared. I think he just knew I had a massive crush on the guy, which was super awkward, because now even my stalker knew I wanted to date Milo real bad. Of course, Dad hadn't been too thrilled about the latest phone call, and kept yelling on the phone to some person from the cleaning company, demanding to know how they had hired someone who was obviously a creep. Kenny had to keep reminding him that it was the police's job to figure those details out, and to keep relaxed. Mom just drank a lot of wine.

I spent the afternoon searching every inch of my room and the house, together with Anya, Jack, Mike and Chris, with no luck in finding where the last bug was hidden. Dad went out for frozen yogurt and kept mumbling something about keeping me in the house forever, and Mom relieved her stress by shopping for new sunglasses. I followed her footsteps and took a break from the detective work, turning to retail therapy for some solace. I didn't exactly have the same freedom of movement as my mother, however, so all my stress had to be relieved via the Internet. Jack had been kind enough to voice his unwanted thoughts on how shopping online for YSL bags wasn't really going to solve any of my problems. But he had also once described Judge Judy as a "national treasure," so I wasn't really inclined to take his opinions seriously.

It was almost dinnertime when Jack and I slumped back to my room, defeated by our loss against the missing listening device. I had barely touched the silky bed sheets when my phone went off, sending my heart into a panic all over again. By now, I was *way* beyond ready to throw the stupid thing in the garbage.

"Well aren't you going to answer it?" Jack asked, standing alert by my side.

I glanced at the screen and flinched. *No Caller ID.*

"No, I'm good," I told him. "It'll stop ringing eventually."

Jack sat on the bed opposite me. "Gia," he said softly. "Just answer it. I'm right here."

I sighed deeply, dreading what was coming next. Now what? Dr. D had forgotten to tell me he had kidnapped Famous and wanted ten million dollars ransom? Just to be sure, I whirled around, watching Famous lie asleep beside Jack on my bed. Nope, still there.

"Hello?" I said cautiously, as if I was trying to walk through a basketball game without getting hit in the face.

"Hi, is this Gia Winters?" I heard a woman's voice reply.

What, was this some new approach to stalking me? Mrs. Dr. D?

"Yes?" I told her, looking at Jack. He mouthed *stalker?* I gave him a palms up to let him know I was just as curious.

"Miss Winters, my name is Carol Beaufort. I'm calling from the Hollywood Foreign Press Association. Do you have a few minutes to talk?"

"Oh. Look, if this is a survey for the Golden Globes, I think George Clooney should win everything. Honestly, the man is a legend."

"Uh," Carol replied, sounding a little surprised. "Not quite. Miss Winters, are you aware of the concept of Miss Golden Globe?"

My jaw dropped. Of course! With all the drama around Milo's perfect dimples and Dr. D trying to kill me, I had completely forgotten about the Golden Globes!

"Oh my God," I said. I stood up, excitement rising in my voice. "Oh my God! Yes! Yes, I know all about it."

Jack, who was looking super bored now that he knew I wasn't being called by a psycho freak, had turned the TV to mute. He didn't really need the sound to ogle Jessica Alba.

"As I'm sure you're aware," Carol continued, her voice as formal as ever. "The title was originally given to someone else. But an issue arose recently that may take months to overcome."

"How many months?"

"About eight and a half."

Oh snap. Ain't no party like a Hollywood pregnancy scandal.

"Okay," I said, pacing beside my bed expectantly. "So why are you calling me?"

Carol sighed, as if she were dealing with someone who didn't understand English. Clearly she wasn't as excited about this as I was.

"We'd like to offer you the role," she said.

"Excuse me a second," I said, muting the phone. "OH MY GOD, YES! YES! YES! YES!"

"What?" Jack said, looking at me in alarm. "What happened?"

"Shh!" I hissed, and Jack rolled his eyes. "I'm on the phone."

"Hello?" Carol's voice said, and I unmuted the call.

"Yes! I'm still here!" I said, a little breathless from my aggressive fist pumping. "Okay, so say for example Leonardo DiCaprio wins an award, which he totally should by the way, he's amazing. Let's say he wins an award. I'm supposed to give it to him?"

"You hold the award and give it to the *presenter*, who gives it to him. Then you usher him off stage." Carol explained, as though she were conversing with a five-year-old.

"Oh my gosh, that's so cool!"

"Look Gia," Carol said in a strained voice, dropping the formal tone she had been using before. "We're getting desperate here. Everyone we choose is either a step away from giving birth, changing gender, or locked away in rehab. This whole thing has been a disaster ever since we had to push the date back to the twentieth of April. You're really our last hope."

Well gee, way to make a girl feel special.

"This is a *very* prestigious title," she continued. "Your parents are extremely well respected in the film industry. The job of Miss Golden Globe is to be taken seriously. You're in your final year of high school, is that correct?"

"Yes, that's correct," I replied, mirroring her pompous accent.

"You'll need to take some time off school these next few weeks. Just for a few days. We need to do a last minute press conference with the President of the Association, and then some much needed rehearsals at the venue. The award show is right around the corner and there are a million things to be done. You think you can manage it?"

Personally, I didn't know why they really needed some fancy title for the people who hold the awards on stage. I just figured they were supermodels that couldn't get work on the runway or in movies. But it was still a huge deal. If they were going to hand me that role on a silver platter, then I wasn't about to say no.

"Can I talk to my parents and get back to you?" I asked.

"Of course," Carol replied, sounding less cranky and more hopeful. "Although I just got off the phone with your mother, who seemed very enthusiastic about this opportunity. I'll text you my number. You can discuss it some more and confirm as soon as you can."

I promised I would and hung up the phone. "YES!" I yelled to the skies, chucking my phone onto the bed, missing Jack and Famous by an inch.

"What are you so excited about?" Jack asked, flipping the channels on the still muted TV.

"That was someone from the Hollywood Foreign Press Association. They gave me Miss Golden Globe!"

"Is that the chick who stands on stage, holding the award and smiling all bright?" Jack asked, looking up as I nodded. "Doesn't seem like that big of a deal."

"Yeah, well," I told him, crossing my arms across my chest. "It's a very prestigious title. I wouldn't expect you to understand."

"Congrats," Jack said, but he looked so insincere, it made me want to hit him.

"Whatever," I said to myself. There was no way Jack was going to bring my happiness down. "There are a billion things I have to figure out. I have to choose my dress! Oh my gosh, and my heels. I need to get this all prepared before the twentieth!"

"Wait a second," Jack said, sitting upright. He turned to me, serious mode activated. "What date did you just say?"

"The twentieth. Why?"

"And what date did Dr. D tell you to save the other day on the phone?"

My eyes widened, as I finally understood what he was coming to. "The twentieth," I told him.

"Well there you go," Jack said, as if he had just completed a thousand-piece puzzle.

"So whatever he's going to do, it's going to happen at the Golden Globes?"

Jack nodded and said, "I guess so."

The idea of me being in the same room as Dr. D and some of the world's best looking men was so overwhelming for me, I actually had to push Famous out of the way and lie down. There was no way in hell Dad was going to let me be Miss Golden Globe if he knew Dr. D was going to show up.

"This is so unfair!" I cried, covering my face with a pillow.

"All I ever wanted was to hand DiCaprio a golden statue without getting killed. Is that too much to ask?"

I felt Jack pull the pillow away from my face, but I didn't resist him. "Don't worry," he said, sounding completely calm. "We'll catch him way before then."

"Oh yeah? How?"

"Well that party on Saturday is a good start," he replied.

Oh crap. I was hoping we wouldn't have to talk about this, like, ever.

"Yeah," I said, sitting up slowly. "About that. I think I should definitely go."

"Good. So we'll go."

"Um . . . I think I should go with Milo. Without you."

Jack blinked at me in silence, his jaw tightening. I offered him a half-assed smile, but he didn't look at all happy to receive it.

"What?" he finally managed to ask, looking pained.

"He knows some people going and he saw the flyer on the desk, so he asked me to come along. I mean it's not a big deal; we were going to go anyway."

"Yeah," Jack said, rising from the bed. "*We* were going to go. I can't keep you safe if I'm not even there!"

"Jack," I said calmly, watching him pace in front of me with frustration. "I'll be perfectly safe! Milo will be right next to me the entire time! He's a police off—"

"He's not an officer yet!"

"Okay fine, he's *almost* a police officer. But it still counts!"

Jack stopped pacing and ran a hand through his hair. He looked like he wanted to jump out of my third story window, run and never come back. I watched him silently. If he was even contemplating the idea I needed to give him some space to come to terms with it. That, and I was scared he might throw a pen at me in rage, or something.

"How exactly are you planning on pulling this off?" he said.

"Your dad is *never* going to let you go to some college party with a guy you barely know."

Yeah, but he was totally down for letting three strangers move into the house to follow his kids around all day. I was going to point this out, but then decided against it. That argument wasn't going to win me any points with anyone.

"It's the same night as Brendan's farewell party, so he doesn't need to know where I really am," I explained. Jack opened his mouth to start yelling again, but I continued before he could begin. "He's not going to stop me from celebrating Brendan moving states. I'm surprised he didn't throw the party himself."

I gave a short laugh, hoping that Jack would join in. He didn't.

"And where does that leave me?" he asked, still looking skeptical.

"That part I haven't figured out yet," I admitted. "But I'm working on it, I swear."

"What do you even know about this guy?" he shot back. "I mean, what if he's a psycho?"

"Don't be ridiculous Jack. The quota for psychos has already been filled in my life."

"What if he's into weird stuff like Christian Grey?"

I paused. "Is that really a bad thing? Christian Grey is hot, rich, and he flies helicopters."

"Yeah, and he also has a torture chamber in his house!"

"Should I be concerned that you know this much about Christian Grey?"

Jack shook his head. "This seems like a terrible idea."

"You always say that, and then things always work out some way or another! It's just one night, Jack!"

Jack did some heavy sighing as he evaluated his options. If he had learned anything about me in the short time he had been around, he would know that I was stubborn as hell. Plus he wasn't going to rat me out to Dad; that just wasn't his style. Jack nodded reluctantly. He seemed like he wanted to argue some more but had evidently decided against it.

"I guess," he said, "I could go visit my sister for a couple of hours. She lives pretty close to campus so I'd be nearby in case anything happened."

I beamed at him, trying to control the urge to hug him. "I promise you, it'll be quick! Nothing's going to happen, I swear."

"If your dad wants to fire me then you have to back me up."

"Done."

"Same goes for suing me."

"He's not going to sue you!"

"And if anything happens to you, I get to beat the crap out of Fells."

"Um, no you don't!" I said, looking alarmed. Jack blinked at me. "But . . . that's negotiable."

Jack blew out a defeated sigh. "Fine. I guess we can make this work."

Seriously. I should write a book or something. I am living proof that you can truly achieve anything in life if you dedicate yourself and persevere.

chapter thirteen

THE NEWS about Miss Golden Globe had divided my house in half. Mom was, of course, completely over the moon and was already planning possible outfits for the night. Dad was a lot less excited, which wasn't at all surprising, considering his favorite hobby was worrying about me. He kept talking about how it probably wasn't safe for me to be in the spotlight at this time, and how he couldn't believe I hadn't mentioned Dr. D's request to "save the date." I'll admit, I was mildly horrified that he didn't tell me he was super proud and throw a lavish party in my honor. Miss Golden Globe was no small thing, but he just kept saying, "I'll think about it" every time I wanted to talk about it. Which basically meant no.

In the meantime, my biggest issue was the UCLA party

and my first night alone with Milo. I had somehow managed to get Jack on board, but there were still a few creases to smooth out. Aria and Veronica had been on my case all day Friday and then Saturday morning, unable to believe I was missing Brendan's party without a solid reason. I didn't even bother pulling the illness excuse this time. I went straight for the parent card and claimed that "I really didn't want to talk about it," while assuring them that yes, I too couldn't believe how much of a nightmare my dad was being. Sorry for throwing you under the bus like that, Dad. Oh, and all the other stuff I was about to lie about, too.

Lying to my friends felt so wrong, and I was tempted to just surrender and tell them everything. But I always managed to hold back at the last minute. It just wasn't the right time yet. Unfortunately, this meant I couldn't turn to them with the biggest issue in my life: what to wear to the party. I needed an outfit that would make me look so sexy that Milo would melt on the spot. Aria's closet *really* would have come in handy at a time like this, but seeing as it was unavailable, I was left with two choices. First there was Anya, who dressed like a pilgrim, and then there was my mother, who didn't dress at all. "Wear a low-cut dress and lots of red lipstick. That's step one." That had been her grand advice when I had asked how to make a guy fall in love with you. I didn't stick around to hear step two, because judging by her experiences, it would only end in divorce.

When it was finally Saturday night, the state of my room had declined by a million. Clothes and shoes were strewn all over the bed and floor, as I kept throwing hangers out of my way. Milo Fells and I were going on the closest thing we had to a date, and goddammit, I was going to look like a freaking sex bomb if it killed me. After trying on hundreds of different combinations that failed to satisfy my ideal look, I finally settled for a little, black, Stella McCartney dress. It was a bit of a safe option, but this was no time to be taking risks.

I had asked Mom if I could borrow her stylist, Kat, to do my makeup, but she had some fancy dinner party she needed to attend in Beverly Hills, and needed her for the night. Left to fend for myself, I curled the ends of my hair and added shimmer and mascara to my eyelashes, careful not to accidently rip off the fake lashes that had taken me a good twenty minutes to put on. It felt like I was wearing umbrellas on my eyes, but they made them look bigger and brighter, which meant Milo could gaze into them all night long as if my life were a Katherine Heigl movie.

By the time eight-thirty approached, my makeup was done, my red heels were on and I was coating my lips with red lipstick, just like my mother had recommended. All said and done, I looked pretty damn hot, considering I had accidently poked myself in the eye with the eye pencil twice and had to stop it from watering like a flowing river. The way I saw it, there were three things that could go down that night. One, I would make a complete fool of myself the whole night, talking non-stop in my ridiculous British accent. Two, I could babble the night away, get kidnapped-slash-killed or worse, break my heel. Lastly, I could be amazing and blow Milo's mind and carry myself as a true lady, casually attending a party for raging alcoholics in the making. I was hoping the third option would work in my favor, but my luck so far hadn't been too promising.

When the clock hit nine, I was considering investing in an asthma pump. Jack and I said our hurried goodbyes and ran out of the house. He did some head shaking and frustrated sighing, reminding me that we had to time our return perfectly. I did a lot of nodding and said, "yes, sir," and watched him climb into his Jeep and drive away. Milo had come to pick me up looking like something out of a Hugo Boss ad, with his leather jacket and perfectly styled hair. Thankfully he had listened to my text that had explicitly stated, in caps, NOT to ring the doorbell, as it was "broken," and to just text me when he was outside. Not a great start to a romantic evening, but beggars can't be choosers. Milo had also adhered to the Halloween theme judging by the batman mask resting on the backseat, which went perfectly with my velvety cat ears headband. Everything up 'til that point had been perfect, until I greeted him by saying "What's up, brotha?" This was apparently my brain's way of telling me that it wanted me to end up miserable and lonely. Thanks for having my back, brain. No, really.

Needless to say, the rest of the car ride to the party consisted of lame jokes and a lot of heavy breathing on my part. I couldn't believe that *any* guy would put up with my crazy like Milo was. Plus, every time I thought I was getting more comfortable around him, my British accent would threaten to resurface and ruin any chances I had with the guy. Which were already minimal. I managed to structure a few sentences and tell Milo about the offer of being Miss Golden Globe. Unlike Jack, he had shared my excitement and told me I'd look so stunning on stage, no one would even bother looking at the award. More heavy breathing on my part ensued.

Luckily, I didn't have to do too much of the talking because Milo seemed to be taking the lead on that front. His small talk gave me the opportunity to gather some interesting facts about him. For example, his favorite dessert was cheesecake, which isn't exactly chocolate mousse, like mine is. But it could have been worse. He could have said he wasn't a "dessert person," and then I would have been forced to jump out of a moving car. His favorite cuisine was Thai, he had one older brother and a German Shepherd named Woody, in honor of the beloved cowboy in his favorite movie growing up, *Toy Story*. Of course, I enthusiastically agreed that it was my favorite as well, but that was a lie. It's adorable, don't get me wrong. But *Anastasia* is totally the best movie ever, no doubt about it. A beautiful girl with a little puppy and big dreams, who one day meets a handsome stranger that helps discover that she's, in fact, the lost Princess of Russia? It was practically a metaphor for my entire existence. Except, of course, that Milo is not a fraud like Dimitri, I am not at all Russian royalty, and I'm pretty sure Dr. D does not have a tiny bat as a sidekick. But I could be wrong about the bat, I don't know.

In between my sad jokes and unattractive breathing problems, Milo also managed to give me updates on the cleaning company that Dad had hired a few months ago. He said that the company had sent over a list of names of the people who had cleaned our house, but the police couldn't a connection to my family or the Dumpling Hospital for any of them. The police also hadn't been able to find the last bugging device, and I didn't know the first thing about spy equipment, so there was no point in me keeping a look out for it. All in all, the investigation was at a bit of a standstill. Dad may have been right about the Golden Globes being a pretty bad idea at this point, but it was also the only chance I had to meet Dr. D. That is, if we didn't find all we needed at the UCLA party, packaged in a little box with a pink ribbon wrapped around it. I hadn't exactly mentioned to Milo my plans for investigation at the party, but if I could manage the colossal issue of Jack Anderson, then this was cake.

We finally pulled up to the party after what seemed like an entire lifetime of shy conversations and nervous laughter. Milo parked a lot closer to the party than Jack and I had on our first trip, and thank God, because Jimmy Choo heels aren't the most comfortable footwear. The last thing I needed was to fall flat on my face and still have another ten minutes to walk before we actually arrived. I quickly texted Jack, reassuring him we were still alive, then told myself everything was going to be perfect as long as I managed not to get killed or kidnapped.

"Are you ready?" Milo asked, as I gently closed my car door behind me.

I adjusted the hem of my dress with a nod and said, "I think so."

Batman mask and kitty ears in our hands, we walked toward the party, which could surely be heard from Guatemala based on the volume of the music. Milo was so close. I could almost hear his heart beating next to me. I desperately wanted to act like a normal human being who could charm him with my natural humor and grace. Instead my tongue refused to move and I had to convince my heart not to break down every time I saw him. The problem was, I was starting to like him a lot. Too much for the amount I knew him. I mean, it was one thing to look at him and be in awe of how an average guy could look that amazing, but it's another thing to have legit feelings for someone. Sometimes I felt that way about Jack too, but Jack was . . . Jack. He was annoying and frustrating and I always felt confused around him. One minute we were best friends and the next I couldn't stand to see him.

But Milo never seemed to get on my nerves. And despite my inability to communicate like a normal human being, we seemed to click. Yes, I didn't know him very well. But I've never actually met Jude Law, and I'm pretty sure we'd click too. I kept telling myself that getting involved with someone days after a break up is just wrong, but come on. The next time your boyfriend leaves for Texas to become a cowboy and the hottest police cadet you've ever seen wants to take you to a college party, why don't you tell me about what's right or wrong.

Club music was blasting from all corners, and tipsy people were dancing all up the street. A girl with hair brighter than Veronica's stumbled past us. She wore leather black plants with stiletto heels and what I could only presume was a top three sizes too small for her. The boy she was with was dressed head-to-toe as Spiderman and was visibly smashed, even though it was barely ten o'clock.

"This must be it," Milo said, and I looked up at the house ahead.

"The flyer did say it had palm trees," I told him.

The flyer failed to mention, however, that the fraternity house was in fact ninety percent made up of palm trees. They were everywhere, completely surrounding the house like a gateway. Cars were parked all up and down the road and through the large glass windows I could see the inside of the house was packed with drunken college students.

A guy dressed as Ronald McDonald waddled past us in his huge shoes and eerie white makeup. His bright red lips curved into a scary smile as he gave me the once-over. I gave him a *never-going-to-happen* look, and I think he took it well because in a matter of seconds he was eyeing up the sexy nurse standing a few feet away.

"Do you and your friends go to a lot of these parties?" I asked Milo, trying to hide the disgust from my tone.

"Hardly ever," he replied. "This isn't really my idea of a good time."

"So then why'd you come?"

"Well I figured it might be worth it if you were going to be there."

Lord have mercy on my poor ovaries.

"Right," I practically squeaked. "Does Detective Reynolds know that we're here?"

"Well," Milo said, looking a little sheepish. "I didn't really mention it. But it's a party that we both just *happen* to be at. Nothing wrong with that, right?"

"You tell me. You're the police cadet."

Milo smiled and held up his Batman mask. "I also happen to be the savior of Gotham. But, whatever. I don't really like to brag."

"Are you sure the city can manage without you for a night?"

I asked.

See? I could be normal if I really, *really* concentrated.

"Let me know if you see any bat signals in the sky. I might have to bail."

"Like Christian?" I asked, and Milo looked at me in confusion. Oh no, he didn't get it. "You know, bail. *Bale.* Like Christian Bale? Batman? No? Not feeling the joke?"

"Oh God," Milo said, but a laugh escaped from his groan. "That was a *terrible* joke. We might need to work on Catwoman's sense of humor."

I had actually been pretty proud of that one, but I smiled sheepishly and said, "I've got plenty more stashed in the cat ears."

"Well then in that case I can't wait to hear the rest of them," Milo laughed.

Yeah, careful what you wish for, pal. But we were flirting! Like actually flirting and not just Milo saying funny and sweet things and me hyperventilating like a weirdo! And if you ask me, I was actually doing a pretty decent job at it, considering my lack of previous experience in such matters. Brendan and I had never flirted. He had just asked me out and I pretty much shrugged and said yes. Jack and I didn't do too much of the flirting game either. We spent most of the time mentally throwing lamps at each other and pretending there was no sexual tension in the room. I had been scared I didn't really know to flirt, but based on how the conversation was going, I was doing a B+ job.

"Dude!" A guy dressed up as some type of Greek god slung his arm affectionately around another guy, right in front of Milo and I. "You ready to get your party on?"

His friend, who was dressed in a red, fluffy onesie that mildly resembled Elmo, smiled. "Dude, hell yeah! I'm gonna get so turnt up!"

Milo and I exchanged glances. Based on how low Elmo had the zipper on his onesie, I doubted his costume would stay on for long.

"So, you ready?" Milo asked me, and I turned my attention away from the boys. "To get 'turnt' up?"

I gave a nervous laugh and nodded. Those thirty seconds of flirting had been great while they lasted, but I waved goodbye to the chance of it occurring it again. Truth be told, I was freaking out. Big time. If Elmo and Zeus were any indication of the crowd, the party was going to be wild inside, and I wasn't sure I was fully up for it yet. It wasn't just the fact that Milo and I were finally alone together without the police or my parents or Jack, which was giving me enough anxiety to begin with. It was also the possibility of Ao Jie Kai being right on the other side of the wide frat house doors, holding all the answers I needed in the palm of his hand.

I did some quick, mental pep talking as Milo and I made our way up to the fraternity house's front doors, where a young guy around Milo's age was sitting at a table with a metal box and a stack of plastic cups. He didn't have any costume on, but we knew he was part of the fraternity because he had the Greek symbols for their house on a small nametag, attached to his flannel shirt.

"Five bucks entry per person," he told us in a bored voice, pointing to the metal box. "You get a free plastic cup. Ten bucks if you want the bigger plastic cups."

Milo and I looked at each other. It seemed the fraternity had conveniently forgotten to mention an entry fee on their flyer.

"Okay, we'll get two small cups," Milo said with a light shrug.

"Sorry," the guy said, not looking apologetic in the slightest. He didn't even bat an eyelash. "We're out of five dollar cups. You gotta take a ten dollar one."

Milo looked at me again with raised eyebrows. I didn't have any loose cash on me, but it didn't matter. Milo was already being a gentleman and pulling his out, handing the guy a twenty-dollar bill.

Flannel shirt guy paused, eyed me up and down, and handed Milo two five dollar bills back. "Here's ten bucks change. You get a discount 'cause your girl is hot."

Well, we couldn't argue with a policy like that. I did some internal flailing and fist pumping when Milo didn't correct him about assuming I was his girlfriend.

"Well," Milo said, pocketing his wallet and change. We moved toward the door so more people could pay for their entry. "I guess your cat ears have superpowers after all."

That was great and all, but he needed to tone down his perfection. Those damn dimples were all I could see, and they were constantly threatening to turn me into a babbling lunatic. By the end of the night, Milo was going to be inquiring about whether or not free therapy was given to police officers, and it would be all my fault.

I was starting to look like the Ronald McDonald I had seen moments before, with my forced smile and fake enthusiasm. It looked like I was scoping out the place for potential victims, when actually I was desperately trying to grab the reigns on my out of control emotions. We walked inside, pushing our way past a group of guys that were dressed in silky robes, boxing gloves hanging around their necks. The inside of the fraternity house was a cemetery for class and dignity. People were everywhere, on the dance floor, on top of each other on the couches, canoodling with others against walls. It was like all the rich high school parties I'd ever been to, only three times more sexual and with cheaper alcohol. There was a DJ dressed as a giant taco in the back of the room playing a remix of a Kanye West song, violently head banging with one headphone pressed to his ear. He stood directly underneath a black, felt sign that read, **Feel A'ite on Frite Nite.** I stood there gaping at the red block letters for a few seconds, amazed that even basic grammar had taken a beating that night.

Well, you have to give them points for creativity.

One thing was certain; I was *majorly* overdressed. And not just because my outfit was expensive. It was because my dress actually covered more than an inch of my body. I've had my fair share of dressing like a stripper, don't get me wrong. But this was something else. It seemed that clothes were just optional, and no one opted for them. I was trying my best not to judge every girl that walked past, but they were giving me so much to raise my eyebrows about.

A pair of girls dressed as vampires walked past holding plastic cups filled with what smelled like straight vodka, which no doubt they would be regretting within the hour. They smiled at Milo when they walked passed and my heart almost stopped. If I saw any fang marks on Batman that night, I was going to lose my shit. Fortunately for me, Milo wasn't even paying attention to the barely dressed vampires. He leaned down close, pulling me away from the entrance.

"Keep close!" Milo shouted over the music, and I nodded obediently. "This place is crazy!"

Milo slipped his hand into the hand that wasn't wrapped around my bag, and I went dead still. He gave me a look as if asking if it was okay, but I didn't move. Milo Fells was freaking holding my hand! He was *actually* making physical contact with me! In what universe was that *not* okay! The feeling was almost indescribable. It was like someone handing you a bag of M&Ms and a plate full of brownies during your time of month, when the cramps have just kicked in and you're dying of pain. Tears of joy just appear out of thin air before you can even rip the bag of chocolate open.

Apparently, Milo took my lack of movement as a go sign, because he tugged on my hand and pulled me further into the crowd. We watched silently as the music got louder and the dance moves made a turn for the worse. There was some weird trance beat playing that was assaulting my eardrums, but everyone else in the room seemed to love it. It seemed that these people thought costumes were a free pass to do whatever with whomever. I had seen young people get crazily drunk before, but I was impressed that most of these people were even standing. The plus side was that even with the mask covering half his face, Milo was easily the hottest guy there, and he was holding *my* hand! It practically took every fiber of strength that I had not to burst out into tears and sing the hallelujah chorus to the heavens. Not that the heavens really needed a reminder of their creation, he was going on the hall of fame list for sure.

"YO BROSEPH!" A guy dressed as fireman called out to Milo.

"Are those your friends?" I asked, and Milo shook his head in confusion.

"YO! BROSEPH! GET OVER HERE MAN." Another pretend fireman yelled.

The college firemen were all attractive with well-toned abs that they were proudly showing off through their lack of shirts. In ordinary circumstances I'd be all over that, but they were nothing compared to Milo, who was hands-down the hottest cop ever after Mark Wahlberg. But really, he doesn't count because he was just acting, and he'd look just as sexy in a KFC uniform.

The group of four firemen walked over to Milo and gave him a manly hug. One of them was trying to jump on his back, affectionately I presume, and I was scared I would have to let go of Milo's hand. But I clung on for dear life, even though I was certain I had pulled a few muscles. No way was I voluntarily going to pass up the chance to touch Milo Fells. That sucker was going to have to get in line.

"Dude! This is our song, man! Where you been?" The blonde fireman asked, beaming at Milo, who looked completely perplexed.

I suddenly recognized him as the guy who had given me the flyer in the first place, and frantically looked around the room, hoping to hide my face so that he wouldn't recognize me. The stupid cat ears were doing nothing for the outfit or a possible disguise, and kept sliding off my head.

"Oh, I've just been . . ." Milo began uncertainly. "Around."

He glanced at me and I shrugged. Neither of us knew who this "Broseph" was, but according to the firemen, he was now Milo. The boys' gazes followed Milo's and settled on me. I looked at them with an awkward smile, avoiding eye contact with the blonde one.

"PETE!" One of them shrieked, and I was about ninety percent sure I had lost hearing in one ear. "TURN THE MUSIC DOWN."

Almost immediately the volume of the music was reduced, but no one seemed to notice. People were still packed on the dance floor like sardines.

"Sup." I said. I needed to stop doing that. It was not helping my cause.

"Well, hello," a brunette fireman said, slipping his arm across my shoulders and pulling me into him.

"So who's this beautiful creature, Broseph?" another one asked Milo.

I gave Milo a desperate look. Behind his batman mask I could see he was just as lost as I was.

"Um—" Milo began, but was immediately cut off.

"Hey, don't I know you from somewhere?" The blonde fireman asked me, narrowing his eyes.

"Nope!" I exclaimed a little too enthusiastically. "That's impossible! I just moved here today from . . . Greenland."

From the corner of my eye I could see Milo trying to suppress a laugh. Greenland? What the hell was wrong with my brain?

"Okay . . ." The blonde guy said, dragging the word out as

he gave me a judgy look.

Milo pulled me closer to him, forcing the brunette fireman to release his hold on me. If I weren't insanely uncomfortable with the whole situation, I would have had some time to concentrate on returning my heart beat to a normal speed.

"She got a name?" one of the boys asked, resting his arm on his friend's shoulder.

"Uh . . ." Milo said, struggling to improvise with the whole situation.

Up until then I had been positive that every police officer should have the ability to make up facts on the spot, but Milo was evidently caught off guard. Any name would have done the job. I doubted any of those fraternity boys would have remembered if my name were Candice, or something like Ethel. Hell, if I had said Roger, they still probably wouldn't have cared. I'd be impressed if they even remembered their own names.

"Well do you want to dance, pussycat?" A fireman yelled over the music, thankfully losing interest in the topic.

"Uh, thanks. But my heels are—"

"What!"

"—killing me."

"Well who says you have to use your feet?" The blonde one asked, grinning.

I gave a small shriek as he suddenly scooped me up and slung me over his shoulder, yanking Milo's hand out of mine. I kicked him slightly, trying to let him know that this was not my idea of fun, but he barely felt it. His fellow fireman friends all cheered around us as if I was a human sacrifice and the ritual was taking place on the dance floor. Milo came into view amongst the sea of partygoers and I shot him an alarmed look, trying desperately to save my dignity and adjust my dress from the back. Milo gave me a lost look behind his mask, clearly trying to figure out what he could do without the use of his police badge. How the hell was I meant to get a hold of information on Ao Jie Kai when I couldn't even get a hold of my date!

My new friend placed me effortlessly down next to him on the dance floor, calling for Pete to turn the music up again. Beside me there were two people who were passionately making out, alcohol spilling out of their cups. The frisky fireman snaked his arm around my waist as I reached up to adjust my cat ears, and my eyes immediately scanned the room for Milo. Where the hell was he? Oh right, he was being mauled alive by a group of girls dressed in sexy Minnie Mouse outfits. Jeez, it had been all of four seconds and all the females in the room had flocked. All I could do was stand and watch helplessly while being violated by some sexed up college boy who was aggressively thrusting his pelvis against me like his life depended on it.

"IT'S COOL.. BROSEPH'S FINE!" The blonde guy assured me, and I forced a smile.

I was holding onto my clutch with such intensity, my knuckles were going white. Thankfully, the frat boys didn't seem too interested in making conversation with "Broseph's" new girlfriend, but they didn't seem to mind getting a little sexual with her. I had always been kind of excited about the idea of a bachelorette party, but my first college party experience was less Magic Mike and more Molestation Mike.

Pete the DJ taco changed the song to a Pitbull remix, and the whole crowd threw their hands in the air. I took the opportunity to move a little away from the firemen, but the dance floor was so packed there was really no point. I needed to get off the dance floor and find Milo, ASAP. Screw Ao Jie Kai, getting out of the party alive and fully dressed was the biggest problem on my mind. I pulled the blonde fireman closer toward me, cringing at his excited look. Clearly Broseph, whoever he was, shared an open relationship policy with his friends. I yelled into his ear, asking where the bathroom was. He pulled away, raising an eyebrow with a smile.

"Not for *that!*" I yelled over the music, and his smile dropped a little. "I need to pee!"

Blondie pointed toward a door near the stairs on the left side of the room. My eyes scanned the crowd for Milo, but I still couldn't find him. There was no use calling him, he'd never be able to hear his phone over the music. I danced my way through the crowd to the bathroom and pushed the door open. Three Powerpuff Girls looked at me questioningly as they coated their lips with gloss. Sitting on the toilet with the lid down was a boy dressed as a pirate, passionately making out with Wonder Woman, who was straddling him.

Well clearly Milo wasn't hiding in there. I headed for the stairway and passed two other girls with similar cat ears, a guy dressed as a giant cockroach, and a smurf before finally reaching the staircase, using the light from my phone to guide me. Dr. D hadn't tried to contact me and I could have passed Ao Jie Kai a billion times already and not known, seeing as I had no clue what he looked like. Was I supposed to find every Asian guy here and ask if he was stalking me? Not a chance. We'd been at the party for about three minutes and I was beyond ready to go home and withdraw all of my college applications.

I made my way upstairs, being careful not to bother a showgirl making out with what looked like a spring roll, and the giant pizza and the Joker who were filming it. I scanned the dance floor for any sign of Milo and that impeccable jacket, but came up short. There was a Minnie Mouse near the DJ table, but Batman didn't seem to be with her. Thankfully, level two of the frat house was slightly less crowded than below, but there were still people everywhere. At least I could actually hear myself think. Everywhere I looked there were people drinking, smoking, laughing, making out or lying unconscious somewhere. At one point I spotted a guy in a very convincing LAPD uniform talking to a girl dressed as a ketchup bottle. I doubted he was a real cop because he was drinking straight from a vodka bottle, ignoring his five or ten dollar plastic cup. On the off chance he was an actual cop, something drastic needed to be done about our legal system.

Aside from the overly sexual college students drinking away their futures and capturing it in a series of selfies, the fraternity brothers definitely had some good equipment going for them. There was a large plasma TV in the living room area upstairs, with an X-Box and a Wii connected to it. Beside the TV, there was a large bookshelf full of DVDs and video games. A big, comfy leather couch faced the TV, and a picture of the Lakers basketball team hung on the wall behind the couch. Heck, I should have just worn that homie outfit of mine, or at least Jack's pimp shoes. I would have fit in much better in that outfit than in the one I was wearing.

"Hey good looking." A guy dressed up as Fred Flintstone in an extremely revealing toga-like outfit sauntered up to me.

I eyed him up and down and raised an eyebrow. "Never going to happen, Fred," I told him, crossing my arms protectively across my chest.

"Oh come on," he said, stumbling a little. Clearly Fred had had one too many bedrock beers. "I'm still looking for a Betty."

I sighed, unable to believe that I was actually at such a stupid party. Not only had he gotten his spouses mixed up, I was shocked that he thought he actually had a chance with me.

"When hell freezes over," I said.

Fred stared at me blankly for a few seconds before walking away without a word. I couldn't believe I had lost Milo so quickly, my stupid cat ears were giving me a headache and there was no sign of Dr. D or Ao Jie Kai anywhere. I dialed Milo's number and wasn't surprised when he didn't answer his phone. It meant that he was probably still downstairs where the music was the loudest and couldn't hear the ringing.

I stopped a passing guy wearing nothing but a Rasta hat and a pair of tiny boxer shorts and asked him where the bathroom was. He pointed toward the end of the hallway and danced away. There were multiple white doors upstairs, all closed and looking exactly the same. I now actually needed to pee, and fake Jamaican guy had been no help whatsoever.

Weaving through the crowd, I headed for the doors. I took a lucky guess and opened door number one. Big mistake. Friendly tip, never walk-in on a closed door during a party. It's traumatic enough to give you mild PTSD.

"EW! Sorry!"

I slammed the door shut, slapping a hand over my eyes in embarrassment, even though I doubted they noticed me. On the bright side, I no longer needed to pee. I did, however, want to soak my eyes in bleach. I was just about ready to begin contemplating the purpose of my existence when I felt my phone vibrating.

Oh crap. No Caller ID.

c h a p t e r
f o u r t e e n

"HELLO?" I covered my free ear with my hand, hoping to block out some of the noise from the party.

"Hey, it's me. Just calling to check up on you."

I sighed with relief. I had grown so used to Jack's voice; it was such a comfort to hear it among all the madness.

"Jesus, Jack! Why do you have your phone on private?"

"I don't!" he replied. "The battery's dead, so I'm calling from Scarlett's."

Well gee. He should probably have let a sista know that before scaring her half to death.

"Well, I lost Milo!" I exclaimed in frustration.

"You what?"

"Actually, he kind of lost me. There were these firemen and

they were all, *hey Broseph*, and we were all, *who*? But then these girls kind of took him while I was being used as a human sacrifice, and now I don't know where he is!"

Jack was silent for a few seconds, and I checked my phone to see if I had accidently disconnected the call while trying to find a quiet spot to talk. There was no way in hell I was opening another one of those doors. It was like opening up a portal to my very own sexually scarring Narnia.

"I'm not even going to ask," Jack finally said. "I'm coming to get you, hold tight."

"No you're not!" I protested, before I could hear the sound of his car keys leave his pocket. "I'm not a five year old! I just need to find him and get out!"

"Well, have you heard from our stalker friends yet?" Jack asked, clearly stifling a yawn. Lucky him, he was probably lying on a couch enjoying himself while I was struggling not to get abducted.

"Not yet," I told him. "I mean, Dr. D hasn't called, but Ao Jie Kai could be standing behind me for all I know. I have no clue what the guy looks like, and everyone here is in costume!"

A muscly guy wearing a pink tutu over his boxers ran past me. He had a halo attached to a headband on his head and sparkly angel wings strapped to his shirtless back.

"TINKERBILL BITCHES!" he yelled to the room, throwing a handful of glitter into the air.

Thanks to my fantastic luck, the glitter seemed to miss everyone else around *but* me. I shook my head, dusting the glitter from my hair, but I knew I'd be spending hours tomorrow in the shower trying to get it all out.

"What was that?" Jack asked, responding my frustrated groan.

"That was Tinkerbill, the gender confused fairy who just glitter bombed me!" I cried, dusting glitter off my black dress.

Great, maybe now DJ Pete could use me as a disco ball. "Are you laughing at me?" I demanded, unable to believe Jack actually found pleasure in my misfortunes.

"Of course I'm laughing at you!" Jack replied, barely able to speak through his laughter. "Damn, I wish I had been there to see that!"

"I hate you," I told him, pulling the cat ears off my head and throwing them on the ground next to me. "And I hate this stupid party! I thought my high school parties were bad. This is just crazy!"

"Welcome to the real world, Princess," Jack said, and I could practically hear his grin over the phone.

"Ugh, whatever! I'm going to go find Milo," I declared with a sigh. "And then I'm going home, taking a shower, scrubbing myself for three days and then going to sleep. I'm so over college."

"Sounds like a plan. Call me when you leave."

I promised I would and hung up. I didn't care who I had to shove out of the way to get out. I would do it. No more Miss Nice Catwoman. Leaving my ears on the floor, with glitter all over my dress and my head held almost as high as fake Jamaican guy was, I marched past the bedrooms and toward the stairs. There was a large group of partiers blocking my way, standing right in front of the staircase chanting something I couldn't quite make out. I couldn't tell what they were so excited about, but damn it, I was going to make it through their rowdy crowd come hell or high water.

"Miranda!" Someone called to my right, stopping me by the elbow.

I looked up to find a guy dressed as Elvis Presley staring back at me with wide smile.

"I'm sorry, do I know you?" I asked politely, raising my voice over the chanting.

Elvis pulled off his black sunglasses and raised his plastic cup to his side as if it would help me recognize him if his hands were away from his body.

"It's Ryan!" he finally said, looking at my blank expression. "We met the other day? You asked for AJ?"

"Oh, Ryan!" I exclaimed in realization. "Sorry, I didn't recognize you in that outfit."

"It's good right?" Ryan replied with a proud grin. He had clearly made use of his plastic cup and five-dollar entry. He kept swaying every time he leaned in to say something. "So, are you having fun?"

"Sure," I replied with a shrug. I was only just getting the hang of lying through my teeth, so I figured I may as well put the skill to use.

"Is your brother here? You know you don't look anything like him."

"Uh, yeah. We get that a lot."

Ryan leaned in close. He reeked of high hopes and cheap alcohol. "We snuck in here," he said. "We aren't cool enough to get invited. But don't tell anyone!"

He clumsily pressed a finger to his lips. I smiled awkwardly and said, "Don't worry, I won't."

"Oh, have you met AJ yet?"

I snapped into attention, scanning the room. That meant Ao Jie Kai *had* come to the party. Holy crap. What was I meant to say if I did see him? *Uh hi, can you maybe not make my life a living hell? Thanks so much, love ya, okay bye.* On the other hand, this whole thing could have been a total misunderstanding. After all, all I had seen was a nametag! For all I knew, poor Ao Jie Kai had nothing to do with Dr. D or this whole thing. Or maybe he was standing behind me with a giant potato sack, waiting to kidnap me and throw me into the Pacific Ocean.

"Is he here?" I asked, my heart racing. I raised my voice over group of people yelling drunkenly at each other on the stairs. I had no clue what was happening, but I didn't have time to check. I needed to concentrate on why we came to the party in the first place.

Ryan swayed some more and took a sip from his plastic cup. "You know, he wasn't going to come," he told me in a hushed voice, as if he were letting me in on some well-protected secret. "He didn't even remember you!"

"Imagine that!" I said sarcastically, patience growing thin. "Any idea where he is?"

Ryan peered around the room and gave it a quick scan, but I doubted he even knew what he was looking for. It was clear he was drunk off his face, and therefore no help whatsoever. He was mumbling something to himself and I rolled my eyes, holding onto his arm tightly so that he wouldn't fall over. The chanting and yells grew into large cheers and I looked at the group, which seemed to have expanded since I last checked. Whatever was going on was obviously happening in the center of the messy circle, conveniently blocked so I couldn't see.

"What's going on over there, anyway?" I asked Ryan.

"They're beating some poor kid up, I guess." Ryan replied with a shrug. "They do it all the time."

Great. Just what we needed to top off a perfect night. Drunk college boys kicking the crap out of each other. I had seen fights happen all the time at the parties I had gone to. Rich boys trying to prove they were hotter, wealthier and generally better than the other. Brendan had gotten into a few himself, but he tried to avoid getting hit in the face as much as he could, given his dreams of becoming an actor. Good thing he did, or else Cowboy Stan would've looked a whole lot different.

When Ryan proved to be completely useless, I dragged him over to the crowd, standing on my toes to see what was happening in the middle of the noise. There were two guys standing on the stairs. I recognized one of them as one of the brunette firemen who had been getting extra frisky with me before, but the other guy was dressed in some kind of martial arts uniform, with a black belt tied around his waist. Unfortunately that black belt didn't actually mean he was actually qualified in any sense, because from where I was standing, he was getting the bejeezus beat out of him.

"Who is that!" I yelled to Ryan, who was standing beside me, swaying on his tiptoes.

For a split second, the karate kid looked familiar, but I didn't have enough time to fully analyze his face. The brunette fireman pushed the karate kid against the stairs railing and I cringed as he made contact with it.

"I think that's . . ." Ryan began, jumping up to see past the large group of people blocking our view.

"Ryan, who is that?" I repeated, holding onto the person in front of me as a giant banana roughly pushed past. I clasped my eyes shut for a few seconds as someone else pulled his arm back, ready to punch the Asian guy.

At this point, even the fake LAPD cop would do. But absolutely *no one* was helping, and Milo was nowhere in sight. No doubt, some idiot was filming the fight so that the whole world would be able to witness it within minutes online. Jeez, what was the point of taking a hot cop along with me to an out-of-control party when he wasn't even going to be around when intense stuff went down?

"I think that's AJ!" Ryan yelled to me, suddenly alert.

I don't know who's luck was worse, mine or Ao Jie Kai's. The first time we would come in contact with each other in person would involve him being beaten up by a jerk, fighting more than just fire, and I couldn't do anything to help him.

"Welcome to K-A-P!" The fireman yelled with a final shove, and Ao Jie Kai grabbed onto the stair railing to steady himself. "Enjoy the party, bitch!"

The fireman gave a triumphant smile to his cheering fans before making his way down the stairs, no doubt to gloat to those who had missed out on the fight.

"See you 'round Miranda!" Ryan called out behind him as he pushed his way through the sea of people who were starting to disperse now that the evening's entertainment had ended.

Tinkerbill came up behind me, grabbing me by the waist. He began thrusting his pelvis against me, shouting out lyrics to "Baby" by Justin Bieber. I spun around and pushed him off roughly, narrowing my eyes at him.

"Beat it, buddy," I told him, giving him my best *don't mess with me* look. "Unless you want your Tinkerballs to suffer."

He thought about it for a beat before nodding. "Sorry, sir," he said, skipping off.

I turned back to the stairs, just in time to see Ryan and Ao Jie Kai disappear into the bottom level of the house.

"Wait!" I called after them, but they didn't hear me.

I ran down the stairs, wincing as my heels cut into my feet and stopped right where Ao Jie Kai had been beaten minutes before. An iPhone was lying on the step next to my foot, and I bent over to pick it up. It was almost as fancy as mine, which was surprising for a waiter who worked at a rundown sketchy restaurant. I pushed the home button and saw a picture Ao Jie Kai and an attractive girl, kissing him on the cheek.

"Gia!"

Milo, minus the mask, was standing on the bottom step with a concerned look on his face.

"Oh my gosh!" I sighed. "There you are."

He ran up to the middle of the staircase, resting his hands on my shoulders. "Are you okay?" he asked, his eyes blazing into mine with concern.

"I'm fine! But there was—"

Milo nodded sharply and said, "Come on. We have to go."

He paused, glancing at my hair. I looked at him self-consciously.

"Tinkerbill kind of got excited with his glitter," I explained, jerking a thumb toward the male fairy.

Milo looked where I was pointing, where Tinkerbill was hitting on a wall, by the looks of it.

"Tinker*bill*?" Milo repeated, still watching him flirt with no one at all.

I nodded. "We better get out of here before he starts making out with the furniture."

Milo pulled his gaze away from Tinkerbill and repositioned it back on me. "Good idea. Hold on a sec."

Milo leaned over the railing of the stairs, scanning the dance floor. I took that opportunity to store Ao Jie Kai's phone out of sight before anyone came looking for it. Unfortunately, my options were pretty limited. I could leave the phone on the floor, where someone would probably steal or break it, keep the phone in my hands and risk running into Ao Jie Kai, which would be slightly awkward, or I could put the phone in my clutch, but it would take at least a minute and put me at risk of being dragged back onto the dance floor by the frisky firemen. Seeing as all of my choices sucked, I decided to do the mature thing and shove the phone into my bra.

I heard Milo let out a frustrated groan as he clearly spotted something in the crowd below. He turned to face me, grabbing my hand, now free of the iPhone. His fingers gripped mine tightly, setting my skin on fire. There was a slight chance my nerves were in overdrive after witnessing AJ get kicked around, and Milo touching me wasn't helping.

"Milo, the fight . . ." I said, but it wasn't loud enough to hear over the music.

Milo and I somehow made our way past the raging partygoers, practically running out of the door and past the bored frat boy dealing with entry fees.

"Why are we rushing?" I asked, trying not to sound breathless.

I *needed* to start working out a little. Not just parading around in tight pants to impress Jack. Milo stopped a little down the road and I caught my breath, adjusting my dress from the hem.

"Sorry," he said. "The firemen wanted to start doing body shots and I was scared they would find us."

"Oh. Well that's . . ." I trailed off. Milo doing body shots off me or anyone else wasn't something my brain could handle.

Milo nodded and gave a light laugh, taking in a deep breath as if he had come into contact with fresh air after living underground for the past ten years. We began walking slowly toward the car, and I turned to look at him.

"Milo, that fight—"

"Yeah," Milo replied grimly. "I only caught the last part of it. It's actually one of the better ones I've seen at college parties."

"That guy was Ao Jie Kai!"

"Who? The fireman?"

"No, the one getting beaten up!"

Milo stopped in the middle of the road, and I checked to see if any cars were about to run us over.

"Wait," he said, looking completely stunned. "*That* was Ao Jie Kai? Did you talk to him?"

I shook my head and said, "I didn't get a chance. He was kind of . . . busy."

Milo ran a hand through his hair in frustration. "I didn't even know he was going to be here!"

"Um, yeah. Me neither . . ."

I was too busy staring at Milo's messed up yet still perfect hair that I forgot to mention I had taken Ao Jie Kai's phone. How was it possible that someone could look so good and be talking to *me* of all people in the world? I was an embarrassment to womankind with the way I acted. Clearly Milo was a direct descendant of God.

"Should we go back?" Milo asked me.

"They'd be long gone by now," I told him.

"But I mean . . ." Milo said, his mind clearly churning out ideas at a million miles an hour. "He obviously followed you here. I mean, we could go to his frat hou—"

I caught onto Milo's arm without even thinking twice, and he looked at me, stopping midsentence.

"He'd never talk to us," I said. "There's no point."

Milo nodded and my gaze dropped to my hand, lightly curled around his arm just above his wrist. I don't know why I had thought it was okay to just reach out and grab him. Obviously my body was finding any excuse to touch the guy. I awkwardly removed my fingers and lowered my hand. Better keep it by my side where it wouldn't cause any more trouble.

"I guess you guys could always officially question him later, right?"

"Detective Reynolds doesn't want to do that yet. But after tonight I think we have good reason to."

I nodded, letting him believe that AJ had followed me to the party, and not the other way around. What he didn't know wouldn't hurt him, right? What really sucked was we really had just missed out on cornering AJ and finding some answers. We crossed the other half of the road in silence, making our way over to Milo's car. "Sexyback" was blasting from the party all down the street, and I mouthed the lyrics when Milo was looking in the other direction. There's just something about Justin Timberlake that sets off a groove reflex in all women. Milo still wasn't saying anything by the time we reached the car, but he hadn't gone around to his side yet either. He looked frustrated and confused, obviously disappointed that we had come so close to a huge lead, only to let it slip away. So I just stood there staring at the door handle, avoiding eye contact with the guy who smelled like a manly daisy field, standing a yard away. I put my clutch on top of the car, running my arm up and down the other to warm myself.

"Are you cold?" he finally asked, and I looked up from my awkward staring match with the passenger's seat door.

"Oh no, I'm dandy!"

Actually, I was not dandy. I was freaking freezing. My feet felt like they were about to fall off and I still had glitter all over my hair and body as if a fairy had just thrown up on me.

"Here," Milo said, taking off his leather jacket and draping it across my shoulders.

I was about to open my mouth to say it was no big deal and that he could have it back, but then I realized he had just given me his leather jacket to wear. I'd have to be a raging lunatic to pass up an opportunity like that! So I gracefully thanked him and tried not to cry tears of joy. I even had to lean against the car door to stop me from melting right then and there.

"Are you okay?" Milo said. "You're not hurt are you?"

Well not physically, but my heart wasn't in a fantastic position. I forced myself to look up at him, because really, the ground can only be interesting to look at for so long.

"No, of course not!"

Milo looked at me seriously and said, "Nobody . . . *hurt* you or anything?"

I thought about it for a few seconds. Tinkerbill had been harmless enough.

"I'm great! Fab! Couldn't be better."

Good God. By that point, I was running out of things to say. Ever had that feeling when you like someone so much, you're so distracted by their mere presence that you completely lose the ability to act like a normal person? It was like that times a billion. I just kept beaming at him like he had told me I had just won a date with Ashton Kutcher.

"Listen, I know it's getting late," Milo began and I looked at him expectantly. "But clearly the party was a bust tonight. And we ran out of there pretty early, so do you want to go grab some frozen yogurt or something?"

"Oh," was all I managed to say. I hadn't been expecting *that*.

"We don't have to!" Milo added quickly. "I just figured in case you were—"

"Yeah," I said. "Um, sure."

Milo and I smiled at each other as he opened the car door for me. Okay, so maybe I should have been focusing on Ao Jie Kai and the fact that we hadn't gotten painfully close to potentially solving this case, and come up completely short. But I always knew the party was going to be a risk. I mean, what if we hadn't shown up at all? We would've wasted our night either way. Besides, he hadn't been kicked around *that* much. I mean, nothing life threatening. And if he was actually stalking me, then he probably deserved a couple of those punches. Frozen yogurt after a night like that was well deserved, if you ask me.

Milo began walking to his side of the car, got half way across the front when the sound of an upbeat, slightly muffled song stopped us both in our tracks. He spun around to look at me, as I stood rooted to the spot, one foot already inside the car.

"Is that coming from the party?" he asked, looking back at the fraternity house.

"Maybe," I told him with a shrug. I pulled my foot out from the car, but left the door open.

Actually, it wasn't coming from the party, because Sexyback was still playing. The aggressive buzzing against my chest told me it was coming from Ao Jie Kai's phone.

I'm sexy, free and single, and ready to mingle.
Yeah, yeah,
Sexy, free and single and ready to mingle!
Milo's lips curved into an uncertain smile as he noticed a

random buzzing coming from inside my dress.

"I—Is that coming from you?" he asked, pointing toward the phone-shaped object, which was still blasting what sounded like a very catchy K-Pop song.

Crap. Once again the options were limited. I could pretend it wasn't coming from me, get in the car and throw the damn phone behind my shoulder. Option number two was to tell Milo what a brilliant super spy I was and how I got the phone and why I chose to put it in my bra. Option two was the mature thing to do, but I was *far* from mature.

"Are you sure it's not coming from you?" I asked defensively, draping my hair over the buzzing.

"Pretty sure."

The catchy ringtone stopped and I sighed with relief. Great, it was all over. I could breathe and pretend that never happened. Unfortunately the ringing started up again after a few seconds and I jumped as the buzzing began once more.

"Oh, come on man!"

I yanked the phone out of my bra and looked at the screen, which read *David*. I refused the call and slapped a hand over my eyes, hoping that when I opened them in a few seconds, that whole incident would have never occurred. When Prince Charming found Cinderella's shoe on the stairs at the ball, he never had to worry about shoving it down his top!

"Is that yours?" Milo asked, clearly struggling to muffle his laughter.

"No, it's Ao Jie Kai's. He dropped it before he ran off."

Milo walked around the car, back to me. He looked at the phone in my hand, then up at me.

"I didn't know you could make a song your ringtone on that phone," Milo said, biting his lip from laughing out loud.

"You can download ringtones," I explained, hoping desperately that David, whoever he was, would have the good sense not to call back. "It's pretty easy."

"I also didn't know you could fit a phone in . . ." Milo said, attempting to look serious. "*There.*"

Oh God, he was actually making fun of me! Which was terrible. Absolutely the suckiest thing that could have happened, short of Milo telling me that he was married.

"You know," I began all serious, as if I were explaining the laws of physics to him. "Bras . . . can be very interesting objects. They're great for those days when you just don't feel like taking a bag."

Even as the words were coming out of my mouth, I knew I was I was digging my own grave. But I couldn't stop them! They just kept flowing out, as if I had suddenly been possessed by the romantically challenged devil!

"Is that so?" Milo replied, giving me a mockingly serious look in return. He took a step toward me.

"Uh-huh," I said, nodding my head violently. "I mean, sometimes you can lose coins in there, but then you just jump around a little, or bend over. Of course, that's always awkward in public, but most women will understand."

I was mentally yelling at myself to abort the whole plan and just stop talking, but clearly some sick part of my brain just loved to watch me crash and burn. It was even worse than the British accent!

Milo shook his head in disbelief, like he just couldn't believe I was *that* big of an idiot. "I just know I'm going to regret this," he said, grinning as he took another step closer.

I had no clue what he was talking about, so I stupidly decided to continue my "Bras for Dummies" lecture.

"You know, they're also useful for storing tissues and bobby pins. You just slide them in and—"

I never got to finish that sentence because Milo backed me into his car, wrapped his arms around my waist and kissed me.

chapter
fifteen

IN FAIRY tales and storybooks, when the Prince kisses the girl at the end, fireworks explode above them and there are violins all around, playing romantic melodies. In real life, there are no violins and no fireworks, but sweet lord, it's pretty amazing all the same. Even though the kiss probably lasted for like, ten seconds, it was probably the happiest I'd ever felt. Brendan had *never* kissed me like that. Compared to Milo, kissing Brendan was like kissing your grandma.

Of course, it was a slight inconvenience that I had two phones in my hands. I was slammed up against his car while Milo kissed the crap out of me, and all I could focus on was not whacking him over the head or dropping one of the phones in case it accidently slid out of my hands. When he did finally release me I had to muster up all the strength I had in my body not to collapse from pure euphoria. Milo and I just looked at each other for a few seconds and we both did some breathing. And then my brain decided it hated me a little more than usual and lifted my fingers up to his lips so I could wipe away some of the lipstick that had smudged onto him. Which, let me tell you, is not easy to accomplish with both hands full. He looked like he wanted to smile, but instead he went all rigid and then suggested we go home. Just like that, as though he hadn't just pressed me up against his vehicle and stuck his tongue in my mouth! I'm not going to lie, that was crushing. I mean kissing me couldn't have been that bad, right? But the look on his face had been that of slight alarm. *And* the ship had clearly sailed on frozen yogurt, which was the most disappointing part of it all.

To make matters worse, Jack hadn't taken the news well at all when I told him. His eyes bugged out so wide, I was scared they might just fall out of their sockets. He kept yelling about how unprofessional that was, and how Milo had clearly taken advantage of me the moment he had gotten me alone. And then he went all meathead macho man and started rolling his eyes a lot. I couldn't tell Aria and Veronica; it would be impossible to explain without getting into detail about the bigger situation. Besides, they already thought it was incredibly suspicious that I had missed Brendan's going-away party, so there was no point even bringing up Milo. I definitely couldn't tell my parents, and I doubted Anya would care. So I was left to cherish my amazing kiss by myself.

In fact, I was starting to question if I had dreamt the whole thing when Milo didn't call me the next day, or the day after that. I mean, it's not like I was expecting him to show up at my doorstep with a dozen roses, get down on one knee and propose or anything. But still, one rose would have been appreciated. Or a text. A post-it note even. By the time I showed up for my first Miss Golden Globe rehearsal on Tuesday, I had driven Jack completely insane with my questioning about why he hadn't called. My favorite theory was that he was so in love with me, he forgot how to dial my number.

Luckily for me, Carol Beaufort was doing her best to keep me busy. I had taken all but one step inside the Beverly Hilton Hotel's grand hall when I had an evening gown two sizes too big for me thrust into my arms, and strict instructions to go change in the bathroom immediately. I gave myself a mental high-five for remembering to wear a pair of heels, just like she had requested, or else she may have had a seizure brought on by stress. Carol was a woman consumed by her stress, and very eager to take it out on me.

Dad had finally decided it was time for me to stop hiding out at home and sent me back to school. I think he figured I was getting into less trouble when I was distracted by algebra. Of course, I'd only returned for like, two days before my first day of training for Miss Golden Globe began. Dad had flat out refused when I finally forced him to make a decision on letting me do it. But Mom had conveniently stepped in and said she already accepted on my behalf, which meant there was no way of backing out. God, I love that woman a little extra sometimes. Needless to say, my father had been less than pleased. But he sucked it up, played some golf, drank some wine, and kept his opinions to himself.

The best part was I had *finally* been able to tell my two best friends about one of the many crazy things that were happening in my life. It also provided me with the perfect excuse for missing school and acting super sketchy. It was all about manipulating the facts, which was something I was getting pretty good at. Aria had practically fainted when I told her Dylan Watson, son of action star Dean Watson, was Mr. Golden Globes. She'd always had a soft spot for him after seeing him at the beach once. I was freaking out too; that boy is *fine*. But of course, my heart was set on a dreamy police cadet that refused to call me after a life-changing kiss. Well done to me.

As it turns out, the role of Miss Golden Globe wasn't nearly as fun as I had hoped it would be. All I had to do was walk, smile, and hand a beautiful person a statue, then repeat the whole process. It wasn't rocket science, from where I was standing. Some people clearly disagreed.

"Gia," Carol sighed, rubbing her temples with her index fingers, trying desperately to keep calm. "That's the seventh time you've almost tripped and fallen flat on your face. I thought you said you were comfortable in heels!"

"I am!" I cried, and Carol sighed again. "It's the stupid dress. It's super flowy and it's way too big."

"Well I'm sorry!" she snapped. "But I didn't have time to get your exact measurements!"

"Jeez, relax!" I told her. "Don't worry, I got this. I was *born* to walk on this stage. It's in my blood."

I gave her what I thought was my friendliest reassuring smile, but she took one look at it at grimaced so violently, I actually had to take a step back so she wouldn't hit me.

"Everyone, take a two minute break. I'll be right back!"

I watched Carol storm off stage, pushing her meek assistants out of the way. I turned to Dylan with a frustrated sigh and he reassured me that she wasn't always that crazy; she was just *really* stressed out. I suggested that she needed to loosen that painfully tight bun she had forced her thin, brown hair into, as it was probably adding to the craziness. Dylan went to go grab himself a bottle of water and I took the opportunity to climb down the stage in the most unlady-like manner and waddle over to Jack, who was immersed in his phone. I sank into the seat next to him with a sigh.

"I'm so done," I declared. "I hate this dress. I hate Carol. I hate it all, and it's only been one rehearsal! Take me home!"

Jack put his phone on his lap and looked at me. "Do it for Clooney."

"Oh trust me, he's the only reason I'm doing this."

"I don't know," Jack said, watching workmen move around lighting equipment across the room. "I kind of like Carol."

"You're kidding, right?" I said.

"I don't know yet."

"This is crazy!" I cried. "Neither Milo nor Dr. D have called and I have to miss half of school tomorrow because dragon lady wants me back here at eight in the morning. I'm supposed to film something stupid about me looking for the right pair of shoes for the award show, or something. Which, may I add, is ridiculous because I don't even have a dress yet! Then I have some press conference on Thursday, which means Dad has to come with me, because Mom's flying out tomorrow. Which also means Dad's going to be a total wreck, as usual, and make me look bad in front of everyone! *And* I have a history test this Friday."

"You know," Jack said, after listening quietly while I babbled, "I have to go to all these crazy events with you. So we're kind of in the same boat here. Plus, I don't get some fancy, prestigious title and a flowy dress. So suck it up, Princess."

"Remind me to hit you later on."

"I'll pencil it into your day planner." Jack's phone rang and he glanced at the screen briefly before lifting it up to his ear. "Cadet Fells, what can I do for you?"

My head snapped to attention, as I looked up to see Jack smiling at me. "Oh my God!" I hissed, and Jack put a finger to his lips, motioning for me to be quiet.

Why had he called Jack instead of me? Probably to ask if Jack knew any good florists so he could send me flowers. Or maybe he'd lost my number and was asking Jack to text it to him.

"Yeah, right now is a good time to talk," Jack told Milo, and I practically jumped onto Jack's lap.

"Is he asking for me? Does he want to talk to me?" I whispered fiercely.

Jack put his hand on my face and pushed me away. I pushed him off me and he replaced his hand on my face immediately afterwards, clearly enjoying my desperation to hear his conversation with Milo.

I watched Jack nod and say, "Uh-huh," "yeah," and "okay, sure" every two seconds as I struggled with his hand. My questions began the moment he hung up.

"What did he say? Did he talk about me? Did he want to talk to me? Should I call him? Should I text him?"

Jack raised his eyebrows and said, "Wow. You're really pathetic."

"Jack!"

"Relax, crazy! No, he didn't want to talk to you. He was calling about Ao Jie Kai's phone."

"What's he saying?"

"He said everything seems pretty normal. No creepy contacts called 'Evil Genius,' no psycho stalker photos of you crossing the street. Your phone number isn't even in there. He definitely works at the Dumpling Hospital, because he's got the number listed as 'work.' And the people he calls most often are his frat brothers, his mother and some girl called Claudia."

"Who's that?" I asked.

"How should I know?" Jack replied, looking at me as if I had just asked him why the sky was blue. "Milo said the police are looking into it, but they have a feeling it's the girl in those photographs with him."

I thought about this new information silently for a minute, hoping desperately something would come from me stealing Ao Jie Kai's phone. I was almost certain that investigating a stolen phone wasn't completely legitimate, but hey, I was no cop. I'd leave all the moral decisions to the men in uniforms.

"So he didn't want to talk to me *at all?*" I asked, trying not to sound as crushed as I was feeling.

"That's it, we're getting you therapy."

"It wasn't supposed to be like this!" I exclaimed. "He was supposed to be adorable and take me to a carnival and buy me a huge stuffed toy while I looked all cute and ate cotton candy!"

"Does L.A. even have carnivals?" Jack asked, looking more pained by the minute.

"Shut up, that's not the point. The point is, it wasn't meant to go down like this!"

I couldn't understand it. Milo definitely knew I'd be around Jack, so to call him and not me just didn't make any sense. He didn't even like Jack! He always called me with updates. Hell, I doubt Dad knew as much as I did about the investigation. As far as I was concerned I hadn't done anything wrong. Or had I? Maybe I injured his spine with my phone when I tried to stop it from slipping. But he would have mentioned something right then, right? Maybe I was a horrible kisser. Brendan hadn't minded it that much. But he was also an aspiring cowboy, so what did he know?

"Alright people," Carol barked, cutting into my self-destructive thoughts. "We only have the venue for two more hours before the rehearsal for the opening monologue starts. So please, let's try to make this work."

I turned to Jack with a groan. "Two more hours? Kill me now."

I rose from my chair to walk toward the stage but Jack caught my wrist, yanking me back.

"Oh, I almost forgot!" Jack said, giving me an excited look. "I was talking to one of those girls with those headsets on, and she told me who the father is. You know, the last girl who got pregnant? Her baby. Want to know who it is?"

I gave Jack an incredulous look. "My life is total mess and

now I have to go make a fool of myself in front of a descendant of the Kennedy family for another two hours, and you want to tell me some stupid piece of gossip?"

Jack blinked at me and said, "Yeah, pretty much."

"Okay, tell me."

"MISS WINTERS."

Carol's vein on her forehead was aggressively pulsing and she looked just about whack me over the head with her clipboard. So I did some exaggerated sighing, collected the hem of the overly flowy dress in my hands, and made my way slowly up the stage stairs.

"One hundred and nineteen minutes to go," I sighed.

"And counting," Dylan whispered back.

By the time Thursday came around and Milo *still* hadn't called, I had gone from crazy obsessed to borderline delusional. I was suffering under the amount of studying I needed to get done and Brendan was clearly mad at me for missing his farewell party because he wasn't answering any of my calls. On top of that, Dr. D hadn't so much had sent me a winky-smiley face emoticon, and I realized that him *not* calling me was far scarier than him actually being in contact. So neither my ex-boyfriend, my future boyfriend, nor my stalker wanted to talk to me on the phone. If that isn't the most depressing thing you've ever heard, then you're lying to yourself.

As if it wasn't bad enough that I was practically being shunned by most of the men of my life, the most dominant male, my father, continued to prove his poor social skills at the press conference for Miss Golden Globe. By the time it was over and the honorary luncheon began, my jaw was about to fall off from all my fake smiling. The press conference itself hadn't lasted long at all, but the flashing camera lenses and eager reporters shooting questions at me made me realize why my dad hates leaving the house. By comparison, I was seriously a nobody. I was popular only by association, yet everyone seemed to falling over their feet to take my picture. I couldn't even imagine how they felt about my dad.

A reporter had asked me about whether or not I was worried that I wouldn't live up to my parents' expectations, to which I replied with slight panic. I hadn't even considered that until they had asked me! It was Freud all over again. So instead I awkwardly told them I was most scared about falling on my face, which was the truth. Hopefully now everyone thought I was endearing and not completely incompetent.

I was standing in a Calvin Klein dress that was probably a size too small, but at least it made me look like I had some body shape, rather than just a twig. The luncheon seemed a little more like a lunch-off, because it had been a good thirty minutes and I hadn't seen a crumb of food. I felt like I had barely eaten in like, a year, seeing as Mom had got us all on a "clean eating" scheme so that I could look "fit and fabulous" for the big day. At least now that she was back in New York she couldn't monitor how many bland salad leaves I had to shove down my throat.

I was pretty much losing the will to live when Jack finally managed to help me escape the tedious conversations with the random celebrities I didn't know, as well as the mini photoshoot done with the Miss Golden Globes from the last three years. They all seemed to think the opportunity was the best thing that had ever happened to them, and kept going on about how prestigious it was. Truthfully, the experience so far had been a bit of a letdown. It was definitely exciting and I knew I would feel differently on the actual night, but Carol never stopped yelling, and with so many distractions buzzing through my mind, I couldn't concentrate. The other girls never had to worry about a Jodie

Foster movie-style stalker and his little waiter minion harassing them at all times of the day!

"I need to talk to you," Jack said, hooking his hand around my elbow and dragging me to a corner.

"Oh thank God," I sighed with relief. "If I have to pretend I know these people for one more second, I'm going to go insane. Plus, they haven't served the food yet, and I'm like dying here."

"Milo called," Jack said.

"What?" I looked at him sharply. "When?"

"Like a half hour ago?"

I widened my eyes in disbelief. "And you're only telling me this now?"

"Sorry, but you were kind of busy, remember?"

A woman who had more Botox than actual skin on her face, sauntered past in her seven-inch heels, threw her hair over her shoulder and congratulated me on landing the role of Miss Golden Globe. I had absolutely no clue who she was and would probably never see her again, but I gave her my thoroughly rehearsed thank you and watched her walk toward the bar. The moment she was far enough away I snapped my attention back to Jack.

"Whatever!" I said impatiently. "Did he ask for me?"

"No, Gia. For the millionth time, no, he did not ask for you."

I looked up at the ceiling and groaned, hoping my unhappiness was making its way across the chandeliers and up to the heavens above.

"Why hasn't he called yet!" I wailed. "Why does he call *you* and not me? He doesn't even like you!"

"Don't hold back. No, really," Jack said, completely deadpan.

"What? He doesn't! That night was *perfect* Jack. It was literally the—"

"As lovely as all that sounds," Jack said in a bored voice. "I can't tell you why he hasn't called. But I can tell you about the girl in Ao Jie Kai's photos, if you want to stop whining and hear me out for a second."

I reluctantly stopped pouting, did a quick check to make sure no one needed me for another photoshoot.

"Ugh, fine," I groaned. "Tell me."

"Her name is Claudia Finch," Jack said, lowering his voice. "Twenty-two years old, two siblings, both younger. Studying journalism at UCLA. She works part-time at some place called the Coco Club. Have you heard of it?"

I nodded and said, "It's a really fancy lounge. It's super popular, and you can always see celebrities in there."

"Have you ever been inside?"

"Nope. The girls and I tried once, but we couldn't get in. You have to be twenty-one."

Jack gave me a half smile and said, "Trust *you* to not be able to get in."

I glared at him. "Shut up! We were like twelve, okay? There was no way they were letting us in either way."

I was such a liar. It was actually a few years ago when I had first gotten my fake ID and had been too wimpy to use it. I backed out when we were literally at the door, and dragged the girls home right after.

"Anyway," Jack continued. "I think we should go pay her a visit. Ask her some questions, do our undercover thing. She might be able to give us some information on Ao Jie Kai."

"Wait," I replied. "Isn't that the police's job?"

"Yeah, but since when have you ever backed out of an opportunity to sneak out of the house and cause trouble?"

I considered his point. "True," I said, nodding. "But I'm surprised you're actually going along with it this time with zero complaints."

"The sooner we find answers, the sooner we can complete

our deal, and I can go back to New York and you get your life back."

I stared at him silently for a few seconds, hoping my surprise wasn't showing on my face. He hadn't said anything wrong; I mean, we did have a deal. But I was only just starting to get used to Jack, and dare I say it, I didn't really hate it anymore. But obviously he still hated being around me, because the only thing on his mind was heading home.

"Right." I forced myself to say with a smile. "Of course. Our deal."

"The real issue," Jack continued, evidently oblivious to how I was feeling, "Is getting out of the house without your dad noticing."

I looked behind my shoulder and watched Dad shake hands with a man I didn't recognize, and affectionately pat him on the shoulder. He seemed completely at ease at face value, but I knew he was bored out of his mind. Kenny, on the other hand, wasn't as great at hiding his boredom. He was standing directly behind Dad, his head to the ceiling as if he was hoping God would descend from heaven and give him an escape route.

"We can't go tomorrow night," I told Jack, turning back to face him. "Dad's at home, and with everything going on lately, he won't believe any excuse I give him for us leaving."

"What if we go during the day?"

"The Coco Club is a bar, Jack! It's not even open before seven!"

"Okay," Jack replied thoughtfully. "Well what about the night after?"

"Dad's got some dinner with Tarantino's people. They want him to play a gangster. Like a legit one, not a homie. He was complaining about it but I was like, that's so cool! 'cause he'd get to wear the old school hat and h—"

"Gia, focus!" Jack exclaimed with an impatient sigh.

"What?"

Jack rolled his eyes dramatically and said, "You said your dad has a dinner! Which means he'll be out."

It took a second for the scenario to register in my mind before I widened my eyes in realization. "Right!" I said. "Which means we can go to the Coco Club!"

"Exactly."

"But what if she's not even working that night?" I asked, biting my nail thoughtfully. "We'll have to figure out when she's working. Saturday is our only chance!"

Jack nodded and said, "We'll work something out."

"Gia! I need you for a moment!" I heard Carol call from across the room, with forced affection in her voice. I watched as she smiled brightly, waving her hand toward her, ushering me in her direction. *Now* she mouthed, dropping whatever fake charm she had displayed seconds before.

I forced a smile back and did an internal sigh. "Dragon lady beckons, so I have to go."

"Leave Claudia to me," Jack assured me. "I'll figure out when she's working."

"How?"

"Just leave it to me!"

"Okay, fine!" I said. "Will you tell me if Milo calls?"

"Probably not, no."

"Jack!"

"I'm kidding! Jesus!"

I frowned at him. "If they bring the food out, save me some. Especially if they bring out those little patty things because, those are incredible! Like *wow.*"

"GIA!" Carol practically barked, and I jumped a little in my Manolos.

"Duty calls," I said, stepping toward my impending doom.

Carol seriously needed to relax, or go on a date or something, because she was uptight to a whole new level. I had enough to worry about without her always breathing down my neck, like gee, my stalker. Or the fact that Milo *still* hadn't called me and it had almost been a week.

If Dr. D didn't end up killing me, waiting for Milo to fall in love with me definitely would.

c h a p t e r
s i x t e e n

THANKS TO Jack and his master planning, our latest secret mission fell exactly on the night of Dad's dinner. After calling up the Coco Club and pretending he was a stranger who found Claudia's wallet and was looking to return it to her, we were able to confirm that Claudia was indeed working on Saturday night. I spent the whole of Friday distracted at school, feeding my friends a lame excuse about why I couldn't sneak out the house and hit up Château Marmont with them that night. Needless to say, they were growing more impatient with my shifty behavior every day, especially when I didn't completely destroy Meghan for starting a rumor that my absences were a result of a Lindsay Lohan-style rehab debacle. Of course I had confronted her about it, asking her what the hell her problem was. She had simply replied by looking down at my Marc Jacobs wedges with a frown and saying, "Those shoes, actually. It's not 2008 anymore, Gia."

Yeah, she was a psycho bitch, but I didn't bother pursuing the matter. I was far too busy scheming with Jack about how we were going to get the information we needed. Truthfully, we could have just waited until the police did their own questioning, or even just asked Claudia out-right. But things were getting a bit boring in Hollywood, if that's even possible, so why not shake it up a bit?

We never did get around to telling Dad about Ao Jie Kai's phone, seeing as it would have raised a lot of questions that I didn't have well-thought-out answers to. If I did mention that I lied about where I was and who I was with, and that we had never actually managed to track down Ao Jie Kai, he would have just yelled about how I had completely wasted my time and put myself in danger for no reason. Plus he might have fired Jack for covering for me, which would have been super inconvenient. Telling him I managed to swipe AJ's phone, which could potentially help solve the mystery, would just give Dad the opportunity to yell at me some more about how he didn't raise a thief. In fact, if I had told him I had saved a one-legged cat from a burning house, he'd have told me I was breaking and entering and was therefore a criminal. There was no winning with that man.

So of course, I was more than eager for him to get out of the house and out of my hair. It had been all of three seconds after Dad and Kenny left for dinner before Jack and I were in full frontal mission impossible mode. At least Dad had managed to rope Al into going to the dinner too, mumbling something about a PR opportunity through his annoyance as he put his suit on. I had done my best to not make it too obvious that I was trying to keep him out of the house; smiling encouragingly and helping him find a tie that wouldn't make him look like a clown.

With all the housekeepers gone for the day or kept busy,

Jack and I snapped into action the moment we heard the car pull out of the driveway. Mike wasn't a problem; he was too busy getting high in his room and kept yelling about how he was "getting those Benjamins, cuz." I considered giving him a lecture, but then decided against it. It wasn't exactly like I was the model daughter. Every chance I got I was sneaking out of the house; so really I was in no position to talk about appropriate behavior. At least this way Mike wouldn't rat me out to Dad. Plus, it wasn't like Chris was going to say anything. He just sat there looking extremely uncomfortable, eyes glued to the television. Someday that boy was going to have a meltdown and yell for fifteen hours straight and then we'd all miss his silence.

With expert speed and timing, Jack and I threw on our disguises and drove to the Coco Club, which thankfully wasn't too far away. It had barely been an hour since Dad left, and I knew those dinners always lasted late into the evening, which gave us ample time to investigate and get home before he arrived back. Jack and I parked across the street from the Coco Club, hid behind his car, and peered over at the bar suspiciously.

"Two bouncers," Jack said quietly, and I nodded.

"Yep."

We watched silently as two tall, scary looking bouncers checked the IDs of a group of girls. They looked more like professional wrestlers than bouncers, which made sense considering how fancy the place was.

"Go for the one on the left," Jack told me. "He looks less scary, which means you'll be able to lie better."

I raised an eyebrow, watching the bouncer that Jack had indicated. "He looks like Kenny."

"Yeah, so?"

"So how is that *less* scary?"

Jack smiled a little and said, "Kenny's a big teddy bear, come on!"

This time I raised both eyebrows. "I don't know what freaky ass teddy bears you grew up with, but that's not exactly how I picture him."

"Anyway," Jack said, standing upright. We had been bending down a little so we were completely hidden behind the car. "Let's go over the plan once more."

I turned to face him, giving him a determined nod. "I go in first," I began, recalling what we had discussed earlier. "Locate Claudia and then give you a signal. Then you come in and I begin questioning."

"Right," Jack continued. "And remember, no probing her too much otherwise she'll catch on. I'll be right there as back up, just in case."

"Got it."

"You got your ID?"

I pulled out my fake ID from the small bag hanging from my shoulder and held it up to show Jack. "Here. But I don't really understand why you changed it. What's wrong with the one I had?"

"Clearly whoever sold it to you ripped you off," Jack said, taking the ID card from me and inspecting it. "It sucked. So I found someone at school to help me fix it for you. Just added a different photo and changed the name. It was the best I could do with a day's notice."

"Who'd you find?"

Jack smiled. "I can't reveal my sources."

"Oh come on! It's not a drug bust!"

"No, but I think he's involved in that business too."

"Fine!" I snapped, snatching the card back. "I'll just take the stupid ID and pretend I'm Roxy Mulligan for a night. Which, by the way, is a terrible name."

"What's wrong with the name Roxy?" he replied.

"Hello—o?" I said, looking at him like he was nuts. "It's

such a stripper name! Might as well have called me Candy and sent me off to the nearest bachelor party."

"Well, we can't change it now, so quit complaining!"

"Whatever!" I sighed. "At least I get to wear a decent outfit."

Thankfully Claudia worked at the Coco Club and not some dump where the homie costume or anything similar would fit in. I was wearing a black, Olcay Gulsen cross-back dress, which I had teamed with a blonde wig I had bought for Halloween last year so I could dress up as Barbie. The wig was high quality, so it didn't look fake, but I couldn't stop checking my reflection just to see how weird I looked as a blonde.

Jack, as usual, looked like perfection in a grey suit. He was wearing a crisp white shirt underneath and looked like an absolute sex god without even trying. It was downright unfair what Baby J was doing to me. He can't possibly have given me Jack, hands-down the most attractive person I'd actually ever gotten to touch, *and* Milo, who was just about perfect in every way. That is if he ever decided to call me back, which he *still* hadn't done. Almost seven freaking days! What, had he died or something? Because that was really the only legitimate excuse for kissing a girl like there was no tomorrow, and then refusing to even send her a hello.

At least I had Jack in a suit to fill the void, which was strong enough for my ovaries to pretty much self-combust. If Jack were a handbag, he'd be Dior. I was Walmart compared to that. Okay, that's a stretch. More like a Fendi purse from 2002. Still worth a lot, but just not as in style.

"Okay, here's your microphone," Jack said, handing me a tiny black device with a clip behind it. "Don't talk through it too much, or you'll raise questions. Hide it somewhere it won't be seen but the sound will still reach."

I took the mic from him and inspected it. "Where do you expect that to be?"

Jack lowered his gaze to my chest and I whacked him as hard as I could on the arm. Of course he was deceivingly strong so he barely flinched.

"I'm not putting this on my bra!"

"It's a convenient spot, Gia!"

"Oh, yeah, I'll bet it is."

"I'm serious!" Jack said, but he was smiling a little. "It'll stay hidden and the sound will be clear."

I did some frustrated sighing while I accepted that he had a point. I whirled around so I had my back to him and clipped the mic into place, right in the center of my bra.

"Okay, done," I grumbled.

"You need me to check?"

"You want to die?"

Jack laughed and pointed at my ear. "You got your earpiece in?"

"Yep," I nodded, making sure it was hidden behind the wig.

"That's how you'll be able to hear what I'm saying to you. Don't talk into your microphone too much, or else she'll get suspicious. And don't touch your earpiece too much; it'll look weird."

"Jeez, have you got enough rules? And how do you even have all this stuff anyway?"

"Gia, I'm a bodyguard," he replied. "The microphones and earpieces come with the job."

"And the suit?"

"Added bonus."

That it definitely was. Jack wished me luck and I took a deep breath, clutching onto my new identity. I kept telling myself to become Roxy, but who was I kidding? I was just going to have to wing it. I took a long look at Jack's encouraging smile before marching over to the bouncers with alarming determination. Given that it was a Saturday night, there were swarms of people trying to get into the bar. Generally, the bouncers could tell who could afford to be seen in a place like that, and who should just give up on trying. I was fairly certain I looked the part of a rich girl. I just wasn't sure if I looked like a twenty-one-year-old rich girl.

I looked over my shoulder to check on Jack, but he was gone. I had no clue where he was, and I was scared to ask because Mr. I'll Do the Talking had made it clear that he could yap into my ear the whole night and not the other way around. I gave up and walked inside, barely breathing from anxiety and excitement. It's not like I'd never used my fake ID before. The stakes were just much higher than usual. A group of paparazzi were snapping shots of someone beside me, but I didn't dare turn around and check who it was just in case someone pulled off my wig and revealed my true identity to the world. Honestly, I didn't think anyone would notice or care, but just in case the news got out, Dad would *definitely* care.

"Hi," I said weakly, handing my ID to the apparently nicer looking bouncer when it was finally my turn. I practically beamed at him as he took it from me, expressionless.

"Smile less!" Jack's voice came through the earpiece, and I immediately dropped my smile. "No not completely! Just a little."

The smile immediately resurfaced as the bouncer glanced up at my face. "Roxy?"

"That's me!"

I thought I could hear a frustrated sigh coming through the earpiece, but I couldn't be too sure. The bouncer took one last look at my beaver smile before handing me back the ID and ushering me inside silently.

With a deep breath and a few nerves, I entered the bar. Out of all the secret missions Jack and I had pulled off, I was enjoying this one the most. The Coco Club was a place I seriously regretted not discovering earlier. No drunken underaged kids pretending they had the maturity levels to be in a nightclub, no tacky disco lights and smoke machines, no seizure-causing club beats. The Coco Club oozed class, with its dark brown walls and reddish lighting. Across the left side of the room there was a long bar that spanned the entire room, with purple fluoro lights surrounding it. You could serve the whole of L.A. at that bar, and still have room for a New Yorker on the end.

The right side of the room was made up of luxury couches and perfectly square tables. There was a medium-sized dance floor among the furniture, but it didn't seem to be in use much. People were too busy looking fancy and sipping martinis at the bar. By social standing, I definitely belonged in a place like this. But if they were letting people in based on personality, I'd be lucky to get into a Chuck E. Cheese.

"Are you in?" Jack's voice came through the little earpiece in my ear, making me jump slightly.

"That's what she said."

"Really Gia? You really want to find your sense of humor now?"

"Okay, sorry. Yes, I'm here."

"Good. Walk over to the bar and see if you can spot her."

I nodded even though Jack couldn't see me and obediently walked over to the bar, passing who I was about ninety percent sure was Lana Del Ray. It seemed a little inappropriate to stop her for a picture, especially if it wasn't her. I slid into a glossy black bar stool and crossed my legs, flipping my blonde wig over my shoulder. There were cute guys *everywhere*. And if Milo wasn't going to call me back then so be it. I was just going to have to find myself a new love interest.

"Do you see her?" Jack asked, and I inspected the bartenders carefully.

I was having a little trouble remembering what Claudia looked like, but I wasn't about to tell Jack that. The last thing I needed was to be arguing into an earpiece with him, making myself look like the *Ghost Whisperer* in the process. The bartenders were mostly men, which helped me narrow it down to two girls, dressed exactly alike in short black skirts, white shirts, a black vest and perfectly aligned black bowties.

"What color hair does she have again?" I mumbled into the mic as subtly as I possible could.

"Brown."

Bingo. Now that I had ruled out the blonde one I could work on getting Claudia's attention.

"She's on the other side of the bar," I told Jack.

"Then move to that side."

"Can I get you something?" A bartender asked me with electric blue eyes and a killer smile.

"Oh, no thanks. I'm not really drinking tonight."

The moment the words left my mouth I wanted to slap myself. The bartender's confused smile didn't help.

"But you're at a bar?" he said.

"I know," I said, struggling to recover from the little blunder. "I meant I'll need a minute to choose."

The bartender gave me a light shrug before moving on to serve someone else and I sighed with frustration.

"You're an idiot," Jack's voice came through the earpiece.

"Shut up! Oh, wait, she's coming over to this side!" I exclaimed.

The man sitting on the barstool next to me raised his eyebrows. I gave him an awkward smile but he shuffled a little further away from me on his seat.

"Get her attention," Jack instructed. "I'm coming in."

"Excuse me!" I practically yelled, and Claudia and another bartender turned their attentions toward me. "Can I have a drink please?"

"Just a sec," Claudia said, pouring amber liquid into a glass.

"I got it," Her colleague told her.

"No, I'll wait, thanks!" I told him, and both bartenders gave me a funny look.

Great. They probably thought I was hitting on Claudia, which I definitely wasn't. But the man to my right had now decided it was probably safer for him to get up and move to a couch rather than sit next to the lesbian ghost whisperer. Smart decision. Claudia handed the glass she had filled to the person in front of her and walked over to me with a tired sigh.

"What can I get you?" She asked with a forced smile. She was clearly exhausted from the Saturday night madness, but knew she was getting paid to keep up good appearances.

"Um," I racked my brains for an alcoholic beverage that would make me sound mature. "A Cosmo?"

"Sure."

"Are you kidding me?" Jack exclaimed into the earpiece. "A *Cosmo?* You can't handle a Cosmo, Gia. You can barely manage orange juice."

"Shut. Up." I hissed into my bra.

"Excuse me?" Claudia said, raising an eyebrow as she picked up a martini glass.

"Nothing!"

I smiled at her brightly and tightened my grip around my clutch. If I hurried, maybe I could escape through the back door and run all the way home before Jack noticed.

"Heads up," Jack's voice filled my ear, and I turned to the entrance, trying to act casual.

Jack walked into the bar and scanned the room, avoiding eye contact with me. I had seen him less than five minutes ago, but his stupid grey suit still floored me every time I looked at him. *He* looked like he belonged in a place like the Coco Club, and the smirk on his face told me he knew it. Women across the room were ogling him as if they were window shopping at Tiffany and Co., and I couldn't blame them. Jack walked right past me, giving me a fleeting look of acknowledgement and a nod only I noticed as he chose a seat at the other end of the club. I was trying my hardest to be cool and casual, but instead I was one of the many women whose eyes were plastered on him

"We get some good ones," I heard Claudia say.

I whipped my head back around to face her and glanced at the Cosmo she has placed in front of me.

"Sorry?"

"The guy in the grey suit?" She said, motioning toward Jack. "We get some really good looking guys in here."

"Oh my God, I think Kate Bosworth is sitting a seat away from me," Jack hushed voice said.

He sounded as excited as he had ever sounded, which wasn't overwhelming, but still decent. I forced myself not to jump out of my seat and shout "WHERE?" There was no way I could compete with Kate Bosworth! It was the eyes. I had no hope.

"I've seen better," I said with a fake smile on my face, making sure I spoke directly into the mic.

"I heard that," came Jack's reply.

"I don't know," Claudia said, taking a look at Jack who was sipping something that looked like whiskey. "He's pretty amazing."

I watched Jack smile and rolled my eyes. The last thing Jack needed was his ego boosted.

"I think I'm off men," I told her semi-truthfully. All this drama with Milo and Jack was doing my head in.

A fifty-something man a few seats down smiled at Claudia and pointed to his empty wine glass. She nodded and returned the smile, reaching over to obtain his glass.

"Oh, yeah? Why's that?" Claudia asked, refilling the man's glass with more wine.

I pulled my drink toward me and ran my fingers up and down the stem of the martini glass. "They suck. They confuse your feelings and never call you back."

"Oh, please," Jack's whisper came through the earpiece, and I forced myself not to shoot a glare in his direction.

"I've been there," Claudia said, nodding at me with a small smile. She handed the wine glass back to the man and leaned in to hear what he was saying to her.

"Get something good out of her," Jack told me, and I watched him rise from the bar from the corner of my eye, and walk over to one of the couches further across the room.

I told him I'd try and watched her nod at whatever the man was saying to her. I took a sip of the Cosmo and felt it burn down my throat. "Oh my god!" I cried, spluttering. "What the hell is in this thing?"

"Keep your voice down!" Jack hissed. "People already think you're crazy."

I coughed some more, trying to regain some control over my esophagus, which felt like it was on fire. I pushed the drink away from me and shook my head. It was practically all vodka! No wonder Carrie Bradshaw never made good decisions. She was always drunk.

"How's the drink?" Claudia asked me, placing a clear drink with a skewered olive through it in front of a woman who had taken the place of my previous companion, in the seat next to mine.

"It's . . . uh, great," I lied, broadening my fake smile. "So you said you've been there? With men, I mean. What happened?"

I knew I was being way perky and super stalker-esque. No one in L.A. cared about your life stories, especially in bars. All they wanted was a drink and to take you home for some sweet lovin', depending on which bars you went to. But still, I hoped she just thought I was being friendly and not nosy.

"Oh, you know," she said, pushing some of her wavy hair out of her face. She gave a noncommittal shrug. "The usual. Weirdos, cheaters, crazy boyfriend."

"Crazy boyfriend, huh?" I said, nodding slowly, easing my way into the conversation. "So what happened there?"

"Good," Jack said, and I diverted my gaze in his direction, reflexively. "Try to get as much as you can, but keep it casual."

"Well," Claudia said cautiously, and I turned back to her. "You know, nothing much. Things just didn't work out."

Okay, so she was clearly not the type who wore a "My Boyfriend is a Stalker" t-shirt and blurted her life story out to anyone who would listen. Admirable on any other occasion, but extremely inconvenient for me.

"I doubt it was worse than mine," I told her, hoping to reduce the level of awkwardness. "He left me because he got some stupid acting job in Texas. Now he's going to be a cowboy."

"Nice to meet you," I heard Jack's voice through the earpiece, and my eyebrows knitted together in confusion. "I'm Jack."

My eyes widened as I realized he was probably introducing himself to some girl sitting on the couch next to him. I couldn't keep looking over at him; it would be too suspicious. But so help me, if Jack ended the night with Kate Bosworth's number I was going to hit someone.

"That's rough," Claudia said, clearly unaware of the voices in my ear. "A cowboy? Wow."

"So, was it worse than mine?" I asked her, contemplating yanking out the earpiece so I didn't have to hear Jack make a move on someone else.

I had to wear an itchy wig, be Roxy, and interrogate the ex-girlfriend of my potential stalker, but Jack got to have an amazing night out and pick up all the girls he wanted! It was by no means a fair deal.

"I don't know," Claudia laughed. "A cowboy is kind of hard to beat!"

"No kidding, I love to surf!" Jack was saying.

Seriously? He was a New Yorker. New Yorker's don't surf. Who was he kidding? I commanded my brain to turn off whatever part was listening to Jack and focus on Claudia's story.

"Uh, so what happened?" I repeated for the millionth time, dropping my smile and trying a more serious approach.

Claudia looked down the bar to ensure that no one was waiting for another round of drinks. But people had started to settle down and the madness seemed to have reduced. The bartenders could actually breathe and were gratefully taking rest breaks as they watched the customers nurse their drinks. She really had no excuse not to talk to me, but getting her to say the right thing was going to be a challenge.

"Well," Claudia began, leaning in as if she was sharing some top-secret piece of gossip with me. "He used to work at this restaurant not far from here. The place was seriously creepy. I mean, it was set up like a hospital! How weird is that?" she asked, incredulously.

"Super weird."

"It gets worse," Claudia continued, and I leaned in closer to her. "We met at a friend's party last year. The party was totally lame and he was kind of geek, not really my type at all. But he was sweet. I mean, everything kind of just worked."

I sent a mental message to Jack saying, *I hope you're getting all of this.* He wasn't saying anything at all anymore, to me or Kate Bosworth, and I didn't know if that was a good thing or not.

"So then what?" I asked, urging her to continue.

"And then . . ." Claudia said. "It all went downhill the moment he got a salary raise at the restaurant."

I looked at her with confusion. "Isn't that a good thing?" I asked.

She smiled and said, "Not if you're an average waiter who somehow gets a five-thousand dollar raise."

"Wait, *what?*"

Claudia laughed in agreement, even though nothing was really funny. "I thought it was strange too. I mean, he was a waiter at some run-down restaurant in some dingy place. Nobody gets paid that much for *that* job! I work here and my pay is still crap!"

"So what did you do?" I asked. "Did you tell him you knew about the money?"

"Nope. I saw it in his bag one day when he came over. I thought he was acting a little jumpy that day, but then the money explained the behavior. But I didn't say anything to him. He could have stolen it for all I know. I didn't want to accuse him of anything without being sure." Claudia shrugged, as if she was having a conversation in her head with herself.

"That's insane!" I said.

"Tell me about it," Claudia nodded. "Then he started working really late and naturally I assumed the worst and thought that he was cheating on me. I mean, the restaurant closes at eleven. What work could he have possibly been doing there until three in the morning?"

Alrighty then, that was super sketchy. Ao Jie Kai had clearly been getting up to no good.

"So was he cheating?" I asked.

"I don't know," Claudia said. "To be honest, deep down, I knew that wasn't it. It still didn't explain the money, right?"

"Wow. That's . . ." I failed to think of an appropriate way to describe the situation.

"Yeah," Claudia said simply.

"So what happened next?"

Claudia shrugged and said, "I told him I had had enough. If he was going to lie to me, then he didn't deserve me. He begged me not end things, but he refused to tell me what he was getting paid so much for. He just said something about the owner being in L.A. and offering him a kind of promotion."

"A promotion? How does a waiter get promoted?" I asked,

trying to fit all the pieces together with unsuccessful results.

"That's what I said!" Claudia cried and threw her hands up in the air with frustration. "He told me to trust him, but I just couldn't. It was all too odd for me. I just couldn't deal with it anymore, so I told him it was over. He calls me all the time though. I never pick up, because I know he'll just beg some more."

We were both silent for a minute as I let that information sink in.

"Ask if she knows who the owner is," Jack's voice suddenly came through my earpiece.

"That's a shame," I said, sympathetically. "Ever find out who that weird owner was?"

Claudia shook her head. "Nope. And frankly I don't care. That guy's out of my life now; I've moved on. I'm trying to at least," she replied with a sad smile.

I smiled back at her genuinely, when a man a few seats down called for another bourbon.

"Listen, it'll be better soon. That guy's gig in Texas probably won't work out anyway," she said with a kind smile. "Who knows, maybe you'll end up with someone like that guy in the grey suit?"

"You never know," I said, rising from my barstool. I tried my hardest to keep the excitement out of my voice. "I need to use the ladies' room. All that liquid is really pressing on my bladder. Where is it?"

Claudia glanced at my basically untouched drink and pointed to the left side of the room. "Straight down 'til the end, first door on the left."

I thanked her and hurried across the room, eyeing Jack as I passed him. He nodded at me and began to rise from his chair. There was young woman in the bathroom when I entered, adding more mascara to her eyelashes. She smiled at me through the mirror when I walked in and I returned the smile as I locked myself in a stall.

"Jack," I whispered as quietly as I could. "Hold on, there's someone else in here."

"Okay, I'm right outside," Jack's voice replied and I leaned against the bathroom stall.

After about thirty seconds I heard footsteps walk away, the bathroom door squeak open, and finally close quietly. It opened almost immediately after, more fiercely this time.

"Gia?" I heard Jack ask the empty room.

"Oh my gosh," I sighed, swinging the stall door open and walking toward the sinks. "This just keeps getting better!"

Jack grinned and put a hand in the pocket of his suit. "I hear that a lot from women."

"Could you not be a pig for like one second and listen to me, please?"

"Jeez, I'm listening. What?"

"Claudia's story! It's going to help us right?" I asked, leaning my back against the sinks.

Jack shrugged and said, "It's definitely more than we had before tonight. At least now we know this AJ guy is definitely involved. Oh and by the way you are a *terrible* spy. You kept talking right into your bra. It looked so obvious!"

"Shut up! I was doing my best. You try having a microphone in the middle of your chest. Whatever, what do we do now?"

"I say we go home. I don't think we can ask her any more questions without looking suspicious. I'm surprised she even went into that much detail." Jack looked around the bathroom thoughtfully, as if distracted. "I've had some good memories in these places."

I rolled my eyes. Great. Now I'd forever have the image of Jack and some twig-like super model pressed up against the inside of the stall door, doing God knows what in God knows where.

"What's that on your hand?" I asked, noticing black ink scribbled across Jack's right hand.

"This?" Jack replied, glancing at his hand. "A phone number."

I glared at the messy numbers. "Whose is it?" I said casually, flipping my blonde hair behind my shoulder.

Jack's lips curved into a smile as he turned to face me. "Laura's." I raised my eyebrows at him and Jack's smile grew wider. "A charming young lady I met on the couches outside. She's on vacation from Australia with her friends from college. Couldn't you hear all of that?"

"No! I was too busy doing what we came here to do instead of hitting on desperate girls at a bar."

"She wasn't desperate! She was cute, so we talked."

"Yeah, I'll bet you two really hit it off over your love of riding the waves."

I turned to face the mirrors with a confident look on my face. Too bad it didn't look confident; it just looked defensive. I could feel Jack's eyes burning into me, that famous half-smile still plastered on his face no doubt.

"You're jealo—"

"I'm *not* jealous!"

"You're *so* jealous."

I whipped my head around to face Jack. I was *not* jealous. If Jack was going to be a player then that was his decision and it had nothing to do with me. He could press anyone he wanted up against the stall door for all I cared. He could freaking break the door. What did it matter to me? I was practically in an almost relationship with the hottest police officer ever. I just needed Milo to call me, but when he did, we'd be together for a very long time. And Jack's life would be a meaningless vacuum of super models.

"I don't have time for this!" I exclaimed, pushing past Jack roughly and swinging the bathroom door open.

I stalked over to the bar and faked a smile as I approached Claudia, who was pouring a drink for another customer.

"Hey, I'm going to head off now. Do I pay here?" I asked, glancing at my untouched Cosmo that remained on the bar top.

"Hey," she replied, placing the margarita mix down. "Some guy settled that for you."

"What?"

"He also told me to give you this," she answered, holding out a napkin with writing on it. "He was kind of old, but I guess it could be worse. He could have been hot back in the day."

I practically snatched it off her, almost ripping the napkin in the process. In the center of the napkin there was a thick black line with a type of box on top of it, and another antenna-like line protruding from the box. In the bottom right corner there was a small "D," as if it were a signature. I had no clue what the black lines meant, but it seemed to resemble some kind of Chinese character.

"Who gave this to you?" I asked her more urgently.

She looked around the room for a few seconds before finally pointing to the main entrance. "That guy. The one who's just about to walk out."

My gaze followed her outstretched hand to the door. A tall man with a brown leather jacket was leaving the club. I couldn't see his face, but I had a feeling I knew who he was.

"Jack!" I cried, twirling around and finding him standing right behind me.

Jack looked at me, the front door, and then back at me. He suddenly took off in a light jog, and I followed in my outrageously high heels. I gripped the napkin in one hand and my bag in the other, trying not to trip over my own feet. Poor Claudia looked at us with alarm, clearly lost as to my sudden change of behavior and association with the "grey suit guy."

Jack pushed the door of the Coco Club open and stopped right outside the entrance. I slammed into his side and grabbed onto his arm to steady myself.

"Where'd he go?" Jack asked, his eyes scanning the few people on the sidewalk.

The man in the leather jacket had completely disappeared. It was hardly a mob outside, so it's not like we had lost him amongst a crowd. But even still, we had no clue where he had gone. The bouncers were looking at us with raised eyebrows and I asked them if they had seen a man with a brown leather jacket on. Both bouncers said they hadn't. There was still a line of people waiting to get inside the Coco Club, so it was easy for him to have slipped past without anyone noticing. Jack ran halfway down the street, scanning the surrounding area with no luck.

My phone buzzed as I walked toward him with a defeated look on my face. It was from Mike.

Dad's on his way home and you isn't home soldier. P.S. buy me chocolate kthanksbye cuz.

Oh great. As if the night needed to get any worse than it already was, yet another obstacle had been placed in our way. We just come agonisingly close to coming into contact with Dr. D and now I'd never live to see him because Dad was going to kill me if he made it home before we did.

"Shit!" Jack exclaimed, running his hands through his hair in frustration. "We came so close!"

He dropped his gaze to the ground, shaking his head. I knew exactly how he felt. The disappointment was practically consuming me whole.

"So now what do we do?" I asked Jack.

For the first time since I had met him, Jack had nothing to say.

chapter
seventeen

TO EXPLAIN the events that took place at the Coco Club would involve telling Dad that I had used a fake ID to get into a club and that I'd left my little brother at home with his bong pipe. Just a few months away from my senior year exams. So Jack and I decided it was probably a better idea to keep that little adventure on the down low.

We had only just managed to run through the doors before Dad and Kenny arrived home. I managed to squeeze in a second to rip the wig off my hair, wincing as the pins dug into my scalp. But I was still all dressed up in my dress and heels, and Jack was in a suit, which raised some questions when Dad walked in. My brilliant excuse had been a complex game of charades, to which Jack, Chris, and Mike all agreed profusely with. Luckily for us, Dad was too tired from complaining about great movie opportunities to delve too deep into the matter.

That night I slept with the napkin Dr. D had left for me under my pillow, as if I would wake up in the morning and the tooth fairy would have left me a ten dollar bill in its place. A clue as to who Dr. D was and what he wanted would have been more helpful, but seeing as I got neither the ten dollars nor the information I needed, I took the napkin with me to Miss Golden Globe rehearsals at the start of the week.

It was just over two weeks to go 'til the big day, and Carol was driving me insane. I just couldn't please the woman. The way I walked was "all wrong," I always missed my cues and I always had a "nervous look on my face. Kind of like a beaver." There was zero appreciation for the effort I was making, including strutting around the house daily, and practicing my award-winning smile. Jack was just about ready to throw me through a window from all my tedious practice of handing pepper mills to him, pretending it was a trophy and he was Ben Affleck. But nothing seemed good enough for Carol. She just kept sighing deeply and rubbing her temples every time she saw me.

As if all of this wasn't bad enough, Milo *still* hadn't called. What, was he in a coma or something? Because other than that, there is NO good excuse for giving a girl a life-changing kiss, offering to buy her frozen yogurt, and then disappearing! Even being abducted by aliens wouldn't cut it; they have lots of communication devices in their little spaceships. I had tried to move onto a new strategy of coping, which mostly involved playing "Independent Woman" really loud while I was getting ready in the morning. As it turns out that was not a great idea, because grooving to Destiny's Child is actually very dangerous in a slippery shower. The fierce finger snapping alone almost cost me my life.

When Carol announced that we should take a ten-minute

break before we had our practice with Billy Crystal, I was just about ready to run away with my maxi dress and four-inch heels on and never look back. I mean, what were the chances I'd actually come into contact with George Clooney anyway? If my dad hadn't gotten me that opportunity yet, I doubted Carol Beaufort would.

"Take me home," I groaned as I sunk into the chair next to Jack.

"You're not *nearly* done with rehearsals yet," Jack reminded me, eyes glued to his phone as usual. "Carol's forehead vein still looks like it's a decent size. You haven't infuriated her enough."

I frowned and picked up my English essay that was lying on Jack's lap. I had asked him to make himself useful and proofread my homework while I was getting yelled at, so I'd have one less thing to worry about when I got home.

"What did you think?" I asked him, hopeful that I had managed to get at least one thing right in my life.

Jack turned to me with a less than reassuring look on his face. "It's not . . . bad."

I gave him a knowing look. "That doesn't mean it's good."

"Yeah, it's not good."

"Jack!"

"Gia," Jack's voice softened, as if he was about to deliver me the news that my cat had died. "It didn't make any sense. You were supposed to be writing about the themes in the *Lord of the Flies*. But it was all over the place."

"It was not!" I cried defensively.

"You spent way too much time on the characters."

"The characters are the important part!"

"Yeah, but the essay is about the themes."

I pouted with disappointment, crossing my arms across my chest like a stubborn five year old. I had woken up early just to write that stupid thing before we left for rehearsals, all for Jack to say it sucked. What a waste of my sleeping time. Now I was going to have dark circles under my eyes and it was going to be all his fault.

"I hate that stupid book. It's so boring!" I exclaimed, watching Dylan talk to a man with a headset on. "And I hate being Miss Golden Globe! Dylan gets everything right, and I'm the massive screw up."

"Boys have it easier," Jack said sympathetically. "They don't have to wear heels."

"Exactly! I'm going crazy here. My mom messages me a photo of a new gown every five minutes. And every time I tell her I like one, she declares that she hates it! Plus, we still haven't figured out what the napkin says, Milo *still* hasn't called me to declare his love, and I'm going to fail English because apparently the characters don't count as a theme!"

Jack watched me silently as I did some heavy breathing and mentally forced myself not to cry. We hadn't informed the police about the Coco Club yet, mainly because we had broken a few laws getting in. But I had no idea if I even wanted to tell the police anymore. Maybe Jack was right. Maybe they were wasting our time and we could figure it all out ourselves.

"Have you calmed down yet?" Jack said, turning so that he was facing me.

"I think so."

"Good."

I blew out another sigh and tipped my head back to look up at the ceiling. "I'm dying under all this pressure! My life is so unfair."

"Seriously?" Jack asked incredulously. "Michael Bublé wrote a song for you on your seventeenth birthday, and you're complaining that your life is unfair?"

I blinked up at the ceiling, nodding sadly. "I tried to get John Mayer, but he was busy. Wait." I cocked my head up and look at Jack quizzically. "How do you know about my birthday song?"

"I Googled you."

"You what?"

"I had to do some research before the job! Make sure you weren't completely nuts."

"And?"

"And you're completely nuts."

I whacked him on the arm, which of course, was a waste of energy because he barely felt it. I groaned and said, "Yeah, well now all I have is tons of stress and a paranoid father."

"Oh come on," Jack said. "Give the guy a break! He's just trying to look out for you."

"He's suffocating me with all his rules."

"Gia," Jack said seriously. "If my dad cared about me half as much as your dad does, I'd never complain."

I watched him silently as he picked up my essay again and began scanning through it. Jack didn't talk about his life much. Or ever, really. Sure, he mentioned New York a lot, and Scarlett was always coming up in conversations. But I had never once heard about his parents.

"You don't get along with your dad?" I asked casually.

"Nope," Jack replied simply, never taking his eyes off the paper.

I considered asking the next question, thought against it, then finally gave in. "Well, why not?"

Jack looked up at me, expressionless. For a moment I thought he was going to get mad, or just walk away. But then his jaw relaxed a little and he shrugged. "We have different ideas about how to run my life. That's all."

I nodded at him, wanting to ask more, but deciding that I had gone far enough for one sitting. Besides, it wasn't like Jack was going to disappear in the next five minutes. There was plenty of time to grill him with personal questions later.

"Miss Winters." I heard a familiar voice call from behind me, and Jack and I turned to look at the entrance of the grand hall.

Jack and I rose to our feet as Detective Reynolds and Milo walked toward us, past the chairs and tables that would be occupied by celebrities' perfectly toned butts in a matter of weeks. I kept reminding myself to act snooty and flippant. Who the hell did Milo think he was? I mean, you can't just kiss the heck out of someone and then pretend it never happened. That's just bad social etiquette. But my heart didn't share those thoughts. It was doing its break dancing thing that's usually followed by a British accent. Milo and his stupid uniform never failed to floor me, even when I was standing next to someone who looked like Jack.

"Miss Winters, Jack." Detective Reynolds greeted us simply, extending his arm so that we could shake his hand. "We stopped by your house but your dad informed us you'd be here. We thought we'd fill you in on the latest developments in person."

"Is everything okay?" Jack asked.

"It's going as well as it can, considering you have a stalker." Detective Reynolds told us, and I stared at the ground so my eyes wouldn't accidently linger on Milo. "We visited Mr. Kai's girlfriend this morning, following up on a lead."

My head snapped up from the ground and turned to face Jack. He gave me a look that told me to be cool, but I always did have a hard time with being subtle.

"What did you find?" Jack said, glancing at me.

I was concentrating so hard on avoiding Milo's gaze, I was practically glaring at Detective Reynolds with squinty eyes as if I was plotting his murder.

"Well," Detective Reynolds began. "She told us that they had recently separated because she suspected he'd been involved in some illegal activity. She informed us that Ao Jie Kai's employer might have had something to do with large amounts of money he was suddenly receiving."

"Drugs?" I asked, throwing my hair over my shoulder with my best *I have no prior knowledge about this topic* look on my face. I could practically feel Milo's eyes burning into my skin, but I kept my eyes away from him.

"It could be anything, really. It needs further investigation."

"Ah," I said unintelligently, with a fierce nod. "Well, thanks for stopping by, we really appreciate it! Okay, see you then."

I spun on my heel, grabbing onto Jack's elbow in an attempt to lead him away before I started blabbing about *our* own encounter with Claudia.

"Uh, just a second, Miss Winters," Detective Reynolds said, and I sucked in some air.

I considered running, or falling to the floor and faking a broken ankle. But I didn't have the acting abilities or speed for either one of those, so facing the police officers was really the only option I had.

I whirled around slowly, forcing a smile. "Yes?" I asked, hoping I looked innocent.

"Miss Finch did mention to us that there were two people who came into the bar yesterday. She said a young blonde woman asked her about her boyfriend and shortly after disappeared to the bathroom, re-emerging with a blonde man whom at first she portrayed as a stranger."

"Really?" Jack asked pensively. "That's interesting."

Detective Reynolds' gaze moved from Jack's blonde hair to my brunette waves. He nodded to himself slightly before continuing. "She said a tall man came up to her while the blonde woman was in the bathroom and paid for her drink. He also left her a napkin to pass onto the blonde woman."

"Did she say what the man looked like?" I asked, flicking my eyes to Milo, who was staring at Jack with a tightened jaw.

"Brown leather jacket, green eyes, salt and pepper hair." Detective Reynolds replied. "Looked to be in his late forties, fairly handsome."

I racked my brains, struggling to place someone with that description. At this rate, Dr. D could have been any forty-year-old average Joe walking down the street. I also recalled Claudia saying, "could have been hot back in the day." I doubted she had used the word *handsome.*

"So where do we go from here?" Jack asked, maintaining his composure while I tried not to give myself a panic attack.

"We've requested that the bar hand over their security footage from last night. Hopefully the cameras caught him, and the two mysterious patrons poking around for information. We're also going to pay Ao Jie Kai a visit today, maybe tomorrow. We're hoping to get a lot of answers from him."

I looked at Jack from the corners of my eyes, gripping onto my maxi dress with such intensity that I was scared my nails would rip through the fabric. If the police got their hands on that footage, they would easily be able to recognize Jack. Considering I barely recognized myself, I doubted anyone would be able to suspect me in that blonde wig. As convenient as that was, it didn't help the case Milo was probably mentally building against Jack, who would be unable to explain his presence at the Coco Club without looking like he was working with an accomplice for Dr. D.

"Well, that's just fantastic!" Carol's voice came from behind me. She marched down the stairs of the stage, eyes narrowed, pushing her hair out of her face.

"Carol, thi—" I began to explain, but she ignored me.

"Officer," she said, approaching Detective Reynolds. "If you're going to arrest Gia for whatever she seems to have done, please do it after two weeks. I'm desperate here, and Gia was already our last choice."

"Hey!" I cried, giving her an offended look. "Why would you automatically assume I did something wrong?"

"Let me guess," she said, shaking her head with an unimpressed look on her face. "Parking tickets?"

"Miss, I assure you Gia is in no trouble. We were just updating her on her . . ." Detective Reynolds looked at me and I shrugged. "Parking tickets. We're just leaving, actually."

Carol's eyes squinted as if she couldn't believe for one second that I hadn't done something wrong, before finally blowing out a sigh.

"Fine. Thank you for your time officers. Now if you'll excuse me, we have a lo—"

"How do they get the curtains up that high?" Detective Reynolds asked, gazing up at the stage, where busy workers were carrying curtains to weave onto rods.

"Uh," Carol replied, following his gaze to her minions. "They have ladders. Very high and sturdy ladders."

"Is that Billy Crystal?" Detective Reynolds suddenly exclaimed, pointing to the stage. His voice had become shrill with excitement, as though he were a teen waiting in line at a Backstreet Boys concert.

"Yes it is," she said, giving him a strange look.

"I'm a big fan" he replied, his eyes widening. "*Huge* fan. If it's not too much trouble, do you think maybe I could introduce myself? Maybe get an autograph for the wife?"

Carol looked at me and I responded with the toothiest smile I had ever flashed in my life. Personally, I thought it was hilarious that Detective Reynolds had turned into a completely different person within a matter of seconds. Carol clearly wasn't as mad as I had first expected, because she actually agreed to introduce him and put our rehearsal on hold. Maybe her forehead vein had finally relaxed, or maybe she was scared to get on the bad side of a cop, but I sent a mental thank you to Baby J for delaying my failures by five more minutes. I wasn't however, thankful for the awkward position I was left in.

"So," Milo said. I could no longer avoid his gaze. "Who knew Billy Crystal had that effect on fully grown men?"

For the first time since I had met him, I actually felt a little relief being around Milo. For once, I wasn't the only nervous one. *He* was too. He kept lightly slapping his thigh with his hand, looking at the floor and then back at me.

"Jack can you give us a minute?" I asked, and Jack's eyes widened in surprise.

"Gia, I—"

"Please, Jack."

Jack looked at me like I had just told him I was having his baby. I gave him a pleading look, puppy dog eyes and all, and he shook his head in disbelief.

"I'm right behind you," he told me, backing away hesitantly. "*Right* behind you."

Evidently that was Jack's favorite thing to say. I turned back to Milo, my momentary burst of confidence wearing off.

"Bodyguards," I said with a nervous laugh. "Whadya' gonna do?"

"Look Gia, I know you're probably really mad at me," Milo began, running his hand through his hair. "I kissed you and then didn't call you for a week. I get it. I'd be mad too."

Of course I had every right to be mad at him! How could he just look that amazing and lead a girl on like that? Only, I wasn't really angry.

"I'm not mad you. I'm just confused. If you thought it was a mistake then—"

"It wasn't a mistake!" he exclaimed. "I just don't know if it was the best decision."

"Okay, you lost me again."

"I probably shouldn't have made a move," Milo said slowly.

"It was crazy inappropriate, considering I'm working your case. I'm *barely* an officer. If I screw this up, I'll never live it down! Detective Reynolds didn't mention anything about us being at the party together, but I doubt he'd encourage it."

"So that's why you didn't call?"

Milo sighed. "Okay, maybe I was using some other work as an excuse to keep myself busy and not call you, which was cowardly. But I felt really bad about leading you on."

My eyes locked with his and everything fell into place. Everything suddenly made sense.

"You're married," I declared.

"What?" Milo said, eyes widening. "No!"

"Single father?"

"No."

"Girlfriend?"

"Gia—"

"Serial killer?"

"No! Gia, I—"

"Gay?"

"Gia, I'm moving to New York!" he cried, probably a little louder than he had wanted because I heard Jack snort with laughter behind me.

I turned to look at him with a steely glare. He really wasn't kidding when he said he was going to be right behind me. Jack clapped a hand over his mouth and held his hand up as an apology, taking two steps further away from Milo and I, struggling to contain his evident happiness.

"What?" I asked, shifting my attention back to Milo. "Say that again, because I'm struggling here."

"I applied for a transfer to the NYPD months ago, long before your case," Milo explained. "I got the call a few days before the frat party saying my application had been accepted and that I should finish whatever major cases I was working on. I graduate from the academy in just under a month, and I'll be out of the city not long after."

"So where do I fit into this?"

"You came along and I couldn't help but feel something. I told myself not to act on those feelings but I kind of had a weak moment at the party. I guess I let myself like you a little more than I should have."

I was so happy on the inside, I could have just died. Officer Milo Fells was standing less than three feet away from me, declaring that he couldn't help but fall for me! It was *definitely* the bail pun that had done it. You can't fight the romantic power of a good pun.

"So right before you, you know . . ." I said, finding myself unable to actually to say the word *kiss* out loud. "You said you were going to 'regret this.' What does that mean?"

"I don't at all regret kissing you, Gia. If I could go back in time and take it back, I wouldn't. But that doesn't mean it was smart, considering our situation. I only meant that I would regret having to explain this all to you later, after acting like a complete idiot and deciding to ignore you instead of facing up to it."

Alright, so he *had* been an idiot. A whole week had gone by and not one word. He had even resorted to communicating with Jack instead of me! But he was sorry. And he was hot. And he said he didn't regret kissing me. And he was hot.

"So," I began, dreading the inevitable question that hung in the air around us. "Where does this leave us now?"

"It leaves you in New York," Jack's voice said. He came up from behind me, looking at Milo with a smile. "And Gia in L.A."

"Nice of you to join us," Milo said sarcastically, and I bit my nails nervously.

I could barely manage to be around Milo or Jack when I was alone with them. I had no hope when they were both in the same room.

"Sorry," Jack said, with the most unapologetic grin plastered on his annoyingly perfect face. "But I couldn't help but overhear the tragic tale you two were reciting to each other."

"Jack!" I hissed, but he ignored me.

"I don't really see how this is your business, man." Milo told him in a strained voice.

"Gia is my business. And the fact that you're going to be in my city in a matter of months is also my business."

"Oh, my mistake," Milo replied with a glare. "I wasn't aware you owned New York."

"There's a lot you don't know yet."

"Jack, stop," I said warningly, but he didn't even look at me.

"Oh, we'll get there soon. Don't worry," Milo replied, his smile unable to mask the challenging tone in his voice.

Shitty shit shit! This was not going well.

"You know what else is my business?" Jack continued, taking a step closer to Milo. "The fact that you're too busy twiddling your thumbs and writing in your journal about lost love to actually focus on the lunatic harassing Gia."

An image suddenly popped into my head of Milo lying on his bed; tongue out with concentration and furiously writing in a secret diary with a feathery pink pen. I had no clue why my brain had decided to form such a pointless thought and at such an inappropriate time too, but I couldn't stop a light laugh from escaping.

"Journal . . ." I whispered, my laughter strengthening.

Both Milo and Jack were looking at me like I was delusional, which only made me laugh harder. I wanted to slap myself for acting like such an idiot, but even that image was funny to me.

"I'll be in touch," Milo said, watching me laugh with a concerned look on his face.

I slapped a hand over my mouth in an attempt to stop the completely uncalled for laughter, but it was no use. Now it just looked like I was having a seizure. Milo raised his eyebrows, shook his head ever so slightly and walked over to Detective Reynolds and Carol, ignoring Jack completely.

"Oh my gosh," I said, wiping the tears from the corners of my eyes. I had just managed to get my laughter under control and my abs hurt. Thanks a lot, brain.

"That was so embarrassing!"

"Can you believe that guy?" Jack asked, shaking his head in disbelief.

We watched Milo approach a beaming Detective Reynolds and introduce himself to the celebrities with a handshake and a strained smile.

"I can't believe *you*! Now I'll never be Mrs. Gia Fells! Especially not after what you just pulled."

Jack rolled his eyes in frustration and turned to me. "Are you an idiot? He made out with you, and now he's conveniently moving to another city?"

"Hey!" I cried, giving him an offended look. "He's not moving to another city to get away from me! We sorted the whole kiss thing out. You should know that, considering you were eavesdropping!"

"It's not my fault you two were talking so loudly!"

"Oh, please."

Jack gave me a pitying look, and I crossed my arms over my chest defensively. "Just wait, Gia," he said. "You're going to figure out that this guy isn't right for you."

I glared at Jack through narrowed eyes. It was just like him to say something discouraging like that. What did he know about Milo, anyway? I was getting *really* sick of Jack caring about me one minute, and then changing his mind the next. The hot and cold act was getting a little old.

"We're taking off," Detective Reynolds told me, making his way down the stage steps with Milo close behind.

Apparently he had gotten all he needed from Carol and Billy. Milo and Detective Reynolds walked up the perfectly plush carpeted floor to where Jack and I were standing, and I thanked them both for the update, being extra careful to avoid eye contact with Milo again. I shook both their hands, tried not to faint when Milo's hand lingered in mine, and watched with a pout as they walked toward the entrance of the hall. Detective Reynolds' phone rang and he answered with a gruff hello, autographs in hand.

"Gia," Milo said, turning around suddenly, as if he had done it on impulse. Detective Reynolds was yelling into his phone so loudly, I doubted he noticed. "I'm really sorry. For what it's worth, I really do like you. And I'm sorry this got so complicated."

I watched him walk away, my heart sinking as Detective Reynolds and Milo disappeared out of the hall. What kind of injustice was this? I had finally found a guy that I genuinely liked (sorry, Brendan), who actually liked me back, and nothing could even happen! For one, he was almost a police officer *working* my case. And two, he was freaking moving states! One reason would have been enough! I didn't need to be smacked in the face twice.

I had three bodyguards, two parents, great friends, a puppy, a dozen housekeepers, and occasionally a pool boy. I even had a stalker, for cryin' out loud. Yet somehow I *still* managed to feel completely alone. I'm pretty sure this is not exactly what Kelly, Michelle, and my girl Beyoncé had in mind.

All the women who are independent, throw your hands up at me.

chapter eighteen

JACK HAD been acting reserved the whole weekend after the little incident at rehearsals. Seeing as he wasn't exactly wearing "I heart Milo" t-shirts under all his clothes, I was surprised he wasn't over the moon that my romance with Milo had come to a standstill. Truthfully, my personal life really wasn't any of his business, so what he thought essentially didn't matter. Except Jack was kind of the only person I had left to talk to about anything, now that the whole Dr. D situation had completely isolated me from my normal life. Without Jack around to hear my complaining, I'd be forced to befriend Chris, who never even spoke. Or even worse my brother, who never shut up. As much as it killed me to admit it, I needed Jack around, and not just for physical protection.

But evidently, even Jack had his limits when it came to

discussing Milo. I guess guys just aren't interested in hearing about other guys, especially if both of them are extremely attractive and don't like each other much. Aria and Veronica definitely would have been interested in hearing about my Milo struggles. They would have agreed that the universe was being a serious bitch, or at the very least bought me some expensive ice cream and put on a Julia Roberts movie. Veronica might have even let me copy her homework, which is what I really needed. But once again, I had to keep them out of the loop. I didn't trust my brain's filter. If I let one thing slip, everything else would come tumbling down with it.

I figured Jack would suck it up and move on when Monday came around. After all, he'd had half of Saturday and the whole of Sunday to be in a constant state of PMS. Apparently, I was wrong.

"I'm not in the mood for this," Jack grumbled. He pocketed his car keys in his jacket with a sigh, instinctively surveying our surroundings.

"For what?"

Jack motioned to the building closest to the parking lot, where we were. "This. School. I did my time, and now I'm stuck here forever like that sparkly dude from that *Twilight* book."

That comment was definitely feeding my vampire theory about Jack.

I rolled my eyes. "You are not stuck here *forever*. I am going to graduate, you know!"

Jack gave another frustrated sigh and shook his head. "Whatever," he said, as we walked toward the entrance to the lockers. "Let's just do this."

Jeez. We hadn't even gotten to first period and Jack was already Mr. Grumpy Pants. It wasn't my fault I was walking on sunshine ever since Saturday. Maybe Jack needed to find someone who made him feel the way Milo made me feel. Which, currently, was pretty shitty. But you know what I mean. Of course, she'd have to be amazing looking to match up to Jack's looks, especially in that black jacket he was wearing. And she'd have to be funny, because he has a good sense of humor. She'd also have to be smart, because Jack is always going on and on about all this stuff I don't know about. Not that I cared about the type of girl Jack would be into. I was apparently "not his type," so he clearly had poor taste.

"Gia!" Aria exclaimed, cutting into my train of thought. We had just reached the entrance when she had appeared out of no-where, smiling widely at me.

Veronica appeared seconds later, a little out of breath but with an equally wide smile. She was cradling a stack of books in her hand, and pushed some hair out of her face, a little flustered.

"Hey Gia!" she said, taking a few deep breaths. "I love your outfit today!"

I looked down at the heeled motorcycle boots on my feet, my ripped, black skinny jeans and fringed tank top with a shrug. I had been forced to throw on the first thing I could find before we left because I had overslept. Yet again. The whole skipping school thing had really taken a toll on my body clock's schedule.

"It's kind of whatever," I said, giving them a strange look. "But thanks."

Veronica and Aria exchanged nervous smiles and I raised my eyebrows. My friends have had their fair share of being weird, but acting like they had just finished burying a body was something new to me.

"Hey Jack!" Aria cried, waving at him even though he was standing less than a yard away.

"Hey Aria," he replied, smiling at me. Clearly he was amused.

"So," I said, after a few seconds of silently exchanging smiles. "I'm going to go to my locker now."

"I got your books for you!" Veronica piped up, thrusting half of the stack in her arms at me.

"Oh, thanks V!" I told her, giving her a touched smile. "But I actually need to go to my locker anyway. I left my jacket in there a long time ago and it—"

"I'll get it?" Aria volunteered excitedly, practically bouncing up and down as if I had told her she would run into Johnny Depp on her way to school.

I narrowed my eyes suspiciously. "Why are you guys being weird?"

"We're not being weird," Veronica replied almost immediately.

"Yeah!" Aria added. "We just thought it might be nice for us to get your books for a change. We're providing a public service."

"Aria," I said, giving her a knowing look. "You can barely find your *own* locker. You have no chance finding mine."

I took a step forward to try and walk past them, but they immediately came closer together, shoulders touching, barricading the entrance. I raised my eyebrows and took a step to the right, thinking I could go around them if not through them, but Aria jumped in front of me, her smile still plastered on her face.

"Seriously, what's going on?" Jack asked from behind me, and I looked at my friends expectantly.

"I—I heard there's going to be a crêpe guy at school today. Flew him up from France and everything." Veronica announced.

"Okay, you guys need to move. You're starting to freak me out a little."

I took another step to the right when Aria was exchanging more worried looks with Veronica, managing to barely slip past her before she stopped me once again.

"No!" She exclaimed with urgency, grabbing onto my wrist.

"What?" I cried.

Aria released my wrist with a frown. I glanced at Jack, who gave me a shrug, and took another step forward, challenging my friends to stop me again. They didn't.

I had taken barely three steps inside the building before I felt everyone's eyes settle on me. Sheets of paper carpeted the floor and were stuck to the lockers, turning the whole building white. The papers had some kind of pictures on them, but I couldn't tell exactly what they were. I was too busy wondering why everyone was looking at me with suppressed laughter. Oh God, why were they all staring? I was definitely wearing clothes; I had just checked. Was there something on my face? I didn't trust Jack, but one of the girls definitely would have mentioned it.

"What the hell is this?" Jack asked, emerging from behind me, looking around the hallway with the same confusion.

"Why are they all looking at me?" I whispered to him.

"Oh shoot!" I heard someone hiss behind me. It sounded like Aria.

"Gia!" Lincoln came rushing up to me, holding a sheet of the white paper in his hand with a concerned look on his face. "Gia, I have no clue who did this. But don't worry. I've taken all the ones down from the boy's bathroom."

Jack took the paper from Lincoln without asking, and I leaned in closer to see what it had on it. There was a picture of the Golden Globes stage from last year. I recognized it from all of my non-stop studying of actress' speeches, trying to find the perfect way to "glide" and not "trot," as Carol had so kindly put it. Except instead of a beautiful actress, there was a photo-shopped picture of a killer whale in an evening gown, standing upright on the stage next to Christian Bale. Instead of its actual head, my smiling face had been photo-shopped onto the body in its place. The picture had probably been taken from one of Dad's premieres a few years ago, because I looked a little younger. Not that anyone was really going to notice that. They were going to be too busy imagining me looking like a humungous underwater mammal on what was perhaps the most important day of my life. My wedding doesn't count, because based on the way I was going, I was never going to have one.

I snatched the poster from Jack, rooted to my spot. I mean, sure I had been eating a little extra chocolate. But that was just due to all the stress from Dr. D and my constant emotional battle with Milo and Jack. Chocolate calms me down, so sue me. I was by no means a killer whale!

"Gia . . ." Jack began slowly, his smile now completely absent from his face.

I pushed him out of the way and tore another piece of paper off the nearest locker. This one had a photo of me smiling, from Aria's birthday party last year, only it had been zoomed in to practically take up the whole page. I recognized it because I had been wearing Veronica's purple feather earrings that I had been in love with, and had gone perfectly with my purple Steve Madden heels. It was a pretty flattering picture if I may so myself. It would have remained flattering if someone hadn't colored some of my teeth in black, added warts all over my face and devil horns on either side of my crown. Scrawled across the top in thick black text was the heading **The New Face of the Golden Globes**.

"It's not *that* bad," Jack said, as if replying to the horrified thoughts passing through my mind.

"NOT THAT BAD?" I practically shrieked. "Jack look at this!" I motioned toward the students pouring out from everywhere, edited pictures of me in their hands. "I'm the school joke!"

"Don't let her see this one," Veronica whispered behind me, and I spun around to face my two friends eyeing a sheet of paper taped to the locker behind them.

"Great," I declared, sarcastically. "There are more than two versions of this! Fantastic! If you'll excuse me, I'm going to lie on a very busy road now."

I tried to head for the entrance but Jack caught my elbow, stopping me from running out the doors and hiding in the bushes for about fifteen years until I was convinced the humiliation had passed.

"No you're not," he said sternly. "You're not going to hide, Gia. It's not even that bad! We'll just take all the posters down and clean up the floors. Problem solved."

"I'll help," Lincoln offered.

"Same," Veronica said.

"Same," Aria agreed.

"Hey, Gia!" I heard Aaron's voice, and I looked behind me to see him running down the hallway toward us. "These posters of you . . . Man, that one with your face on that obese body is really harsh."

"You mean the killer whale," I corrected him with a sigh. "Yeah, I saw."

He raised an eyebrow and said, "No, I mean that obese body stuffed into a bikini. What's this about a killer whale?"

I slapped a hand over my eyes as if that would help shield the embarrassment and sudden trauma my poor brain had been forced to deal with.

"Oh my God!" I wailed. "Make it stop!"

"Okay," Jack said, uncertainly. His confidence in just how bad the situation was had clearly faltered. "I'll get Gia out of here, you just deal with the posters."

My friends all nodded aggressively, swapping pitying looks that I knew were meant for me. Lincoln stopped a group of freshman boys picking up a pile of papers off the floor and grabbed the posters off them.

"What are you even doing in our hallway?" he asked a scrawny one with big, green eyes.

"There were some on our lockers as well," he explained in a nervous voice. "But we heard the good ones were on the senior lockers."

"In the *freshman* hallway?" I yelled, my voice becoming shrill. "WELL GEE. That's just freaking fantastic!"

"Beat it, kid," Lincoln told the scrawny boy. "And take down all the posters in your hall and throw them away."

"Come on," Jack said, tugging on my hand as he led me toward the entrance. "We'll skip first period. I'll get you a Krispy Kreme to make you feel better."

"I can't eat a Krispy Kreme, Jack!" I cried, fighting back tears. "People already think I look like a whale! What, are you trying to ruin my life completely?"

Jack sighed as Veronica pulled Aria toward a set of lockers, ripping off sheets of paper as she went along. I gave my friends what I hoped was a grateful look, but probably came across as majorly depressed, because Aaron and Lincoln exchanged frowns.

"Come on, Gia," Jack said, tugging on my arm lightly.

"SHOW US YOUR TEENY WEENIE BIKINI GIA!" Someone yelled out from behind me, and I was certain a part of my insides had died.

"Yeah, we all know you're an expert in teeny weenie things, aren't you Carter?" Aria yelled back, and the crowd *ooo-ed* and *aaah-ed*.

Carter flipped Aria the bird, to which she replied by blowing him an air kiss.

"Just ignore them," Jack told me firmly, and I bit my bottom lip to stop from crying.

It was easy for him to say that. His social status hadn't been murdered in front of his own eyes.

"Who would do something so horrible?" I heard someone say from a little behind me.

It was a good question. Who would capable of pulling off such an extravagant prank? More importantly, who hated me that much they actually wanted to pull the prank in the first place.

"Hey Gia," Meghan said sweetly, walking through the entrance of our hallway just as Jack and I were ready to make our escape. She placed her sunglasses on top of her head and beamed at Jack, her two sidekicks by her sides. "Hi, Jack!"

"Hey," Jack replied, with a pleasing amount of disinterest.

"Meghan!" I snapped, pulling my hand away from Jack's grip.

She spun around to face us and I narrowed my eyes at her. "Can I help you with something?" she asked, her fake smile still on her heavily made-up face.

"Yeah, I hope so," I said with a fierce nod. "Maybe you could do me a favor and go fu—"

"Far out, Gia!" Lori said with an offended look. "What's with the ambush first thing in the morning?"

"Gia, come on," Jack said calmly, stepping beside me and putting a hand on my shoulder.

I shrugged it off with a steely stare directed at Meghan. "Look around you, Meghan," I told her, pointing at floor where my edited pictures lay scattered below our feet.

Meghan, Lori and Mischa obediently looked at the ground, craning their necks to get a better look at the papers on the floor. Lori bent down and picked a few up, handing them to Meghan. The three leaned in to inspect the posters while I crossed my arms over my chest, seething.

"That's horrible, Gia!" Meghan cried, placing a manicured hand to her chest. "I can't imagine why anyone would be so cruel."

"Yeah, neither can I. So why'd you do it?"

Meghan faked a shocked expression and turned to her friends, as if to reconfirm that she had heard me correctly.

"You think I did this?"

"I *know* you did this," I told her. "You're the only one evil enough to pull it off."

Meghan's shock turned to sympathy as she reached out and lightly patted my arm. "It's alright, Gia," she said. "I know you're upset and you just want someone to blame, so I won't take this absurd accusation personally."

"Yeah," Mischa added. "We'll just attribute this to your substance abuse problems, poor thing."

I gave her an incredulous look. First she went and made all these terrible photo-shopped pictures of me, then she spread them all over the school, and now she had the nerve to deny all of it in the world's most condescending tone ever *and* bring up an addiction I didn't even have?

"Gia," Jack said quietly, sensing the volcano of anger was ready to erupt. "You don't know that Meghan did this."

"Exactly, Gia," Meghan agreed, fake sympathy dripping from her voice. "But if you'd like, I can go to Principal Morris with you. I'd be more than happy to help you find out who pulled this hideous prank."

"You want me to hit her?" Aria asked, coming to my other side with a pile of ripped up posters in her hand.

"I don't think that's the best idea!" Veronica piped up with a concerned look, standing with Aaron a few feet away.

A crowd was forming around us. What with my furious looks and my well-known rivalry with Meghan, everyone else seemed to have figured out that I was pointing fingers at Meghan Adams, and began to gather around us to hear the conversation better.

"Are you sure?" Aria asked me, ignoring Veronica. "Because that World History textbook you're holding can do a lot of damage."

"Excuse me?" Lori exclaimed. "You can't just go around hitting people, Aria! Especially when they didn't even do anything wrong."

"Exactly," Meghan said, looking at Aria with disgust. "If anything, *I'm* the victim here."

Jack sucked in some air and my mouth dropped open. If Meghan Adams was the victim in all of this, I was the new Pope.

"Okay, hit her," I told Aria, taking a step back and thrusting my textbook in Aria's hands.

"Violence never solves anything, guys!" Veronica cried, running up to us and snatching the book from Aria's grasp. A few spectators groaned with disappointment. "Can't we just talk this out?"

"You lay a fingernail on me and I will slap so many lawsuits on you, your plastic surgeon daddy will have to give up that shoebox you call a mansion." Meghan's eyes turned cold and predator-like.

"Oh, you're going to need my plastic surgeon daddy after I'm done rearranging your face!" Aria shot back, taking a step forward, challenging Meghan to retaliate.

Veronica immediately stepped in the middle of both of them, desperately trying to reason with Aria as she and Meghan exchanged some not-so-nice nicknames for each other. The bell signaling that it was time for first period rang and everyone stopped shouting at each other.

"Alright guys!" Jack said, with a hint of amusement in his voice. His bodyguard instincts apparently kicked in as he pulled me back toward him. "As much as I would love to see this fight . . ." He turned to Aria with a grin. "And trust me, I would *really* love to see that fight, I think it's time to dial it down a notch."

"Whatever," Meghan announced, flicking her hair behind her shoulder and pulling her handbag higher up on her shoulder. "I don't have to stand here and deal with you barbarians. Gia, if you can't prove that I pulled this little stunt, then I really have no reason to keep looking at your face right now."

I desperately tried to think of a good comeback, but my mind had shut down. So instead I stared at her through squinty eyes. When I finally couldn't think of anything good to say, I continued to glare at Meghan and her sycophants as they walked all the way down the hallway in their inappropriately high heels and disappeared inside a classroom. Around us, disappointed students began to disperse, heading to their classes and giving up hope for a good catfight.

"If that didn't cheer you up a little bit, I don't know what will," Jack whispered, and I pouted.

Personally, I didn't feel any better. I had just missed an opportunity to watch Aria release hell on my arch nemesis, so disappointment was at an all-time high. On top of that, Meghan was right, which is a scary thought in itself. I didn't have any proof that she had printed out those edited pictures of me, let alone spread them all over school. All in all, there was nothing to make me feel better, and now I was late to my first class.

"Screw it! Buy me a damn sugary treat," I declared, grabbing onto Jack's leather jacket sleeve and pulling him toward the entrance roughly.

"Don't worry, Gia," Veronica assured me. "We'll deal with the posters."

"And Meghan," Aria added, winking at me. "You go home. We got this."

"I'm actually starting to like L.A.," Jack said, smiling at me as we left the building and headed back to the car park.

It had been all but three minutes and I was beyond done with school for the rest of the year. I needed to go home, crawl under my silky covers and not come out until I was pushing sixty. I hoped the embarrassment would have subsided by then.

"Nice to know you're enjoying my humiliation," I said, returning his grin with a glare. "I was *insanely* close to slapping her."

"I think Aria had that part covered," Jack laughed, putting a hand in his jacket pocket as we approached the car. "She's a keeper, I'm telling you."

That much was true. If there was a silver lining coming out of any of this, it was that I had some pretty amazing friends. But even still, I could seriously do with a calorie-filled dessert right now.

"Oh shoot," Jack said, stopping next to the driver's door.

"What?"

"I think I dropped my keys when I was trying to break up the catfight. My jacket pocket was open."

I widened my eyes, panicked. "I'm not going back in there, Jack! I can't!"

"You don't have to. I'll be back in a second. Stay here."

"You can't just leave me here!"

Jack rolled his eyes. "Relax, Princess. I'll be back before the big bad wolf can eat you."

I watched Jack jog back to the school with another sigh. Great timing for losing your car keys, Jack. Right as I'm trying to make my great escape. I leaned against his jeep and crossed my arms over my chest, glaring at my boots. I was considering possible lawsuits against Meghan when I felt my phone ringing in my pocket. I pulled it out and looked at the screen, squinting in the sunlight.

"Milo," I said, answering the phone with forced happiness. "Hi."

"Hey, is this a good time?" Milo asked, with slight urgency in his voice.

That was an interesting question. It was pretty much the worst time possible, but if Milo Fells was calling me, I was pretty sure things were looking up.

"Yeah. Sure, what's up?"

"Is Jack with you?"

"Um," I looked over at the school entrance, watching a few latecomers rush through the doors. No Jack. "Kind of. He actually just ran inside to—"

"Gia, listen to me," Milo said, cutting me off. "We watched the security footage from the Coco Club. The blonde guy Claudia was talking about was Jack."

Oh shoot. It's not like I didn't see this coming, but I had

kind of forgotten to think of an excuse for that.

"Um, really?" Was all I managed to mumble, but Milo didn't seem to be paying attention.

"We're still trying to identify the blonde girl, but it's definitely Jack in the video. Look, I'll explain everything soon. We're coming to your house, I'll be there in like half an hour."

"Wait, Milo!" I cried out, before he hung up. "I know Jack was at the Coco Club!"

"What?"

"I'll explain when you get to my house," I told him.

"Wait, you know he was at the Coco Club?" Milo repeated, as if he was still processing that fact.

"I wasn't . . . entirely honest with you the other day."

My phone began beeping, cutting into our conversation and indicating I had another call waiting.

"Gia w—"

"Sorry! I'm sorry! Look, I'll explain soon. I'll see you at my house. Okay bye, thanks!"

"Wai—"

I cut the phone before he could ask more questions and I could make even more of a fool of myself.

"Hello?" I said, answering the second call, not bothering to even check who was calling.

"Gia. It's been a while."

"Hello?"

Oh shoot. Dr. D.

"Sorry I haven't been in contact. Did you miss me?"

Gee, let me think about that one. Nope! I covered my free ear with my hand, trying to block out the sound of a car that was parking nearby. Dr. D had clearly decided his Darth Vader voice was more effective at scaring me than his auto-tune, and he was absolutely right.

"You were at the Coco Club the other day," I said, asking

more than declaring a fact.

My voice was shaking and I kept looking over at the school, but Jack was nowhere in sight.

"I was," came the reply, and I pressed my phone tighter against my ear, straining to clearly make out what he was saying. "I'm glad you received my message."

Sixty seconds was all I needed to nail his location, and I knew Milo would be listening closely.

"Thanks for the drink by the way," I said.

"You barely had any of it."

"I'm not much of a drinker," I replied, desperately trying to keep the fear out of my voice.

It had barely been fifteen seconds. I needed to keep him on for longer, but honestly what were we supposed to talk about? Hair products and Taylor Swift's new boyfriend? Yeah. I doubt it.

"Neither am I," Dr. D replied. "But I hope you can make it to my after party."

"After party?"

Still no sign of Jack, and my heart was pretty much threatening to burst out of my chest from anxiety.

"Yes. It should be quite spectacular."

Something about the way he said "spectacular" with his creepy voice sent a chill down my spine. Suddenly it hit me that in a tiny amount of time, the most important day of my life so far would involve me coming face to face with a person who had been watching me for lord knows how long. If the pressure of not falling flat on my face or looking like a whale in my dress wasn't bad enough, I also had to deal with the possibility that I may get kidnapped. Or die. Or rip my dress. Shoot I didn't even have a dress yet! I paced around Jack's car, fidgety and quite possibly suffering from some kind of an anxiety attack.

"What does the napkin say?" I demanded, transforming my panic over the lack of a gown into what I hoped was confidence and power.

"You're a smart girl Gia. Except, of course, when it comes to your math homework. You can figure out what it says."

"Hey!" I cried, putting my free hand to my chest. "I'm trying my best, okay? You try being me for one day! I had to deal with Meghan Adams ruining my life this morning, I don't have a gown yet for the Golden Globes, the guy I really like is moving away and I *really* don't need this from you right now!"

Okay, so I wasn't particularly using my brain. Yelling at my potential murderer was probably not the best idea. A low, grumbling laughter came from the other end of the line and I looked up at the sky in frustration. Where the hell was Jack? What, was he cutting a new car key or something? And why was there a random group of people standing way on the other side of the car park holding massive cameras, looking all lost?

"I've got my tux ready," he said, in an almost patronizing way, and I turned my attention away from the group of photographers. "I'm looking forward to the night."

"Wait!" I cried. I pulled the phone away from my ear to check how long we had been speaking for fifty-one seconds. "What does the napkin say?" I practically yelled into my iPhone.

"In the meantime," Dr. D continued in his Star Wars voice, "Smile for the cameras."

"Wait, what?"

Fifty-six seconds. He had managed to slip away again.

"GIA!" I heard a girl call my name out, and I spun around, coming face to face with a camera flashing in my face. "Is it true you've been receiving threats from a mysterious caller?" she asked.

"How does your dad feel about this?" A man beside her asked, resting a bulky video camera on his shoulders, the lens pointed at me.

"Where did you even hear that?" I mumbled, backing away toward the car.

There were about eight or ten of them, some had tape recorders, and the others had cameras. They were all swarmed around me, eyes widened as they expectantly waited for me to reply to their questions.

"Is it true that your father is planning on moving you to live with your mother in New York?"

"Have the police been notified?"

"Any comments on who you think this person is?"

All the questions were coming at me with speed I couldn't handle. I felt like I was being backed into the corner of some weird experiment, poked and prodded at by evil scientists.

"I—I really can't comment," I told them, spinning on my heel and pulling on the car door even though I knew it was locked.

How did they even know all of this? And who decided it was a good idea to ambush a girl in her school parking lot? I felt like yelling but I didn't know why. I felt like crying but that didn't make any sense either. And stupid Jack, who had completely vanished, had the car keys!

"Gia! Just one more question!"

I could hear their footsteps hurrying behind me, flashes of cameras bouncing off my back. Maybe I should call someone. Who, though? If my own bodyguard wasn't around when I needed him then why would any else be? I pulled on the car door handle again, just in case Baby J decided now would be a good time to grant me a miracle and have it magically unlock. Nope. No miracles for me today.

"Oh!" I called out in a completely animated voice. "I am just taking my car keys out of my bag. So I can drive away now. I have car keys in my bag."

The reporters stopped throwing questions at me for a second, giving me strange looks. Great. Even the paparazzi thought I was weird.

"Gia!"

I snapped my head up, along with my eight new companions, and watched Jack jog toward the car with a confused look on his face.

"What the hell is going on?" he asked.

My eyes slid back to the momentarily silent reporters standing in front of me. Three. Two. One.

"Gia, is this your new boyfriend?"

"Does he know anything about the stalking?"

"What about your relationship with Brendan Miller?"

Jack grabbed my hand and tugged me toward him protectively. Bodyguard mode had been switched on.

"Gia is not answering any questions. Excuse us," he said in a voice so formal, I wanted to laugh.

Jack put his hand on the small of my back, leading me closer to the passenger's seat. He unlocked the car door, and I yanked it open, struggling to fight off the questions and camera flashes that were being hurled my way. Jack had his hand in front of my face, shielding me from whatever he could long enough for me to slide myself inside the car, pulling the door shut behind me.

I sat in the car with my hand replacing where Jack's had been over my face as I waited for him to come around the other side of the car. Tape recorders and video cameras were pressed against my window, and I told myself to do some breathing. My heart was thumping against my chest and I kept looking at my lap and shaking my head with disbelief. Being the daughter of Harry Winters, I had definitely had some encounters with the paparazzi. But never before had they sprung out of nowhere in my school parking lot. The driver's door opened and the sound of the reporters' questions filled the car.

"Let's move," Jack said calmly, the car door shutting with a light thud.

"I don't even—"

"Don't worry," Jack said, clicking his seatbelt into place.

"You're safe now."

chapter
nineteen

WHEN I was in sixth grade, we had a "Secret Santa" thing in class for Christmas. It was around the time of the birth of my fake British accent, and I was used to doing some pretty heavy breathing in class. You can only imagine the damage my lungs incurred when I pulled Colin's name out of the glass bowl filled with roughly folded pieces of lined paper. Remember him? The reason I now live with the mortifying fake accent every time I get nervous? Yeah. That guy.

Needless to say his eyes widened with fear and I had to be sent to the nurse because I was sweating an abnormal amount. The poor guy thought I had probably rigged the whole thing just to get close to him. Which I didn't, I promise. But after the project when he had requested another partner, I really should have rigged it just to spite him. I decided that was my moment to make amends. Colin was going to love me and give up that restraining order his parents were probably considering. So naturally, I did what any twelve-year old would have done, and stole my dad's favorite Cartier watch and gave it to Colin. In glittery, pink wrapping paper.

Dad found out pretty much the next day and almost had a heart attack. He had this bug-eyed look on his face and he kept yelling that I was absolutely insane. Which I clearly was. But I was also a woman in love, which has to count for something. And I was like twelve, so he was also being little harsh. In the end the situation kind of worked itself out because Colin's parents mailed the watch back with a frosty thank you, but leave us alone letter. Colin moved schools about a month after, and my parents got divorced. Yeah, it was probably karma.

That was the one time I had seen my dad at his angriest. Not even during his arguments with Mom did I ever see him as red-faced as he was that day. That is, until I told him about the reporters at school.

"MAYBE YOU SHOULD JUST LET PRISON INMATES WALK AROUND YOUR CLASSES WHILE YOU'RE AT IT."

Dad had been yelling at our poor school principal for twenty minutes, threatening to take legal action if the lack of safety wasn't explained. I mean, he kind of had a point. With a school like ours, reporters shouldn't just be allowed to walk in and out whenever they please. But even still, it was totally embarrassing the way he was going on and on.

"Can't you get him to stop?" I whispered to Tori, Dad's assistant.

"Unlikely," she replied.

"I think it's good," Jack said, and I scowled.

We were all listening to the shouting coming from the TV room across the hall. Tori, whom I liked to consider my thirty-year-old "sister," had been on leave for the past three months, so I hadn't seen much of her in a while. What a day for her to come back. Al was somewhere else in the house too, speaking to news channel and magazine editors, trying to figure out who sent the reporters and why.

If things hadn't already hit the fan enough, Milo, Detective Reynolds and some guy called Officer Donovan were standing in the front hall, talking quietly amongst themselves. Every little while though, Milo would flick his eyes in my direction and I'd have to remind myself to breathe. Jack's phone buzzed and he picked it up off the counter, checking the screen.

"Mike and Chris are on their way back from school," he informed us, placing his phone back down and casually reaching over to grab an apple from the fruit bowl.

"Great!" I exclaimed, throwing my hands in the air in frustration. "We're back to the house arrest."

"G, I reckon it's probably better this way," Tori said, placing a hand on my thigh comfortingly. "This guy is clearly off his rocker. You're safer in the house."

I knew she was right, and let's face it, worse things could happen than staying at home with a full supply of wifi and Anya's baked goods. But I would have liked to open a damn window without an invisible ankle monitor sending alarm sounds to my dad's brain.

"Where's Kenny?" Jack asked, swallowing a bite of the apple.

I shrugged, fixing my eyes on Milo. He looked up and I diverted my gaze to the ceiling. Good one, Gia.

"No clue," I mumbled.

Jack leaned against the fridge, taking another bite of the apple. "Maybe he's with Anya."

I narrowed my eyes at him as if he were insane. "What's that supposed to mean?" I asked him.

He gave a light shrug in return, tilting his lips up in a

half-smile. "Nothing. They just get along, that's all."

Okay, I had seen a lot of crazy in the last few months. Enough to last me a lifetime, in fact. But an Anya and Kenny romance wasn't something I was ready to stomach.

"That's . . ." I began, failing to find the right words. Jack raised his eyebrows expectantly, and Tori gave a quiet laugh. "Just, not okay."

"Gia," I heard Milo say, and we all turned to look at him standing in the doorframe, looking all adorable in his uniform. "Can I talk to you for a second?"

I froze on the spot, glancing at Jack. I couldn't go talk to Milo by myself! I'd blurt out the truth about the Coco Club and then Dad would find out and his hair would probably start falling out from anger or something. Is that even possible? Who knows, it's a weird world. On the other hand, I kind of needed to tell Milo about the Coco Club or else he'd continue to think Jack was somehow involved with Dr. D. Besides, I would be covered by police officer-client privilege, which I'm about eighty percent sure is a real thing.

"Gia?" Milo repeated, and I snapped out of my thoughts.

"Yeah, sorry! S—sure. Give me a sec."

Milo nodded and gave me a tiny smile, disappearing back into the front hall. I turned to Jack, who had temporarily given up on the apple in his hand and was watching me thoughtfully.

"I need to tell him, Jack," I whispered.

"Ooo, tell him what?" Tori said, leaning in closely. "By the way, he is *gorgeous.*"

"Yeah, just swell," Jack said under his breath.

"Sorry?" Tori asked, looking up.

"Nothing," Jack said, shaking his head. "Gia, tell him what you want. Honestly, it's not a big deal."

There he went again with his infuriating disinterest in anything that concerned Milo. One of these days, when I wasn't being stalked by a psycho or the paparazzi, I was going to sit the two of them down and have a mediation session. Maybe. Probably not. I took a deep breath and walked out of kitchen. I was suddenly craving chocolate cake, and not just because it was almost my time of month. The way I was going, I was going to end up with no boyfriend and forty extra pounds.

"Did you want to go somewhere private?" Milo asked almost immediately as I approached him.

"Sure. We can go to the study."

"OH YEAH?" Dad was shouting, and I cringed with embarrassment. "WELL SAME TO YOU, BUDDY."

I led the way down the hall as quickly as I could, giving Detective Reynolds, who was also on the phone, an embarrassingly childish wave.

"So how's it goi—" I began, attempting to make light conversation.

"We really need to talk," Milo interrupted, as I swung the study door open.

Okay then. No time for pleasantries. No place for hello, hi, how are you, let's get married. Milo looked around the room, seemingly impressed. I never went to the study, but it was private enough for the conversation we were about to have. Plus, the burgundy leather couch was super shiny and the room looked like something out of a Sherlock Holmes novel, which only seemed fitting. I closed the door behind us, but left it the tiniest bit ajar.

"Listen, about the phone call . . ." I said.

"You need to stay away from Jack," Milo cut in. He said it so simply, as if I had asked him the time.

"I'm sorry, what?"

"Look," Milo told me, his voice softening just a little. "I'm not really supposed to be telling you this stuff, but I want you to be careful. He's not who you think he is."

"Milo, I know he was at the Coco Club," I said, shaking my

head at how messy this whole situation had become. "I was there too!"

"No you weren't," he said, as if he knew the events of the night better than I did.

I let out a little sigh. "Yeah I was."

"But you weren't on the security footage."

"You know the blonde girl talking to Claudia?"

"Yeah . . ."

"That would be me."

Milo's eyes widened in surprise and his gaze moved to my hair.

"But you're not blonde" he said, and I nodded at him like he had just discovered the cure for cancer.

"It was a wig," I explained. "And then we went and asked Claudia some questions about Dr. D, and she told us pretty much everything she told you."

Milo took a minute to process this silently, and I bit my lip. Hopefully he thought I made a hot blonde and wasn't concentrating on the totally insane plan.

"You're underage," he said finally, and I was sure there was a question in there somewhere.

"Yeah, I don't think you want to hear those details."

Milo shook his head at me and massaged the bridge of his nose with his thumb and index finger in frustration. Poor guy. I was seriously pushing some boundaries here.

"Wait a minute," he said, snapping his head back into attention. "The napkin. Claudia said there was a napkin she gave to the blonde girl. Which is you, I guess."

"I still have it," I assured him. "It's in my room. I have a photo of it on my phone if you want to see."

I pulled my phone out from my pocket and opened the photograph up. Milo shook his head at me again as he took it. Good one, Gia. He was definitely going to need therapy after this case was over.

"Any clue what this says?" he asked me, his eyebrows knitting together with concentration as he tried to decipher the message.

"No, but I think it's Chinese. My skills are kind of lacking in that department."

"I'll get it checked out." Milo replied, turning the picture sideways.

Milo handed my phone back to me. "I'm going to need that napkin. And I need to take another look at the footage. Now that we know the blonde woman is you and not an accomplice, we can try to get a clear shot of the man in the brown coat. Did you see his face at all?"

I shook my head no. "He disappeared the moment Jack and I chased him outside."

"Yeah, I saw that on the tape."

"Did you manage to get a good look at Dr. D on the video footage?" I asked him hopefully.

"Not as good as we would have liked," Milo told me, and I tried not to show my disappointment. "He was pretty good at hiding from the camera's view."

"Damn it!"

"Yeah," Milo agreed grimly. "Unfortunately we don't know the specific details of all the times he's visited the place. We can't exactly pull the footage for every single day. We would be here for months."

"You're not going to tell my dad are you?" I asked him, suddenly remembering the cost at which this revelation would come. "Technically we weren't supposed to be at the Coco Club that night."

"I kind of have to, Gia," Milo said with a frown. "I mean, I can try to be delicate about it. But I would recommend that you don't try to question anyone else while this investigation is going on. It could be dangerous."

"No more personal investigations, I swear," I told him, only half believing it. Besides, Dad was already furious. There was no point in hiding anything now. "How do you think Dr. D knew we were going to be at the Coco Club that night?"

"Well," Milo said. "It's possible he trailed your car without you noticing, although I doubt it. The security at the front of the house would pick up on any suspicious cars parked right outside."

"The last bug," I said, the thought suddenly popping into my head. "The one we never found."

"Where did you and Jack discuss the details for the Coco Club?"

I cast my mind back, fully aware I was going to be no help. "Initially, at one of the Golden Globe events. After that, all around the house really. The kitchen, the TV room . . ." I paused, flicking my eyes to the ground. "My bedroom."

"It was probably the bug that told him," Milo said. "Which, unfortunately, could be anywhere."

I looked up at him. "Sorry," I said, as if I was causing such an inconvenience. It definitely felt like that.

"Gia, there's no need to apologize!" he replied, almost laughing. "None of this is your fault! And you were honest about the Coco Club."

"Yeah but—"

"But this doesn't change things about Jack. He's still a person of interest."

Hold up. I had watched enough NCIS episodes to know that wasn't a good thing.

"Milo," I said calmly, leaning against the back of an armchair. "Jack isn't a person of interest. He's not a person of anything. He's . . . Jack! He's my bodyguard."

Milo gave me an *oh really* look and raised his eyebrows. "Fine," he said, even though I knew it so wasn't fine. "Then tell me why every time Dr. D has called, Jack's never been around."

"Yes he has! He was around that one time when . . ."

I racked my brains, trying to think of all the times Dr. D had called.

"Yes?" Milo asked expectantly, as he watched me prove his own point.

"Oh I got it!" I cried, throwing my hands in the air in excitement. "The first time Dr. D called! Jack and I were in the kitchen and the phone was on speaker! There!"

I did an internal victory dance, and then told myself to snap out of it. Defending Jack was not meant to give me that much pleasure, especially when it involved Milo on the receiving end.

"Fine. What about that time he was supposedly in the shower?"

"Remind me of that time again."

"The time when he even mentioned me right at the end of the phone call."

"Oh," I said. "He really was in the shower!"

Or so he said. It's not like I could guarantee it. I'm pretty sure that would have involved crossing some boundaries.

"Okay," Milo said, accepting my lack of proof. "What about today? Where was Jack when he called today?"

"Jack dropped the car keys in sc—" I thought about saying school. It made me seem childish. Although I was talking to a police officer. If he couldn't figure out that I was still in high school then we've got ourselves a problem. "Inside the building. He went back to get them when Dr. D called."

"He was gone pretty long, don't you think?"

"My friend Veronica saw the keys lying on the floor and took them with her. Jack had to chase her all the way down the hallway to get them back."

Milo looked at me sympathetically, as if he felt sorry that I actually believed Jack was with Veronica.

"Did you know," he began slowly, "That if Jack's father dies, he stands to inherit millions?"

I opened my mouth and closed it again. Nope. Wasn't aware of that one.

"I don't understand. What?"

"And I don't mean one or two million," Milo continued, pleased that he had hit a nerve in my Jack is Innocent campaign. "I'm talking *hundreds* of millions."

"But that's just cra—"

"Crazy?" Milo finished for me. "Yeah, it does seem a little odd. Ask yourself this, Gia. Why would someone who has a *trust fund* need a job as a bodyguard for celebrities?"

"Trust fund?" I repeated incredulously, and Milo nodded. "No, you've obviously made a mistake. Jack's not rich. He can't be!"

I thought back to what Jack had said about his father. If they didn't get along then why would his dad have set up a trust fund for him? That didn't add up.

"Can't he?" Milo said. "Dr. D's got to be getting his money from somewhere, right? That restaurant isn't worth anything! Of course, I don't know what Jack's motive would be, but—"

"Motive? Wait, what? Slow down!" I cried, backing away from Milo, my head spinning in confusion. "This doesn't make sense. Jack . . . he's not Dr. D."

"He could be working for him?" Milo said, and I shook my head fiercely.

"No. No, that's not possible! That doesn't make any sense."

And it didn't. I mean, not really.

"Gia," Milo said softly, taking a step toward me. His tone sounded like he was telling a five-year-old that her puppy died. "There's a lot more about him that you should probably know."

"Well I don't want to know!" I declared, holding my hands up in attempt to stop him from continuing.

It was absolutely insane. Jack couldn't possibly be involved with Dr. D. He was Jack! He was *so* not a criminal mastermind. Although he was pretty slick. I mean, he wasn't Bruce Wayne, let-me-keep-my-identity-hidden, but he wasn't exactly handing out autobiographies to strangers. He couldn't possibly be the bad guy in this equation.

"Alright," Milo said quietly, accepting defeat. "I understand that. But I'm going to keep looking into this, whether you approve or not. My job is to keep you safe, from whoever."

"I can't stop you from doing your job," I told him with a sigh. "But I can't know about anything you find."

"Your dad's asking for you," Jack's bored voice came from behind me, making me jump a little.

Milo and I turned to look toward the study door, where Jack was leaning casually against the frame, arms loosely crossed. I had no idea how long he had been standing there, or how much he had heard, but there was no way he would have been pleased by our conversation.

"I'll see you in a minute," Milo said to me quietly, taking a long stride to the door and pushing past Jack without making eye contact with him.

"How much of that did you hear?" I asked him finally, after a few seconds of silence.

"How much of what did I hear?"

I opened my mouth to elaborate, then closed it again. He clearly hadn't heard. I mean, that was a pretty relationship-damaging conversation. If he had heard Milo talking about his little research plan then he would have said something. Besides, if he *had* heard and was playing the fool, I wasn't going to go announce what we were talking about. I'd just play along. Cool as a cucumber.

"Never mind."

It was only just noon and I was ready to crawl back into bed and never get out. Between getting mobbed by a group of paparazzi and being photo-shopped onto a whale, I was having the worst day in the history of the world. Oh, and finding out my hot bodyguard and dare I say it, *friend*, might also be evil wasn't much help either.

"I had to tell Milo about the napkin," I told Jack, fidgeting nervously with the fringe on my shirt.

He shrugged. "Alright."

Jack's phone buzzed in his hands and my heart skipped a beat. What if that was Dr. D giving him further instructions? What if some other rich guy was transferring millions into Jack's account as I stood there watching him? Suddenly a million possibilities were swimming around in my mind, and I didn't know how to make sense of them all.

"You're on E! News," Jack said, raising an eyebrow.

"*Already?*"

Okay, I'm not an idiot. I knew news of the reporters ambushing me wasn't going to stay hidden for long. But damn, the E! Network moves fast!

"Turn on the TV," Jack said.

I reached for the remote and turned on the plasma across the room. Jack moved into the room beside me, just as I found what we were looking for. My heart sank as I watched my shocked face stare back at me on the television screen.

"*I—I really can't comment,*" I was saying, and I covered my eyes my hand, as if I were watching a horror movie.

"Oh lord," I groaned, sinking onto the leather sofa.

"It's not that bad!" Jack assured me, taking a seat next to me. He leaned in, resting his elbows on his knees. "I mean, your hair looks cute."

I groaned some more, watching my embarrassingly dumbstruck face on TV through parted fingers.

"Dear God, why?" I wailed, as footage of Jack shielding my face with his hand came on screen.

"Is that really what I look like from the back?" Jack asked himself more than me. "Wow, I look *good.*"

I lowered my hand and forced myself to watch the television screen, muting the TV so that I didn't have to hear the questions being flung at me all over again.

"Your hand," I said, pointing at the TV screen in horror. "Is ridiculously low on my body! You're practically groping me!"

Jack watched the screen with concentration, a grin threatening to appear on his face. I pointed again as his hand rested on my lower back, as he eased me into the car.

"I was protecting you!" Jack replied, the grin fully evident now.

"You were protecting my ass."

"And I succeeded. Nothing happened to it."

"There you are!" Dad said suddenly, appearing in the doorway. "I was yelling out your name. Why are there pictures of you with colored-in teeth stuffed into our mailbox?"

I looked at Jack with widened eyes. Meghan, the spawn of Satan, had resorted to tormenting me on a domestic level!

"Oh God . . ." I picked up a cushion and buried my face in it.

Hopefully if I clasped my eyes shut for long enough, I'd be floating on a rainbow when I opened them.

"Oh fantastic," I heard Dad say sarcastically. "News has spread."

I guessed he was looking at the TV screen. This was worse than cramps and math tests put together.

"Just ignore the flyers, sir," Jack said. "They're not important."

"Good. Because right now, I've got a bigger problem to deal with," Dad replied.

"What now?" I cried, looking up at the chandelier in disbelief. "What could possibly be wrong now?"

Dad took a deep breath that told me he needed a drink, and

blew out a sigh.

"Your mother is flying in tonight," he told me. "She heard about the reporters and is *furious*. But more importantly, she's worried about your outfit for the Golden Globes."

Rehearsals! I had completely forgotten that I had rehearsals that afternoon. Now I had to go and get barked at for three hours while I stumbled like an idiot across the stage. And now I had to deal with Mom? She was all the way in New York! Which meant my friends and the rest of the school would have heard about the reporters by now as well. News travels faster than STDs amongst teenagers in L.A. I just couldn't deal with my friends asking questions about being stalked and me moving to New York. Which reminded me, was I actually being shipped to New York to live with my mother like that reporter said?

At this stage, I didn't care if Dad was ready to ship me to Madagascar in a wooden box. I needed a break. Big time.

c h a p t e r
t w e n t y

"OW!"

That was the fifteenth time I had been poked by a pin in the last hour, and I was less than pleased. My bedroom had been transformed into a makeshift boutique, and I was clearly the mannequin on display. My mother stood watching me from across the room, hands on hips, eyeing me uncertainly as I stood there with my arms stretched out by my side, while two Filipino women continued to use me as their human pincushion. Jack was sitting on my couch, occasionally looking up from his phone to laugh whenever I got poked. It seemed Jack had officially become less of a bodyguard in the house, and more of an adopted son. I was on my way to being replaced.

"The top needs to be tighter," Mom said, more to herself

than anyone else.

"Can't I just pin it?" I asked, knowing fully well the answer was going to be a flat no. "It's better than becoming Swiss cheese."

"Gia!" Mom said sharply. "Monique was kind enough to do this fitting in our house rather than her boutique to avoid the media. The least you can do is suck it up and quit complaining while these kind ladies sew you into this dress that cost me thousands."

Couldn't argue with that. I dropped my eyes and looked at gown that was pinned all over. It *was* beautiful. I mean, worse things could have happened. Well, for some. Mom had been in the house three days and Dad was already on the verge of having an anxiety attack. She cared far less about the reporters coming to school than she did about that little Photoshop stunt. She'd spent an entire day yelling about how she was going to make the Adamses pay, laughing at Meghan's mother's "botched nose job." It was pure luck that while my life was in shambles in L.A., my mother had busied herself in New York with finding the perfect dress for me to wear at the Golden Globes. And boy, had she found it.

Mom's friend Monique Lhuillier had been working on a collection that hadn't been released to the public yet. The collection was every girl's dream, and I couldn't believe I was standing in a part of it. Mom practically cried every time she was reminded that the dress wasn't made especially for me, but with such short notice, I was beyond a lucky Cinderella.

The one-shouldered, deep purple gown was breathtaking. It just looked out-of-place on me, especially with the messy bun positioned high up on my head. The silk felt cool against my skin, and I fingered the flowing net material, careful not to lower my aching arms too much and get poked again.

"We'll have to go get you some jewelry," Mom said, biting her thumb fingernail thoughtfully.

I winced as one of the ladies poked the skin under my breast. Hopefully that would be a less painful process than this.

"I need heels too," I reminded her.

"Jesus, Gia," Mom said, shaking her head. "You really have no breasts at all!"

"*Mom!*"

I glanced at Jack, who was looking back at me with a wide smile on his face. His gaze lowered to my chest and he feigned a thoughtful look. I rolled my eyes. Good job, Mom. Go ahead and announce my lack of endowment to the world.

"I need to get you a new push-up bra."

"Kill me now."

"I mean, honestly," Mom said, clearly talking to herself. She looked at my chest, shaking her head some more. "Here I am, desperately try to get you to cut back on junk food, and no breasts is how I'm being rewarded."

"Mom!" I snapped in horror, and she looked up at me. "Less junk. No breasts. Got it. We don't need to keep talking about it."

"Oh!" Mom cried, as if she had suddenly remembered something. "I need to make sure your outfit is ready for tonight's *W Magazine* event."

Of course. The magazine event. It seemed everything was being sprung on me last minute, and I was just expected to show up and look pretty whenever I was told to. Mom had actually been invited to the event to "celebrate style icons," but the editors had suddenly decided that it would be good publicity to invite this year's Miss Golden Globe to come along and make an appearance, maybe even get an informal interview out of her.

Mom whipped out her phone, business face on, and walked past me as she typed away furiously.

"Wait!" I cried, as she reached the bedroom door. I craned my neck as best as I could in my statue position to see her. "Don't leave me here with the pokey twins!" I hissed, motioning toward the dress fitters who were working away like mad scientists.

"I'll be right back," Mom called behind her shoulder, strutting out of the room in her Louboutin pumps.

Jack stifled a laugh as I blew out a frustrated sigh.

"Quit laughing at me!" I whined. "My arms are going to fall off!"

"You look like a giant grape" Jack said, tilting his head to one side as he eyed me up and down.

My mouth dropped. "How dare you? This dress is amazing! Or at least it will be once it fits."

"The push-up bra will help, no doubt."

"If I ever get out of this, I'm going to kill you."

The two helpers exchanged words in a language I didn't understand and stopped pinning my dress.

"One. One minute," one of them said, with a heavy accent.

She held up her index finger, pointing it at the sky, as if indicating the number one. I nodded to let her know I understood, and she smiled. They left the room together, leaving me in my hanging grape costume.

"This is just fantastic," I grumbled.

I could barely move my body and now I was stuck in a room with Jack, who would undoubtedly continue to make fun of me. And Famous didn't count, because all he ever did was lie there. Plus he couldn't stick up for me, and he probably wouldn't have even if he could. Even *he* liked Jack more than me.

I shuffled around so that I was facing Jack. A few seconds later, my brother walked slowly past my room, stopped in the center of the doorframe, eyed me up and down and shook his head. He then proceeded to disappear out of sight, doing what looked like The Robot. Chris was right behind, glancing in my direction and then quickly averting his gaze to the floor as if I were Medusa, ready to turn him to stone. I watched as they walked away, shaking my head.

"We need to get him checked out."

Jack looked up. "Who?"

"Chris. He doesn't speak at all! It's not normal."

"Oh, I thought you meant your brother," Jack replied, turning his attention back to his phone.

"Yeah, him too actually."

The pokey twins re-entered the room, and a few seconds later, Mom followed.

"Here's your dress," she said, holding up a pink and silver dress on a hanger.

"Mom!" I cried, eyeing the dress up and down. "I can't wear that!"

She looked at the dress in confusion. "Why not? It's Balmain!"

Yeah, which was exactly the problem. I waddled closer to the hanger she was holding, feeling the material that was perfectly bandaged into a one-sleeved mini dress. There was no way in hell I'd be able to pull a dress like *that* off. The sad thing was, my mother probably could.

"It's very . . ." I trailed off, and Mom rolled her eyes. Clearly she knew where I was headed.

"Gia, you've got the body." She eyed me up and down. "Well more or less. A few more carrots wouldn't hurt. I don't understand why you don't flaunt it! Tell her Jack."

I turned to Jack with raised eyebrows. He smiled in reply, nodding his head in approval.

"Hot." Was all he said, and my mother nodded enthusiastically.

I widened my eyes in embarrassment. There was no way I was ever allowing my mother and Jack to interact again.

"You have male approval." Mom declared, as if it emphasized her point. "Now we can all move on with our lives."

"You take dress off," one of the pokey twins said.

"Um, how exactly?" I asked, turning to mom.

"They'll help you out," Mom replied, hanging the Balmain dress on my closet doorknob. "Just hold very still."

Easy for her to say; she could just stand there and watch.

"Anything else, mother dearest?" I asked her sweetly.

"You have an appointment for hair and nails at six. Go straight from rehearsals, and don't be late," she said, pulling out her phone from her pocket.

"Dad will never let me out of the house," I told her.

"I told Anya to make Italian tonight."

"Using his favorite food as a distraction. I like it."

"I've had a lot of experience manipulating your father."

Yeah, I didn't doubt it.

"Okay, time to change," I announced, waddling toward my helpers. "I need to get a stack of homework done before rehearsals today."

"I'll go supervise the boys in the kitchen," Mom said, walking toward the bedroom door. "Your father's making crème brûlée and I'm scared he's going to blowtorch Mike's eyebrows off."

I watched her walk out the room, lifting my arms so that the pokey twin could start relieving me from the dress.

"Jack," I said, suddenly remembering he was still in the room.

"Yes?"

"Get out. I'm changing."

Jack lay back against the couch pillows, resting his head on his fingers that were intertwined. He yawned, and one of the seamstresses unzipped my dress from behind.

"You take off dress," she said. "Slow. Slow."

"Jack!"

"I'll shut my eyes, I promise," he said innocently.

I knew there was no point in arguing with him. If I had learned anything from my time with Jack, it was that he was almost as good as me when it came to getting his way.

"Fine!" I snapped. "Close them. And if you even *accidently* blink, I'll set the pokey sisters on you."

He squeezed his eyes shut, making a big show of it as if it was such a complicated task. I rolled my eyes and let the gown sink to the floor; making sure Jack's eyes were closed. I grabbed my leggings and sweatshirt off the edge of my bed and put them on as fast as I could.

"Okay, three, two, one, I'm opening my eyes," Jack said, his eyelids fluttering open.

Thankfully I had managed to get the sweatshirt over my head and just past my bra in time. The last thing I needed was for Jack to see me half naked, especially after the macaroni and cheese I had demolished yesterday. The seamstresses carefully placed the gown on a hanger, holding it as if it were glass. I watched them carry the dress out of my bedroom, yelling out a thank you behind them.

"They seemed nice," Jack said. "Bit talkative though."

My phone buzzed on the couch beside Jack, who reached over to pick it up.

"Who is it?" I asked, removing stray strands of hair from my sleeve. "It's not one of the girls again, is it?"

The last few days had been a complete nightmare to deal with. My friends had been amazingly sweet and supportive about the whole flyers incident, and it killed me that I had to keep lying to them. They had called about a billion times after hearing about the reporters in the school parking lot, wanting to know if I was actually getting stalked. I had come inches away from telling them the truth, but decided not to at the last minute. The last thing I wanted was for Dr. D to target them as well. So instead I pretended that the rumors were completely baseless, and that Meghan had probably orchestrated it to drill home her Photoshop prank, and scare me right before the Golden Globes. I think they only half believed me. When they had come to drop off some homework and notes on what I'd missed, I'd hid in my closet like a coward and begged Jack to get rid of them for me. I know, I know. Not one of my proudest moments.

"Nope. Lover boy," Jack replied, as my phone continued to ring.

I paused for a second, trying to place the nickname in my memory. "Who?"

"Our favorite, Mr. Fells."

My eyes widened and I could feel the panic start to creep over me. Oh no. What if he was calling to say he had more information on Jack? I hadn't heard from him since our conversation the other day, and I spent the rest of the time trying not to think about Jack and his mystery trust fund.

"Give it to me!" I cried, launching toward the iPhone.

Jack moved out of my reach, answering the call. He was apparently trying to get me to die of shame.

"Well hey there, Cadet Fells," he said brightly, winking at me.

"Jack!" I hissed. "Give me the damn phone!"

Jack covered the speaker with his hand and whispered, "Say please."

"I'm going to hit you."

"Is Gia here?" Jack said into the phone. "No, sorry. You just missed her actually. You can tr—"

"Jack!"

"OW!"

I pounced on Jack, wrestling my phone out of his hands. His laughter had now become uncontrollable.

"Hello!" I practically yelled into the phone, a little breathlessly. I was still kind of sitting on Jack, who had buried his face in my pillow to muffle his laughter.

"Uh, hi," came the reply, and I could tell Milo was probably battling some Jack-hatred within. I could tell because I was doing the same.

"How's it going?" I asked, sliding off Jack and pushing the hair away from my face.

"Good," Milo replied, still sounding tense.

"Is everything okay? Any . . ." I glanced at Jack, who was still composing himself. "Updates on anything?"

I mouthed a *shut up* to Jack, who was still laughing a little as he fiddled with Famous' ears.

"We're tying up some leads actually. Ao Jie Kai's managed to slip away from us a few times, but I think we're getting close to getting some answers."

"That's good."

There was silence for a few seconds while I waited for him to continue, sitting on the edge of my bed in anticipation. Jack looked at me, but didn't say anything. His laughter had even died out. Evidently he was waiting to hear the rest of the conversation too.

"I guess," Milo said, "I just wanted to call to make sure we were cool. We left things kind of weird the other day."

"Um, yeah. We're cool," I replied, biting my thumbnail. Thank God I had a manicure at six.

"I'm sorry for coming down hard on you with the Jack stuff. I just want you to be safe."

I looked at Jack. He was still playing with Famous' ears but I could tell he was listening.

"It's okay. I get it."

This was *so* awkward! Why was this so hard? It was like I was six-years-old, talking to my crush in the sandpit. Apparently Milo felt the same.

"I'm just going to say it," he said. "This whole thing kind of sucks, right?"

I smiled, even though it was kind of depressing how right he was. "We're definitely a bit messed up."

"Plus, we had to share our first date with a pack of frisky firemen and a guy dressed like a taco. Not particularly ideal, if you ask me."

"Should have kept it simple with a dinner and a movie," I laughed.

"I'll have to remember that for next time."

My heart rate picked up speed. "Next time?" I repeated.

I dropped the smile when I suddenly remembered Jack was still in the room. He wasn't sitting close enough to hear what we were saying, but his gaze made me want to pee my pants. He was better at the disapproving dad face than my own father. Milo sighed. The fun and games had apparently stopped. There was obviously not going to be a "next time." Story of my damn life.

"I better go," he said. "We'll keep you updated on any new developments."

"Right." I said.

"Stay safe."

Could Jack, like, chill with his intense staring? His blue eyes were swallowing me whole!

"Thanks, old bean. See you!"

I hung up the phone, throwing it on the bed as if it had set fire in my hand.

"Did you just call Milo an old bean?" Jack asked, gathering Famous in his lap.

I buried my head in my hands. I was hoping by some miracle of the heavens above, Jack hadn't heard that last part.

"Oh God. Oh God. Oh God!" I groaned, shaking my head in my hands. "This is your fault! You were making me antsy with your staring!"

"Hey, don't blame me for your poor conversation skills."

"I'm trying my best here!"

"Princess," Jack said, raising an eyebrow. "That's your best?

Now you've got me worried about your worst."

"Don't you have anything else to do other than eavesdrop on my conversations?"

"I wasn't eavesdropping," he said, not even trying to mask his pleased smile. "I was just sitting here, minding my own business like the gentleman that I am."

Right. And I was the next Bond girl. I threw another pillow at Jack, who caught it in the air before it could land on him.

"Go away," I snapped. "I have a ton of homework and you're distracting me."

"There's something I don't like about Milo," Jack said. He wasn't smiling anymore.

I sighed. "I know. You've told me about a billion times."

"He takes advantage of you," Jack said, stroking the top of Famous' head. "He's practically a cop and you're vulnerable right now. It's just wrong."

"You're my bodyguard," I reminded him. "And I'm your client. You still flirt like there's no tomorrow. Isn't that wrong?"

Jack thought about it for a second. "Not the same thing," he said simply, placing Famous down next to him.

I rolled my eyes. "Jack, my practice essay isn't going to write itself."

"Okay, consider this," he pressed on, clearly ignoring my attempt to change the conversation. "What would you do if he wasn't in the picture?"

I rose from the bed, stretching my arms to the sky, stifling a yawn. "What do you mean?" I asked.

"I mean, what would happen if you didn't know Milo?"

I looked at him blankly. "Then I wouldn't know Milo?"

"No," Jack replied impatiently. He stood up, walking over to me. "Like, what would happen between us?"

My jaw almost hit the floor. Was he seriously asking me this? Did he not know that I was physically incapable of dealing with awkward situations?

"Us?" I echoed. "What? N—nothing. I mean . . . nothing! Yeah."

My flustered reaction was obviously exactly what Jack had been looking for, because he smiled some more, taking a step closer. Alarm bells were going off in my head. Abort mission! I repeat, this is not a drill!

"I guess I should be thanking Milo," Jack said, faking a thoughtful expression. "I mean, if it wasn't for him you'd probably be in love with me right now and *I'd* be on the receiving end of your terrible flirting skills."

They were not terrible! Sure, they were *questionable.* But hardly terrible.

"Get over yourself," I said with a scowl. "Not every girl is just *dying* to declare their love for you."

Granted I may not be on that list when Jack is wearing his leather jacket, but the message was still widely applicable. I turned to face my desk, thinking the conversation had ended, when he caught onto my wrist and pulled me onto the edge of the bed again. We sat facing each other, his hand still gripping mine, not allowing me to move. My heartbeat began to pick up speed as I tried not to look directly at Jack. I had no idea what had suddenly possessed him, there were little stop signs popping up left, right and center in my brain.

"What do you think you're doing?"

"So you're telling me that *nothing* would happen here?" He ignored my question, giving me a knowing look. "I mean, look at me Gia. I'm a Greek God. There's no way my flawless looks don't make you crazy."

Yeah, actually, they did make me crazy. Beyond the British accent crazy. At this rate, I was impressed I was even functioning with any normalcy.

"Nothing would happen," I declared, convincing myself

more so than him.

"Why?"

I gave him an incredulous look. His smile told me he was kidding—being the egotistical flirt he always was. But we'd never had a conversation like this before. And it felt like I was going down a black rabbit-hole.

"Because!" I cried, not yet knowing how to finish that sentence. "Because you don't see me that way."

"So you're saying *you* see *me* that way?"

"Of course not!"

"So then why not?"

"Because it just wouldn't!"

I had given up on making up excuses. It's what he did best; flirting, enchanting, making you fall in love. I had seen it first hand and I knew no one was immune from it. People like Jack are incredible at playing games, but aren't so great at the commitment thing. He couldn't care less about me before Milo was in the picture, but now suddenly he was asking me what ifs? I wasn't willing to risk falling for him only to get slapped in the face with disappointment. Better not follow that rabbit down the hole. I don't care how fancy his waistcoat is.

Jack's smile widened, as if portraying victory. He released my hand and said, "Alright."

"Well what would you do if Milo wasn't in the picture?" I asked him.

I wasn't entirely sure I wanted to hear the answer, but I didn't want to give him the satisfaction of winning. Fake it till you make it, Gia. In Hollywood, they practically drilled that into you the moment you left the womb. Jack cocked his head to one side, eyeing me thoughtfully. The smile remained on his face, but faltered slightly as he thought about something with evident concentration.

"Well . . ." he began finally. "If Milo wasn't in the picture, then you and I—"

My phone began ringing from behind me, and I held my breath. Seriously? Seriously! You and I what? You and I would be together forever? You and I would start a rave club? You and I could go grab some kebabs for lunch? There were millions of ways to finish that sentence!

"Aren't you going to answer that?" Jack asked, pointing to my phone.

Actually I was just about ready to scream in frustration.

"Um, yeah," I mumbled, reaching for my phone.

If it was one of the girls, I wasn't going to answer. If it was Dr. D, I was going to throw the damn thing out the window. It was Milo, ironically.

"Hello?"

"Gia, we're on our way over," Milo told me, his voice pressed with urgency. In the background I could hear the sound of cars.

"What's the matter?" I asked, glancing at Jack who was watching me carefully.

"We got him, Gia. We know who Dr. D is."

chapter
twenty-one

THE MOST important family meeting was held in the grand living room, which we only ever used for fancy parties. I sat nervously on one of the sofas, squished between Jack and my brother. My dad stood by his bar, glass of whiskey in hand, and Mom next to him. With the whole family, all the bodyguards, the housekeepers scattered about and three police officers, our massive house seemed to be running out of space.

The moment we had all been waiting for had finally arrived. Dr. D had been found. I was ready to put it all to bed, but I was petrified. My thoughts were running frantically across my mind. What if he looked like Hannibal Lecter and wanted to make a purse out of my skin? What if he was some fourteen-year-old kid who had way too much free time on his hands? Or what if he was actually a woman? Or an evil genius cat!

"Are you sure it's safe to speak in the house?" Dad asked the officers. "There might still be a listening device somewhere."

"I'm pretty sure the stalker knows his own identity, Harry," Mom said, and I suppressed a smile.

"Yes, I'm aware of that. Thank you Evelyn. I just meant—"

"It should be okay sir," Officer Donovan, the same cop from the other day, said. "At this stage it hardly matters."

"Sir," Detective Reynolds said to my father. "Does the name Gregory Mills mean anything to you?"

I racked my brain. That name sounded distantly familiar, but I couldn't quite place it.

"It's the name of a character I played once." Dad replied. "Way back in the day."

"And Jeremy Boyd?" Officer Donovan asked.

"I played him in a Wild West movie."

"What about Michael Barnes?"

"Another character," Dad replied almost instantly.

Detective Reynolds turned to Officer Donovan, giving him a nod as if confirming something they had discussed before. Milo was standing next to his colleagues in silence, his face expressionless.

"Mr. Winters," Detective Reynolds said, "We had to follow a long trail of aliases to finally get to where we are now. It seems this Dr. D was managing the Dumpling Hospital under a number of pseudonyms, all of which seem to be characters you've played in movies."

"So you're saying he stole these names from Harry's movies to keep changing his identity?" Mom asked.

"That's right," Detective Reynolds nodded. "The ownership of the Dumpling Hospital has changed three times since its opening five years ago. Each time, it's the same person who owns it, but under a different name."

"What's the point of that?" Mike asked, leaning forward on the couch. "Why would you sell yourself a restaurant you already own?"

It pained me, but I actually agreed with him for once. The whole thing didn't make any sense. It was like me putting up an autograph from my dad on eBay and then bidding on it myself. Why wouldn't I just keep the damn thing in the first place?

"It covers his tracks," Officer Donovan answered for the detective. "He probably knew the Dumpling Hospital was a good way to catch him. But by making it seem like ownership has changed three times, no one presumes it's the same person. And no one suspects anything's off because the person selling is also the person buying. There's no third party to raise questions. Management stays the same, so the staff don't care either."

Okay, I had *seriously* underestimated how crafty Dr. D was.

"So who is he?" Dad said, asking the question that hung in the air.

I held my breath, praying to the heavens high above that Milo wouldn't point a finger at Jack in reply.

"His name is Frank Parker," Detective Reynolds told him.

All eyes in the room fixated on Dad, waiting for his reaction. His eyes widened as he tightened the grip around his glass.

"You've got to be kidding me," Dad whispered, massaging the bridge of his nose between pinched fingers.

"Frank Parker?" Mom repeated, looking confused.

"Who is that?" I said, looking from one parent to another.

"S—surely there's some mistake," Dad said, almost pleading with Detective Reynolds to confirm it was all a misunderstanding.

"Hello?" I cried, waving my hands to try and get his attention. "Dad! Who is that? Who's Frank Parker?"

"He was . . ." Dad began, looking at Mom nervously. "He was my best friend in college. We went to Tisch together."

"Seriously?" Mike said, as my mouth dropped open in

surprise. "You actually know this guy?"

"Frank Parker," Detective Reynolds read off the paper in his hand. "Forty-eight years old. Never married. No kids. Moved to L.A. six years ago."

While Detective Reynolds was speaking, Milo handed Dad a piece of paper. As it crossed hands, I caught a glimpse of an enlarged photo, as if taken as a screen shot from a video. The photo was blurry but I recognized the brown jacket. It must have been from the Coco Club footage.

"We captured this from cameras close to a payphone he used," Milo added.

I looked at Milo, but he didn't look back. I wondered if he was thinking about when he had accused Jack of being behind the phone calls. Looks like he was majorly wrong about that one.

"So you're saying Frank is Dr. D?" Dad clarified, like he was being Punk'd.

"Yes, sir," Detective Reynolds replied. He turned back to the paper and continued to read. "Bought the Dumpling Hospital a year after its opening. The place was on the verge of shutting down. Apparently they didn't even have enough money to pay their staff."

"Okay, hold up a second," Kenny said in his deep voice. "I think one of y'all needs to explain why this so-called best friend has gone crazy ass on us all."

"Yeah, Dad," Mike agreed. "Why has he gone crazy ass on us all?"

"Us all?" I repeated, glaring at my brother. "I don't recall you being stalked! Crazy ass on just me, more like!"

"Okay can everyone shut up for a second so your father can explain?" Mom said, and everyone fell silent. "Because I think we *all* need an explanation."

"Frank and I were like brothers," Dad began, shaking his head in disbelief. "He never had a lot growing up, but he was in love with movies. He was a bit of a loner back then. I was really his only friend."

"So what happened?" Kenny asked.

"Well," Dad said. "We shared the same the agent. A man named Martin Fulbridge. One day the call came for my first ever movie, my big break. I mean, I was so excited! But Frank wasn't happy for me. He was angry, and I couldn't figure out why, and he would never tell me. We had a huge fight and that was it. We fell out of touch and we never spoke again. I heard a few years later that he went overseas."

The room was silent for a few seconds as we all played out Dad's story in our heads. None of it made any sense. Dad had a best friend who randomly stopped talking to him when he was finally becoming successful? Actually it did make sense.

"So he was jealous?" Mike asked, reading my mind.

Dad shrugged. "I couldn't tell you for sure, Mike. He never told me."

"I have a question," I announced, raising my palm to my side like I was being sworn in at court. "Why am I being stalked if he's got a problem with Dad? Why not Mike, or Dad himself?"

"Gia!" Mom said sharply, as if I had just called someone a fat cow.

"What?" I replied. "I'm serious. Why am I being stalked and no one else? That doesn't seem very fair to me."

Beside me, Jack stifled a laugh.

"Actually," Officer Donovan said. "Your daughter has a point. Do you have any idea why he would choose to target Gia, and *only* Gia?"

"Maybe he thought hurting Gia would be the easiest way to get to him," Kenny suggested.

"But hurting Mike wouldn't?" Jack replied. "That can't be it."

"Maybe he didn't know about Mike," I said.

"I highly doubt he didn't know about Mike. This guy's clearly done his research," Jack said, looking at me like I was an idiot.

"Maybe he thought I was too awesome to stalk?" Mike proposed.

"Or maybe he didn't think you were smart enough to know you were being stalked," I replied.

"Fascinating theories," Detective Reynolds cleared his throat. "But we can really only speculate at this point."

"So now what?" Mom asked. I hadn't seen her this stressed since there was talk a few years ago of potentially closing the Chanel store on Rodeo Drive. "Can't we catch this Frank guy now that we know who he is?"

"We've sent officers to his address, but someone who plans this carefully isn't going to be stupid enough to live at home. I wouldn't expect much."

"So where would he be living then?" Kenny asked.

"Probably a relative's house. Possibly a friend, or someone he trusts," Officer Donovan said.

"Do you know if he had any family living in L.A.?" Detective Reynolds asked Dad.

"Not that I'm aware of," he replied. "Frank's mother left when he was twelve and his father must be long gone by now. He was never in good health. As far as I know he was an only child."

Oh great. Mommy issues. Just what my stalker was lacking.

"We'll continue our investigation," Detective Reynolds assured us, nodding firmly. He lowered his voice to almost a whisper, most likely trying to avoid the hidden device catching any information. If the situation wasn't so screwed up, I'd have laughed. "We've put out an APB on the UCLA student. His roommates say he hasn't been around for over a week now, and his mother hasn't heard from him."

"In the meantime," Officer Donovan continued in an equally quiet voice. "I suggest we discuss plans for the Golden Globe ceremony."

"Why can't we arrest him now? Why do we have to wait until the Golden Globes?" Mom asked, not bothering to whisper.

"Yeah," Kenny added with a nod. "And what exactly does this guy think he can pull off at such a high-profile event? There'll be security everywhere; even more now that we know he's planning to do something on the night."

"We can only arrest him if we find him," Milo replied. "As we said before, its unlikely Frank Parker is living at home. We'll investigate his work place as well, but right now it seems like our best bet is the Golden Globes."

"I'd have to agree," Detective Reynolds said grimly. "It's not an ideal situation, but as you said, there'll be security everywhere."

"I'm sorry," Dad said, looking at Milo in confusion. "What did you say your name was again?"

Oh my God. NOT cool Dad. I know Milo was just the quiet cadet, but my dad should at least be aware of his future son-in-law's name!

"What guarantee is there that he won't strike before then?" Jack asked, breaking into the awkwardness. "What if the entire Golden Globes thing is just a distraction so we'll all be caught off guard when he makes a move?"

"Yeah," Kenny added with an enthusiastic nod. "Who's to say this guy won't try something before?"

"This man is all about timing," Detective Reynolds said. "The phone calls all cut *just* before he knows we can trace it back to him. The reporters at the school appeared almost immediately after he hung up. This man is extremely particular about time."

"It's about the performance," Officer Donovan added with a nod. "Theatrics. I don't think he's going to strike before he says he will."

"Gia," Mom said with an exhausted sigh. "Are you sure you want to do this, kiddo? People will understand if you pull out.

They brought you in so last minute anyway."

I shook my head at her before she had even finished speaking. "I'm not going to just sit here and hide. I'm not running away from this guy, and I'm *definitely* not giving up an opportunity like this for some psycho!"

I also didn't want to pull out because Carol would most likely stab me, and I was way more scared of her than I was of Dr. D.

"So then it's settled," Jack said. "The Golden Globes is where we catch the guy."

"Where *we* catch the guy," Milo corrected him quietly, and I looked at him awkwardly.

He didn't return my gaze. Instead his eyes were fixated on Jack.

"Yeah, that's what I just said," Jack said.

"Now we just have to wait until he makes contact again," Detective Reynolds said. "Or else we won't know what he's planning for the day. I doubt he's the type of guy who would parachute down on stage and hold Gia hostage in front of a room full of celebrities."

He chuckled to himself, obviously imagining that scene playing out in his head. Boy was he going to be sorry if that happened.

"I'll tie up some loose ends," Officer Donovan declared. "We were able to get the napkin figured out. It's the number five in Mandarin. Does that mean anything to anyone?"

"Not really," I replied, confused. Nothing important was standing out.

"Wait, what napkin?" Dad asked. Obviously Milo hadn't told him about the Coco Club.

"I'll explain later, Dad," I told him quickly, giving Jack a nervous glance.

"Hold on a second," Mike said, leaning forward thoughtfully. "Is this Frank guy the reason we got the bodyguards?"

I looked at Mike, then at Dad. Everyone else in the room did the same.

"Actually," I said, nodding. "Yeah. You said you hired us protection because our lives could be in danger. You have to have known something was happening to do that!"

"I . . . got a photograph in the mail," Dad said casually, but he wasn't making eye contact. I could tell he had been put on the spot. "It was an old photo of me and Frank. Only, there was a giant red cross drawn across my face."

He said it so matter-of-factly, as if I had asked him if anything good was on TV that night.

"Oh my God!" Mom cried, putting a hand to her lips in concern. "Harry!"

"You didn't tell us this?" I exclaimed, my eyes widening in disbelief. "Dad, how could you keep something like that from us? That could have helped get him a long time ago!"

"I know!" Dad replied, throwing his hands in the air. "Look, I know! But I didn't know for sure if it was him. I didn't want to jump to conclusions."

Or, he wanted to protect his psychotic best friend because my dad was far too much of a nice guy.

"We'll need to see that photograph, Mr. Winters," Detective Reynolds said calmly, clearly trying to restore peace to the conversation.

Dad nodded grimly, his face becoming pale. I felt kind of bad, but I also felt furious. We had been running around in circles for weeks while I continued to be tormented, and all this time Dad had the biggest clue of all hidden away somewhere in the house.

"We'll let you know when we find anything else," Officer Donovan said, eyes shifting around the room awkwardly. I was a hundred percent certain the LAPD had never experienced craziness to this level before.

"I can't *believe* you kept this from all of us!" Mom practically exploded. She looked just about ready to chuck the whiskey bottle at Dad's face.

I rose from the sofa and did some heavy breathing as my parents argued. Watching their divorce sort of set off instant dread the moment they so much as disagreed now. But this wasn't a disagreement. Mom was livid, and I couldn't blame her. Detective Reynolds was trying to calm the situation down to the best of his abilities, but his luck was running short. Mike decided that was a good opportunity for him to start arguing with Officer Donovan about why we couldn't just "get the asshole when he was in the shower, or something," to which the officer calmly explained that they didn't actually know *where* he was showering. Jack and Kenny began a hushed conversation to my right, as Chris silently watched on, which left me staring right at Milo. As usual. His eyes met mine and he crossed the room toward me. No one was even paying attention amidst the commotion Mom was causing by the bar.

"Hi," I said softly.

"Hi."

"Sorry about all of this," I told Milo. "We're all nuts."

"Listen," he said seriously. "I know this is a lot. But we know who he is now, and we're close to getting him. We're not going to let anything happen to you."

I stared at him for a few seconds, not really knowing how to respond. Usually when Milo was standing inches away from me, my thoughts involved removing items of his clothes. But this time I just wanted to hug him. Instead, I gave him a half-assed smile.

"You trust me right?" he asked.

"Of course!" I replied, without a second thought. "We found the guy! I couldn't have done that without you. Plus, now we know Jack isn't involved."

"Well—"

"Milo."

The look on Milo's face was a giving away pretty good hints that he was pretty certain Jack was still involved, but just didn't want to make a scene in front of everyone. After all, that hefty trust fund was still a mystery worthy of Scooby-Doo.

"Well," Milo said. "Do you trust him?"

He looked over my head, and I followed his gaze behind me. Kenny was saying something to Jack, but he wasn't paying attention. His gaze was locked on me, jaw tightened.

Did I trust Jack? Boy, wasn't that the burning question in everyone's mind.

c h a p t e r
t w e n t y - t w o

"LADIES AND gentlemen, this year's Mr. and Miss Golden Globe!"

I took a deep breath and gave myself a nod of encouragement. This was it. No more time to waste.

Carol pointed at the curtain and impatiently hissed, "Go! That's your cue!"

Dylan and I walked toward the curtain, with the sound of thunderous clapping making my ears ring. I kept telling myself it wasn't hard. All I needed to do was walk on stage, smile a little bit and then walk off. Really not groundbreaking stuff.

I did some more excessive breathing right as my Hermés pumps touched the stage floor in a feeble attempt to calm my nerves. I, Gia Winters, was sharing the same air as a room full of people I had idolized my entire life. The weight of that thought was crashing down on me a lot faster and harder than I had expected.

In the background I could hear Tina Fey say something that was obviously hilarious and witty because light laughter rippled amongst the audience, as Dylan and I stopped in the center of the stage and smiled. But I couldn't hear anything. Everything felt like a blur, like it wasn't even happening for real. I felt like I was competing in a pageant, or I had just gotten married and we were about to begin our first dance as husband and wife. Which, you know, wasn't terrible. But I was about ninety-six percent sure I was in love with Milo, so the fake marriage was a little inconvenient. I couldn't even see where Milo was in the crowd, even though I was desperately scanning the room for him. He was definitely in the room, right? Had he said he was going to be there? It was like a thick cloud of fog had consumed my brain, and I couldn't think straight. I could see everyone in the room, but I couldn't really tell what they looked like. I squinted a little, thinking the lighting was probably just hitting my eyes. But it wasn't that. Something was off. Plus, I was smiling so much I was scared my jaws were going to crumble under the pressure.

Someone was speaking into a microphone, but I couldn't really tell whom. They were doing a good job because the crowd kept laughing. Only I couldn't really hear anything over the sound of my own heartbeat. Dylan and I slowly made our way toward the other end of the stage, carefully walking so that I wouldn't do something stupid like trip on the bottom of my dress and rip it.

A loud bang suddenly went off and everyone in the room gasped. I whipped my head around to face the crowd, unconsciously digging my nails into Dylan's tuxedo sleeve. The stage lights were still kind of blinding, but I scanned the audience through squinty eyes.

"GUN!" Someone yelled and I heard some people cry out

in panic.

My eyes frantically searched the room, trying to make sense of what was happening. Everyone had jumped into action, celebrities scrambling to and fro. Security guards were emerging from everywhere as another shot went off.

"What the hell?" someone yelled.

"Oh my God," I whispered, my eyes finally fixating on a revolver that was pointed to the ceiling. My eyes slowly traveled down the arm that the gun was attached to, to find out who it belonged it.

I yanked on Dylan's arm, pulling him further back from the front of the stage. Standing a few yards away from me, staring me dead in the face, was Frank Parker. Only I wasn't sure that it was Frank. I only had a vague sense of what he looked like, so I couldn't be sure. Plus, everything was still blurred, and I was scared my eyes had suddenly gone wonky. Maybe my tears were the cause of that.

"I WANT EVERYONE DOWN. RIGHT NOW," he yelled, and fired another shot into the ceiling.

There was more screaming and panic as everyone crouched down. Some people hid behind chairs, others crawled underneath tables for safety. In that moment no one was a celebrity. No one was special. We were all vulnerable, and in extreme danger. Dylan and I reflexively hit the stage floor, still clutching onto each other. Oh my God, I was going to die in the same room as George Clooney and never get to tell him I love him.

"Not you, Gia," Frank said with a smile. He slowly lowered his arm and pointed the gun at me. "I have other plans for you."

This cannot be happening to me, I thought. *Not like this. Not now. Not here. Not him.*

"Pleas—" I began to say, with strength I didn't know I had in me.

Frank's blurred face distorted and suddenly a face I was

extremely familiar with replaced it. Jack's.

"Gia," he said, calmly, pointing the gun at me.

"No," I said, shaking my head fiercely. "NO."

"GIA!" Jack was yelling, but his voice sounded distant. "HELLO? GIA!"

Wait, what? I looked around the room in confusion. The whole room was disappearing and Dylan wasn't next to me on anymore. Jack and the gun were gone too, but I was still lying face down on the stage.

"GIA!"

"WHAT!" I yelled out in confusion, and suddenly I could see my bedroom ceiling.

I blinked a few times, feeling completely dazed. What had just happened? Oh right, I was about to get shot. Wait, so what was I doing in my room? Oh God, maybe he shot me and they took me to hospital and said I would survive but I would lose my memory for like, three months, and now it was three months later and I was home but I couldn't remember anything!

"Jesus, can you wake up already?" Jack's annoyed voice filled my ears.

I shot upright, frantically scanning my pajamas for any signs of a gunshot wound. Nope, nothing. I touched my head. No massive bandage around it.

"Gia, what the hell?" Jack said, looking at me with concern. "Are you okay?"

"I—" I looked down at myself. "I think so. What happened?"

"You were dreaming or something and then suddenly you started yelling real loud. It really freaked me out! I could hear you from downstairs!"

"I was dreaming?" I repeatedly stupidly, slapping my palm against my forehead.

"Yeah! It was really weird."

Thank you Baby J! It was all just a stupid nightmare. No

gunshot wounds, and my memory was still intact. I think. I glanced at my doorway, where Nadia was standing with a concerned look on her face.

"We're okay. Thanks, Nadia," Jack said, without casting a look over his shoulder. She nodded at me and walked away, looking unconvinced.

"What was I yelling?" I asked, running my hands through my hair.

Jack took a seat on my bed next to me. "You first started calling out for someone named George, and then randomly started yelling out 'no!'"

Well, Clooney should be flattered that in my final moments I called out for him and not my own parents.

"Oh my gosh, that was the worst dream ever," I groaned, burying my head in my hands. "I was at the Golden Globes and yo—"

I paused. Telling Jack that he shot me in my nightmare didn't seem like the best idea.

"Who?"

"Frank," I replied, looking at my hands. I couldn't bring myself to look at him as I lied. "Frank showed up and shot me."

I was expecting Jack to say something insensitive like, "how stupid is that?" Or, "suck it up and move on, Princess." But instead he sighed and said, "Gia, it's okay. Nothing's going to happen to you tonight. Not when I'm around. Don't worry."

"Jack," I said softly, terrified that I might start crying. "I'm really scared."

"I know."

"What if he shoots me?"

"He won't."

"But what if he does?"

"Gia!" Jack said impatiently. "Then I'll shoot him back. Okay?"

"Are you kidding me? So you're going to let him shoot me, but then fix it by shooting him back? That's ridiculous!"

"I'm not a psychic. How am I supposed to know that he's going to shoot you until he actually does? And I can't shoot him if he doesn't shoot you. That would make me look like the bad guy."

I glared at him and his frustratingly logical reasoning. "I hate you."

Jack smiled. "I can make it up to you by telling you about the paternity scandal with the previous Miss Golden Globe. That is, of course, if you're interested."

I stared at him in disbelief. "Are you insane?" I exclaimed. "I'm practically having a heart attack over here, and you want to exchange gossip?"

"Suit yourself," he replied with a shrug. "Let's just say her boyfriend won't be too pleased."

Okay, *now* I was interested.

"No, wait! Tell me! Whose is it?"

"Up and at 'em!" Jack ignored me, his smile widening as he ruffled my hair. I pushed his hand away and kicked the blanket off me. "Your mom has you on a tight schedule today. The makeup artists are already here."

I pouted as I watched Jack leave the room. Everything else in the dream may have been fake, but the date wasn't. Today really was the day of the Golden Globe awards. I had barely finished processing the nightmare I had just endured, and now Jack had just sprung another one on me. I forced myself out of bed and into the shower, doing some mental pep talking as the water hit my skin. Today was quite possibly the most important day of my life, and I wasn't even close to prepared to face it. I spent some extra time washing my hair, climbed out of the shower and threw on whatever clothes first caught my eye.

"Jesus what are you doing, building a new shower?" Jack cried, bursting into my room.

I ran the towel through my wet hair with a scowl. "Oh my gosh, it's been like ten minutes! I needed to get dressed."

"If you've finally awoken and are bright and fresh," Jack said sarcastically. "Then can you please join me in the living room? Your mom has turned me into her personal secretary for the day and I'm not okay with that."

"You're such a complainer," I told him, chucking the wet towel on my bed. Anya would deal with it later.

"I'm just getting started."

I followed Jack down the elevator and into what used to be a living room. Instead it had been turned into a full hair and makeup studio. Mom's makeup artist Kat was holding an eye shadow palette in one hand, mixing two shades of colors together. Three strangers beside her seemed to be struggling to work a curling iron. My mother was sitting in one of our throne-like armchairs with huge rollers in her hair. She was holding her hands out in front of her with her fingers apart from each other, waving them lightly so her nail polish would dry. She was cradling her mobile between her shoulder and ear, yelling at someone to "get it done *right now.*" Tables and chairs had been completely rearranged and there was a full-length mirror resting on a wheeled base sitting in front of Mom.

"Holy mother of—"

"Yep," Jack said, nodding his head. "Beauty apocalypse."

"Mom," I said, to let her know I was in the room.

She reflexively turned to look over her shoulder, her phone accidently dropping onto her lap and onto her silky robe. Her massive rollers bounced up and down as she turned her head.

"Gia! Finally! Come over here, we have to get started on you," she exclaimed, picking her phone up and replacing it to her ear. "Oh damn, I messed up my nail polish. You'll have to do this one again, Kat."

"Hey Kat," I said. I gave the strangers an awkward wave.

"Hi guys."

"Hi sweetheart," Kat said warmly. Her blonde curls were layered with baby pink streaks. "This is Tom, Chloe, and Ruby, my assistants for today. Gosh, you've become even more gorgeous since the last time I saw you."

I gave her a small smile, but my concentration was still on the makeup and hair products scattered all over the place. Dad wasn't going to be pleased.

"Well, go on," Jack whispered, nudging me with his shoulder. "What are you going to do?"

"Security stuff. Make a plan. Remake it. Watch some TV. Knit a sweater. Adopt a kitten. I don't know, anything but this."

I watched as either Ruby or Chloe—I didn't know who was who—pulled out eyebrow tweezers from a black pouch.

"Take me with you?" I whispered hopefully.

"Sorry, Princess," he replied. "No way you can escape those tools of torture."

Jack left the room just as Mom hung up the phone, looking more hassled than ever.

"Those idiots still haven't delivered your dress yet," she told me, before I could ask her what was wrong.

"Seriously?" I gave her an incredulous look. "Why do they even have it? I thought all the alterations were complete!"

"I had to send it back to Monique to get the hook changed. It was tacky."

I put my palm to my forehead in frustration. "Mom! I need that dress! What am I going to wear tonight?"

"Don't worry, I just gave them an earful. They said the driver would be over within the hour."

I did a silent prayer that the traffic in L.A. would magically disappear and the dress would arrive in one minute flat. The last thing I needed was something else to stress about today.

"Chloe, you can get started on her eyebrows," Kat told the

girl holding the tweezers. "Tom, you can fix Eve's nails."

"Oh, Gia I almost forgot," Mom turned to me as I lowered myself into an armchair next to her. "Aria and Veronica will be over in a half hour or so. I invited them to come help us get ready."

I gave a sigh of relief. Finally, some comfort through the madness of Golden Globes preparation.

"Wait, but they obviously don't know about . . ." My eyes flickered to the makeup artists, who seemed less than interested in our conversation.

"Of course not," Mom assured me. "But Detective Reynolds and his band of merry men will be over in a while, so make sure you keep the girls busy."

Chloe told me to lean back so she could start on my eyebrows and I started to question what was more painful: getting shot at the Golden Globes by a deranged stalker or getting my eyebrows plucked.

With two hours left to go before we were meant to leave, I was well on my way to becoming a human Barbie doll. My hair was resting in rollers slightly smaller than what my mother's had been, and I had been plucked just about everywhere a hair was brave enough to grow. My skin felt raw from all the scrubbing and I smelled like a mixture of nail polish and eucalyptus lotion, but all in all I was pretty happy. Plus my dress had finally arrived, so all peace was restored in my mother's heart. Kat was on the phone somewhere in the house, and Mom was in Dad's room helping choose the right bowtie, something I knew would take forever because they'd be arguing over every shade of red. Mike was in his room with Chris, probably doing something illegal. Hopefully he was teaching Chris to speak. Kenny was who knows where. He was a slippery one for such a big guy.

Unsurprisingly, Jack had been no help through the whole process. He'd come in only twice: once to tell me that the mozzarella sticks in the fridge were "the bomb," and the second time was to laugh at me when I had my face mask on. He told me I looked like Shrek and I threw a hairbrush at him. Thankfully, I had Aria and Veronica to keep me sane through the whole glamathon, reading magazines, experimenting with Kat's makeup, taking selfies and catching me up on school gossip.

"So, how's my bestie Meghan?" I asked.

I couldn't see my friends because Chloe was doing my eyeshadow and was already annoyed that my eyelids kept fluttering.

"Oh my gosh," I heard Aria groan. "I almost punched her the other day."

"What happened now?"

"Now that you haven't been around," Aria said. "She's running out of lives to mess with. V and I caught her doing her dragon-lady thing on some poor freshman the other day."

"Seriously?" I scoffed.

"Yep," Veronica continued. "Some girl called Cecilia something-or-other. Anyway, her dad is *super* loaded. I heard he's like the Simon Cowell of Sweden. Only, bigger!"

"Open your eyes," Chloe told me. I opened my eyes and watched her as she carefully studied each eye. "Close them."

I obeyed. "So what did she do?" I asked.

"She was basically threatening her!" Aria cried. "She was all, 'just remember that this is L.A., and in L.A. you're nobody until Meghan Adams says you are.'"

We all laughed at Aria's dead-on impression of Meghan's high-pitched, self-righteous voice, and I heard Chloe sigh as she held my head still.

"That poor girl," Veronica said. "She looked terrified! It was pathetic."

"Done!" Chloe announced, relief clearly evident in her voice.

My eyelids fluttered open and Chloe studied them once more, pleased. She asked Tom to pass her the eyelash glue just as Jack strolled into the room.

"Speaking of pathetic," he said, easing into the throne armchair similar to mine. I wondered how long he had been sneakily listening. He had a tendency to do that. "How's Brendan doing?"

"He's doing fine," I snapped. "He sent me a letter the other day."

"A letter?" Jack repeated.

"Yes," I replied, sticking my nose up defensively. "Don't look at me like that. I think it's cute."

Lord knows why I still bothered defending Brendan around Jack. It was probably just instinct.

"Oh yeah, sure!" Jack said, feigning an understanding look. "I forgot we had traveled back to the 1800s. Silly me!"

Aria laughed and even Veronica smiled. A whole lot of help they were.

"Well, I think it's sweet," I said.

I looked up at Chloe who was expertly applying glue to a set of fake eyelashes. Her eyes flicked to me and she raised her eyebrows and gave me a little headshake. Clearly Chloe wasn't a fan of letter writing either.

"How's his TV show going?" Aria asked, painting her thumbnail an electric blue color.

"Yeah," Jack piped up. "How's his great, cowboy adventure going?"

"Good. Fantastic, actually," I replied. "It got picked up for a season."

"Seriously?" Aria asked, raising her eyebrows in disbelief.

"Yeah! On selective channels only, of course."

Personally, I was just as surprised as Aria. A part of me was scared the TV show was actually a huge disaster and no network was willing to pick it up and he was just lying to convince me, and possibly himself, that moving to Texas was a good decision. But as likely as that was, he genuinely seemed happy. Well, at least his writing seemed happy. He even drew smiley faces at the end of each paragraph. In fact, what was more surprising was that he actually paragraphed.

"Jack," Kenny said, appearing in the doorframe. "They're here."

Veronica and Aria exchanged looks, and I turned to Jack. "Who?" I asked him.

"Detective Reynolds," Kenny replied for him, and disappeared back into the hallway.

"Who's that?" V asked.

"Yeah, and why is there a detective in your house?" Aria added, reaching for a nail file.

"Gia, close your eyes. The glue's going to dry!" Chloe told me, waving the fake eyelash lightly in her hand.

I looked at Jack. Too much was happening at once for my brain to function normally. If Detective Reynolds was in the house that meant Milo was in the house. And if Milo was in the house that meant he would have to see me in a silk dressing gown with rollers in my hair and fuzzy slippers on my feet.

"That's Jack's father," I told my friends, and from the corner of my eye I saw Jack's jaw drop. "We're just going over some basic security stuff. The paparazzi have been nuts lately."

Aria's eyebrows rose so far up her head, they practically disappeared into her hair. "Jack's father?" She repeated slowly. No one seemed to be bothered about the police anymore.

"Yep."

Veronica and Aria turned their heads toward Jack, who was doing some heavy breathing. I shot him an apologetic look, and he shook his head ever so slightly.

"Um, yeah. That's my old man."

"Seriously?" Chloe asked, lowering her hand that was holding the eyelashes. She had temporarily replaced her annoyance for shock, by the looks of it.

Tom and Ruby, her fellow assistants looked at each other with light shrugs, and went back to looking busy.

"Uh, yeah," Jack said, rising from his armchair. "Gia, a word?"

"Nah, I'm good."

"Gia!"

"Fine, jeez."

Jack glared at me and left the room. I gave Chloe and her eyelashes my best *sorry I'm such a pain* look and rose from my chair.

"Gia!" Aria hissed.

"What?"

"Jack and his dad are . . ." Veronica said quietly. "Different."

I straightened my back and shrugged casually, as if I couldn't tell why they were so surprised. "Yeah, I guess. I mean, I haven't really noticed."

"You haven't noticed that his dad looks like a professional wrestler?" Aria asked incredulously. "Or that he's African American?"

"Aria," I said. "Jack's from Guam, remember?"

"Yeah, bu—" Veronica began, but I cut her off before the questioning could deepen.

"I'll be right back, guys!" I exclaimed, my rollers bouncing around on the top of my head.

"I'm pretty sure Guam isn't in Africa," I heard Tom say as I left the room, and bit my lip.

I knew that wouldn't be the end of that discussion. Veronica was definitely smart enough to pick up on something being wrong, but at least I was safe with Aria. She once asked me if the Burj Khalifa was a rapper, so she'd believe anything. I followed the sound of voices coming from the kitchen and found Jack stand-ing outside the room with his arms crossed.

"Kenny's my *dad?*" he exclaimed, grabbing onto my elbow and pulling me closer to the wall.

He dropped my elbow and I rubbed it where his fingers had dug in. "Ow! Sorry! It's all I could think of in the moment."

Jack gave me a frustrated look, like he was trying to train a disobedient puppy. "Okay, fine whatever. Can we just sort this security stuff out now please?"

"Calm down! You're so hyped up all the time."

And he thought *I* was high maintenance! Jack and I were about to walk into the kitchen when my parents emerged, usher-ing me toward the front door. Behind them I could see Detective Reynolds, Milo, and a man in a suit I didn't recognize.

"What's up?" I asked as my dad led me out the front door. "What are you doing? I'm in my robe!"

"Gia," Mom said. "We're just going over security details for tonight. We can't do it in the house if there's still a listening device somewhere."

We all gathered around in a circle, as if we were holding a daytime séance in the front yard. Thank God our house was gated, or else I'd be dying of humiliation. I hadn't entirely been lying about the paparazzi situation, particularly after the parking lot incident. But we seemed to be covered pretty well by the ex-pertly landscaped bushes.

"The driveway? Really?" I mumbled.

Jack smiled, taking a spot beside me. Of course he was find-ing this whole thing hilarious. Jerk. Detective Reynolds did a quick scan of the immaculately trimmed garden to make sure it was safe. By now it was probably just reflexive.

"Gia, good to see you again," he said, giving me a nod.

"Hi," I replied, giving him a small wave. I glanced at Milo, who was trying to hide a smile by looking at his shoes.

Oh no, my rollers. He was probably smiling just to be polite, but there was no way my alien hairstyle wasn't freaking him out a little. I was in fuzzy slippers for God's sake!

"Gia, this is agent Joseph Walker from the FBI." Dad motioned to the man in the suit.

Agent Walker extended his hand so I could shake it. "Nice to meet you, Gia."

I surveyed him quickly. He was definitely balding and he looked like the type of guy who complained about his salary a lot, but he seemed nice enough. I put my freshly manicured hand in his and shook it.

"FBI?" I repeated.

"Yes."

"That sounds intense. Is everything alright?"

Agent Walker dropped my hand, giving me a reassuring nod. "Everything's fine, Gia. Our involvement is purely on a worst-case-scenario basis."

"The bureau decided to lend a helping hand for tonight," Detective Reynolds told me. "Just to be safe. Frank Parker's location is still a question mark, so we need all the security we can get."

"So you didn't find anything at his house then?" Jack asked.

"Nothing," Detective Reynolds replied. "Neighbors said they hadn't seen Frank for almost two months, and nothing in his apartment seemed too out of the ordinary. The amount of dust on his possessions would indicate that he hasn't been in there for a couple of months, like the neighbors said, and there weren't many clothes in his closet. Lots of bills under his door though."

"We think it's safe to conclude Frank hasn't been in his apartment since he's starting harassing Gia," Milo finished.

Sweet lord Milo looked hot in that LAPD uniform, and whenever he said my name my heart would do its break dancing thing. At the rate I was going, installing a pacemaker might prove to be a necessary precaution.

"So where has he been staying all this time?" Mom asked.

"Probably the Dumpling Hospital," Detective Reynolds replied. "But we did another check of the place and it's been closed this entire week. We didn't find any sign of him living in the restaurant."

"So then where is he?" Kenny said.

"It's most likely," Agent Walker said, "that he's living in his car. He may have been at the restaurant on and off for the past few months, but this week he's definitely been on the move."

"We've managed to identify his car, and we've got everyone's eyes open for it," Detective Reynolds assured Dad, who looked like he was going to faint from all the stress. "It wouldn't be surprising if Ao Jie Kai was with him."

"So what can we do in the meantime?" I asked.

"Unfortunately, nothing for now," Agent Walker replied, and my eyes flicked to him. "Frank Parker clearly has a plan for tonight. It's our job to stop him from carrying out. It's your job to let him come to you."

"Security will be tight," Detective Reynolds added. "We've got a good number of men assigned to help out tonight."

I looked at Milo, as if asking if he was a part of that assignment. He gave me a nod that was so small, I would have missed it if I had blinked. Somehow knowing he'd be there was a huge comfort, even if he wouldn't be close.

"Plus we'll be there," Kenny said, motioning toward Jack.

"And so will I," Agent Walker added, and I gave him an appreciative nod. "Don't worry, Gia. We're going to get this guy."

"Thank you."

"Where will your son be tonight?" Agent Walker asked, directing the question to my parents.

"He'll be staying at my sister's house tonight," Mom replied. "His bodyguard Chris will be with him for security."

"We'll have a police car patrol up and down the street every hour just in case," Detective Reynolds added. "I doubt we'll need it, but it's better to be safe than sorry."

"Smart decision," Agent Walker said with an approving nod.

Yeah, it was a smart decision! How the hell was Chris going to take down a crazed psycho if something were to happen? Every time Famous barked he would jump up so high in his seat, it looked like a cartoon. Besides, Mike and I may not be besties for life, but he was still my brother and I loved him, even if it was just out of obligation. I looked at my parents, who were actually holding hands. Hopefully in a way that was friendly and said *I'm so concerned for my daughter's safety, but I'm consoling you because she's your daughter too.* If it was a *let's go rekindle the fire* type of thing, I would have to call an emergency family meeting. That is, of course, if I made it through the night in one piece.

"We'd better let you get back to your grooming," Detective Reynolds said with a chuckle, and I put a hand to my rollers with an embarrassed laugh. "Sit tight. We'll see you at the venue in a few hours."

Agent Walker gave everyone his card with his phone number on it, as if he was an air-conditioning salesman and everyone was burning in the L.A. heat. Everyone shook hands, signifying that our little ritual had been successfully completed, and my parents walked the men to their cars. Milo and I exchanged looks before he walked away, but nothing more.

"Gia," Aria said, appearing suddenly at the front door. "That chick with the lashes is getting real antsy. Should I tell her you're coming, or should I just kick her out?"

"I'll be there in a sec," I told her, forcing myself to behave as normally as I could.

"Hey Mr. Anderson!" Aria said to Kenny, giving him a small wave. With that, she spun on her heel and disappeared into the house once more.

"Mr. Anderson?" Kenny repeated, looking from me to Jack with a raised eyebrow.

"Trust me," I told him. "You don't want to know."

chapter
twenty-three

IF YOU ask me, Aladdin had it all wrong with his impressive singing skills and fashionable monkey. If he really wanted to get into Princess Jasmine's harem pants, he should have traded up the flying rug for a red carpet. It's hard to resist a man when he's standing in the middle of Hollywood with a hundred cameras aimed at his Armani suit. This was by no means my first red carpet experience, but it still felt overwhelmingly new.

As a kid I had always hated the strangers behind the camera lenses. I always thought of them as bloodthirsty wolves, that I could only escape by clinging onto Dad's neck and burying my face in his chest as they called out my name. Who were these men? How did they know my name and why were they bothering me? "It's like brushing your teeth," Mom had told me once.

"Just part of the daily routine." At eighteen, I'm only just starting to understand the casual approach my parents now take to
these affairs. It's a career, nothing more and nothing less. They're
just doing their jobs every time a photo is snapped. Being Miss
Golden Globe was sort of like being their intern for a day, only it
came with a little extra stress and higher stilettos.

As if the nerves weren't bad enough from the FBI getting
involved and the horrific scenarios I had conjured up in my mind,
I was *so* not prepared for Jack in a tuxedo. He looked incredible.
Like *wow-ee*. When he had emerged from his room fixing his cuff
links, I actually did a double take. Where the heck had that outfit
been hiding all this time? If I had known sooner, I might have
yelled at him a little less when he was being annoying. A good
tuxedo is the real life "get out of jail free" card. Of course, Mom
had ruined the whole thing by insisting on taking photos as if I
were going to prom like some dorky fourteen-year-old. I was half
expecting her to hand me a corsage and make me pose in front
of the limo. She would have tried too, but Dad was getting antsy
about leaving on time. Saved by the punctuality bell.

The person I was actually most pleased with was myself. The
dress fit perfectly, my hair was up in a fancy, loose bun that I
would never have been able to do by myself, and I had managed
not to accidently rip any of my fake lashes off yet. So far so good.
Even Mike, who I'm about ninety-four percent sure hates me,
told me I looked beautiful. Not even "pretty" or "alright," but
beautiful! So clearly I was doing something right. Jack on the
other hand, had practically crushed me with disappointment. He
gave me an once-over and said, "You look nice." Nice! Really?
That was all he could muster? I mean, it's not like I was expecting
to slowly descend from the staircase with some lame 90s love song
playing in the background while Jack watched me with his eyes
bugged out in love. Actually, yeah that was pretty much exactly
what I was expecting. Unfortunately real life is nothing like a

Freddie Prinze Jr. movie.

But I didn't have time to focus on impressing Jack. Instead, I needed to work on keeping calm and collected, even though my nerves were building up and threatening to explode at any moment. If I managed to survive the evening, then I would majorly regret my nervous fidgeting and potential eye twitching when I watched the ceremony back at a later time. So every time a reporter would ask about how excited I was to be given the title of Miss Golden Globe, I would take a deep breath, smile gracefully and tell them I was over the moon.

"Congratulations!" A reporter exclaimed, flashing her perfect set of teeth at me. She had mentioned where she worked, but it hadn't registered in my mind. "Miss Golden Globe is definitely something to be proud of. How are you feeling tonight?"

I was just about ready to throw up all over her hideous green gown, but I held it together. Lime green and sequins? What was this, Shrek goes to Broadway?

"I'm just thrilled!" I replied with a smile so big, I looked like I could swallow her whole. "This is such an honor, and I was so excited to even be considered."

Dad gave my shoulders a comforting squeeze and said, "Her mother and I are very proud of her."

Mom was definitely proud of me. But based on the way she kept posing sexily in her Zuhair Murad gown, she was prouder of something else.

"Any plans to follow in your parents' footsteps and get into showbiz?" The reporter asked.

I gave her a forced laugh and said, "Who knows? Anything could happen."

Yeah no, that was *never* happening. Because years after you've become the most famous actor ever, some scorned friend from the past will show up and start stalking your kids. So no. Showbiz was definitely not for me.

I did some more scary smiling and repeated a rundown of my outfit for what felt like the millionth time before Dad and I posed for some more photos, Kenny and Jack close behind of course. Jack now looked the complete part of a bodyguard, standing tall and tough in his tux. He had a little telephone wire looking thing attached to one of his ears, and kept scanning the crowd for any signs of trouble. All business, no play. If he decided to throw on some Ray Bans at some point, I was going to have a severe case of heartburn. There would definitely be questions about Jack at school after the awards, but by then everything would be resolved and I could come clean. Granted I got through the night in one piece. Dad leaned in so he could whisper in my ear, ignoring the questions and instructions being hurtled our way.

"Your mother is going to give someone a heart attack tonight," he said disapprovingly.

I watched her wink at the cameras, throwing her hair over her shoulder like she was in a GQ photoshoot. I think I actually heard someone pass out in the crowd.

"I don't think there's much we can do about that," I told Dad.

He sighed. Sometimes being around my mother was like having a cold. It was better to just let her run her course and fade away until the next time she visited. We continued to make our way up the carpet, smiling brightly, giving air kisses to fellow celebrities and making small talk about their outfits. Dad was clearly growing agitated, but never let it show. He was a pro at this. Me? I needed a little more practice. I was quickly running out of ways to stick my chest out and smile, and I couldn't pull off a wink like my mom. Dad had left me alone to go talk to Martin Scorsese, and the noise was only growing louder as more stars arrived. I was about ready to give up acting like a lady and sprint into the hall for some peace and quiet when I spotted a uniformed Milo a little further away, walking closely behind an officer I didn't recognize.

"Milo!" I called out. He stopped abruptly, scanning the crowd. "Behind you!"

His eyes settled on me after a few seconds of searching, and he gave a small smile. I glanced at Jack over my shoulder, who was watching me expressionlessly. The only thing worse than Jack giving his two cents about Milo was Jack *not* giving his two cents about Milo.

"Hi," Milo said loudly, over the sounds of excitement and anticipation. We were almost at the entrance now, partially sheltered from the cameras that were now focused on the new arrivals.

"Hi."

Milo looked me up and down. "Wow," he said. "You look incredible! That dress! It's . . . wow."

See! That's all I wanted, Jack. A little appreciation for my hotness once in a while wouldn't kill you!

"Thanks," I replied, almost certain I was blushing. "You look great too."

Milo looked down at his uniform with a smile. "Yeah, it's custom made LAPD. I think the silk is Italian."

I gave a short laugh at his joke, playing along with an impressed look. It could have been silk from Compton for all I cared. If the end result was *that*, it was value for the money.

"So how are you holding up?" he asked, his dimples disappearing from view.

How was I holding up? Gee, let me think about that one for a second. I was standing in one of the most beautiful gowns I'd ever seen, the world seemed to be dying to know every detail about my life and there was a great chance Clooney was in the vicinity. Oh, and I wasn't able to enjoy *any* of that because somewhere in the sea of unfamiliar faces was a potentially violent lunatic who was intent on getting revenge for reasons that were still a mystery to me. How was I holding up, you ask?

"Great!" I lied. "Fabulous. Fantastic."

"Are you sure?" Milo asked uncertainly. "You look a little nervous."

"I'm a *tad* nervous. Tiny amount. Miniscule, really."

"That's understandable," Milo said with a nod. "But we've got a lot of people watching out for you tonight. Plus, you're killing it on the red carpet, so you've got nothing to worry about on that front."

I gave an embarrassed laugh, as if the idea of fame suddenly seemed ridiculously over-the-top. "The cameras are blinding me! I think they might have done some serious retinal damage."

"Quick!" Milo said, holding up two fingers in the shape of a peace sign. "How many fingers am I holding up?"

"That's a tough one. Five?"

"Close! Seven."

We both laughed as he lowered his hand to his side, hoping it would buy us some time to evaluate our next move. Jack seemed to have made that decision for me when he came up beside me.

"Gia," was all he said.

"Jack," Milo greeted him with no emotion in his voice. "Nice tux."

Jack's lips curved up into a smirk as he gave a nod of acknowledgement. "Gia," he said. "Carol wants to see you. Something about you taking photos with Dylan."

"Right now?" I asked, giving him a disappointed look.

"Like, yesterday now."

There was a girl standing a foot away, dressed in a wine colored evening gown that was definitely off the rack. She had a clipboard in her hand, and fear in her eyes, nodding at me intensely as if confirming the urgency of Carol's request. Goddammit Carol! I was having a moment!

"Don't worry about it, "Milo said in response to my apologetic look. "I have to go anyway. I've got to sort out some security stuff."

"Right," I said. "I've got to go get shot. By photographers, I mean! Like, with cameras. Not the guns."

Oh good God. Apparently I could speak to James Franco just fine, but any more than thirty seconds with Milo would cause my brain to stop functioning.

"Stay safe," he said, suppressing a smile as he walked away.

"Shut up!" I groaned, watching Milo get swallowed by the crowd.

"Are you talking to yourself or talking to me?"

"Both."

"I didn't say anything."

"It was a pre-emptive shut up."

I looked at the smug smile on Jack's face. "Get shot?" he said, not bothering to stifle a laugh. "You wanna talk about what's happening in your subconscious?"

"No, but you're going to be *un*conscious in about two seconds if you're not careful."

"If it makes you feel any better," he said sincerely, "I never freeze up around hot girls."

I put my hands on my hips. "How exactly is that meant to make me feel better?"

"Oh, no wait. You're right. That's meant to make *me* feel better."

"Miss Winters." The woman with the clipboard said, looking more fearful by the minute. "I really need you to come with me. Carol says we're already behind schedule."

"Well good luck," Jack said, patting me comfortingly on the back. "Be brave."

"Good luck?" I repeated. "You're my bodyguard! You have to protect me in case Carol throws a stiletto at my face!"

Jack shook his head, taking two steps away from me as if I were about to bite him. "Oh I'll be there, but strictly as an observer," he said seriously. "No one takes on Carol's forehead vein and lives to tell the tale."

Yeah, well, only the brave get pay checks.

With barely ten minutes before the ceremony was going to start, my heart decided it was a good time to complctely fail. The heavy breathing was no longer working, and I was about a million percent sure the nerves weren't because I got to hand famous people trophies on stage. It was bad enough that I kept forgetting which direction of the stage I was supposed to lead the winners off, my anxiety attacks weren't exactly helping. My parents had come to visit me backstage, wishing me luck and telling me how excited they were. They were clearly as tense as I was, but we didn't even hint at the possibility of anything going wrong. We did what normal Hollywood families do and swept our problems under the rug for as long as we could get away with it.

Backstage was packed with people, finalizing last minute details and shining the globes on the awards. I was in the same room as Hugh Jackman and all I could think about was stupid Frank Parker and his psycho revenge mission. We had heard nothing from him the entire day, and I was secretly hoping he had forgotten, or he was just bored and decided to move to Botswana. Both were highly unlikely, but I kept praying anyway.

"Gia," Jack said softly, but I jumped anyway.

"Oh my God, don't sneak up behind me like that!" I cried, whacking his arm.

Jack rested his hands on my shoulders and looked me square in the eyes. "You need to calm down."

"I am ca—"

"No you're not!" he replied, cutting me off. "Listen to me Gia, you are going to be fine. You've got Milo, Detective

Reynolds and a bunch cops looking out for you. There's security everywhere, and Agent Walker has eyes all over the place. Besides, I'm *right* here for you."

"Yeah but you can't come on stage with me!" I argued. "What are you supposed to do if he comes jumping out of nowhere and grabs me?"

Jack looked around carefully, his hands still on my shoulder. "Not that I think that'll happen, but I've got a gun," he whispered.

"You've got a gun?" I cried, and Jack slapped a hand over my mouth.

"Will you shut up?" he hissed, removing his hand from my lips.

"Ugh, you ruined my lip-gloss! What are you doing with a gun!"

"It's licensed, Gia! I'm a bodyguard, remember?"

I dropped my gaze to his waist. "Can I see it?"

Jack gave me a look like I was insane and said, "I thought you hated guns! They make you queasy?"

"Yeah, I'm terrified. But I've always kind of wanted to see one someday."

"Well today is not going to be that day."

"FIVE MINUTES!" Someone from the crew yelled and everyone suddenly went into fast forward mode, bustling around backstage.

Close behind Jack was a man who looked exactly like Gerard Butler. My heart rate picked up.

"Oooo, is that—"

"Gia, not right now!" Jack said. "I don't need you any more hyped up than you already are. Just do some more heavy breathing."

"Jack!" I cried, trying not to hit him. "I'm fine, okay? I'm just freaking out a little! It's perfectly normal! If I do anymore heavy breathing people are going to get me an oxygen tank."

"Don't you think I'm freaking out too? Jon Hamm is standing less than two yards behind me, and I have a *huge* man-crush on Don Draper!"

"Oh why didn't you say so? He's a family friend, I can totally introduce you."

Jack's eyes rounded in disbelief. "You've known me like, two months, and you choose *now* to tell me this?"

"Hey! I've offered to introduce you to other people!"

"Actually," he said, giving me a knowing look. "You haven't. I mean, even your dad invited me to lunch with Cliff Richards."

"Who?"

I did some frustrated sighing and waited for Jack to get his *I can't believe you don't know who Cliff Richards is, that man is a legend* look off his face. It's not like I didn't know who he was, I just really didn't care. Like, at all. A woman dressed in the all black uniform of the backstage staff stopped abruptly as she was passing by.

"Excuse me," she said, looking at Jack uncertainly. "Are you authorized to be backst—"

"Yes! For the millionth time, yes! I *am* authorized to be backstage! This is the sixth time I've been asked that question. What, do I need a visitors pass or something?"

She gave me a fleeting look, and then cut her eyes back to a now very annoyed Jack.

"I'm sorry," she said curtly, looking more frazzled than apologetic as she walked off.

"Anyway!" Jack said, shaking his head in frustration. "I know you're nervous and this whole thing kind of sucks. But like I said before, we've got you covered. It's just a waiting game now."

I knew he was right, and I did feel bad that I was acting like a hyped-up maniac. But the waiting was the worst part. As much as I was counting on the Botswana plan, I was also just hoping the whole thing would be short and sweet. Dr. D would appear and the police would slap cuffs on him. The end. Bye forever.

"Maybe it doesn't have to be," I said slowly, letting an idea form in my mind.

"What?"

"What if we drew him out?"

"Wait, what?" Jack repeated.

"Jack," I said impatiently, excitement rising in my voice. "We'll just dangle me in front of him so he appears and then bam! You do your thing, the cops can arrest him and this whole thing ends!"

Jack blinked and took a deep breath. "Okay, firstly no," he said. "Secondly, *hell* no."

"Why not?"

"We can't just *dangle* you! You're on stage with over half of Hollywood's biggest stars. How much more dangling can we possibly do?"

"Yeah bu—"

"Plus," Jack continued. "We can't even reach Frank! We can't trace any calls to him, we have no location, and only he contacts us!"

"Okay, bu—"

"Which he hasn't done so far. Which means he could be anywhere. Doing anything!"

"Jack, listen to me!" I hissed, before he could cut me off again. I lowered my voice as Seth Meyers walked by. "Alright fine, so I don't really have the specific details. But this could work if you help me!"

Jack slapped his hand across his eyes and groaned. "How is this going to work Gia? You have *no* specific details. What do you want to do, huh? Go on stage, grab the mic and politely ask for Frank Parker to raise his hand?"

I scowled. "No! Wait, why? You think that would work?"

"No!"

"Look, everyone is expecting me to come on stage, right? What if I just don't come on stage? It'll throw Frank off his game!"

"I think you're forgetting that Frank was planning his grand finale for today even before you became Miss Golden Globe," Jack reminded me. "So, personally I don't think his plan involves you being on stage. And even if it does, there's no guarantee it'll change anything if you just decide to not show up! Besides, if you screw up the stage plan now, Carol is guaranteed to throw a chair at you and I won't be able to save you."

I crossed my arms over my chest and pouted. "Why can't you just be helpful for once?"

Here I was, trying to help us all out of a sticky situation, and Jack was doing nothing to show me he appreciated my efforts. So what if it was just the base of an idea. All buildings need foundations!

"JUST OVER TWO MINUTES," I heard someone yell, and I knew Carol would be going crazy if she couldn't find me.

"Not helpful?" Jack echoed my words. "I'm out here dealing with your stupid suggestions and trying to calm you down so you don't break down on stage! I'm practically keeping you upright! And *I'm* not helpful?"

"Instead of yelling at me," I told him, "you could be helping me with my plan. So that this whole thing is just over and done with!"

"There is no plan!" Jack cried, and we looked around as people started to take notice of our fight. Jack lowered his voice and said, "Gia, we're not discussing this anymore. Stick to the actual plan."

"I bet if I told Milo he would be a lot more understanding," I said under my breath, but loud enough for Jack to hear.

Jack scoffed. "Yeah of course he would. Officer Perfect would high-five you, and then give you a gold star for coming up with the world's dumbest idea!"

"You know what?" I said, shaking my head in disbelief at Jack's audacity. "He probably would! Because he's a nice guy. You should try it sometime! Maybe I *will* go tell Milo!"

"You have about a minute before the ceremony starts," Jack said, starting to look amused. "By all means, go find Prince Charming and let him in on your mission impossible."

Okay he had a point. There was no way I had time.

"Well maybe I'll just text him then!" I told Jack haughtily. "I left my phone on one of these tables, but the moment I find it I'll just message him my brilliant idea."

Maybe I'd even add some emojis just to *really* get under Jack's skin.

He laughed. "Yeah," he said, feigning encouragement. "You do that."

"Gia!" A male voice called from behind me. "We need you over here. We've got about ten minutes before your entrance!"

"Coming!" I yelled back, but I stayed where I was. "Whatever, Jack. I'm not just going to sit here and do nothing. I'm ready to end it right now! And if you don't want to help me then I'll do it alone."

I lifted up the hem of my dress once more, spun on my heel and stalked off toward Dylan. I had taken all but two steps when Jack had caught me by the elbow and yanked me toward him.

"Gia," Jack said sternly, no longer laughing. "I'm not kidding. Agent Walker was very clear. Just act normally and wait it out. You're not building on this stupid idea of yours, okay? I forbid you."

I pulled my elbow out of his grasp and gave him an incredulous look. "Oh, I'm sorry *Dad*, you forbid me? I already have two parents, Jack. I don't need another one."

I was ready to walk off again but Jack caught me by the arm once more.

"That's funny," he said, even though he was dead serious.

"Because it kind of seems like you do! You never want to listen to anything anyone else says! You're so damn stubborn, and it's really starting to piss me off!"

I glared at him so intensely, I was scared I had done some damage to my eye. He was calling *me* stubborn? If the whole world wasn't falling over themselves to give Jack what he wanted, the way he wanted, he was unhappy. I wasn't the one with the problem here! He had been looking for a way out ever since he walked into the house that first night, and had been all too obliged to keep reminding me how much of an inconvenience I was to him. If he was so pained to be around me, he could leave whenever he wanted. I wasn't exactly dead bolting the door shut.

"You're fired," I snapped, yanking my arm away.

"What?"

"You're fired!"

"Nice try," Jack said, looking unimpressed. "But you can't fire me, remember? I work for——"

"My dad?" I finished. "Guess what? I don't give a damn! Whatever this is, our deal, our friendship. It's over, okay?"

"ONE MINUTE TO GO!"

"No!" Jack exclaimed angrily, over the increasing chatter of backstage. "No, not okay! If you do anything in your immaturity, it's on me! I'm responsible for keeping you safe. So if you get killed, your boyfriend comes for *my* throat first!"

I was so furious; I thought I might just slap him. So if I died the only thing he would care about is saving his own ass. That hurt like a bitch. Of course it might have had something to do with that fact that deep down, a teeny tiny part of me had some feelings for Jack, which is messed up, I know. It's the hair! Nobody is immune. But he apparently didn't share that teeny tiny feeling because he was emotionally trampling all over my face with his shiny black shoes.

"Don't worry, Jack," I said, giving him a humorless smile. "If

I die tonight, no one's coming for you. You can just *buy* yourself an alibi. We both know you have the funds to do it."

Jack looked at me, stunned, and I felt a minute of pleasure for catching him off guard. "What did you say?"

I took a step closer to Jack, lowering my voice so only he could hear me. "Why would a person devote their career to protecting stuck-up rich kids, when they have a trust fund full of millions lying in the bank?"

"How do you know about that?" Jack asked, his expression growing more aggressive by the second.

"Does it matter how I know, or *that* I know?"

Jack and I glared at each other in angry silence for a few seconds, before I stalked off, just as the sound of applause from the audience hit backstage. Alright. So maybe I overdid it a little. I may have gone a little soap opera on him there with my dramatic whispering. And yeah, maybe it was a bit dumb of me to bring up his trust fund. Clearly it was a touchy topic. But he was being a jerk face, so he deserved it. Besides, why was he so determined to stop me from straying from the original plan? I was beginning to highly doubt that it was to keep me safe. It sounded more like he was following a plan of his own, and I was getting in the way of that. Could Milo be right? Could Jack have something to do with Frank Parker?

"Gia!" I heard Jack call out my name.

"WHAT!" I practically shrieked with irritation, stopping and looking over my shoulder.

Jack was arguing with two burly men who I guessed were security guards. "This is getting a little ridiculous!" he was saying, "I don't know how many times I have to tell you guys. Ask her yourself, she's standing right there! Gia!"

Jack motioned toward the guards, as if asking me to corroborate his authorization to be backstage. I watched this unfold thoughtfully. If Jack really was on Dr. D's team then it was probably best that the guards throw him out. If he wasn't, well then he was still an asshole. Even more reason to throw him out.

I gave a nonchalant shrug and turned my back to him, almost immediately colliding with a guy dressed in the black backstage crew uniform. He was wearing a baseball cap that was sitting a little too low on his head as it shadowed his eyes, with a headset and microphone resting around his neck. Jet black hair peeked through the sides of his cap. He looked a little familiar, but I couldn't be too sure if I really knew him. Behind me I could hear Jack's angry yells growing further away. They were probably leading him to an exit.

"Oh my gosh!" I cried, putting a hand over my heart. "You scared me."

The crewmember didn't apologize. Instead, he held up my phone and said, "Is this yours?"

"Yes!" I sighed in relief, clutching the phone to my chest. "I was looking for this. Thank you so much!"

Finally. Something that was going right in my life. The young guy nodded and gave a half-assed smile, walking away without another word. Carol clearly had everyone on high stress mode. I had barely unlocked my phone when I heard the same voice speak again from behind me.

"Uh, Gia?"

"Yeah?"

I turned to face him, looking at him expectantly. I had *definitely* seen him before, but where? He seemed a little nervous, almost reluctant to be speaking to me.

"I'm really sorry about this," he said.

And then everything went black.

chapter
twenty-four

RED. IT'S all I could see when my eyes finally fluttered open, as if the sky had been painted in the color. At first, when I snapped back into consciousness, I was scared it might have been blood, but there were gold lanterns dangling above my head, which didn't make any sense. Where was I? Wasn't I meant to be at the Golden Globes, or did that already happen? It was definitely night time; everything else besides the lanterns was dark. But what day was it?

And then suddenly everything came screeching back. The red carpet, my fight with Jack, the mystery guy in the baseball cap and the overwhelming sensation of being suffocated. I straightened my head so I could get a better understanding of where I was, even though it was still spinning and I was partially seeing double.

"Oh good, you're awake," I heard a man's voice say, and I turned my head in the direction of the sound, still groggy from whatever had happened to me.

"Where am I?" I croaked.

I tried to move the hair falling onto my face from my loosened bun, but found that I was unable to lift my hands. I forced my eyes to widen long enough to realize I was sitting on a chair with my hands tied together behind my back. I tried to move my feet, but the same thing had been done to stop me from running away. My gown was still on me, its fabric covering my legs so I couldn't see my feet. It was still in fairly good condition, although it looked dirty now, and some of the netting had been torn.

"Gia Winters," the man said, coming into view from behind the shadows. "Pleasure to finally meet you."

It took me no more than two seconds to figure out who the mystery man was. Frank Parker. He didn't look much older than my dad, but his face showed weariness and exhaustion. Frank Parker was definitely a man who would have had Hollywood good looks back in the day, but now the stress of his life was painted across his face. He was fairly tall, and was dressed in creased blue jeans, a white shirt and the same leather jacket he had worn at the Coco Club. His brown hair had traces of grey in it, and his smile seemed friendly. If I had run into him at the grocery store, I would never have been able to tell he was capable of kidnapping.

"Frank Parker." I said. "Dr. D."

"The one and only," he replied. "Welcome to my humble abode."

I scanned my surroundings. The chair I was tied to seemed to be in the middle of a deserted street. There were shops on either side of me, all labeled in Chinese characters, but every one of them was closed. There must have been a hundred lanterns woven through string above my head, lighting up the otherwise dim street. The sidewalks were empty and unusually clean. There was no sign of life around. No one to help me out.

"Are we in China?" I asked, my voice feeling hoarse.

Frank gave me a pleased look and said, "Close enough. I'm glad the set managed to convince you."

I turned my attention back to him. "Set?"

"Gia, we're on a film set. Welcome to Universal Studios."

Suddenly everything clicked into place, and I saw things as they really were. Of course the street was deserted. None of it was real! The shops began to look like paintings and the sidewalk completely fake. The ceiling may have been shining with golden lights, but it wasn't a real parade. I was in a movie.

I looked down at the chair I was sitting on and felt the strings that were wrapped around my feet and hands dig into my skin roughly. I tugged on them desperately, but they only scratched my skin harder. My heels were still on my feet, which felt like they were about to fall off, and the hair continued to tumble down my face.

"The Golden Globes?" I asked, trying to keep the panic out of my voice.

"Happening as we speak," Frank replied, pacing around in front of me.

"Listen . . ." I struggled to find the right thing to call Frank. "Mr. Parker . . . Sir. I'm really sorry about everything that happened to you. But kidnapping me isn't going to solve anything! I swear if you let me go, I won't press charges."

Yeah right. I was going to go straight to Milo and the Feds and not looking back for one second.

"How noble of you," Frank said, feigning appreciation. "But I think I'll stick to my plan for now."

I heard footsteps come from my right, and the guy from backstage appeared from the shadows. This time I had a pretty good idea of how he fit into the puzzle. He was the waiter at the Dumpling Hospital. He was the karate kid from the UCLA party.

Ao Jie Kai. My gaze cut into him, intensely watching the almost helpless look on his face. He was trying to keep his eyes ahead of him, but every few seconds he would glance at me tied to the chair. Oh, so now you're sorry for helping a crazy guy kidnap me? Thanks. A fat lot of help your apology will do now.

"Ah," Frank said, patting AJ on the back. "I see you've recognized my right-hand man."

"How did you even get me here?" I asked, my voice threatening to give way to tears.

"Through a lot of careful planning, and this guy," Frank replied, proudly looking at AJ.

"You drugged me," I said, helplessly tugging on the ropes once more.

"Uh, kind of," AJ mumbled, staring at his feet.

"You see," Frank began, "AJ here managed to slip backstage through the hustle and bustle. Everyone was so fixated on the award ceremony going smoothly no one would notice the people in the black uniforms. Then, when you had your little tiff with that bodyguard of yours, AJ called security and had him thrown out. All we needed was a little distraction to keep him busy while we dealt with you."

"Yes, but how did I end up *here?* Someone must have noticed you drugging me in the middle of a crowd!"

"That's the best part, Gia!" Frank exclaimed, clapping his hands together in excitement. "It was all about the timing. You turned, he chloroformed, you collapsed and he told everyone that you had fainted due to the pressure of the awards. Besides, everyone had seen your fight with the bodyguard and how upset you were. It was *such* an honor to be named Miss Golden Globe. Everyone could understand the stress that came with it."

Chloroform? This kind of stuff didn't happen in real life. There was no way Frank's story was true, yet the evidence was damning. I was strapped to a chair in a dimly lit warehouse with nobody to help me. I wasn't sure if that was terrifying or impressive.

"So then . . ." I began, playing the scenario out in my head.

"So then the kind helper volunteered to help you out, get you some fresh air and some water before you went on stage. After that it was just a matter of sneaking you out of the nearest backdoor emergency exit. And here we are."

Staring up at Frank Parker's almost manic smile had made something very clear: he was a total nut job. And quite possibly a genius. That plan had so many opportunities to go wrong, and yet he had managed to pull it off. He had managed to snatch me up in front of a room full of people, and get away without being caught.

I opened my mouth to plead with him once more, but the muffled sound of my ringtone stopped me. Frank pulled out my phone from his jacket pocket and smiled at the screen.

"Oh look, it's Blondie!" he said, holding the phone to show me. The screen told me it was Jack calling. "This must be call number twenty four. That's three more times than that cop. Makes you wonder what that means."

I had no idea how long it had been since I had been gone, but at least people were out looking for me. It was no use if I knew where I was if I couldn't tell them. All I needed was a few seconds with Jack to yell out our location, and that was it.

"Please let me talk to him!" I cried over the sound of the ringing.

Dr. D ignored me and answered, looking at Ao Jie Kai. He cocked his head toward me and AJ walked over to my chair, putting a hand aggressively over my mouth.

"Gia's phone!" Frank chirped in a singsong voice. I shook my head from side to side desperately, and AJ's grip hardened. "I'm sorry, she can't come to the phone right now. She's a little . . ." Frank paused, taking a moment to smile at me. "Tied up."

I'm not sure what was more painful; being tied to a chair or having to listen to Frank's lame joke. I bit AJ's finger as hard as I could, causing him to sharply remove it from my mouth and yelp out in pain.

"JACK, WE'RE AT—" I screamed as loud as I could, and AJ immediately pulled out a handkerchief from his pocket and wrapped it around my mouth, between my parted lips.

Frank shot AJ a look that read *get it together* and turned his attention back to Jack on the phone. Tears were streaming down my cheek and I sobbed into the handkerchief. It tasted foul, its fabric brushing against my tongue roughly. The ropes on my feet and hands were cutting into my skin with every second that passed, and there was nothing I could do about it.

"You have half an hour to bring me five million dollars at Universal Studios. And for every minute you're late, I cut off one of her fingers. Does that sound fair?"

Oh. HELL. No. I needed my fingers, big time. What the hell was Milo going to do if he ever decided to propose? I wasn't going to wear the ring on a necklace like some girl whose flaky fiancé couldn't commit to a wedding date. Plus I had just gotten my nails done, so that would have been a complete waste of time. I tried to scream, but it was muted by the handkerchief. I wriggled harder in my chair. It was almost as useless as just asking Frank to kindly let me go. If I only I had practiced telepathy with Jack before I got kidnapped. All my life's problems might have been solved.

"Oh, you're smart. You can work that out for yourself," Frank was saying into the phone.

I had no idea what Jack had asked him, but I knew he wouldn't be happy with his reply. Frank thrust the phone to my ear and pulled the handkerchief down roughly.

"He wants to make sure you're alive," Frank told me, in an almost bored voice.

"Jack, please!" My sobbing was practically hysterical now.

"Gia! Oh my God! Are you alright? Of course you're not alright, what am I saying?" Jack was yelling into the phone. His voice was frantic, as if he couldn't get his thoughts in order. "Don't worry! I'm coming. We're going to get you out of there and we're going to—"

The phone and Jack's voice were yanked away from me, as Dr. D placed the phone back to his ear and replaced the handkerchief over my mouth.

"No police. Just you and Harry. You've now got twenty-eight minutes. Tick tock," he said, and cut the phone abruptly. "For your sake," Frank said, putting my phone in his jeans pocket. "I hope your boyfriend's punctual."

I rested my back against the chair again, wriggling my wrists around and trying to loosen the strings with no luck. I tried to steady myself but I couldn't stop crying. I didn't care that Frank was pacing in front of me, looking completely disinterested in my pain. I cried because I was helpless. I cried because I wanted to go home. I cried because I had been immature and spiteful, and maybe Jack could have stopped this if I had been smarter. I cried because I was completely alone and absolutely terrified. But crying wasn't going to get me out of there alive. So when I had given myself enough time for self-pity, I concentrated on composing myself as best as I could so I could review my options.

I sniffled, shaking the tears off my cheeks. Through my blurred vision, it looked like there might have been a door in the far corner of the room. I couldn't tell for sure because it was mostly hidden by a large, red dragon; the kind used in Chinese parades which needs people to make up its body within the long fabric. If I could somehow get myself off this chair, I might be able to make it to the door and out of the studio. It was a long shot, but I had less than half an hour to try to save myself.

"You can go," Dr. D told Ao Jie Kai, who was standing

behind my chair, out of sight. "But I may need you later."

I heard footsteps walk away into the distance, and forced myself to concentrate. AJ was clearly going somewhere, which meant there was another possible exit route behind me.

"You know, it's pretty lucky you got chosen to do that thing at the Golden Globes," Frank said, and I stared at him, concentrating on keeping my breathing steady. "I was going to go through with the plan with or without the whole fancy title, but I guess life throws you a bone once in a while."

I stared at Frank silently. I couldn't reply even if I wanted to. Not with the stupid cloth in my mouth. Clearly Frank had chosen it as a symbolic date, and had gotten lucky with me being crowned Miss Golden Globe. He was right. Sometimes luck does change. Sometimes it's not for the best.

"I'm bored," Frank continued, giving a small sigh. Now that I had stopped crying, he had run out of entertainment. "We've got all this time, and there really isn't much to do on a half completed film set."

I looked at Frank in disbelief. How could he just sit less than a few feet away from me and tell me he was bored, while I furiously tried to untie myself? I wriggled my hands once more, but the rope wasn't budging. Frank looked at me thoughtfully, as if contemplating something in his mind. He finally leaned over and removed the cloth from my mouth.

"Please!" I begged, the moment I could move my lips freely. "If it's money you want, then we have plenty! A lot more than five million. Just *please* let me go!"

"Easy there, kid," he replied with a scoff. "I only took that out of your mouth so you could actually reply when I said something, and it didn't feel like I was talking to a wall. The begging isn't going to help."

If begging wouldn't work, then I would try reasoning. Either way, I wouldn't stop trying.

"I get it," I said slowly, carefully choosing my words. The tears on my cheeks were beginning to dry. "I understand why you're angry. You've had a crap life that you didn't deserve, while my dad got super lucky. Bu—"

Frank gave a humorless laugh and said, "Lucky? Winning the lottery is lucky, Gia. No, this wasn't luck. Your father took my big break from me. He *stole* my life from me and claimed it as his own."

"You must have made a mistake! My dad would never do that to someone. Especially someone who was his best friend!"

"Why," Frank demanded, looking at me with cold hatred in his eyes. "Do you think I felt so betrayed? I was his best friend. He was like my brother! Why do you think it hurt so much, huh?"

I didn't answer. There was no way my dad would do that to someone. Yes, we didn't always get along. Yes, things had been the rockiest recently given all his secret keeping, and mine too, to be fair. But there was no way Dad was capable of what Frank thought he had done to him all those years ago. Frank blinked and suddenly his friendly smile reappeared, as if he had flicked a switch in his brain. I yanked on my ropes one more time, not expecting anything to come of it. Sure enough, they remained tightly wrapped around my wrists and ankles.

"Well, can I ask you a question?" I said, not giving him time to respond before continuing. "What are you going to do with the five million? I mean, how is it going to fix everything?"

"Ah!" Frank said, as if he were conducting a magic trick. "I'm glad you asked. I'm going to add it to my movie fund."

"Movie fund?"

"Gia, I didn't bring you to this set randomly. Everything I'm doing, everything I've done has had a purpose."

I looked at him, confused. "I—I don't understand."

Frank extended his arms by his side, a proud look on his face. "This," he said. "This is all mine."

I looked around at the set, eyeing the lanterns and painted shops one more time. His? There was no way someone like Frank Parker could afford a set like this. The Dumpling Hospital was on the verge of going out of business, he'd been living out of his car for the past week and his apartment wasn't exactly a Beverly Hills condo. None of this was adding up.

"This is for *your* movie?" I asked, turning my attention back to Frank, who had resumed pacing in front of my chair.

"Yes, Gia. This is my movie. And to answer your second question, those five million dollars aren't going to change the past. But it'll certainly help the future."

"No offense," I said slowly, being extra careful not to say the wrong thing. "But five million is kind of a small budget for a movie. And this set is . . ." I trailed off, hoping he'd understand what I was saying.

"I'm not a fool, Gia," Frank replied. "Admittedly I've had some help on the money front. I did some work back in China for some men who offered to help me out a little."

My thoughts immediately shifted to Jack and his mysterious trust fund. There was no way Jack was involved, like Milo thought he was. Or else he'd be in Ao Jie Kai's place instead of panicking on the phone. That, or he was an excellent actor.

"Some men?" I repeated, raising an eyebrow.

"Powerful men."

"What kind of work?"

Frank stopped pacing and looked over at me thoughtfully. "You ask a lot of questions."

"I'm just trying to figure out how it came to this," I told him.

And I meant it too. Also I had managed to loosen one of the ropes off one of my wrists and was tugging on it gently so that it would give way. My skin underneath the ropes felt raw and ached every time I moved my hands, but if I could manage to get them off me then I had a chance to get away. That was only a possibility if I kept Frank distracted.

"I think I've already made it pretty clear how it came to this, and I think you have your father to blame for that."

If this were a movie, I would have managed to get the ropes untied, picked up the chair and smashed it into Frank, managing to look sexy the whole time. But this was real life, and real life sucked. There was some revenge-driven psychopath who hated my dad and wouldn't stop talking about it, and then there was me. Helpless little Gia, tied to a chair with a ripped gown and mascara probably running all down my face and ruining my perfect contour.

"How did you manage to bug my house?" I asked. "I know you infiltrated that cleaning company, but h—"

"Infiltrated?" Frank echoed with a genuine laugh. "You make it sound like a spy movie."

Really? At a time like this he was going to be iffy about my word choices?

"Was it Ao Jie Kai?"

"Yes, actually, it was" Frank said, beginning to sound impatient. I knew there was only so much more I could ask, but I pushed on.

"How did he manage it?"

I cast my mind back to the day the cleaning crew were in the house. I had been fighting with Dad that day about something or the other; I couldn't even remember. Ao Jie Kai, however he managed to get into the cleaning company undercover, would have had plenty of opportunity to plant the bugs all over my house. He was an IT specialist after all, so it probably wouldn't have been that hard to break apart my phone. Dad and I were so distracted yelling at each other I wouldn't have noticed for one second if he had cracked my phone open in front of me. Now whatever we had been fighting about seemed so stupid and insignificant.

"You know," Frank said, narrowing his eyes at me. I turned

my attention away from my daydream and back to the nightmare playing out in front of me. "It was bad enough that I had to listen to your nonsense all day long through the bugs. And now this interrogation? Do you ever just keep quiet?"

Not going to lie, he had bruised my feelings a bit with that one. I mean, wasn't it bad enough that he had tied me to a chair? It's not like I had asked him to eavesdrop on me all day long! Now he was just getting personal.

"That final bug . . ." I began, suddenly remembering that it was still somewhere in my house.

"And it continues!" Frank exclaimed, an amused look on his face.

I ignored him but tugged on the ropes a little harder, wincing as it dug further into my skin. I tried to be subtle, not moving my body too much to raise suspicion. Luckily I had loosened one to the point where I could almost release my hand.

"Where's that last one? The police never found it."

"That's because you never bothered to check your dog's collar."

"My dog?" My jaw dropped, and I momentarily forgot the ropes.

"Clever, isn't it? Although sometimes very inconvenient. That dog spends most of his time hiding in bushes, by the sounds of it."

Okay, messing with me was one thing. But touching my dog was a whole different game. If I ever got out of the ropes, I was going to kill him.

"And I guess you were behind the paparazzi ambush too?" I asked, and Frank nodded.

"Bad publicity is still good publicity, Gia," he said simply.

"You didn't by any chance have a hand in the Meghan Adams prank did you?"

Frank looked confused. "That one I can't take credit for."

It was worth asking. Evil people run in the same crowds.

"Tell me about the poisoned dumpling," I demanded. "If you say my dad did all those things to you, then I deserve to know everything from the beginning. How else can I believe you?"

Frank sighed and checked his watch. I didn't know how much time had passed, but judging by his impatience, it hadn't been long. He looked at me reluctantly, and gave another sigh as he launched into his explanation.

Frank began his story about how he approached Brendan after school, a few days after Jack's first day. He told me about offering him a discount on catering, telling Brendan a sob story about how he worked in the school cafeteria and heard about the party, and how he was a restaurateur, struggling to make ends meet. Brendan, being the nice guy he was, gave him a chance. That became the point where he roped Ao Jie Kai in as a "waiter" at the party, offering him a little extra cash for his troubles. He had all the technology experience necessary, and needed the money to pay for school.

"But there was poison in that dumpling," I cried, waiting for him to finish. "You could have killed me if your original plan had worked!"

"Oh calm down, it was a tiny amount. It was just meant to send a message," Frank said, waving a hand dismissively. "Such an over actor, just like your father."

Careful Frank, your jealousy is showing.

"So how come you went after me, and not my brother?"

Frank slapped a hand over his eyes and groaned in frustration. "You *seriously* never stop talking!"

"I'm just curious!"

"I swear, I'm going to shove that handkerchief back in your mouth."

"No! Okay, sorry! I'll shut up."

I clasped my lips together, and looked down at my lap.

Anything to stop that filthy cloth from being thrust between my lips again. After about a minute of silence, Frank rolled his eyes dramatically.

"I called your brother first," he said, and I looked up in surprise. "Tried to threaten him a little; scare him. But he kept laughing and calling me Brody. He must have thought I was his friend prank calling or something. It must have been the voice-altering app that AJ suggested I use on my phone. It didn't always make me sound as threatening as I would have hoped."

Well there you have it folks. Mike was literally too dumb to stalk.

"I still don't get why you went after us and not Dad. If he's the one who betrayed you, then why didn't you do anything to him?"

"Gia," Frank said. "Targeting your father would have done nothing. What could I have possibly taken from him that he truly cared about? A car? A watch? These material things come and go. But his kids, on the other hand, are irreplaceable. Possibly the only people he loves more than himself."

I hated to admit it, but he was right. Frank wanted Dad's suffering to be long and extensive, just like his had been. It's not like he could snatch Dad's career away from him. The damage was already done in his eyes, and there was no turning back time. His only option was to make my dad feel so scared of losing everything he cared about, despite having it all.

"Can I have one more question?"

"You're going to ask it either way, right?"

"That depends. Not if you're going to kill me for it."

"One!" he said, throwing his hands up in frustration. "You get one more question and that's it."

It was as if we were playing celebrity heads and I couldn't guess which celebrity he had appointed me. I racked my brain for a good question to ask him, something that would hopefully make a difference to my situation in some way.

"Can I save it for later?" I asked.

"No."

"Who's going to be in your movie?"

Nice one, Gia. You didn't bother to ask him if he could pass you a bottle of water or maybe an apple or gee, I don't know, something to help untie you. Instead you asked him who his fantasy cast would be. There was no way in hell Frank Parker was going to get away with what he did fast enough to round up a group of actors. Even if they were all unemployed and desperate for work, the chances of Frank having more than just himself and his pal AJ as the leads, was slim to none. And I didn't think anyone would want to watch *The Adventures of a Crazed Lunatic and His At Times Uncertain Sidekick.*

"I was thinking about asking your mother to play the lead role opposite me," Frank said with a smile that made me want to knock him out. "Think she'll agree?"

I didn't dignify his sick question with a response. Instead I carefully squeezed my hand through the loosened rope and began freeing my other hand as discreetly as I could. My legs were still firmly tied and hidden underneath my gown. But at least if I got my hands free I would have a better chance of fighting back if necessary.

"Just over ten minutes to go," Frank said, tapping on his watch. "I hope they're close."

"They'll never make it here on time," I replied, trying to keep the defeat and panic out of my voice. "You're setting them up for a loss."

Frank nodded sympathetically and said, "What a shame for you."

"I don't suppose you want to untie me?"

"I don't suppose I do."

Okay, worth a shot.

"Frank," Ao Jie Kai's voice came from somewhere behind me, his footsteps growing louder as he approached us.

I quickly slipped my hand through the rope once more, wincing as it roughly grazed my skin. I sent a little prayer to Baby J, hoping that AJ hadn't noticed, and that Jack and my dad were close by. With lots of backup.

"What?" Frank asked AJ, who was still standing behind me and out of my sight.

"The car won't start."

"You're kidding me, right?" Frank said, with an incredulous look on his face.

"I don't know what happened," came Ao Jie Kai's voice. "But it won't start. I think something's wrong with the engine."

"Well fix it!" Frank snapped.

"I—I don't know how," Ao Jie Kai replied.

Oh lordy. I actually felt bad for Ao Jie Kai then. Frank was not having a good day, or two decades, to be exact. And AJ was about to become minced meat if he didn't get that car running. As much as he had it coming, I was scared enough of Frank for the both of us. I could lend him some of my terror.

"You literally had *one* job!" Frank cried, clasping his eyes shut as if he was struggling to accept his current bad luck. "Forget it, I'll do it!"

Ao Jie Kai remained silent, but after a few seconds his footsteps began to fade until I couldn't hear them anymore. *One job* seemed a little inaccurate. I mean the poor weirdo did have to do most of his dirty work for him.

"Wait—" I began, as Frank gave a frustrated sigh and headed toward the exit.

"I'll be right back," Frank said gruffly. "Don't try anything smart! You'll get yourself killed."

I opened my mouth to say something and then closed it again when I saw how scary Frank looked. I nodded to tell him

I understood and sat there silently until I heard his footsteps disappear behind me just like AJ's had. I counted to five in my head after I couldn't hear anything except my own heart in my chest, and craned my neck to look behind my shoulder. No Frank hiding behind my chair, ready to scare me. Just more lanterns, shadows and pretend Chinese shops.

I whipped my right hand out from rope and examined it carefully. The skin around my wrist was red, and the rope had cut in so far that it was almost bleeding. I blew gently on the raw skin, not knowing how that would help, but doing it anyway. Forcing myself to not burst into tears, I twisted my torso uncomfortably so I could see where my other hand was behind the chair.

"Come on!" I hissed, as I pulled the rope wrapped around my left hand.

It finally began to loosen and I sighed in relief. I yanked on it a little more, only enough so that I could slide my hand in and out of the loop like I could with my other one, but not enough that Frank would notice. Unfortunately there was no hope for my legs. Each one of my ankles had been tied to a separate chair leg and not together like my hands were. If I tried to untie them then I risked exposing the fact that my hands were free. There was no point even attempting to run for it. I'd never free myself in time, and there was no saying what Frank would do to me if he caught me trying to escape.

I did some breathing exercises and carefully took in my surroundings, trying to figure out what could help me in my escape. Finally, by the large dragon in the corner of the room, my eye caught a door handle. I leaned to the left on my chair, squinting to get a better look in the light from the lanterns. Yes! Definitely a door handle. All I needed to do was get past Frank.

I suddenly heard distant talking and I sat up straight in my chair, pushing my hands closer together.

"They're here!" Frank called from behind me in an almost

singsong voice.

My heart began to race as I clasped my eyes shut in a mixture of anxiety and relief. Finally, Frank would get his money and leave us alone forever. Hopefully. I heard footsteps walking from behind me, and my eyes fluttered open just in time to see Frank reappear in front of my chair.

"Where are they?" I asked.

"Timing, Gia. It's all about the timing. You should know better," Frank said, as if he were telling his child he was disappointed in them.

I waited silently, holding my breath as Frank mouthed *three, two, one*. Sure enough, after only three seconds I heard the very same door I planned to escape from, open.

"Oh, thank God," I whispered, as my dad and Jack came into view, still in their tuxedos.

I tried desperately to hold back my tears, but they sprung to my eyes anyway. I had never been so glad to see Jack in my life, and never as appreciative of my father until that moment. We watched in silence as they approached, Ao Jie Kai re-emerging like a ninja from the dark corners of the set. Dad's face was painted with worry lines. He looked about twenty years older than he actually was, and was taking deep breaths as he walked over to us. Jack seemed a little calmer, but not at all relaxed. More than anything he looked ready to battle, which I hoped was something that would get us all out alive.

"Welcome!" Frank said with a cheerful smile. "Harry, old pal. Long time, no see."

"Jesus, Frank!" Dad practically exploded in reply. "That's my daughter you've got tied up there! She's just a kid!"

"She's close enough to how old you were when you—"

"When I what?" Dad cried, clearly expressing all the frustration he had managed to keep bottled in until then. "I didn't do anything to you! This whole vendetta you've got against me is ridiculous!"

"Check them," Frank said, and we all gave him a confused look.

AJ seemed to understand that the instructions were direct-ed toward him, because he stepped into view and began patting down Jack, checking his pockets for any weapons. Jack extend-ed his arms in compliance, locking eyes with me as Ao Jie Kai searched him. He gave me a nod so subtle that I would have missed it if I had blinked, just as AJ moved onto my father to do the same. When he was satisfied that neither had brought in any weapons, he stepped back silently into the shadows.

Fantastic. Jack had brought nothing along to defend us from a lunatic who had me tied to a chair. I know half an hour isn't much time, but the planning on his part was seriously shoddy. I knew we should have hired John Cena instead.

"Question," Jack said. "What exactly am *I* doing here?"

"Are you serious?" I said incredulously, still half-crying. Jack cut his eyes to me, expressionless.

Typical. I was strapped to a chair in the middle of fake China and Jack wanted to know his role in the whole situation.

"You're here to make sure she cooperates," Frank told him, cocking his head in my direction.

"Which means?" Jack said.

"So where's the money, boys?" Frank asked, ignoring Jack.

My gaze dropped to Dad's hands. No briefcase, so plastic bag, no nothing. I looked at Jack. His hands were empty too.

"I have a check in my pocket," Dad told him, slowly pulling out a piece of paper from inside his tuxedo coat.

Frank snatched the check from Dad the second it came into view and inspected it thoughtfully. I sniffled.

"Did I not say five million cash?" he asked Dad.

"No," Jack replied roughly. "You didn't."

"Oh silly me," Frank said, handing the check to AJ. "That

check's not gonna cut it."

"What?" Jack exclaimed. "No bank just hands you five million dollars on such short notice! It doesn't work like that!"

"It's okay, Jack." Dad said in a surprisingly calm voice. "I'll give you whatever you want, Frank. Just please let my daughter go."

"Well that doesn't seem fair," Frank replied. "First, you show up late—"

"We're early!" Jack cried.

"Then you don't even have what I asked for. And now you want me to give you the one thing I have over you, right now? Yeah, no thanks. I think I'll keep her tied for a bit longer."

"Come on, Frank!" Dad said, his desperation beginning to show. "What happened to you? We used to be best friends. Brothers. And now this is what it's come to?"

"Really breaks your heart, doesn't it?" Frank sneered, stepping closer to Dad. "Poor Harry and his poor little girl. Well guess what? You got yourself into this mess the moment you chose your fame over your best friend. Your so-called *brother.*"

Frank spat the word "brother" out like venom. All his cheeriness had disappeared from his face, and in its place was only hatred. It was at that point that I realized Frank was beyond the hope of reason. We just needed to figure out a way to get around him and run.

"I don't even know what you're talking about!" Dad cried, throwing his hands in the air in frustration. "You keep yelling about how I betrayed you, when all I did was support you!"

"Support me?" Frank said with a scoff. "So you were *supporting* me when you convinced Marty to give you a once in a lifetime role that made your career? A role that was given to me first!"

"What role?" Dad cried out in exasperation. "I don't understand!"

"*Piece of My Heart!*" Frank shot back, his loud voice echoing off the set walls. "That role was mine and you took it from me! You left me with nothing!"

Dad's face filled with confusion. "You were offered the lead in *Piece of My Heart?*"

"Oh come on!" Frank exclaimed, glaring at Dad. "Don't act so surprised. You're not that good of an actor."

"Frank, I swear," Dad said firmly. "I didn't know!"

"So you're telling me," Frank began. "That you *didn't* know I was offered the part? And that you *didn't* know Marty came to me, told me they decided to go with you instead. That they held another audition for you upon your request for a second chance, and they gave it to you instead of me."

"Yes!" Dad cried. "That's exactly right. I didn't know any of that! And they never held another audition for me!"

Frank shook his head in disbelief. "You're lying."

"Frank," Dad said, steadying his voice. "I swear to you. I didn't know you got offered the role. You never even told me!"

"You never gave me a chance!" Frank snapped. "Nobody did. They just handed you the role like you got handed everything else."

"That's not fair!" Dad said angrily.

"Oh give it a rest!" Frank replied, his irritation growing. "We both know that if you hadn't gotten that role then you would have made it big anyway! Your father was huge in the theatre! He probably helped you get that second audition."

"Frank, be reasonable," Dad said. "If what you're saying is true, then why did I need to steal your role? Why did I need another audition?"

Everyone fell silent as we thought about how logical his argument was. I made eye contact with Jack, who just stared back at me. He was as lost as I was.

"I don't need to know your reasons," Frank finally said. "All that matters is that you stole my life from me! I was completely invisible to everyone after that! Every audition, every opportunity! It was just taken away!"

Dad opened his mouth to say something but Jack got there first. "If I may," he said, holding up his palms so that the argument would stop. "I think you should talk to this Marty guy. Clearly he seems to be the cause of this misunderstanding."

"We can't," Dad replied with a sigh, looking at his hands. "He had a heart attack about twelve years ago and died."

"Karma, I'd like to think," Frank said, a hint of a smile across his lips.

Fantastic. The one man who seemed to really be at fault here was conveniently not alive to deal with the mess he created. Just swell.

"Well," Jack said, awkwardly. "Okay then."

"It wouldn't have mattered anyway," Frank scoffed. "Marty always played favorites with Harry."

"He was our agent, Frank!" Dad exclaimed, frustration growing in his voice. "If he really liked me more than you, then he wouldn't have even told you about the audition in the first place!"

"Ye—" Frank began, but Dad cut him off.

"And maybe he would have like you better," Dad continued. "If you hadn't been messing around with his wife!"

I inhaled sharply without realizing, and whispered *oh snap* to myself. Frank had his very own Mrs. Robinson situation! I knew there had to be a more scandalous aspect to the whole equation. Ao Jie Kai, who had been so silent I had forgotten he was there, shifted uncomfortably from one foot to another.

"What?" Frank said, his voice becoming dead quiet. "What did you say?"

"Oh come on, Frank!" Dad said, shaking his head lightly. "We were best friends! You think I didn't know you and Monica were doing something?"

Frank's body went stiff as he looked at Dad in surprise. "T—That's . . . Y—You never said anything."

"You were happy," Dad replied with a light shrug. "I mean, I didn't think it was a great idea, but I figured it was none of my business."

Suddenly everything became clear. Frank must have been offered the lead role in *Piece of My Heart* and in his happiness, he went and told Marty's wife first. Somehow, Marty must have found out about his wife, who I was desperately hoping was not like a sixty-year-old woman back then, and taken his revenge on Frank by blacklisting him. He probably called the producers, made up some story so they would drop Frank, and convinced them to go for my father instead. I guess it was just easier for Marty to lie to everyone than confront Frank and let him know the truth.

My theory clearly seemed to be shared by Frank, who was shaking his head as if rejecting the possibility that he could be the one to blame for his own misfortune.

"It doesn't matter now," Frank said, shaking his head even harder. "None of it matters anymore."

"Fran—" Dad began, calmly extending his hand toward his ex-friend.

"No!" Frank cried, slapping Dad's hand away. "Don't you dare pity me!"

In what seemed like a blink of an eye, Frank reached for something tucked into the back of his jeans hidden under his jacket and pulled out a revolver, aiming it at my dad.

"Frank!" AJ exclaimed, shooting him an alarmed look. "What the hell?"

"The money isn't going to cut it anymore," Frank declared, his hand shaking a little as he tightened his grasp on the gun.

"Frank!" AJ hissed, coming up next to him in a panic. "Come on man, this wasn't part of the plan!"

"Let's be reasonable, Frank," Jack said, his voice surprisingly steady. "No need to do anything stupid."

"I'm done being reasonable!" Frank snapped. "Someone has to pay for what happened!"

Everyone was quiet for a few seconds, as Frank considered his options. I watched carefully, moving only my eyes. It's one thing to watch someone point a gun at your dad in a movie. It's a whole other thing to watch it play out in reality, where the possibility of him getting killed is a lot higher. Every part of my body was aching with fear.

"Frank," Dad said calmly. "If you want to shoot me, then do it. But please let Gia go."

I gave Dad an *are you serious* look, but he wasn't looking at me. His eyes were now glued to the gun that was pointed at him.

"Fine," Frank said. "Works for me."

"Wait, what?" I exclaimed in alarm, and everyone looked at me. "Are you insane?"

"Gia!" Jack shot me a warning glare, but I ignored him.

"No!" I cried. "That's ridiculous! You didn't even do anything wrong, Dad! He can't just shoot you!"

Jack mouthed my name angrily and shook his head. I probably should have listened to him and calmed down a little, given that I was yelling at a guy who was pointing a gun at my father. But it felt like a little part of me had snapped. Although the timing was inconvenient, I was getting real sick of being stalked, scared and tormented. Especially now that I knew it was all done by a maniac who really only had himself to blame for everything that went wrong in his life. And if I'm being *really* honest here, *Piece of My Heart* was a pretty lame movie. Dad couldn't pull off the doctor look, and the scene transitioning was nothing to brag about. If you're going to hold a grudge, at least make it worth your while.

Plus, the way Frank's hand was shaking as he held that gun,

it was clear he didn't really want to shoot any of us. He was good at making threats, but not great at acting on them. He had been stalking me for over two months, with multiple opportunities to make a move, and he still hadn't done any major damage. If he wanted to hurt me, he would have by now. It was definitely a crazy risk to take, but the way I saw it, I didn't have too many options.

"Gia, it's fine," Dad said.

"How is it fine?" I practically yelled. I turned my attention to Frank, who was still aiming the gun in my dad's direction. "None of this is fine! Even *you* know he didn't do anything!"

I didn't care about the dangers at that point. Frank's hand was beginning to shake again violently, which meant my words were hitting home. It even began to lower ever so slightly. There was still hope.

"Gi—"

"Shut up, Jack!" I said while I glowered at Frank, "You don't get to stalk me for months, ruin my life, kidnap me, tie me to a chair, destroy my dress, steal my phone and now shoot my dad all because *you* couldn't keep it in your pants a million years ago!"

"GIA." Jack's voice had risen in volume.

"You really think that killing my dad is going to make it all better?" I demanded angrily. "At the end of the day, you'll still know the truth. You'll know you only have yourself to blame for your life!"

"That's enough, Gia," Dad said quietly, but there wasn't enough strength in it to stop me from finishing.

"He's had a full career. Everyone will mourn him. The whole world will cry! Everyone respects him! That's something you'll never have, even if you try to take it from someone at gunpoint. At the end of the day you'll always be what you are inside."

"GIA!"

"Nothing! A completely worthless *nobody!*"

My words echoed across the set walls, as I snapped my mouth shut. I may have overdone it slightly, and made him more angry than before. Which isn't great because if he shot my dad it would be my fault. If he shot me, it would suck an equal amount. If he shot Jack then Jack would probably shoot me in revenge. So either way the plan wasn't looking so great anymore.

"It seems," Frank finally said, eyes locked on me. "That bringing the blonde one here was a bit of a waste. He couldn't shut you up after all. Should've tried the cop."

Frank's gun slowly rose once more so that it was staring at my dad's chest, eager for someone to pull on the trigger. I stopped breathing, not daring to look at Jack. My heart had constricted so much, I was scared it had shrivelled up completely and evaporated. I had officially sealed my father's death, and there was no emotion to describe the pain that brought with it.

"Shut her up," Frank snapped at Ao Jie Kai, his eyes still on me.

AJ reluctantly walked over to me, mumbling something to himself. If there was anyone who felt unhappiest about this whole thing, it was probably Ao Jie Kai. But he had gotten himself into the mess, so my sympathy levels were pretty low.

"There's no need for you to keep Gia," Dad said, as I watched AJ approach me almost sheepishly. "You're already getting your revenge."

"I'll be the judge of that," Frank replied, his eyes narrowed with fury.

"Yeah, I don't think so," Jack said, launching at Frank and knocking the gun out of his hands.

Frank watched his gun hit the floor in surprise, but Jack wasn't done yet. He grabbed Frank by neck of his jacket and dragged him backward.

"What the hell . . ." AJ said, turning to face Jack, who was struggling with Frank.

I did some quick thinking and slipped my hands out of the rope as fast as I could. I clasped one hand on each side of the chair seat and lifted myself up as though I was awkwardly bowing. With my ankles still tied to the legs of the chair, I clumsily launched at Ao Jie Kai, ramming my chair into him as hard as I could. I gave out a small yelp as he crumpled to the floor in surprise, clutching his arm in pain. I watched him roll around in pain for a few seconds, slightly apologetic for coming at him full force with a chair. But then Dad came rushing up to help and I realized I didn't feel so bad any more.

"Untie your legs!" Dad instructed, and I obediently placed the back legs of the chair back on the ground. "I'll deal with this."

Dad punched AJ in the face, and blood immediately began spurting out of his nose.

"Dad!" I cried in disgust, but I didn't blink once. "You've got blood on your Givenchy suit!"

Once Brendan had gotten into a fight with some guy he met at a party, and kicked the crap out him. But in that moment, I was glad Brendan had never gone head to head with my dad. My father had a mean punch.

"Untie yourself!" Dad barked, flexing his hand.

There was blood on Dad's knuckles, and I watched as he wiggled his fingers with a wince. He had probably broken his hand, or cracked something at the very least. Ao Jie Kai was in a slightly worse off situation, as was his nose, which was most definitely a goner.

I snapped myself into attention and began clawing at the ropes on my ankles. In the distance I could hear Jack and Frank struggling with each other, but I forced myself to work on freeing my ankles from the ropes. I wasn't much help if I was still tied up. I wasn't much help period, but the freedom to walk would definitely come in handy.

"I'm going to go help," Dad told me hurriedly. "Are you

okay here?"

"I'm fine."

"Are you su—"

"Yes! Go!"

I watched as he rushed over to Jack, who was wrestling with Frank on the ground, trying to keep the gun out of reach. If Frank got his hands on that gun, he would be far from willing to let us go without a scratch. I wrenched my left leg free from the rope, ignoring the pain my foot was in. The heels didn't exactly help the raw skin around my ankles, identical to that on my wrists. One ankle was free, just one more to go. And now thanks to Dad, AJ didn't seem to be much of a threat anymore. He was struggling to just stay conscious.

"Finally!" I whispered in relief, as I tugged the remaining rope off my ankle and threw it on the ground.

I jumped up from the chair, my gown falling to floor length again. Beautiful as it was, it wasn't really appropriate attire for kicking ass. I pushed the chair away; ready to help in any way I could when I felt something yank my gown so hard that I almost fell over. I looked down to see Ao Jie Kai, writhing in pain but attempting to hold me back with a surprisingly strong hold.

"Get. Off. My. Dress!" I cried, enunciating each word with a tug.

AJ was badly hurt, and slowly running out of energy. He would probably give up in a minute, but that was a minute I didn't have. I sank to the floor, yanking on the dress in frustration.

"Seriously?" I looked at him with exasperation. "You and I both know you don't even want to be here! So just let go so we can all move on with our lives!"

After a few more pain-filled groans, AJ's bloodied hand unclenched and moved to his nose, which was looking worse by the second. If he thought a broken bone and a prison cell were going to get him out of the dry cleaning bill I'd be mailing him, he had another thing coming. I was in the process of scrambling to my feet when the sound of a loud bang stopped me. I hit the ground instinctively, clenching my eyelids shut as I lay my cheek onto the cold set floor.

My heart was beating so fast; I was scared it would burst through my chest. I was no expert, but my dad had been in enough action movies for me to immediately recognize the source of the noise. A gunshot. After a few long seconds of heavy silence, I sat up breathlessly. Jack and my father rose slowly from the ground, backing away from Frank who had the gun pointed at the ceiling. Thankfully the bullet had hit the roof and nothing or no one else. Jack was bleeding a little near his right eye, Frank's cheek looked a little too red and Dad's shirt was ripped. They looked like they were part of some well-dressed fight club, breathing heavily with bowties and clenched fists.

In what felt like a millisecond after, the sound of chaos filled the set. I turned to look behind me, as police officers and men in black uniforms came swarming in from doors I didn't even know existed.

"FREEZE," one yelled.

"PUT YOUR WEAPON ON THE GROUND," another instructed, rushing closer to us.

I turned once again, just in time to see another team of men making their way through the door I had first spotted as my best escape route. They were all yelling out instructions to Frank, who was looking around the set with a panicked look on his face. None of the agents were nearly close enough to wrestle the gun out of Frank's hand like Jack had done before, but they were getting there.

"SIR, I SAID DROP YOUR WEAPON."

I had time to only blink once when I head another gunshot, then another and another. I clapped my hand over my eyes and let out a scream. The ringing in my ears was so harsh I wanted to cry. It was finally the sound of something clattering to the floor that forced me to face Frank again, the yelling around me growing louder. I removed my hands from my eyes cautiously and saw Frank was on his knees, his fingers laced together behind his head. He didn't look injured at all. My eyes trailed to the gun lying next to him, and the body lying a few feet away from it.

The chaos around me became a blur as I focused on Jack and his lifeless body. He lay next to my stunned father, who thankfully seemed fine, albeit a little bruised. A police officer knelt down and helped my father up, as two more crouched down near Jack. It was Detective Reynolds. I pulled my gaze back to Frank, my ears unable to register any sound around me. There were two men dress in black from head to toe holstering their guns, pulling Frank to his feet. I assumed somewhere behind me, Ao Jie Kai was getting the same treatment. Everyone's lips were moving but I couldn't hear anything. I couldn't feel anything. All I knew was Jack had been shot, a pool of blood escaping from beneath his body.

I felt someone place a hand on my shoulder, but I didn't move. They were asking me if I could stand up, whether or not I was injured. There were voices speaking above me, but I couldn't stop staring. It was like I had momentarily forgotten how to function. Then suddenly Milo came into view, kneeling down in front of me with concern.

"Gia," he said as calmly as he could. "You're in shock right now; it's perfectly normal. But we need to get you out of here. Do you think you're okay to stand?"

I blinked, snapping back to attention. Suddenly every sound in the warehouse was crashing against my ears. I could hear the officers and agents scattered everywhere, calling out instructions, handcuffs clicking into place, someone calling for an ambulance. Everything was catching up with me so quickly, it felt like I was suffocating.

"J—Jack!" I cried, and I realized I was crying.

Milo cupped my face in his hands and looked at me straight in my eyes. "Gia, I want you to listen to me." He said, sounding more strained. "I'm going to need you to stand up for me. Can you do that?"

I wrapped my hands around his wrists and shook my head frantically. "Milo, we can't just leave him here! We have to help him! We have to—"

"He'll be fine, Gia! The ambulance is right outside. So are the FBI." Milo interrupted before I could argue. "Right now, you need to get out of here. Are you listening?"

I nodded meekly, and Milo removed my hands from my face. He took my hands and helped me to my feet slowly. Ten seconds ago I was ready to make the floor my permanent home, but now I was desperate to break through the walls. Milo put his arm around my waist, holding me upright as I hobbled forward in my heels. An officer who I vaguely recognized held my other arm supportively, watching me apprehensively as if I were going to collapse any second.

"Careful," Milo said, like I was made of glass. I wasn't sure if he was talking to his colleague or me.

I let them lead me out the exit without a second look back. I was already having a hard time breathing, and I didn't entirely trust what my heart would do if I did sneak a glance of the scene behind me.

Milo and the officer exchanged wary glances. Neither of them mentioned the grim possibility looming over our heads. Neither of them acknowledged that Jack might be dead.

c h a p t e r
t w e n t y - f i v e

FOR THE second time that evening, I awoke in a complete daze. Thankfully this time I hadn't been drugged; my body had just decided I had been freaking out way too much lately and needed a minute or two to reboot. My vision steadied as my gaze fell onto Milo, who was looking down at me with furrowed eyebrows.

"Gia?" he said softly, and I felt a hand rest carefully on my shoulder.

I looked past Milo's head. It was all black, with only specs of silver scattered around. I tried to lift my head but it felt like it weighed a ton. I dropped it back again, resting it on something surprisingly soft. I heard footsteps hitting the floor as someone came running up.

"Oh good, she's awake," said a voice I didn't recognize.

I turned my head to the side slowly, groaning in pain and confusion. Milo, who was evidently the soft object I had been resting on, carefully propped me up to a sitting position. I looked up at him and he gave me a tight smile.

"What happened?" I asked.

Before he could answer, my brain snapped into action and everything hit me like a tsunami. Frank, the lanterns, a gun, three loud bangs, handcuffs and being unable to breathe. It seemed like weeks ago, but I knew it had only just happened.

"You fainted," Milo told me. "I think you had a bit of a panic attack."

"Oh."

I turned my head in the direction of where the unfamiliar voice had come from a moment before. There was a middle-aged paramedic standing in uniform with a bottle of water in one hand. She gave me a warm smile and knelt down next to me.

"Hey, honey," she said kindly. "Here, have some water."

She handed me the water bottle but my hands stayed by my side, looking down to examine where I was. I seemed to be lying on the pavement, right where I had fainted before. Which, may I add, is not exactly the same as landing on Egyptian cotton sheets. Either I hadn't been unconscious long, or no one had bothered to move me to a more comfortable position. Milo's right arm was wrapped around my waist; his left hand reaching over to take the water bottle from the paramedic. I mumbled a thank you as I took the water bottle from him, and the paramedic rose to her feet. She told us she would send someone to assess me and walked off toward the flashing lights, coming from the police cars and ambulance vans.

"How long have I been out?" I asked Milo, uncapping the water bottle with shaky hands.

I tried to sit up a little straighter; suddenly feeling very conscious of the position Milo and I were sitting in. But he didn't budge. Instead he tightened his grip around my waist, and my body stiffened.

"About a minute the first time," he replied.

I put the water bottle to my lips, but paused before taking a sip. "First time?"

"Yeah," Milo said. "You woke up and then kind of collapsed again. But you haven't been out long."

I took a sip of water and gulped it down. I felt the water go down my throat slowly, and I put a hand to my chest as I choked it down. I forced another few sips into me and immediately began to feel a bit better. I capped the bottle and placed it on the floor next to me, watching as a police car slowly backed out of the parking lot and drove off out of sight.

"Was that—"

"Frank," Milo finished for me, and I turned to look at him. "Ao Jie Kai is probably in one of the other cars. We'll be taking them to the station now."

"So . . . it's over."

"It's over."

"My dad!" I suddenly exclaimed, remembering that the last time I had seen him was on the floor in the warehouse behind me.

I slapped my palms to the floor, knocking the water bottle over as I attempted to push myself off the ground. Milo pulled me closer to him, lifting my hand up from the concrete floor and squeezing it in his own.

"Gia, calm down! He's safe. He's getting checked by the ambulance over there."

Milo cocked his head to the left and I followed his gaze past all the police cars and chaos until my eyes finally caught my dad sitting on the edge of an open ambulance van, talking to Detective Reynolds and Kenny. His face looked weary and exhausted, like he had just walked a hundred miles in a desert without stopping. I felt relief crash over me.

"My mother?" I asked.

"On her way," Milo told me. "She should be here any minute."

"Is Mike okay?"

"He's still at your aunt's house. He's safe, we just checked."

I looked at Milo. There was one person still unaccounted for, but I was nervous to even ask about.

"What about Jack?"

Milo let out a soft sigh and I prepared myself for the worst. I hadn't seen him anywhere around, so either he had already been carted off in an ambulance or he hadn't been moved out of the set yet. Or worse, but I didn't want to think about that.

"He was shot," Milo said cautiously, and my heart sank further into the pit of my stomach.

"But he's okay?"

Milo opened his mouth to reply, but a voice behind me answered for him.

"Well I mean, that depends," Jack said and I looked up. "I took the bullet, so it's okay for *you*. But my arm is killing me!"

He smiled as I examined him frantically. His tuxedo jacket had been taken off, and his white shirtsleeves were rolled up over half way up his arms. His right arm was bandaged a bit above his elbow, the rim of his rolled sleeve stained with his blood. The cut above his eye was no longer bleeding. I pulled my hand out of Milo's grasp and pushed myself to my feet before anyone could stop me. Half tripping over my dress, I threw my arms around Jack, pulling him into the tightest hug I had ever given anyone.

"Ow!" Jack exclaimed, and I pulled back almost instantly. "My arm, Gia!"

"I'm so sorry!" I cried, taking a step back. "Oh my gosh, I'm sorry!"

Jack shook his head and laughed lightly. "It's fine! Don't worry."

Milo stood up awkwardly, dusting off his uniform. He straightened his cuffs and gave me a tight smile.

"I'm going to go check on your dad and make sure everything's alright."

I gave him a warm smile in reply, my emotions still on dangerous highs, and watched him walk toward the sea of uniforms.

"He seems overly enthusiastic about my safe condition" Jack said sarcastically.

"I can't believe you!" I cried, giving Jack a light shove. Oh fantastic, the waterworks were back. "Can you imagine if you had died? Can you imagine what that would have felt like for me?"

"Hey!" Jack said, catching onto my hand that was braced to shove him once more. He tightened his grip and pulled me closer to him. "Can you imagine what that would have felt like for *me*?"

I pulled my arm away and gave him another hug, careful not to injure his arm any further. Who would have thought Jack Anderson and I would be hugging in a parking lot, blood and smudged makeup everywhere?

"I can't believe you're alive."

"The bullet-proof vests were a good idea, I'm not going to lie," Jack said, patting my hair comfortingly.

I broke away from the embrace and looked at him. "You were wearing a vest?"

Jack nodded and said, "So was your dad. I guess our pal AJ isn't too great at checking for these things."

I wiped my wet cheeks with the back of my palms, wincing at the sight of my injured wrists. "That's so smart!"

"Well, I still caught a bullet!"

"Yeah, but it could have been worse!"

"True. But Milo wasn't wrong about the vests; they're freaking uncomfortable! Thank God, they just pulled mine off."

"Uncomfortable?" I repeated, giving him an incredulous look. "They saved your life! Wait a second. When I looked over at you after Frank fired the shots, you looked dead. Like, big time dead. You weren't moving at all!"

Two FBI agents immersed in conversation walked past us, without even giving us a second glance. Jack waited for them to pass before he spoke.

He lowered his voice and said, "Don't tell anyone 'cause it hurts my manhood. But I passed out. I hit my head on the floor really hard and freaked, and I guess I just fainted for a second."

I put a hand over my mouth, desperately trying to stifle my laughter. "Wow. I really feel for your manhood."

"Shut up!" Jack replied, but he was smiling so I knew he was playing along with the joke. "You fainted twice!"

"Yeah, but I had a legit reason!"

"I got shot in the arm! Isn't that legit enough?"

I looked at his arm with a grimace. Even through the bandage you could see the blood from where the bullet had hit him. "You should go to a hospital," I told him, my smile fading.

Jack looked back at the ambulance vans and said, "Yeah, they're trying to get me to go. Apparently I got lucky; the bullet just grazed the skin and didn't actually go through. But I probably should get some morphine or something."

I winced as he described his wound, imagining a bullet hitting his arm in slow motion.

"Yeah," I agreed. "Hey, Jack I'm sorry for ever—"

"Don't even worry about it."

I shook my head at him firmly and said, "No! I was way out of line."

"Gia," Jack said, looking troubled. "That money . . . It's complicated. It's not mine. I mean it is. But I don't use it."

I waited for him to continue, but it looked like he was kind of struggling so I cut him off. "Jack, I don't need to know. It's your business, and I completely trust you."

Actually I was majorly curious and I would probably be

Googling this later. But it *was* his business, and he had saved my life and taken a bullet for my father. I wasn't really in a position to ask for anything more.

"I've been meaning to tell you something," Jack said, looking serious. "But I guess I've just been putting it off."

My heart picked up speed. "Yes?"

"I . . ." Jack paused, looking at his shoes dramatically.

Dear God, was this the moment I had been waiting for? Was Jack about to say what I thought he was? I wasn't sure I was ready for this.

"Go on," I said nervously.

"Ivan Moore."

I blinked at him in confusion. Did he say Ivan Moore or "*I want more*" in a really weird Russian accent? There was so much noise in the background, I couldn't be too certain.

"I'm sorry, what now?" I asked.

"Ivan Moore," he repeated with a grin. "The mystery father of the Golden Globes baby. And get this, he's her agent's younger brother."

My jaw dropped. Not quite what I was hoping to hear, but I can't say I was too disappointed.

"No. Freaking. Way!"

"Yes freaking way."

"NO."

"Yeah. Apparently they met at some luncheon or a party or something. Anyway, the rest was history."

"This is like, life changing. Seriously. Why hasn't MTV made a TV show about their lives yet?"

"They're clearly missing out."

"GIA!" My dad called out from somewhere in the distance. I turned to see him half-sprinting toward me in his ripped shirt, Kenny close behind him.

I ignored my tortured feet, still squeezed into the heels, and ran up to him. I launched at him with so much force, he stumbled a bit as he hugged me back.

"You're okay," he whispered, as he ran his hand soothingly down my now completely loose hair. "You're alright, sweetheart. You're safe now."

I pulled apart from him a little, still resting my hands on his shoulders. The tears were definitely on their way, but I held them in. Mom had once told me that crying a lot creates wrinkles. I wasn't about to be kidnapped *and* look ten years older all in one night. No thank you, sir.

"Dad!" I exclaimed. "You're safe! For a minute there I was sure I had lost you!"

"I'm not going anywhere, Gia."

I removed my hands from his shoulders and looked at him square in the eye. "Dad I'm really sorry! I've been so difficult lately. Lashing out, not listening to you, hiding things from you. You're the best father anyone could ever have, and I'm just sorry for everything."

Dad opened his mouth to say something and closed it again. He was silent for a few seconds before he smiled and patted my arm with the hand that wasn't bandaged.

"Thank you." He looked over my head to where Jack was standing and added, "And you too, Jack. You saved my life; pushing me out of harm's way like that. That was very brave. I'm forever indebted."

"It was my job, sir," Jack replied, with a gracious nod. "And my pleasure."

Jack had officially beaten me on the list of people my father loves, and rightfully so. Pushing him out of the way of three bullets and catching one himself kind of puts him in first place. I mouthed *thank you* to him and he winked at me, his lips curving into a half smile.

Almost as if it were a sixth sense, I could suddenly feel that my mother had finally arrived. Sure enough, just a few seconds later I could hear her frantically calling out my name, rushing toward me. Jack, Kenny, Dad and I watched her run toward us, half-waddling because of her heels and the train on her gown.

"Oh my gosh!" she cried, practically slamming into me. She hugged me so tight I could barely breathe. "My baby!"

"I'm okay, Mom!" I assured her, my voice muffled amongst her still perfect looking hair.

Mom pulled away from me before I had a chance to hug her back, examining me up and down just as I had done to Jack when I realized he was alive.

"Are you hurt?" she practically yelled. "Turn around! Are you alright? I am going to murder that man!"

A police officer walking past stopped momentarily, an eyebrow raised.

"She's kidding," Kenny said. "Nothing to see here."

"Mom, I'm okay!" I replied, pulling my arm out of her reach so she couldn't turn me around.

"You!" She cried to a paramedic coming up next to her.

"Y—Yes?"

I gave the paramedic an apologetic look. She looked too young and inexperienced to be dealing with my mother's harassment.

"Check her!" Mom demanded, pointing at me. She stopped, eyes fixated on the hem of my dress. "Is that . . . *blood* on your Monique Lhuillier gown?"

"Mom!" I said in alarm. She looked on the verge of passing out. "It's fixable. Chill."

"That's alright," Dad told the paramedic calmly. "We'll send Gia over in a second."

"Uh, yeah, you can check me instead," Jack said, motioning toward his injured arm. "Come on, Kenny."

Jack stood between my mother and the paramedic, practically

pulling her away before Mom could scare her anymore. That boy seriously deserved a fruit basket or something. Or, I was completely wrong and he was making a move on the paramedic. It was probably the second one.

Mom ran her fingers through her hair and blew out a sigh. Dad opened his mouth to say something but before he could, Mom turned and whacked him in the arm as hard as she could.

"OW!"

"Mom!"

"This is all your fault!" she exclaimed. "We should have never let Gia out in such a public place like that."

"My fault?" Dad replied, giving her a look of complete disbelief. "I was the one who said it was too dangerous for Gia to do the whole Golden Globes thing. *You* insisted that she do it!"

"And whose choice was it to befriend the Chinese lunatic, huh?"

"He's not even Chinese!"

"His nationality isn't actually what I'm concerned about, Harry!"

"Guys stop!" I interrupted, before they could continue their argument. They both looked at me. "Seriously! Whatever happened, happened. It's over now! It's no one's fault but Frank's. So let's just move on and stop blaming each other!"

My parents looked at me sheepishly, as if they were two kids being told off for some act of mischief. It was quite possibly the only time I could act like the parent without someone shutting me down, so I smiled a little, enjoying the power.

Unfortunately that was cut short when Dad said, "When you said you were hiding things from me, what did you mean?"

Oh shoot. There was no way I was going to tell my dad about the Coco Club, sneaking out of the house and using a fake ID. I was definitely sorry for all that, but I hardly thought it mattered now. No need to dwell on the past.

"I'm going to go get some medical help," I told him, smiling innocently.

Dad gave me a knowing look, but stepped aside so I could move past him. I smiled at both my parents, sent a mental message to Baby J to thank him for doing me a solid and saving all our lives. That was going in the *I owe you* book for sure.

Ten minutes later, I was sitting in an open ambulance van running my fingers softly over my bandaged wrists. It was past one in the morning and the exhaustion was starting to hit me. I had been briefed by about twenty different agents in the last five minutes, and my energy levels were running dangerously low. What did a girl have to do to get a Mars bar and a silky cushion around here?

"Hey," I heard Milo say softly, and I looked up at his grim smile.

"Hey."

Milo leaned against one of the van door, putting a hand in pocket of his LAPD jacket. "How are you feeling?"

Truthfully, I had no clue how was feeling. Relieved, tired, disturbed, grateful, sad, scared. Everything rolled into one. But because the dictionary didn't actually have a name for that emotion, I just lied and told him I was good.

"Listen," Milo said, watching a pair of police officers walk over to their police car. "Some reporters caught wind of this, and I think they're on their way. So we should probably get you out of here."

"Yeah of course," I replied, nodding understandingly.

"Your parents will go with one of the agents. Jack's going to the hospital." He eyed my bandages. "Do you need to go too?"

"The paramedics said I should be okay to go home."

Milo nodded and watched me slip off my heels silently. He extended a hand to me, helping me climb out of the van. I took his hand and jumped out, my heels in my other hand.

"Thanks," I told him, giving him a tired smile.

"No problem." Milo dropped my hand and pulled off his jacket, handing it to me. "Put this on. You must be freezing."

I took it from him gratefully. I hadn't noticed how cold I was until he had just mentioned it. Plus, the jacket smelled like him, which was a scent I was trying to figure out how to bottle. I caught my father's eye as he was easing his way into a shiny black car. He stopped and nodded at me, as if checking if everything was okay. I gave him a thumbs-up to signal I was fine.

"You sure you're okay?" Milo asked, eyeing me uncertainly.

"Yeah, I'm good," I replied with a half-laugh.

"Just checking!" Milo replied, his own lips curving into a smile. "I don't want you collapsing on me again."

I cringed, clasping my eyes shut for a second. "Sorry about that."

"Don't be silly," he replied seriously. "I think you're holding up pretty well, considering everything that just happened."

"Yeah, well, don't get too excited. If I hit the floor again, I'm going to need your help."

"Fair enough."

"Miss Winters."

I turned around to see Agent Walker and Detective Reynolds walking toward us. Both men looked exhausted, but still smiled.

"Hi," I said, giving them a little wave with my free hand.

"Firstly," Agent Walker said. "I'd like to apologize. We were really hoping to avoid this outcome tonight."

"It's okay," I replied truthfully. "I think we all underestimated how much Frank wanted this."

"Agent Walker will be taking you home tonight," Detective Reynolds said. "I'll be following your parents in a separate car. Just a safety precaution, no need to worry."

"The car will be here in a few minutes," Agent Walker said. "Sit tight, and we'll get you home safe in no time."

I said my polite thank you's and both men turned to leave.

"Great work tonight, Fells," Detective Reynolds added to Milo, giving him a quick handshake. "You're going to make a great officer, kid."

"Thank you, sir."

Milo gave an embarrassed smile as they walked away, as if the idea of pride was shameful.

"You really did do great tonight," I said, and his smile widened a little. "I don't think I would have gotten off the floor it weren't for you."

"I didn't really do anything. It was Jack who figured out which lot you were in."

"Oh yeah!" I exclaimed, looking around. "This place is huge. How'd he manage that?"

"Do you remember that napkin from the Coco Club? The one that Frank left for you?"

"The one with the number five on it?"

Milo pointed to the side of the wall ahead of us. On the top-right, a huge number five was painted in block, dark blue.

"Lucky guess?" he said, lowering his arm.

"Oh," I replied, as everything clicked into place.

"Yeah."

"Wow, Frank really planned this whole thing out!"

"He definitely has some evil genius vibes going for him."

"So," I said, rocking back on my heels. "Looks like you and Jack did a bit of collaborating tonight."

"I think I owe him an apology," Milo said sheepishly. "I got a bit caught up with my conspiracy theory, didn't I?"

Yeah, lil' bit. But I wasn't about to tell him that. Now that Jack had proven just how innocent he was, all that research on him seemed a little over the top. I didn't even want to imagine what had been happening between the two boys on the way over.

"Well," I said, fiddling with the zip on Milo's jacket. It was hanging off me a little, but it felt like I was being hugged. "I guess it's all over now."

I tried to look relieved, but it must not have worked because Milo was looking at me like I was about to cry again.

"I know what'll cheer you up," Milo said, and the corners of my lips lifted an inch. "Frank's terrifying nickname actually stands for Dr. Dumpling. If that doesn't make you feel a little better, then nothing will."

"I'm sorry, doctor what?" I asked, even though I had heard him.

"Doctor Dumpling," Milo repeated, grinning at me. "I guess it was influenced by the role he always wanted and his time overseas."

"How do you know what it stands for?"

"I asked him," Milo said casually, and I began to laugh as I pictured it. "Just after they read him his rights, of course. The LAPD take those very seriously."

"You're kidding, right?" I said in-between laughter. On the phone it sounded so scary. Now, it sounded ridiculous.

"No, it's true!" Milo replied. "I was really curious!"

"That's a terrible villain name!"

"I mean, it's not as good as Tinkerbill. But I'll give him points for effort."

I cast my mind back to the fraternity party I had gone to with Milo, where the random frat boy half dressed as a fairy had been throwing glitter at everyone and yelling about how drunk he was. Just the thought of comparing Frank to someone as stupid as "Tinkerbill" made me laugh uncontrollably. I was laughing was so much, I had to lean against Milo's car door and clap a hand over my mouth. It didn't feel like it was appropriate to be happy for some reason, but laughing just felt so good.

"Hey, Gia?" Milo said, as my laughter began to die down slowly. "I'm really sorry your big night got ruined. That kind of sucks."

My smile faded. "Yeah," I said. "It does."

"And I really am sorry about the whole Jack thing."

"Just so you know," I said. "There's nothing going on between Jack and I. Like . . . you know. In *that* way."

If Jack was secretly in love with me, Frank almost killing us all would have been a good time to admit it. Seeing as that didn't even come close to happening, I was going to take a wild guess and say he probably didn't share those electric currents I always felt around him.

"Is something going on between us in *that* way?" Milo asked, and I blushed a little. "I mean, I know the timing isn't great, but—"

"I don't know," I interrupted. "You're leaving soon and it's . . . complicated."

There wasn't really an easy way to say *oh my God please love me forever, I don't care if you're moving to freaking Norway.*

"Well, maybe we can just hang out sometime?" Milo suggested, looking hopeful. "Nothing fancy."

"Milo," I said with a sigh. "You don't want to get involved with me. Like, seriously. This is the danger zone."

"Oh come on."

"No, it really is! I have an unhealthy addiction to shoes and I crave chocolate to the point where I actually dream about it at night."

Milo look amused. "Everyone loves chocolate," he said.

"It's not just the eating habits. My mom is probably going to hit on you occasionally, and my brother is a complete weirdo. And if you think that you're going to have one *second* of peace and quiet after all of this, then you're wrong. The paparazzi are going to be up in your grill every time we want to grab some gelato!"

"I think my grill will survive."

"Not to mention Meghan Adams and her minions, who are

going to have plenty to say about us. Which, trust me, is not a good thing!"

"Should I know who Meghan Adams is?"

"If that's not bad enough," I continued. "My dad is going to go full on CIA mode! He was protective enough to begin with, and now he's going to be a complete nightmare. Like, he's probably going to know which brand of hair gel you use."

Milo put a hand to his head and said, "L'Oreal mostly."

"Plus, there's always the issue of you going to New York."

"I don't leave for a couple of months!"

I blew out another sigh. "Yeah but you *are* going to leave."

Milo nodded thoughtfully, watching as two paramedics walked passed, engaged in conversation. "You're right," he said finally. "We shouldn't make things messy."

He smiled, but I could tell his dimples weren't really feeling it. I could relate. Milo Fells wanted to date me and all of a sudden my brain wanted to become Mrs. Practicality? I bet Audrey Hepburn never had to deal with this crap. Oh, screw practicality. It had never done me any favors in the past.

"But," I said, "I suppose we could still hang out sometimes. You know, platonically."

Milo raised an eyebrow. In the background I could hear Agent Walker's car approaching us.

"Platonically?" Milo repeated.

"Yeah. Casually. Platonically. I know I said that already, but I'm not great with synonyms."

"Right," he said, nodding. "That could work."

"Great," I smiled, holding out my free hand so he could shake it. "So . . . friends?"

Milo curled his fingers into his jacket, still draped around my shoulders, and pulled me close. He kissed me, quickly but with lots of feeling.

"Sure," he said. "Friends."

chapter
twenty-six

ARIA AND Veronica were lying sprawled across my bed, flipping through magazines and filing through a pile of clothes dumped next to them. It had been three weeks since the Golden Globes, and three weeks since the little *incident*. We tried not to bring it up too much in the house. It wasn't exactly great dinner table conversation. I had finally been able to tell my friends everything, which hadn't been easy to relive. But it was a relief to not have to lie anymore. Everything had changed in such a short amount of time. College acceptance letters had been mailed, I had planned my future and I had a brand new replacement for my phone. Plus, my house was bug-free, as was my dog, and I was officially out of harm's way. Oh, and Dad had let me go shopping to "relieve my stress," so I had a brand new wardrobe too. I knew there was only so long I could milk the "remember when your ex-bestie stalked and kidnapped me" card, but I was going to use it for as long as I could.

More importantly, *I* had changed. I refused to dwell on things I couldn't change, and instead busied myself with anything that would take my mind off that stupid night. As far as I was concerned, Frank Parker didn't exist. He was just a terrible nightmare I had, here one minute and gone the next. I'll admit, Ao Jie Kai had proved to be a little more interesting to learn about. His mother apparently worked in the cleaning company that we hired the day the listening bugs were planted. Frank had found that little fact particularly interesting when it came up in conversation with his favorite waiter, building his diabolical plan from there up. It was thanks to her that Ao Jie Kai got the job for a few shifts, claiming he needed some extra cash and was willing to help his mother out. The cops said his mom had no clue what was happening. That made two of us.

But that chapter had finished, and I was ready to move on. No more worrying about guns and warehouses. My biggest dilemmas were going to be wardrobe related from now on.

"I can't choose!" I cried with frustration, throwing another pile of dresses onto the bed.

Lincoln was throwing a "Pre College" party at his house to celebrate everyone's acceptance into college, even though I'm pretty sure a fair few of our year level hadn't even applied. With bulging wallets and sturdy trust funds, college wasn't a necessity for everyone at LAC Elite.

"Why don't you wear this?" Aria asked, holding up my Yves Saint Laurent strapless dress.

I took it from her uncertainly, running the silk through my fingers. "I don't know. It seems a little much for this crowd."

"Personally," Veronica said, holding Famous in her left hand. "I like the Chanel leather shorts."

I made a face and said, "Meghan was wearing those the other day. I can't stand to have the same taste as Meghan Adams."

Meghan had been abnormally nice ever since the Golden Globes debacle. Everyone at school had, to be honest. But there was something extra weird about kindness coming from Meghan. It just seemed wrong, like the other shoe was about to drop at any time.

"It's Chanel! It's everyone's taste!" Aria argued.

"Even still, I think I'll pass."

"What about this?" Veronica asked, pulling a black dress out of the pile.

It was the same one I had worn when Milo and I went to the frat party to find Ao Jie Kai. I took it from her and clutched it to my chest, as if I were holding an autographed poster from the Backstreet Boys.

"I was wearing this the first time Milo kissed me," I told my friends, unable to keep the love-struck look off my face.

"Ugh!" Aria cried, resting her head against the headboard. "Your boyfriend is so hot, it's like, painful."

"He's not my boyfriend, remember?"

"Yeah, yeah," Aria said, rolling her eyes. "You're still into the whole no labels thing. But if you guys make out every time you go to the movies, then he's your boyfriend. Hate to break it to you."

"Are you an expert on boyfriends now?" I asked with a smile.

Aria winked at me cheekily. "Actually, I'm an expert on no labels."

Milo technically wasn't my boyfriend, but honestly those lines were getting pretty blurred. We were trying to be realistic about all the things going against us. And trust me, there were plenty of them. But if Milo and I wanted to "hang out," then damn it, we were going to hang out. No point being young if you can't have some fun with it.

"Um," Veronica said, holding up the cut up basketball jersey

Jack had given me the first time we visited the Dumpling Hospital. "What the hell is this?"

Aria sat up and took the unevenly cut t-shirt from her, eyeing it uncertainly. "Gia, why do you own this? If *this* is your taste, we need to get you some help."

I snatched the t-shirt from her defensively and put it on top of the black dress I had folded a minute earlier.

"It's a really long story, but Jack got me that," I told them, shrugging.

It was definitely great that I could tell my friends the truth about everything, but there were some things they just didn't need to know. They wouldn't understand all the inside jokes, so I had just omitted them when I told them the stories. I guess I thought the memories would remain as they were if I left it that way.

"Okay . . ." Aria said, raising her eyebrows.

"I still can't believe Jack was your bodyguard!" Veronica said, placing Famous carefully on the floor. "Bodyguards never look like that."

"I think Jack is the love of my life," Aria added seriously, and Veronica and I exchanged knowing glances. Aria thought everyone was the love of her life.

"I wouldn't mind hiring him full time, if you know what I mean," Veronica said. "I could do with some twenty-four-hour body protection."

"Not sure how Aaron would feel about that," I said.

Veronica held up her hands in front of her and wiggled her fingers as if she were trying to dry nail polish. "Do you see a ring on this finger?" She asked me.

I picked up the nearest piece of clothing and threw it at her playfully. She caught it right before it hit her face and held it up in front of her.

"Hey, I kind of like that," Aria said, as we all inspected my long-sleeved Victoria's Secret dress.

"Me too actually," I agreed.

"Same," Veronica added with an approving nod.

"Knock, knock!" came Milo's voice from the door. "Everyone decent?"

It had been way too long for me to still get butterflies every time Milo was around, but it happened anyway. Especially when he was in his uniform. Every man needs to invest in one of those.

"Hi Milo!" Aria chirped, giving him an excited finger wave. "You look really good today."

I cringed and gave Veronica a *handle her* look. The smile on her face told me she was having way too much fun to save me from the embarrassment.

"Hey girls, how's it going?" Milo asked. He was getting used to the level of craziness that followed me around.

"Good!" Veronica replied, before Aria could say anything else. "We're planning outfits for the party tonight."

Milo eyed the pile of clothes carpeting my floor and bed. He nodded and said, "I can see that."

I held up my chosen outfit and held it against myself to show him what it would look like. "Do you like it?" I asked him.

Milo eyed the dress up and down and said, "On a scale of one to the Oscars, how fancy is this party?"

"I'd say it's at least a Paris Hilton Birthday Bash."

Milo smiled and said, "Well then it's perfect. You look good in everything."

I smiled so widely, I think my jaw snapped in two. When life gives you lemons, throw them back and ask for a hot police officer instead. Trust me, you won't regret it.

"I see you made it past LAX," I said, referring to the new guards Dad had hired to pretty much sit outside the house and make sure no one kidnapped me or anyone else.

"It helps when I'm in the uniform."

"Good things happen when you're in that uniform," Aria

told him with a nod.

"So are you going out tonight?" I asked him, shooting Aria a warning look.

"Yeah, I've got drinks with some guys from the academy, to celebrate graduation," he replied. "I just stopped by to check in on you. Make sure everything was okay."

Milo had been doing that a lot lately. Actually, everyone had been doing that a lot lately, even when I told them I was fine. And I was fine. I mean, okay, I may have had this nightmare where Frank was breaking out of his prison cell and yelling out my name like a maniac. If he was going to break out of jail, he may as well have brought Wentworth Miller with him. And yes, I kind of freaked out when I was alone for too long. But everything was still raw, so you could hardly blame me. Dad had suggested I get a shrink, but I had replied with a categorical no. I wasn't going to pay some stranger to tell me I was traumatized. I had already figured that out myself. Thanks, Dr. Phil.

"I'm good," I told Milo. "Don't worry about me."

"Hey listen," he said, lowering his voice. I glanced at my friends who immediately made themselves busy, poring over a magazine as if they had just discovered it was made of gold. "I found out some more stuff about Frank and those guys he was working for in China. It pretty grimy stuff. Do you want to hear about it?"

"Um," I replied, fiddling uncomfortably with the ring I was wearing. "Not really."

"Okay," Milo said, nodding understandingly.

"I'm sorry! I just don't think that I'm . . ." I trailed off, not sure how to finish that sentence.

"No, I get it," Milo said, taking my hand and giving it a squeeze. "Whenever you're ready."

I gave him a grateful smile as he released my hand. It's not that I didn't appreciate all the effort he was putting into following up on everything to do with Frank. But hearing all about Frank made it a lot harder to forget he existed. It was like going through a really tough breakup, when all your friends keep talking about your ex and how he's doing. Oh, and your ex tried to kill you on a movie set. You know, standard relationship drama.

"I better head off," Milo said, turning to the girls. "Nice to see you again. Enjoy the party!"

Aria basically threw the magazine out the window, flipping her hair. "Bye Milo!" she said, batting her eyelashes.

I practically shoved Milo out of the room, desperate to get him away from Aria. When she bats her eyelashes, boys go nuts. And I wasn't about to let that happen this time around.

"Okay, time for you to go before Aria starts getting frisky!" I told him, placing my palms on his chest and pushing him out of my room.

He laughed, trying to keep his balance as I backed him out with all the strength I had. "She's nice," he said.

I dropped my hands and shook my head. "She's marking you as her next victim as we speak, so you better get out of here."

"I heard that!" I heard Aria called from inside my room, and I smiled.

"Oh, I almost forgot," Milo said. "I ran into your dad downstairs."

"And?" I asked nervously.

"We mostly talked about the weather, which is actually great progress from a few weeks ago. At least he didn't call me Melvin this time."

"Oh God."

"Is he like this with all your boyfriends?"

I paused. "Are you implying that you're my boyfriend?"

"Of course not," he replied, but his dimples were showing. "That would be breaking our no labels agreement."

"Yes, it would."

"Okay, but this isn't a free pass to date some guy from like, the CW or something."

"Don't worry," I assured him. "Teenage werewolves don't really do it for me. But if Henry Cavill comes knocking on my door, I can't guarantee I'll turn him away."

"Fine by me," Milo laughed. "He can put up with your terrible Christian Bale puns instead."

I feigned an outraged look and said, "Firstly, that joke was hilarious and you secretly loved it."

"Debatable."

"And secondly, my Superman puns are even better than the others."

"Oh no," Milo said. "You've already thought of some, haven't you?"

"I wonder if he's Hen-*free* tonight."

"I am in actual physical pain right now."

"I *Kent* believe how hot he is!"

"Wow, these are actually getting worse."

"You cops have no appreciation for creativity."

Milo looked at his watch and said, "Actually, us cops have no appreciation for being late. I better run. Detective Reynolds is expecting a whole lot of paperwork, and I don't even know how to do half of it."

I made a face. "Have fun."

"You too," Milo said, hooking an arm around my neck and pulling me against him. "Remember, drugs are bad, and don't take candy from strangers. I can give you a pamphlet if you want."

"Pass."

Milo smiled, giving me a quick kiss before letting me go. "Stay out of trouble," he said.

"Yes, sir."

I watched him disappear down the staircase with a happy sigh. If this were a Disney movie, you would have seen hearts in place of my eyes and tiny blue birds circling my head.

"I freaking love witty banter!" I announced, re-entering my room. "Seriously, my life is like a Meg Ryan movie right now."

"If I didn't love you," Aria said. "I would hate you so much right now."

I moved the pile of clothes out of the way and flopped down onto the bed in between my friends, staring up at the ceiling with a smile.

"I bet Brendan was great at witty banter," Aria said sarcastically, resting her head next to mine.

"Brendan probably thought *banter* was a type of cardboard," I replied, and my two friends cracked up. "He sent me another few letters after the incident, saying he was super freaked out. He even wrote in capital letters and drew shocked smiley faces."

"Oh my God," Veronica cringed. "I think it's time to give him a fake mailing address."

"I hate to admit it," I said. "But you might be right."

"Hey Gia," Aria said, propping herself up onto an elbow. "You're friends with Zac Efron right?"

"If by friends you mean we've met twice, then yes. We're best buds."

"You think he'd want to date me?" Aria asked.

Veronica and I both turned our heads toward Aria, who looked dead serious.

"Come again?" I asked, just to make sure she wasn't kidding. She wasn't.

Aria shrugged. "What? Can you put in a good word or something? I happen to think we'd look bangin' together."

"The key word being *banging*," Veronica added with a laugh.

"Aria, if I had that kind of influence over Zac Efron, don't you think I'd put in a good word for myself first?"

"Oh shut up!" Veronica said, and I turned to face her. "You have Milo."

"Yeah!" Aria agreed from behind me. "You don't need anyone else. You have witty banter, remember?"

I looked up at the ceiling, my smile widening. "I'll see what I can do for you."

A muffled buzzing noise came from somewhere on the bed as the mattress began to vibrate lightly.

"Is that my phone?" Aria asked, pulling her phone out of her jeans pocket and checking the screen. "Nope, not mine."

I sat and listened closely to the buzzing. It sounded like it was coming from underneath the pile of clothes. I shoved my hand in the pile, tossing clothes out of the way until I found it, lying hidden underneath a Taylor Odetta dress.

"It's mine!" I told my friends, checking the caller ID. "Oh, it's Jack!"

I answered as quick as I could, before he hung up, putting the phone to my ear.

"Hello?" Jack's voice came through the phone.

"Hey Jack!"

"Gia!" he replied, and I smiled. Something about Jack's voice was so familiar and comforting.

"HI JACK!" Aria and Veronica yelled in unison behind me. They were so loud, people in Uzbekistan could have heard them without a phone.

I turned and shushed them, sliding off the bed. "The girls say hi," I told him, pacing in front of my bed.

"Aw, I miss the girls!" Jack replied.

"Jack says he misses you," I told my friends, the phone still to my ear.

Aria clutched her chest like she was having a heart attack, and flopped back onto my pillow dramatically. Veronica chucked a pillow at her and I turned around, trying not to laugh.

"So what's been happening?" Jack asked, his breath sounding a little uneven, like he was walking quickly.

"I messaged you like a billion times yesterday. You never replied!"

"I know, I'm so sorry!" Jack apologised. "I've been super swamped at work lately. I just didn't get any time."

I gave a disappointed pout, but I guess I couldn't blame him. He didn't really have much of a choice if work was busy. I just missed him a little more than I liked to admit.

"It's okay. I just wanted to tell you some exciting news!"

"Dinner with Clooney?"

"Oh my gosh, no that's next week! I just about died when Dad told me he had set it up. I couldn't believe it!"

In fact, there were plenty of people in the celebrity world that had sent my family messages. They all said the same thing; how they couldn't believe something so horrible had happened. It felt so odd, like a family member had died. Even Carol had sent me a basket of chocolate. I'm not going to lie; I got some of the housekeepers to try it first, just in case it was poisoned. Harsh, but a risk I was willing to take. So far the causality count was at zero.

"Try not to go British at dinner," Jack said. "He'll never love you then."

"I still have Leo."

"You're not blonde, or a supermodel. You don't have Leo."

Sadly, he was right. I was going to have to rule him out.

"Anyway, whatever," I said, pushing the hair out of my face excitedly. "I just wanted to tell you that you'll be seeing me in New York pretty soon."

"Oh, how come?"

"I'm going to NYU in the fall!"

"Seriously?" Jack's voice came through the receiver. "Congratulations!"

"Thank you!" I replied, giving the phone a pleased smile. He sounded genuinely excited. "I mean, Aria's going to UCLA and

V's at Berkeley, so I'm going to miss them. But I'm still happy!"

"You should be," Jack said. "This city is incredible. You're going to love it!"

"I better! You sure talk about it enough. Dad was pretty set on Brown, but I did some research and NYU ranks higher on the list, so he couldn't technically say no. Plus, Mom will be there after she gets back from filming in Greece, although who knows how long that could take."

"Well, nothing's better than New York. Not even Greece," Jack said, matter-of-factly. I heard a car horn beep in the distance as Jack continued. "So have you thought about what you want to major in?"

"I don't know yet," I told him, sitting on the edge of my bed. Famous walked past, nudging his little ball with his nose. "Maybe something do with psychology? It sounds pretty badass."

"Oh good choice!" Jack replied. "You're going to need some experts to help figure out what's wrong with you."

"Ha ha," I said dryly, rolling my eyes even though he couldn't see. "The joke's on you buddy. You're stuck with me for at least another three years. Just you and your bestie, Gia!"

"Lucky me!"

"Yeah, lucky you!"

"I'm going to take a wild guess and say Milo's going to be around a lot."

"It's not that much of a wild guess if you ask me."

"Great! Can't wait to hang out with him," Jack said wryly.

"Can you at least *try* to be nice?" I asked him, seriously. "He's important to me."

"Fine, but I'm not making any promises," Jack said, sounding a little breathless.

"I'll take it," I said. I'd break down his walls eventually. There wasn't much he could do about it once I moved to New York.

"On that note, when you get here I want to introduce you

to Lucy."

"Who is that, your cat?" I joked, eyeing the chipped nail polish on my free hand.

"Very funny, smartass," Jack replied. "No. She's my girlfriend."

I opened my mouth and closed it again. Did he just say what I thought he said?

"Your what?" I said, as more car horns blared in the background.

"My girlfriend!" Jack replied, raising his voice over the noise of the traffic.

"Since when?" I asked, not fully believing it.

"Since always. Listen, I need to go. I was out for my break but I'm just heading back now."

"Wai—"

"I'll message you later, okay?"

No, not okay! He couldn't just drop a bomb like that and then disappear!

"Wait, Ja—"

"Talk to you soon!" Jack said cheerfully, and hung up before I could protest.

I lowered the phone and stared at the screen for a few seconds, gaping at the photo of me and Jack that Mom had taken before the Golden Globes. It stared back at me, sitting next to Jack's name and contact details on my phone.

"What did Jack say?" Aria asked from behind me.

"Uh," I said, trying not to sound as flustered as I felt. "Nothing much. He said he wants to introduce me to his girlfriend."

"His girlfriend?" Veronica repeated in surprise, and I nodded.

"Are you kidding me?" Aria cried. "All the good ones are taken!"

"I guess you guys could double date now." Veronica said.

There were about a billion things I would rather do than

double date with Milo and Jack's girlfriend. Number one on that list involved throwing myself out of a plane without a parachute. It's not like he wasn't allowed to have a girlfriend or anything, but it was Jack! He wasn't exactly a commitment kind of guy. Besides, if he had a girlfriend, why hadn't he mentioned her until now? And what does "since always" even mean? That wasn't a clear answer! Maybe that's why he was always glued to his phone. Maybe he was sending her updates about how annoying I was being, and how he couldn't wait to see her again.

But, you know, whatever. My New York adventure would just have another person involved. And I could do that much for Jack, after all he'd done for me. Besides, I am a very accommodating person. Mostly. Sometimes. I would accommodate the heck out of her. Okay but, like, who is actually named Lucy nowadays? All I'm saying is, she sounded like a cartoon farm animal.

Whoever she was, she was probably really nice if Jack was putting up with her. And really attractive. Like, unfairly attractive. At least now I wouldn't feel lonely in a new city without my two best friends. I'd have Milo and Jack. And Jack's girlfriend. And his secret, bottomless bank account; let's not forget about that.

Just the four of us pals together in a new city. Without my parents always watching me like a hawk. No Dr. D. No rules. College life. College parties. College boys.

What could possibly go wrong?

a c k n o w l e d g e m e n t s

First, a massive thank you to Amberjack Publishing, who took a chance on a young writer who was just about ready to give up. And a special thank you to my lovely editor, Jenny Catanese, for all of her guidance and support.

I'd also like to thank Anastasia Hantzis, for teaching me that books will never let you down, even when people do. Thank you to my always excited friends, for never being any of those people who let me down. I promise I'll try to make you famous (but I can't guarantee anything, sorry Uma).

I'm forever grateful to my parents, who patiently watched me obsess over my manuscript for three years and never once let me lose faith.

And of course, to my sister Rahat, for crying before every one of my school dances and graduations. You are perhaps the only person I would choose over George Clooney.

about the author

Saba Kapur is a 20 year-old writer based out of Melbourne, Australia. Her passion for storytelling developed at a young age, born from a deep-seated love of books. *Lucky Me* is her first novel and an ode to her favorite things: fashion, romance, and mystery.

Born in India, Saba spent her childhood in Indonesia and Kiev, Ukraine. She is currently in her final year of college, studying International Relations and Criminology at Monash University. She hopes to one day become a fabulous lawyer in New York City, with a closet full of stilettos.

In her spare time Saba enjoys reading, watching anything to do with Ryan Gosling, and pretending she's Beyoncé. She currently lives with her parents, her older sister, and a large supply of chocolate.